SHIKAREE

Shikaree

M.J. Oelkers

Arnstead Press

For those who helped me climb after I fell.

1

Spelunking

Channeled light cut through the void of the World Below. Oppressive darkness weighed on those who dared tread the cavernous depths. Chandra felt the shroud rest on her shoulders like a veil of night. Had she not been so used to clambering about the darkness, the environment might have terrified her. The Flow-infused light Chandra channeled, however, rendered the dark as mere inconvenience.

The intrepid explorer maintained the small orb above her right shoulder. It cast enough golden light to reveal what lay directly ahead: Two stone passages carved by centuries of water flow. Rough-cut walls marked the passage of the Federation through decades of labor. Rock, rock, and yet more rock. Not sights Chandra would write home about.

Where Chandra looked, light followed as a conical beam. She maintained the convenient source of light with little thought. The act was about as challenging for her as was breathing or walking. Years of practice made it so.

"Let's see if we've gone far enough," Chandra murmured.

Chandra placed her left hand on the nearest cavern wall. The light at her shoulder fluttered and went out, released from its duty. A deep breath lifted Chandra's mind from the darkness and focused her attention on the Flow. She reached out with her mind to the crackling river of purple light. One light tug was enough. Energy filled her like a vessel, pooling in her core before Chandra directed the energy to the wall.

Nothing.

The sequence was repeated with Chandra's right hand on the opposite wall.

Nothing.

The lack of any visible reaction elicited a sigh from the young channeler. Chandra clicked her tongue against the back of her teeth in frustration and rolled her eyes.

"Right then," Chandra muttered in a conciliatory tone. The familiar light popped up over her shoulder once more. "Guess I'll just have to pick one, then."

Chandra looked back and forth between the two different pathways. Though she was no stranger to the World Below, these paths were new to her. On the right was a gentle, sloping decline. Additional forking paths were just visible at the edge of Chandra's light. On the left was a steep drop.

A confident grin widened into a mischievous smile. Chandra felt her nose wrinkle with delight at the notion of a challenge.

Leather straps swished over her cotton shirt as Chandra removed her backpack. The wooden staff fixed to the side of her pack was decidedly less quiet. A tool made of red maple that stood as tall as Chandra at a little over five feet, it struck the ground with a thunk that echoed down the corridor. Chandra grimaced at the tool before rolling the sleeves of her shirt up tight over her elbows. Light-brown arms probed deep into the bag. Angling light proved to be a waste of time. Chandra was able to fish for what she needed by feel.

"Aha!" Chandra ripped a length of rope from her bag. "There you are. Just what I need."

Chandra shouldered her bag and unfurled the rope, looking over the ledge as she did so. The drop was not too far. The bottom could be seen clearly thanks to her Flow-infused light. There was plenty enough rope to reach the bottom and more besides.

The next item Chandra required was one of the half-dozen manarail spikes that dangled from her hips. Which she grabbed did not matter. They were little more than hunks of iron. Chandra settled for one from her right hip without giving the matter much thought. She tied one end of the rope to the spike with a sturdy hitch. Two tugs at the rope established confidence in her work.

All that remained was to find a home for the spike. Though the drop was short enough to see the bottom, it was not so short that Chandra felt comfortable making an unassisted leap. She knelt by the ledge. Her empty hand probed for a nook or hole in the rocky floor. Something into which she could embed the spike held in her other hand.

A slight divot in the floor yielded to Chandra's probing touch. It was about as wide around as her thumb, perhaps made by a pickaxe or the piton of another explorer. The slot was too large for the manarail spike to fit into as it was. If Chandra were to let go of the spike, it would tumble over the nearby ledge. Not the sort of hold she could rely on if her goal was a safe descent.

"Well, that won't do," Chandra whispered without losing her grin.

Another call went out to the roiling river that was the Flow. Yet more energy was needed, this time for a different task. Something more complex than the simple light at Chandra's shoulder. More concentration was required.

As Chandra pulled at the Flow and channeled its power, she envisioned the manarail spike growing soft. She saw in her mind the tip of the spike become almost like liquid. It was as if a smith were working the raw metal without the need for fire or heat. The metal seemed to pour into the stone crevice of its own accord. Once the hole had been filled, the remainder of the spike curled at the opposite end into a hook.

"Better safe than sorry." Chandra tugged at her rope. The refashioned manarail spike did not budge. Chandra gave the improvised piton a light kick with her booted toes. Still no movement. Firm resistance held the hook snug in place. "Excellent."

Satisfied with her handiwork, Chandra tossed the rope over the ledge. It uncoiled as it fell, hitting the ground with a hearty thump. Plenty of slack remained when the rope came to rest. Chandra slid herself over the ledge after securing her backpack. The spike made for an excellent handle as she took hold of the rope. In less time than it took to fashion the spike into a hook, Chandra was down the full length of the drop.

"I'll be seeing *you* later," Chandra said playfully as she tugged at the rope. She decided to keep the rope in one piece. If she needed more further down the passage, she could return to cut a length as warranted.

Light scoured the new passageway for signs of any kind. There were no support beams. No immediate evidence of tools having worked the stone. It was a smooth, natural passageway. The sight refueled the broad smile that covered Chandra's face.

Her steps were light as she wandered down the passageway. Sometimes she was stooped. At other times she was lucky enough to stand at full height. When her luck waned, she was forced to slide and crawl her way forward.

It was during one of the patches of bad luck that Chandra came to a complete stop. She felt her luck shoot from the floor to the low, cumbersome ceiling. Nestled against the wall just ahead of her was a pile of bones, with remnants enough to loosely be called a skeleton. What mattered most to Chandra was that the skull was intact. There were no fangs to indicate that the skull had belonged to a katarl. No snout gave the impression of a harn. It certainly wasn't human.

Perfect, Chandra thought, her smile incapable of growing any larger.

Four narrow slots for eyes. No perceptible place for a mouth. The rough shape of a human skull, but slightly elongated. It was the most intact specimen of Those Who Came Before that Chandra had ever encountered. If Chandra was not the first person to pass by the centuries-old display, then this was the luckiest day of her entire life. To find an unmolested site such as this was unthinkable so near a middle strata checkpoint.

One of the skeletal hands gripped the hilt of an ancient sword. Light danced on the silvery metal in misleading fashion. Any weapon this long-dead creature would carry must have been upward of three or four hundred years old. That it reflected light as if it had been polished yesterday was a testament to the skill of the artisan. There were none in the Federation that could make blades like these. Chandra pulled herself close to the pile of bones. Her eyes roved over the pristine surface of the blade. It bore a gentle curve with a single edge.

No runes.

Chandra pulled herself closer. Her gaze probed the hilt of the sword. It was small and offered little protection to the owner's fleshless hand.

No runes.

As Chandra pulled herself further still down the passage, nearly atop the skeletal remains, she accidentally bumped one of the bones. A crackle and a pop were followed by a tense moment of silence. Then, as if time had slowed, the teetering bones fell into a genuine pile. Chandra recoiled at the noise and remained still for the space of a few timid breaths.

"Sorry, friend," Chandra whispered. Her composure returned as if it had never left. "Just gonna borrow this for a minute."

Chandra brushed the pile of bones off the sword and sat up as best she could. The weapon was light in her hands. It was not the first sword Chandra had the pleasure of holding, and this one was certainly the most elegant of the bunch. A fact irrelevant to her interests. What gleefully pushed Chandra's heart into her throat was tucked into the pommel of the sword.

"That's what we're after," Chandra uttered in a breathless whisper.

A runic symbol that covered the entirety of the pommel. Characters for wind and fire, among others that Chandra did not recognize. The wavelike formation of lines enthralled her. Chandra forgot for a painful moment that what she held was indeed sharp. Sharp enough to leave a small cut on her left thumb. Chandra shook away the pain and wiped the light trickle of blood on her pantleg.

Tucked under the pile bones was a moldy sheath. Though nowhere near as exciting as the blade, it could still serve as useful housing. Chandra fitted the blade into the time-worn scabbard and slotted the whole package between her hip and belt.

"Now," Chandra muttered, passing a glance at the foreign, unrecognizable skull, "let's see if you have any friends down the way, shall we?"

Chandra did not have to crawl far.

The way expanded so that Chandra was able to stand. Three Bangeli katarl could have walked shoulder to orange and black-striped shoulder without discomfort. At the end of the passage was a natural chamber. In the center of the chamber was a man sprawled on his back and still as the stone that surrounded him. The sight forced a gasp from Chandra. Her light went out and the chamber fell silent.

Blood pounded in Chandra's ears as she crouched motionless in the chamber. She felt her heart try to escape her chest. The sight of flesh had set her mind racing. *Am I caught? Will he find me? Will I be left for dead?* These thoughts, and many more, flashed through her mind. An errant hand wandered to the hilt of her newest prize.

Locked in darkness, Chandra waited.

And she waited.

Chandra agonized over the time wasted in idle terror. She was not sure whether it had been ten minutes or a full hour. The only sounds she could decipher in the gloom were the trickle of water somewhere in the distance and her hushed breathing.

Nothing moved.

The ball of light reclaimed its place over Chandra's shoulder. Golden hues revealed the walls of the cavern. Shadows danced among stalactites as the orb flickered.

The man's eyes did not open.

Chandra felt the stranger's grip on her heart ease. Breaths calmed and found a regular pace. Dread drained from her chest to disappear among the shadows. Confident equilibrium reestablished its presence.

A pair of hesitant steps turned into three steps more. As Chandra approached the body sprawled faceup on the floor, she unfastened the staff fixed to her backpack and used it to prod the body.

The man did not move.

"Hey," Chandra called with uncertainty. Her prodding with the staff moved from the man's shoulder to the man's head. "You alive, mister?"

The man did not respond.

A heavy sigh escaped Chandra as relief washed over her like a wave of sunshine.

"He's dead."

Not wasting any time after the vital discovery, Chandra set both her pack and staff on the ground and knelt next to the man. She pressed two fingers against the man's neck to check for a pulse. Another, smaller sigh left Chandra when she felt the cold flesh had no pulse.

"Yup." Chandra nodded. "Dead as a doornail. All right, fellow Shikaree, let's make sure nothing you've got on you goes to waste, huh?"

Practiced hands ran along the body in search of anything that might prove useful or, better yet, turn a profit. The man's pockets were empty. *Not the best start,* Chandra conceded. His breast pocket was empty as well. A dagger sheath was fixed to the man's belt, but it lacked a dagger. Chandra clicked her tongue at the misfortune as she continued her search of the body.

On the man's right arm was a band with a patch. The letters *BB* were stitched onto the fabric. Jammed between the letters was a sword that pointed downward. It was a familiar piece of iconography.

"Baylocke Battalion, huh? Definitely a good thing you're not still kicking," Chandra said with a pat to the man's chest. "Oh, but what's this now?"

Crumpled in the man's death grip was a piece of parchment. Chandra carefully plucked at the morbid fist, peeling each finger away from the curio. Despite being dead, Chandra noted that the man had a surprisingly firm grip. It took a few minutes' struggle before the hand was open and the parchment was free to be taken.

Chandra smoothed the parchment out on the dead man's chest. Her light moved to hover directly over top. The golden light revealed an absolute mess. Poorly written Federal common surrounded the edges and was occasionally found elsewhere amid the two-by-two-feet collection of foreign characters and hastily scrawled arrows. Ugly lines seemed to forge passageways that led between proportionally absurd chambers.

"Some kinda map?" Chandra whispered.

What caught her attention more than anything else on the piece of parchment was the repeated mention of a single word: cache. Her eyes widened at the notion. *A cache of relics, maybe?* Chandra thought. *Must be worth a fortune if someone from the Baylocke Battalion was willing to die over it.*

"Well, I think this tops the day off nicely." She gave the dead man's chest a celebratory pat as she furled the map and stowed it in her backpack. "Time to get out of this place in one piece."

* * *

Memory glass faceted into the cave walls guided the way to the middle strata checkpoint. A foreboding crimson, the lights served as a warning to those who would pass unprepared. At the same time, the lights welcomed home any Shikaree who survived their expedition into unknown territory. The sources of light stretched a hundred feet or so through the four passages that connected to the checkpoint. Everything beyond the light was considered to be wild. An ungoverned expanse of stone and shadow.

Chandra ran her fingers along the red glass. Each time Chandra passed she channeled a small amount of energy into the light sources. She thought of it as doing her part for the Shikaree community. A way to give back a little at a time.

Walking along the final stretch felt something like coming home to Chandra. The checkpoint was the closest thing to a guarantee of safety she had seen since entering the middle strata of the World Below. The upper stratum was a quiet place by comparison. A zone where people had picked clean any trace of memory glass. Where Shikaree had combed over every rock and crevice in search of relics.

Warm familiarity wrapped Chandra in a blanket of satisfaction as she approached the checkpoint. A single soldier stood watch over the important passageway, their undivided attention on the upper stratum-side of the way.

"Garett!" Chandra called as she approached, waving the whole way. "What's on the menu today? Melissa pack something delicious like usual?"

The figure at the checkpoint did not respond to the greeting. Their attention was fixed in the opposite direction.

Chandra cocked her head to the side. She had expected a warm hello from her favorite soldier of the 4th Federation Army. Garett, Chandra thought, was not the type of person to spurn a pleasant greeting. Chandra covered the pommel of her newfound sword to obscure the runes it housed. The sense of familiarity had gone, replaced by a frosty suspicion that furrowed Chandra's brow. Her steps became thoughtful and guarded as she came within reach of the soldier.

"Garett always has this post on odd days," Chandra said to the soldier. "Is he not well?"

"Private Garett Watson has been reassigned."

The soldier's tone was gruff, his words coarse and cold. Chandra craned her neck to see that the soldier's features perfectly matched his tone. She gave the man a look up followed by a look down.

"Awful shame," Chandra replied. "Why the transfer?"

"Negligence," the soldier snapped. As he spoke, his gaze fell to Chandra. "I haven't seen your face before. How did you enter the middle strata?"

Chandra felt the cold of the soldier's voice penetrate her chest. Ice gripped her heart and hampered her breathing. *He hasn't found you out yet,* Chandra tried to convince herself. *Stay calm.*

"Trade secret," Chandra stammered after taking a moment to find her breath. "If I tell you how I got in, the passage will be swarmed by other Shikaree before I could blink. That's my livelihood on the line, thank you very much."

"Show me your license," the soldier demanded.

The cold dread inspired by the man's voice tightened around Chandra's throat like winter freezing a river. She did her best to maintain an outward sense of composure as she unshouldered her backpack to retrieve the requested documentation. No amount of charm, however, would hide the black-and-white nature of her licensure. Chandra handed the soldier a small rectangle of thick paper with a cracked smile.

"Chandra Pattal," the man read aloud. He flicked his eyes up to Chandra now and again as he read. "Residence: Pattal Farmstead, west of Arnstead. Fifteen years old, judging from the birth date. Registered as a *novice* Shikaree."

Chandra winced at the word *novice*. Her age was enough evidence of her status without reading the actual title. She nodded in affirmation.

"Yep, that's me. Chandra Pattal. Shikaree. And if you don't mind," Chandra added as she reached pleadingly for her license with both hands, "I'd like to be on my way. People to meet, you know. Relics to sell."

"Novices aren't permitted in the middle strata, Pattal," the soldier stated matter-of-factly. "Not allowed to sell relics from the middle strata either. I'll need to see your permit for that sword."

In her haste to retrieve her Shikaree license, Chandra had exposed the runes on the pommel of her prize. Chandra gave the soldier a wide, toothy smile as she removed the sword and scabbard from her belt and handed it to him. The man's expression did not change as he received the relic.

"Hand me your bag," the soldier said as he rested the sword on the checkpoint table. A metal mug bounced, spilling some of its steaming contents. "I need to perform an inspection."

"It was a light day." Chandra pouted as she handed over her backpack as her smile spoiled into an unfettered frown. "Nothing left in there but tools and supplies. You've already stolen my meal ticket for the week."

Knowing she spoke the truth of the matter gave rise to a bitter venom in Chandra's voice. The sword *had* been the only thing that she found on this night's expedition. Something was demeaning about the way the unfamiliar soldier rifled through her backpack. It was clear that he bore no trust for Chandra.

Garett wouldn't have searched my things, Chandra mulled. *Wouldn't have thought to take the sword. Wouldn't have asked for a license. Would have wished me a good day and that would have been the end of it.*

Chandra kicked an errant pebble and watched it bounce down the red-lit corridor beyond the checkpoint.

"Looks clean." The soldier offered the pack back to Chandra.

"How kind." Chandra wore a new smile born of contempt. The sort of smile you gave a thief who had just returned an empty purse.

"Right," the soldier grumbled, "everything's in order. Now get out of here before I report you for working the middle strata without a proper license."

Chandra bowed low as she stepped backward. She maintained steady eye contact with the soldier through the entire gesture. Up until she backed into someone else. Chandra yelped and jumped in surprise at the unexpected contact.

"Whoa there, youngblood!" came a shrill voice. Chandra whipped around to find that it belonged to a sneering Nirdac katarl. "Mind your elders. We're trying to walk here."

"Cut her some slack, Alyssa," said another stranger. This one was a Zumbatran human, who leaned over the shoulder of his feline counterpart. "She's barely old enough to hold a novice license. Give her a few years to mature, and she might learn a thing or two."

The pair shoved their way past Chandra. They were not about to wait around for Chandra to concoct a response. The pair flashed professional Shikaree licenses to the soldier at the checkpoint, who nodded his assent for passage.

Armbands that bore the patch of the Baylocke Battalion caught Chandra's attention as the two Shikaree passed her by.

"Hey, Bootlick Battalion," Chandra mustered. Not her best, but it was enough to garner a bemused look from the dismissive Shikaree. "I found one of your ilk downstairs taking a dirt nap. You might want to go hunt him down so you can tuck him in. I think it was past his bedtime."

The human Shikaree adopted the sneer of his katarl counterpart. Both departed the checkpoint without another word.

Chandra smirked at her minor victory before turning to make her way topside. Further delay and her absence might be discovered. To be sure, Chandra dug into her pocket for her timepiece.

Worn brass caught the fading light of the checkpoint as Chandra produced a weathered pocket watch. Little nicks and scratches marred the surface. Some of the letterings on the front cover had become diffi-cult to read, though Chandra had memorized the scant text. The words *Magic in Moderation*, repeated three times, formed a circle around an engraving of an open book. A harsh click cut through the sound of Chandra's footsteps when she released the catch.

Hairline cracks ran across the glass face of the small watch. One larger crack made it particularly difficult to determine when it was half-past any given hour. Despite the abuse the watch had seen, it never slowed. The device kept time as well as the day it had been crafted. Opposite the glass, on the back of the front cover, was inscribed a name: Trayni Mangal. The surname had been scratched out. Below the original, Pattal had been crudely inscribed as if with a nail.

Trayni Pattal. The name ran through Chandra's mind as she rubbed her thumb over the inscription. Brass shined bright and clear from such repeated gestures. *Mom.*

"Oh. Oh!" Chandra thought aloud, her eyes widening when she bothered to check the time. "Cutting it close. Sisir, guide my feet and get me home before dawn!"

With that, Chandra snapped the pocket watch closed, shoved it into her pocket, and took off through the tunnels of the World Below at a sprint.

2

Breakfast

Predawn light rendered the sky gray and murky, clouded glass that yawned over fields of green. Enough light to see by, but only so far into the distance. It was all Chandra needed to find her way home. She turned her horse, named Alabaster after his white coat, off the main road that led west from Arnstead. A northward stretch served as the last obstacle before she would reach the Pattal family farm.

The road north was not as wide as the road that led west, but the dirt was packed just as well. Hard, settled earth allowed the pair to ride hard for the farmhouse. A casual pace from the main road would have Chandra arriving home as the sun rose fully from the east. With the current stride she forced on old Alabaster, she hoped to be back before the gray light turned to gold.

"C'mon, Alabaster," Chandra whispered to her horse. "We've beaten the sun dozens of times. I know you can do it again."

Chandra could not tell if the gentle coaxing made Alabaster ride harder. Excited whispers of challenge between old friends. She liked to think that it did.

Tall grasses gave way to low, grazed-upon plots that surrounded a small wooden farmhouse. The exterior of the house was nothing special. A simple structure that served a simple purpose: to house a family.

A great red barn stood to the north of the farmhouse. Chandra guided Alabaster to the looming structure, slowing pace as she did so. Their path was one chosen out of necessity. It led the long way around the back of the farmhouse. Chandra would not allow herself to be found out by a mistake so simple as being seen or heard through the front windows of the house. That would not do at all.

Chandra walked Alabaster into his stall. It lay between the stalls for Mortimer and Patra, the Pattals' two draft horses kept for field work. Chandra patted Alabaster on the cheek and removed an apple from her backpack. She placed it in Alabaster's trough as she mouthed the words *thank you.*

Having seen to Alabaster, Chandra moved as quickly as silence would allow to the back of the farmhouse. The southernmost window on the back of the house whispered her name as she approached.

"Chandra. Chandra, hurry!"

Chandra made a shushing noise to the small girl leaning out the window.

"Quiet, Omala," Chandra said in a hoarse whisper as she slung her left leg over the windowsill. "You'll be the end of me! Keep quiet."

Omala took the backpack offered by her older sister and hid it under a pile of dirty clothes. Chandra focused on getting herself inside and stripping off her boots. The pair flung themselves into their wide bed as footsteps approached the door to their room. To the untrained, unsuspecting eye, the girls were fast asleep.

"Chandra, Omala," their father called between raps on the wooden door, "time to rise. The boys have already started making breakfast, sleepyheads."

Chandra and Omala giggled at each other in nervous excitement. Their father was none the wiser.

"So?" Omala asked in her wispy voice. "Find anything good last night?"

"Hush, hush, hush," Chandra replied. "Let's get up and get dressed. We can talk when we're in the fields. Fewer prying ears."

"That bad, huh?"

"Yeah," Chandra conceded. "Not great. I'll tell you later. Now, come on!"

Chandra whipped the blanket off the bed, pulling a playful squeal from her sister. Omala disappeared under the blanket. A morning game of catch the mouse seemed to be in order. Not one to shirk a challenge, Chandra growled as she dived under the blanket after her sister. It was not long before Omala, giggling as she squirmed, was caught in the clutches of her sister. Being twice Omala's age gave Chandra a considerable advantage in such silly games.

Omala acquiesced to the standard morning ritual once caught. Both girls changed out of their considerably different apparel into clean working clothes. Faces were washed in a basin next to the window. Once the girls were fresh and dressed, they opened their bedroom door and strode into the main room of the simple home.

The inviting smell of breakfast pummeled Chandra the moment she opened the door. Eggs fresh-plucked from the chicken coop between their house and the barn. Sundried tomatoes and green chilies, harvested from the garden behind the house, spiced the air in succulent fashion. Crisp dosa made with batter set out the day before. There was no better smell in the world to Chandra than breakfast at the Pattal home. It was the sort of smell that warmed her to her very soul. Simple and hearty. A meal to power Chandra through the day without weighing her down. The way the spice clung to her nostrils almost let her forget she had spent the whole night up and about.

"Look who's out of bed, at last," said Kumail. He was the older of the two brothers, but younger than Chandra by two years. A tall and wiry boy. Black hair curled over his ears in a shaggy mess.

"Respect your elders," Chandra shot back with mock criticism. She could not help but smile as Kumail placed a large tray of bacon on the dining table. It was a plain piece of circular furniture. Much like the house, the table knew its purpose and sought no extravagance.

"You need more beauty rest," called the younger brother, Najran. Only two years older than Omala, the boy shared his younger sister's feisty energy. Round cheeks lent the spicy words an air of innocence.

His was a face with which Chandra struggled to remain angry. No matter how cutting his remarks might be. "You've got purple under your eyes."

"Well, if Omala would quit with her snoring." Chandra chuckled.

Omala leveled a slighted glare at Chandra. Avoiding the young girl's eyes, Chandra tousled Omala's hair in recompense.

Chandra's father, Nitesh, was sat at the table. His fingers were knit together with palms facing upward. He was ready to say the morning's prayer and get on with the day. One curious eye cracked open to see whether his children had finished joining him at the table. An appreciative grin curled the corners of his mouth as he watched the family adopt the same position. The Pattals were ready to pray.

"Lucina, hear our prayer," Nitesh said with due reverence. "We thank you for this bountiful breakfast. For blessing the chickens that lay our eggs and the pigs that give us their flesh. For the grain in our bread and the spice that grants us flavor."

Nitesh gave a slight nudge to Najran, who sat to his father's left.

"Lucina, hear our prayer," the boy mimicked. His words faltered, giving the boy the air of a lost duckling. "We thank you for our fields. For the... the harvest. For making sure our fruit grows and our wheat... grows."

Nitesh unknit his fingers to rustle the boy's hair. A tacit sign of appreciation for a job well done.

It was then Najran's turn to nudge the person to his left.

"Lucina, hear our prayer," Chandra followed.

Chandra said her piece, as did Omala and Kumail in turn. There was no word or phrase to signal the time to eat. The family knew to begin their breakfast as soon as the last prayer had concluded. Kumail spoke quickly for the sake of their stomachs and was the first to reach into the bowl of eggs with his hands.

Breakfast was served.

A rush of hands flew about the table. Some grabbed eggs and bacon to plop on their plates. Others went first for the flatbread. Chandra herself was partial to getting a hefty portion of eggs before the bowl was empty. Kumail made the best eggs in the house, and Chandra was sure to get as much on her plate as she could get away with. They were soft and creamy. Not like the bricks her father cooked. It was like tossing a cloud of flavor over her tongue each time she put a pinch into her mouth.

Chaos eventually settled into the members of the household eating off their plates. Hands were kept to themselves. Mouths were too busy eating to speak. Each person knew there would be time enough to chat as they worked the fields. Time at the table was time meant to be savored. Only when the meal was near its end did the family converse.

"So," Nitesh began, the first to finish his plate, "what's all this talk about snoring, Omala? Keeping our Chandra awake? I might have to build you a bed next to Mortimer and the other horses."

"I do *not* snore," Omala protested amid a collective chuckle.

"Of course not," Nitesh replied. "You do look tired though, Chandra. Are you not sleeping through the night? You're not wasting your time in town once everyone has gone to bed, are you? That Arnstead is a hotbed for thugs and the like."

"No, Father, I'm not wasting time in Arnstead." The fact that she spoke at least half a truth gave Chandra a sliver of conviction. "It's probably worrying about you that keeps me up at night. I'm not going to see another delivery person from Westinghouse today, am I?"

"Nonsense. The Westinghouse people are nothing to worry over," Nitesh said, dodging the question. "Everything they bring helps the farm grow. You just wait until next season. That automated tiller is going to save us so much time in the fields. You won't even know what to do with yourself next spring, you'll have *so much* time."

"I'm serious, Father. We've talked about this. We don't have the money to afford another pig from the Hartsfields, much less go off and buy another new contraption every year. Still haven't paid the last three off."

"They're *investments*, Chandra. The people at the Orland Bank have got us a proper payment plan now for the loans. Soon, these machines will be paying for themselves."

"If you say so," Chandra mumbled through the last bite of her eggs.

"That's enough out of you two," Kumail interjected. "All this doom and gloom sours our breakfast. Let's talk about the festival. It's only a week or so away!"

"Oh, yes!" chimed Omala. "I can't wait for the music."

"If you have time to flap your mouths, you have time to make the harvest a reality," their father said flatly. "Out to the orchards with you, boys. Girls, that leaves you with cleaning. You'll be cooking tomorrow."

"Fair enough." Chandra collected plates from the table. "And what about after? Are Omala and I out in the fields today as well?"

"No, my dear. You're taking a loaded cart into town. The baker is waiting for some fresh fruit for his pies. Everything he doesn't take needs to be sold at the market. I planned on letting you go since you love that blasted town so much."

"Can I take Omala with me?"

"Can she, please?" Omala begged. "I'm good at helping Chandra at the market. Can I go? Please?"

"She does make convincing puppy dog eyes." Chandra chuckled. "Hard to tell this little one no."

The sound of wooden plates being scraped and submerged filled the plain room while Nitesh thought on the proposal. It was all for show. A game to see how long he could wait before Omala broke down into crocodile tears. It brought a smile to Chandra's face as she placed the plates on the windowsill to dry. The window shutters creaked as she popped them open to welcome the morning breeze.

"Yes, all right," Nitesh said as Omala reached her whimpering limit. "It never hurts to have two sets of eyes at the market. Wouldn't want anyone wandering off with something that wasn't theirs, after all."

Omala exploded with excitement. Words failed to convey her joy. Instead, she scampered off to the barn to ready one of the draft horses for the journey.

"Care to help your favorite daughter load the crates?" Chandra lightly placed a hand on her chest. "Something about extra hands and what not."

"Oh, you want me to give Omala a hand?" A wide grin plastered itself on Nitesh's face.

Chandra let out a surprised gasp, then gave her father a light push on the shoulder. Her free hand covered her astonished mouth in feigned heartache. "You're so bad, you know that? I suppose it's no wonder where I get my attitude from."

"Oh no, no, no." Nitesh laughed through his smile. "You are your mother's daughter. To this day, your true father is a mystery. There's no way any daughter of mine could be so free-spirited."

"Gods rest her soul," Chandra said.

The mention of her mother tugged at the corners of Chandra's smile. A light blanket of sorrow wrapped the pair in a moment of silence. The rest of the children had already left the house to go about their tasks. Only Chandra and her father remained in the sparsely furnished room.

Nitesh leaned against the table and folded his arms. He nodded, at last, in agreement with Chandra.

"She was a hard worker in life," Nitesh said. "I am sure she serves the gods well in death. No doubt about that."

"Yeah." Chandra nodded back. "So, help me load the cart, then? After I grab my backpack?"

"Of course. Let's get you two loaded up and ready to go. A shame to waste daylight while we have it."

3

Market

The Pattal family's cart liked to show its age during transit. Both back wheels squeaked and were in desperate need of lubricant. These were no quiet sigh-and-you'll-miss-it squeaks. They were the loud groans of a cart with bones that had gone unattended for years. Cracks in the spokes threatened to shatter like twigs underfoot on a forest floor. The bench at the front of the cart was in no better shape. It bowed prominently in the middle and was always willing to endow riders with a sliver or two. Even the arms of the cart seemed to bow slightly as they reached out on either side of Patra the draft horse.

Nothing about the cart would suggest that the Pattal family owned a single piece of technology from Westinghouse Industries, much less four.

Chandra was able to sleep despite all the cart's negative qualities. Her long night caught up to her the moment the family farm disappeared. Nestled in the back among crates of apples and pears and figs, Chandra was rocked to sleep by the sway of the cart on the road.

The trip from the Pattal farmstead was made at a much slower pace when against the sun. Omala ensured that her sister was allowed at least two hours of much-deserved rest. She loved her sister too much to deprive her of sleep.

While the road south was quiet and empty, the Pattal cart encountered many other travelers once it hit the main road. Most were farmers with the same goal as Chandra and Omala: ride into Arnstead to sell their harvests. The year was already deep into autumn. Fruits and vegetables were taken to market every day. Some sold directly to businesses in town, while others went to those looking for something fresh in their homes. There would be no shortage of competition for the Pattal girls when it came to vending their crops.

Fortunately for Chandra, the gentle hellos were not enough to interrupt her deep slumber. It was not until the golden fields of grain had been traded for the perimeter warehouses of Arnstead that Chandra woke. A small handful of carts became a torrent of traffic on Main Street. Quiet and polite well wishes were supplanted by irritated cries of cart drivers that could not find a way through densely crowded streets.

It was the sounds of Arnstead that finally brought Chandra, kicking and wholly against her will, back to the world of the waking.

"Glad to see you're finally awake, my queen," Omala chided as Chandra made her way up to the riding bench. It groaned woefully under the added weight. "I hope you're quite rested."

"I'm better than I was a couple of hours ago, to be sure. Thanks for driving, Omala. I really appreciate it."

"Yeah, yeah." Omala struggled to hide the grin that grew from her sister's appreciation. "Sure, you are. Hey! Out of the way, furball!"

A Nirdac katarl scuttled out of the way of the Pattal cart, her attention caught by the raucous call of Omala.

"Omala," Chandra chided half-heartedly, "language."

Omala clicked her tongue at the notion. The pair didn't give the discussion a second thought. There would be plenty more shouting and hollering at pedestrian traffic. As with any day in Arnstead, the streets were choked with people of all sorts going about whatever business they had.

The first sorts to get through were the storage workers. Colossal warehouses dominated the western edge of Arnstead, places to store raw goods for construction around town. Lumber from the Flickerwood to the west and Oswyn to the north. Stone from the memoryglass quarry just northwest of Arnstead. Anything a builder might need to raise a new structure if they could afford the means to do so.

Mixed in with the storage folk were people making their way out of town. Their business was typically obvious to anyone who had a moment to look. Miners, with their picks and sieves, headed for the mountains to the southwest. Smaller, independent ventures could be spotted among the more concerted efforts of the O'Hara Mining Company. Lumberjacks due for the Flickerwood could be spied with their axes and spiked boots. Hunters and trappers ready to brave the wilds of the Great Expanse between Arnstead and the Flickerwood. Some bore bows, while the more well-funded of the hunters carried caster rifles suited to their prey.

All types had business out west. An endless stream of hopes and dreams that thundered its way out into the wilds of the New World. Chandra sometimes wondered how many of these men and women would ever see their homes again.

Omala wondered how much she would have to pay to get the crowds to part for the Pattal family cart.

Weaving the cumbersome vehicle through crowds of people became no easier as they pushed into Weststead. Traffic near the perimeter had the courtesy to move either east or west. Into town or out of it. There was no such method to the madness in Weststead. North. Southeast. West by northwest. Everyone had somewhere to be, and the traffic followed no rhyme or reason.

The type of people that frequented Weststead made the problem worse, Chandra felt. When she looked around the western third of Arnstead, she almost always saw the same thing: money. An overabundance of coin that showed itself in needlessly fancy dress or an excess of gold and silver. The people who owned the warehouses where the citizens of Arnstead slaved away for meager pay. Chandra saw bankers and magnates. Tycoons marking their territory. People who came from money and knew nothing but.

"And there it is," Chandra could not help but mutter as the Orland Bank came into view. The primal urge to spit her dissatisfaction at the building was barely suppressed. Her detest instead manifested itself as an ugly sneer.

Omala kept her thoughts to herself, but mirrored the look of disgust that played across her sister's face.

"One of these days," Chandra began. "One of these days, Omala, I'm gonna pull something out of the World Below that's worth a damn. Then I'm gonna drop a fat bag of coins in front of a teller and laugh in their stupid face. I'll laugh all the way home. No more late fees. No more thugs banging on the door asking about money. We'll be done. Done, I tell you."

"If I had a dollar for every time I've heard that rant, we'd be paid off. You know that?"

"Yeah, maybe…" Chandra paused for a moment in thought. "Doesn't make it any less true, ya know?"

"Well for now we've got fruit to sell. Right?"

"Actually, I was going to ask—"

"Oh boy," Omala sighed. "What is it this time?"

"Didn't find anything to sell this last time, but I did find a map. It's got a bunch of weird markings and notes on it. I was going to pop over to Robin's and ask if she's seen anything like it before. You don't mind watching the cart for a bit while I'm gone, right?"

Omala, familiar with this sort of request, squinted at her sister. Amber eyes scanned the sympathetic front that Chandra manufactured. Chandra felt as though her essence was being picked apart by those eyes.

"Just going to pop off, then?" Omala confirmed. "Can you tell me when's the last time you sold something while we were in town together? Months? Years, even?"

"I'll be gone no longer than necessary," Chandra answered, dodging the question. "I can even take a crate of apples along with me. The baker next door to Robin's is the only set delivery we have today, right? Everything else is for the market. It's like we're killing two—"

"Two birds with one stone, yeah, yeah, yeah. At least think of something original next time you plan to ditch me, okay?"

"Perfect!" Chandra said. She leaned back into the cart to grab her backpack and a crate of apples before sliding off the side of the cart. She met the ground with a hearty thud and started to push through the crowded street. "Faster if I go on foot, I think!"

"I'll be on the eastern bank of Sisir's Run," Omala called after her sister in exasperation. "At least *try* to get back before lunch!"

Chandra heaved her pack over a shoulder, waved an excited hand back at Omala, and disappeared into the dense crowd of bodies that blocked the Pattal cart's way. She was now just another head in a sea of unfamiliar faces. Uncaring shoulders bumped and jostled her as she walked. She had to raise her elbows to get any sort of breathing room in the dense crowd.

She loved every second of it.

The claustrophobia brought on by the crowd. Having to mind every footstep lest she become the target of some person's ire. Protecting the few goods she carried from thieves and careless passersby. All of it reminded her of exploring the World Below.

At least, it felt like exploring the middle strata. Chandra began to draw comparisons between the different levels of the World Below in her head. The upper stratum, where the actual mining of memory glass was done, had to be Weststead. It was a place where people slaved for pennies, while the real profits went to some ass who was sitting in an armchair and sipping on their best brandy.

The middle strata were Eaststead. A place where the honest work got done. People made fortunes there with their own two hands. Sure, there was some fierce competition between Shikaree companies. Sometimes a body might show up in a place where it was neither expected nor appropriate. That could happen when exploring in search of riches from bygone eras.

That just left the lower strata, places of ancient danger where even Shikaree feared to tread. There was no better description for the place than Oldstead. Both were out-of-the-way places that nobody went to willingly. A Shikaree only traversed that deep if they knew there was something worth finding, as it could take a day or more just to climb that far down.

A place nobody wants to be, Chandra thought. *Somewhere no one goes unless they absolutely have to. No better comparison than Oldstead, I'd say.*

Halfway across the Bridge on Main, Chandra paused for a quick rest. She placed her crate of apples up on the northern railing and looked up-river toward Oldstead. There was no real contempt in her heart for the place. It was just another place to live as far as Chandra was concerned. Her only real interaction with the place was to pray at the House when the occasion presented itself. The white belltower glistened in the light of a cloudless day. It was as if the hand of a god had reached out to touch the very tip of the tower, so beautiful and refreshing the sight was to Chandra.

Chandra took a deep breath through her nose before filtering back into the traffic of Main Street. The sight of the tower kept her in a state of elation across the bridge and into Eaststead.

There were by no means fewer people in Eaststead than in Weststead. Chandra was still jostled about as she navigated shoulders and elbows. She still had the distinct feeling that she needed to be mindful of her pockets as well. What there was less of were robes, fine and fancy, that would do nothing but collect dirt and dust. Here in Eaststead, she saw more work boots. Suspenders and rolled sleeves were the common attire, worn by people ready to do some honest business.

Eaststead was the place in Arnstead where Chandra felt most like she was at home. A place where she could hold her head high, where she was not glared at over pointed noses.

Now that Chandra was tucked into the secure folds of Eaststead, her first order of business was the baker across from Robin's Field Goods. It was a nondescript little shop. The simple name, Kamotho Bakery, suited the simple tastes of the man who ran the establishment: Kamotho, an elderly Zumbatran human. There was nothing in the shop that did not need to be there. The ever-present line out the door and around the corner spoke to the man's continued success.

"Excuse me," Chandra said in the politest tone she could muster. "Pardon me. Business delivery. Coming through."

Most moved out of the way without a word. Some required an elbow. Others required a swift kick in the shin, for which Chandra made no apologies. She weaved and ducked until she was at the counter. Wide eyes stared at her from the other side.

"Ahh, Chandra!" Kamotho exhaled with the warmth of freshly baked bread. "Always good to see my favorite apple farmer. And with a package, no less!"

"Oh stop." Chandra chuckled. "I'm sure you say that to all the young girls that bring you nice things."

"I would never dream of it! Can I take a peek?" Kamotho dusted some flour from his hands as he pointed at the crate Chandra bore.

"Sure, sure. Do you have the silver?"

"I would never dream of shorting you, my dear." Kamotho reached his still-whitened hand into a pocket on his dough-caked apron. Coins jingled as he fished for the right amount. "Here we are! A silver dollar for a full crate. Per the usual."

"Excellent." Chandra palmed the coin as she set the crate on the countertop. She then cracked the crate of apples open with practiced hands. Light glimmered on the red and green surfaces of the fresh-picked collection. "As promised, a mixture of sour and sweet to help make mouths water. Only the best for repeat customers."

"This I see, Chandra. I thank you from the bottom of my heart."

"You are most welcome, Kamotho. And if anybody else wants some delicious apples or pears," Chandra added, raising her voice as she made her way back to the door, "look for Omala on the eastern bank of Sisir's Run! Ask for the Pattal girls!"

"Goodbye to you too, dear." Kamotho chuckled as Chandra waved goodbye.

Chandra bounced her way through the door of Kamotho Bakery. No longer burdened by the cumbersome crate of apples, she was able to slip by the line that crowded the entryway with little effort. Her obligations for the day were done. Chandra was confident that Omala could handle sales at the cart. The youngest Pattal sister had proven her mettle in the mercantile space. Chandra knew that all the produce would be gone from the cart by the time she returned.

Torrents of people whipped and whorled around Chandra as she crossed the crowded street. Robin's Field Goods, her next destination, was just across the way from Kamotho Bakery. A happy convenience that Chandra had taken advantage of many times before.

There was no line spilling out the entryway to Robin's Field Goods and onto its wooden porch. That is not to say that the two-storied building was empty. Packs of people moved up and down cluttered aisles. A staircase that led up to the second floor was constantly in use. Young attendants with bright eyes made suggestions to would-be pioneers, pointing to backpacks and tents and many other things besides.

There was no shortage of activity within the confines of Robin's Field Goods. It was a well-oiled machine that gave the outward impression that the place was empty. New faces arrived as the old, invariably satisfied with their purchases, were shuffled out.

Busiest among the handful of employees that attended customers was by far the namesake of the establishment: Robin Rutherford. Short for a Nirdac harn, it was difficult to keep track of the woman as she dashed about the store. All the shelves in the place stood well above her head. The mazelike nature of the aisles, a tactic devised by Robin to ensure her customers saw as many potential purchases as possible, made it no easier to spy the harn. It was only through occasional bouts of excitement that Robin was visible from the entryway of her store. Even then, it was just the tips of her black-and-gray ears that could be seen.

Chandra bobbed and weaved through the aisles, waiting for one of these moments of visibility. She politely waved away employees that approached her to offer guidance. Robin was the only person in the store that would be able to assist Chandra. This was something that Chandra knew well.

Fortunately, Chandra did not have to wait long. Two long ears popped over the top of a shelf that was stuffed with oats, dried fruits, and other bits of food appropriate for a wilderness expedition.

"Robin!" Chandra called over the shelving. "That you, Robin?"

The ears twitched, then turned to face Chandra. Both ears rocketed upward as the harn leaped into the air. A pink nose and big black eyes hung in the air long enough for the harn to develop a welcoming smile.

"Chandra!" Robin replied as she returned to the ground. Another hop allowed for a few short words. "How are ya?"

"Fine, thanks. Do you have a minute?"

"Oh ho!" the harn said as one hop transitioned into another. "Something to share?"

"Yeah." Chandra snickered. "I'll meet you at the teller?"

"Perfect!"

Large feet, wrapped in leather sandals, padded their way across the floor to the teller. Robin was looking smart, as she always did. A purple vest with gold stitching bound a pressed, white shirt to the harn's small frame. She ducked and bobbed potential customers and dutiful employees alike to reach the teller at the front of her store. Robin produced a golden pocket watch from her vest. Satisfied, she slid the engraved piece back into the pocket from which it had been taken.

All of this was done before Chandra could take so much as a single step toward the teller.

Robin did not stand behind the actual register. It was manned by one of her people, who was in the middle of finalizing the sale of a spacious tent to a trio of prospectors. Robin stood to the left of the transaction. She rolled a small stretch of red velvet over the countertop and flattened it so there was no hint of a wrinkle. Her hands slid in opposite directions from the center of the velvet to give it one final preen.

There was something about the way Robin prepared for a transaction that tickled Chandra. No matter how many times she saw the harn roll out that patch of velvet, it never failed to crack the suggestion of a smile. No foul mood could dissuade Chandra from indulging in the spectacle that was dealing with Robin.

"All right, then," Robin began before Chandra had even sidled up to the counter, "what do we have today, Chandra? Front of house?" Robin tapped the stretch of red velvet. "Back of house?" Robin said a bit quieter, cupping one hand around her mouth with a suggestive wink.

"Front of the house today, I think." Chandra set her backpack down next to the low counter and fished out the map she had taken from the dead Shikaree. She set the piece onto the velvet and began to unfurl it as she continued speaking. "Found this while I was down in the middle strata. Was on a dead fellow from the Baylocke Battalion. Was wondering if you might... Robin? Is everything all right?"

The formerly loquacious woman's mouth had sealed itself tighter than a sarcophagus. Not even Robin's ears twitched. All that moved were her eyes. They focused intently on Chandra before snapping back to where she had originally come from.

Chandra, unable to stifle the curiosity raised by the uncharacteristically quiet harn, turned her head to follow Robin's gaze.

"No!" Robin hissed, grabbing Chandra by the chin and wrenching her head around. The two locked eyes hard as Robin hissed again. "No, don't look."

"People from Baylocke?"

"People from Baylocke." Robin nodded in response. "This is backroom talk. Come on, before they notice anything."

Robin flipped up the slab of wood that barred guest entry to the teller. Behind the counter was a solid oak door. Chandra knew the portal well, one that remained closed save for the passage of furtive customers. The sort of door that hid dark deals from eyes that poked and pried. A place where a Shikaree could sell relics that far exceeded her licensure.

Both Chandra and Robin tucked through the doorway into an empty office. All manner of ancient tools hung from the walls. Shovels that moved soil by the ton. Swords that shattered armor like it was glass. Bits and baubles that granted invisibility or the power to breathe fire. Hair pins that befuddled minds and opened wallets.

There was no shortage of the type of relics that Robin had acquired. Some were for resale. Others would never leave the office so long as Robin lived.

Chandra's chest always swelled with pride when she noticed her contributions to the collection. Jobs well done that helped keep the Pattal family in the black with the local Orland Bank.

"So, what's the big deal?" Chandra asked after Robin had closed and twice-bolted the door. "Wasn't expecting a backroom discussion today, if I'm honest."

"Have a seat, dear." Robin gestured to a pair of chairs in front of a small, harn-sized desk. The office was in keeping with the front of the house: designed for those of small stature to be comfortable.

The design, however, made sitting in one of Robin's chairs an uncomfortable experience for someone of Chandra's size. She only remained seated to avoid being rude.

"We're in the backroom," Robin began in a grave tone, "so be straight with me. You didn't kill him, right? The person you plucked this map off of?"

"Gods above, no." Chandra would have taken offense at the question if it had come from a stranger. "I may not like the bunch, but I'm not about to go killing them over a scrap of paper."

"They might not say the same." Robin pointed through the door to the members of the Baylocke Battalion that browsed her wares outside. "Came in asking about a Bangeli girl that murdered one of their own and made off with company property. That's how they're spinning it. Asked me if I'd had any backroom dealings that involved a map of the middle strata. Map with some funny markings."

"Wait, they're saying I... saying I *killed* the man?"

"I know they're full of it, Chandra, but... yeah. They're saying you killed the guy and robbed him. At least, that it was a Bangeli girl about your age. If they know your name, they weren't sharing it."

"Atherea, give me strength." Chandra sighed. She felt a wave of heat rise from her chest and roll across her face. Though she had no hand in the man's death, Chandra suddenly felt a pang of guilt. She buried her look of exasperation into receptive hands. "The last thing I needed. What am I gonna do?"

"Probably stay out of the World Below for a few days," Robin chimed in, trying her best to sound helpful and without reproach. "Come on, now. Let's have a look at this thing that's causing so much fuss."

"Right." Chandra sniffed. The moment of panic had passed. A lump of dread remained in her stomach, but Chandra was in control again. "Sure, let's have a look."

Both women worked to clear space enough for the map on Robin's desk. Scraps of paper were whisked aside and fell to the floor like feathers. Writing utensils were moved with a bit more care. Larger bits and baubles were handled with yet more care, especially by Chandra. An impressive room filled with such wondrous items could prove to be as much a danger as a boon for the unwary.

Even with the desk cleared of all odds and ends, it was barely large enough to accommodate the square map. It was a close fit from side to side. The top drooped over the lip of the desk.

This was the first time Chandra had been able to take a good, long look at her find. There had been no time or guarantee of safety in the middle strata of the World Below. She could not have afforded the distraction. Time was also a luxury in short supply on the ride home. Chandra might have been able to fight the wind on the cart ride to Arnstead, but catching a few winks of sleep proved the more enticing option.

Now that time was on her side, Chandra conjured up a small orb of light to compliment the dim glow cast by a brass lantern hung from the ceiling. Both Chandra and Robin allowed themselves a few moments to inspect the peculiar piece of parchment before voicing any of their initial thoughts.

The whole of the map was a mystery to Chandra. Most of the chambers appeared to have been scrawled by an unsteady hand. That or the cartographer had been dedicated to capturing every nook and cranny of each peculiar room. Such attention to detail would not have explained why there were no connecting passages that linked the rooms. The map favored large, expansive chambers over connective tissue.

Inside the chambers were markings unfamiliar to Chandra. Symbols arranged like letters that were not actually letters. Not that Chandra recognized. They could have been runes from ancient languages.

"Can you read it?" Chandra asked hesitantly.

"Read what, the appalling handwriting?" Robin gestured to the collection of notes written in Federal common that surrounded the edges of the map. "Sure, if given some time."

"No. No, I mean these." Chandra pointed to a set of the odd characters. She picked a set and tapped them with a gentle finger. "Can you read what this says? I've never seen these runes before. Was hoping you might know, with how many runes you see come through here and all."

"Was afraid you might say that. No, none of that chicken scratch means anything to me. Might mean something to Olu, though. Only person I know around these parts that can speak the old languages. The ones from before the Upheaval. If anybody would know about weird words and symbols, it would be him."

"Olu?" Chandra cocked her head as she asked, "Somebody around these parts?"

"Yeah, he runs a shop in Eaststead. North of Main Street. It's called Frontier Finds. Sells books and such."

"Well, while we're talking language… there's one word that *does* jump out at me: cache." Chandra touched the word on the map. It was in a chamber at the bottom right corner of the map, next to a crudely drawn skull.

"That's enticing." Robin tittered. The prospect pulled the harn forward from her chair.

"Wager it's at the end of the map then?"

"What makes you say that?" Robin asked. "Makes sense, but I don't see any passageways to suggest it's not in the middle. Whatever the middle even is. This whole thing is a mess."

"Well, up here in the top right must be the checkpoint between strata." Chandra pointed to the corner of the map. The chamber she noted was the only one on the map that seemed to have been drawn by a steady hand. It had small red circles that lined the narrow passage, like little rubies protruding from ink-black walls. "What with the lights down there being red and all. The only place I know down there that looks like that, and it makes sense as a place to start a map. Don't you think so?"

"Couldn't argue with that logic," Robin replied with a smile. "Well, now that we know what it is, the next question would be... how much do you want for it?"

It took a moment for the words to settle from Chandra's ears and into her brain. She was so preoccupied with understanding what it was she was looking at that it had not crossed her mind to sell it.

"What do you mean, sell it?" Chandra asked. "There's stuff hidden at the end of this map. Stuff the Baylocke Battalion was interested in finding."

"So interested," Robin interjected, "that they're offering to pay for its safe return. Now I don't normally share secrets for free, Chandra, but they're offering a hundred silver for the map. That's easy money right there. We can split it right down the middle."

"That's... not a small amount of money."

"Right?" Robin sidled around the desk so that she was on the same side as Chandra. The women were shoulder to shoulder when Robin continued. "How much do you normally get out of me for the trinkets you find in the World Below? I can't recall a find that's ever gotten you more than five silver dollars in one shot."

"That's two payments to the Orland folks," Chandra mumbled. An errant pair of fingers wandered up to touch her face, then her sealed lips.

Realization shot through Chandra like a bolt of lightning.

"If they're willing to pay a hundred dollars *just* to get the map back, imagine what's waiting down there to be found?"

Disappointment was the first reaction that flashed across Robin's face. The first, but also the briefest. The harn shook the disappointment from her face and allowed a bright chuckle to diffuse the room of tension.

"I'll write you directions to find Olu's shop," Robin said through her chuckle. "But you better bring what you find down there straight to me. I won't hear about you talking to some other fence. Especially not Randall, gods forbid."

"Have I ever done you wrong?" Chandra asked with a laugh.

Robin shook her head again and began to jot some notes onto a scrap of paper.

* * *

"Hello?" Chandra called for the third time. "Is anyone here? The door was unlocked!"

A calm silence settled over the odd establishment as Chandra waited near the front door. Something about the place kept her from wading to the back of the store in search of the shop owner. The way that dust hung about in the air without ever finding a place to rest. Bookshelves that cluttered the floorplan with odd angles, out of which hung books of all sizes and colors.

The building felt old. Old, and fragile. Like speaking above a whisper might cause some ancient tome to vaporize from the vibrations in the air.

Chandra wondered what association Robin could have with this Olu. Robin's place was organized chaos meant to entice customers to stay. Her demeanor gave a similar impression to the store itself. This place, Frontier Finds, was just plain chaos.

Uncomfortable wasting time, Chandra approached the nearest bookshelf and stood on her toes. The act revealed that even the bookshelves were of different proportions from one to the next. She could see clearly over the bookshelf in front of her, but could not see more than three shelves down. Chandra moved to a neighboring bookshelf but achieved no better results.

"Hello?" Chandra inquired in a more conversational tone. She had thought she spied some movement to her left. A shape disappearing around a corner. Chandra followed the suggestion of a presence.

Nothing.

No customers to turn a curious head.

No employees to answer a question.

Nothing.

"I'm just going to have a walk around, then."

Chandra was unsure of herself as she began to wander from the front of the shop to the back. It was a long shop whose only clear landmark was the wall on the opposite side. There were no section markers to denote things like mystery or fiction. Just shelf after shelf after shelf of books. Some were bound in leather, while others had cheap backs of paper. Both types were mixed without any apparent rationale.

Books were not an everyday affair for Chandra. Time not spent on the farm was spent tending to the Pattal family's needs. Sometimes that meant visiting neighboring farmsteads to trade goods. Other times she might be channeling energy into one of her father's Westinghouse Industries *investments*. On rarer and more exciting occasions, it meant delving into the World Below to help offset her father's terrible financial decisions.

The only books Chandra had spent much time reading were the scriptures of the House. Stories of the exploits of gods and their heroes that had been documented before the Upheaval. They were the sort of thing that the family would read by candlelight before bed. Chandra's father would read one of his favorite stories every Sunday. Her mother used to do the same, a recollection that brought with it a bittersweet smile.

"Oh, hello there," came a musty voice that matched the atmosphere of Frontier Finds.

Chandra started at the words. She had been caught in a pleasant reverie and woken from it a little too soon. The culprit stood before her behind a pair of wide spectacles. A Zumbatran human whose warm voice felt like hot chocolate and a down blanket. He gave Chandra a polite wave with one hand. The other was preoccupied with an uneven stack of books that threatened to crash to the floor.

"Uh, hi," Chandra replied, her heart still fluttering from the surprise. "I'm, uh… I'm Chandra Pattal. Would you be Olu?"

"Olufemi Bradly," the man said as he extended his free hand. Chandra took his hand and received a surprisingly firm handshake. "A pleasure to meet you, Chandra. How might I be of service?"

"A friend of mine referred me to you. Robin, from Robin's Field Goods. She said you're good with languages?"

"I've learned my share," Olufemi mused. "Do you have something from the Old World that needs deciphering, perhaps? Some forgotten tome from centuries past resurfaced in your possession?"

"Not exactly. Do you have a table we could spread some paper over?"

Olufemi nodded and guided Chandra to the front counter, stopping here and there to deposit the books balanced in his hands.

"Oh my." Olufemi's brow knit into a quilt of intrigue as Chandra unfurled the map over his counter. Roving eyes devoured the foreign markings that plagued the tattered scrap of paper. "Varmint symbols, then."

"Excuse me?"

"You know. Varmints. The people-sized rodents beneath our feet. Nasty little buggers, if you ask my opinion."

"I know what varmints are, sad to say. I've seen plenty. Didn't know that they wrote stuff down, is all."

"Oh sure, most folks that can speak end up figuring a way to catch it on stone or paper. Federation managed it. The kin can do it. Why not the rat people?" Olufemi chuckled. "So, I'm guessing you wanted someone to read the markings, then?"

"If you could."

"Give me a week with this map of yours, could you?"

"Wait," Chandra began in dismay, "I thought you said you could read it? How could it take you a week to read a page's worth of text?"

Olufemi did not respond immediately. He took a moment to look Chandra over, to take in her agitated expression. Chandra felt the examination and recoiled. Not because of the piercing gaze or lack of response, but because she realized the tone she had taken with a complete stranger. One that she was asking a favor of uncertain difficulty.

"I'm sorry," Chandra muttered, deflated.

"I can see it means a lot to you." Olufemi's expression softened somewhat. "There are bits of the varmint language I know offhand, yes. Others I will have to seek references for." He gestured to the library of books that filled Frontier Finds. "I hope you understand."

"A week, then, you said?" Chandra accepted with a nod.

4

Cider

Three days had passed after Chandra gave the map to Olufemi to decipher. Three days of unbearable quiet, filled with nothing but meals and work around the farmstead. These periods of calm hung like a saddle over her shoulders. A burden of duty to the family. The weight of not being able to access the World Below until the heat around the Baylocke Battalion cooled.

No matter how many apples or pears or figs she managed to pick in those times of quiet, Chandra knew they would not be enough to assuage the hunger of the Orland Bank. The ravenous beast would continue to consume what meager profits the family could pull from their simple farm work.

Four more days, Chandra told herself. *Four more days until I'm back below, making the real money for the family.*

These patches of quiet were not all bad. If Chandra could quiet her mind and shut out the family's dire need for hard cash, the wind was cool. A concentrated effort could filter thoughts of the Orlands out and let the rustle of the apple trees sink in.

Peace was possible. Chandra just had to work hard to achieve it.

"Hey, sis," Omala called out. The tone of her voice was of one ignored. "Are you listening to me?"

"Hmm? What's that, Omala?"

Chandra had not heard a single word that her sister uttered. She had been too busy filtering her thoughts as she picked apples and placed them into the nearby cart. The silent flow Chandra had achieved came to an abrupt halt as she focused on her little sister.

"I said I've picked the low hangers clean from this one. Can you make one of those picker things? I can't reach the higher stuff."

Omala lifted herself onto her tiptoes in adorable futility.

"Maybe if you jumped?" Chandra asked, half hoping her sister would make an earnest attempt. The suggestion was met with an icy stare. Further amusement seemed to be out of the question. Chandra chuckled all the same. "All right, all right. Don't get your knickers in a knot."

No further explanation was needed beyond the "picker thing." Chandra knew that Omala was asking for a picking tool: a metal basket with prongs on the end of a staff or pole. Something to reach the upper boughs of an apple tree to grab those pesky fruits that hid beyond an arm's length. It was a simple request that Chandra fulfilled regularly for whomever she happened to be picking with that day.

Chandra brushed some apples aside in the cart to reveal a pole brought for this purpose. She pulled the length of wood out. At the same time, she used a free hand to pull a manarail spike hung from her belt. Handy bits of metal that were easy to carry. Useful both above ground and in the World Below.

Energy pulled from the Flow pooled within Chandra's chest. The process was second nature to her. So practiced was the effort that it began without thought. The solid spike softened. A faint light, nearly imperceptible under the afternoon sun, split the metal spike from tip to top. Both slid apart from one another like an empty banana peel. Violet light bisected both halves of the spike down the middle, whereupon those halves split into quarters. The process continued until a basket, roughly the size of an apple, had been formed out of the spike.

Chandra channeled one last burst of energy to affix the metal basket to the wooden pole, then handed the newly crafted device to Omala.

The younger sister smiled her appreciation and returned to her tree empowered by the effort.

Another basket was formed so Chandra could snag any apples that Omala was still too small to reach, though Chandra made sure that Omala did not spy the cleanup effort. A third and fourth repeat occurred when the boys tracked down Chandra for assistance with their picking efforts.

"I still don't understand why you can't just leave a couple spikes attached to the poles," Omala said after picking fruit for a few minutes in silence. "Seems like a waste of effort to always havta undo what you made. Don't you think so, sis?"

"Nonsense," Chandra replied offhandedly. "There have been plenty of times down below where I found myself needing just one more spike. I can't afford to leave any of them behind for convenience. Besides, it keeps my channeling skills sharp. I like being able to do this sorta thing without having to think about it."

"If you say so." Omala shrugged and went back to picking. A comical endeavor when the girl rose onto the balls of her feet to fight an apple that was just out of her reach. The grunts of effort, accompanied by Omala sticking her tongue out to one side, were the sort of memories that Chandra lived for.

There would be no further distractions for quite some time. The sun crawled across the sky like a brilliant snail leaving a trail of warmth. Shade from the apple trees ensured that the autumn day remained tolerable.

Chandra fell into a quiet rhythm: clear out the low-hanging fruit by hand, snag the higher apples with her crafted picking tool, then pick the last couple of apples Omala could not quite reach. It was a peaceful sequence. If Chandra looked over her shoulder, it was just to monitor the progress of her sister. There was no fear of encountering a stranger who might attack without provocation. No rat people the size of a human to charge and hiss when Chandra least expected it.

Short breaks came in the form of scratching Mortimer's neck. Chandra loved all the horses on the Pattal farm equally. They all served a purpose, and did so with steadfast consistency. An occasional apple was snuck from the cart up to Mortimer's mouth. Chandra felt it was only fair to reward the draft horse as he pulled the apple cart.

Of course, such peace could not last forever.

"Hey there, Chandra!"

The voice was immediately familiar. Though it was quite a soothing voice, low and like silk, it caused Chandra to cringe. She knew who the tempting sound belonged to, and she was in too good of a mood to deal with him.

"We're busy, Jacob," Chandra replied mildly without bothering to look at the boy who approached. "As I imagine you should be. Back at your family's hog farm."

"Come on, Chandra," Jacob pleaded. There was something in the earnest way he spoke that annoyed Chandra. Polite insistence that made no demands, but instilled guilt when ignored. Chandra groaned whenever she felt the boy tug at her attention. "Wouldn't be here if Father needed me. Everything's fine back at the farm. I see there's plenty to be done around here, though."

"What do you mean? We're just picking apples here." Chandra finally turned to look at the blond-haired, brown-eyed boy. The brightness on his tanned face was matched only by his curiosity. "Out with it, Jacob. What's going on?"

"I just saw a Westinghouse Industries wagon out by your house. Looks like your dad bought a new toy, did he? What's he dipping his toes into this time?"

Chandra felt her heart hit the bottom of her boots. Arms went slack. A pair of apples fell from the basket of her picking tool and bounced on the root-gnarled ground. She felt her grip on the pole tighten as rage welled in her gut.

"If you want to make yourself useful, you can help Omala pick some fruit," Chandra said, jamming the picking tool into Jacob Hartsfield's rough hands as she shouldered past him. "I'll be back."

"You sure you don't need a hand talking with those business types?"

"They're not the ones I want to talk to," Chandra seethed.

Peace abandoned Chandra as she stomped her way through the orchard rows. She was on a warpath. Sticks and twigs crunched underfoot as she plowed her way. The odd apple that had fallen from a tree was sent flying, subject to the force of a frustrated kick.

It did not take Chandra long to reach the farmhouse. If there was one thing she hated most about the Hartsfield boy, it was his penchant for being right.

Between the farmhouse and the red barn was a covered wagon. The sort of wagon that families used to start their journey out into the western frontier. It was also the sort of wagon, Chandra had learned, that companies used to transport expensive merchandise. Goods that needed to stray dry and avoid too much direct sunlight. Things that might set the mouths of highwaymen to water.

Emblazoned on the wagon's canvas was an all too familiar logo. The letters *W* and *I* had been lovingly stenciled on either side of a depiction of a memory-glass crystal. Both letters were flat black, while the crystal was depicted in a cool sky blue. The logo was known well by members of the Pattal family. By now, it likely was to their neighbors as well.

The mere sight of the Westinghouse Industries company logo was enough to put Chandra in a cold fury. Despite her abhorrence for the company, however, Chandra's target was not the two massive Bangeli katarl that were unloading some ill-conceived device and carrying it inside the barn. No, Chandra knew where the true blame for whatever this machine was rested. All her attention was focused on her father.

"Father!" Chandra called across the yard before coming to a stop between him and a woman with a clipboard. The woman had Orland Bank written all over, and Chandra did not need her interceding in what was a family matter. "What is this?"

"A fermenter, my dear," Nitesh replied. His bright demeanor was unphased by the wroth Chandra bared. "We're moving into the cider business! For both the apples *and* the pears."

"That's not what I meant, *Father*," Chandra hissed. "You *know* that's not what I meant. Tell them to pack that thing up and take it back to wherever it came from."

"He can't." The words came from the familiar woman with the clipboard. Her frigid tone was the opposite of Chandra's poorly contained rage. "The loan paperwork has been signed. All the necessary places. The Westinghouse Industries Express—"

"Nobody asked your opinion, Vic."

Victoria Chandler, a well-dressed Nirdac human with a fiery mane of red curls, waited to be sure that Chandra had finished with her outburst before continuing. Thin, emerald-green lips formed a slew of carefully calculated utterances that jabbed like knives.

"The Westinghouse Industries Express Fermenting Device has been officially paid for by the Orland Bank. Mr. Pattal has assured us that the increased productivity guaranteed by the Westinghouse machine will allow payments to be made on time and in full. We look forward to your future success in all endeavors."

Rage boiled over. Chandra tried her hardest to keep back the tears of anger that welled in her eyes. Tears filled with disgust at the predatory woman's nonchalance, and disappointment at the decision her father had made.

"When I said get this thing out of here, I meant it, Vic," Chandra spat.

"Or what?" Victoria asked. It was not a challenge. The Orland representative spoke without malice. Genuine intrigue drove the question. Victoria was curious what Chandra might have up her sleeve. When it became clear that all Chandra had to offer were fumes, Victoria continued. "Look, Chandra. You know I can't do anything. Once a contract is signed, it's signed. Cynthia Orland honors all her contracts, and she won't let one go just because someone made a bad decision. I'm just a collector."

Chandra understood the iron-clad nature of an Orland contract without explanation from Victoria. Years of crippling debt had made that clear. What confused Chandra was why the collector was on her property in the first place.

"What are you doing here, Vic? Collection isn't for another week. You're early."

A deep breath expanded Victoria's slight frame. She cast a glance toward the Pattal barn and closed her eyes. Her distraction was brief. As a sigh slid out from her lungs, she looked back to Chandra with renewed focus. The momentary show of emotion had passed. Business was back on the menu.

"Nitesh was presented with two options. He could either pay the same rate on a reduced timetable, or he could keep the same timetable with an increased rate. Whatever might be most convenient for your family. He chose the former, so… I'm here to collect. Gave you an extra day, in fact, so I could come out with the Westinghouse people."

"You people are disgusting," Chandra replied. What little moisture she had in her mouth collected on her tongue. Chandra spat the congealed blob next to Victoria's boot, then sniffed derisively at the woman. "Orlands. Their lapdogs. *All* of you."

The collector shuffled in place. Ill at ease, she looked away from Chandra. Not that Chandra could blame the woman. She felt the aura of violence that emanated from her quaking fists. The desire to reach out and strike Victoria was overwhelming. Chandra knew it would not solve the matter, but that made the thought no less enticing. It took all the willpower Chandra could muster to turn away from the collector.

Thinking better of assaulting a member of the bank, Chandra ripped herself away from the situation.

"I'll give you some time to talk to your father, Chandra," Victoria called after Chandra, "but I can't leave without some form of payment. The bank has given me strict orders to accept no more delays."

"Shove it," Chandra murmured to herself as she stalked over to the Westinghouse workers. The device they delivered was too large to be carried by hand, so the men operated a dolly. One katarl pushed while the other ensured the device remained balanced. Chandra reached them just as they were entering the barn.

"Take it back," Chandra demanded. She struggled to calm the rage in her voice as she begged leniency. Her tone grew brittle, injected with bitter sorrow. "Please. We don't need it. We can't afford it. *Please.* Take it back to where it came from."

"Not our call, miss," replied the dolly operator. "We just push the things where they need to go."

Chandra fell to her knees in the path of the dolly. The pair of katarl came to a sudden halt that caused the Westinghouse device to wobble. Up front, one katarl did his best to steady the object and bring it back under control. The dolly operator looked around the device and down at Chandra. She heard a defeated sigh escaped the man. Her face was pressed too firmly into the ground to see the fractured mix of sympathy and duty that spiderwebbed across the operator's features.

"Hey, kid," the operator began, notes of melancholy seeping into his voice. "I really am sorry, but it's just not up to us. We just move the stuff to where it has to go. The folks at the bank would still be crawling all over you even if we took the thing back to the warehouse. I can promise you that. Might as well try and make the thing useful, huh?"

Halfway through the katarl's suggestion, Chandra began to sob. Impotent rage fell to heartbreak. She pounded at the ground with one limp fist. Her other arm hid her tears from the powerless onlookers who shrugged their shoulders and wheeled their way around Chandra.

"Come now, Chandra," came the voice of her father. "There's nothing to be sad about. Today is a happy day. We're starting a new business venture! The debt will dry up like a puddle under the sun. Believe me."

Chandra felt a hand on her back. Each digit was heavy with calm reassurance. The sort of fatherly gesture Nitesh made whenever his decisions further fractured Chandra's heart. Chandra ripped away from the hand in disgust. Dust kicked up at the sudden movement and caked her tear-stained cheeks.

"Why?" was all Chandra could manage to respond.

"Why start the new venture?" Nitesh asked. "There are so many people in that town you love so much. Those people love their booze, and we never manage to sell *everything*. Now we'll be putting the extra fruit to good use instead of feeding it to the horses. It's a win, Chandra."

"We were stable, Father," Chandra sputtered. "We were *stable!* For the first time since Mom died, we didn't have to worry about money."

"Do you know how long we would be paying the Orland folks at the rate we're going, my dear?" Nitesh ventured a wary hand onto Chandra's shuddering back. She did not push him away this time. "Your children's children would have been paying for the loans. This way, we'll get the loans paid off in *my* lifetime. We might even be able to hire some hands. Get the young ones into town for some proper schooling. Teach them more than what the traveling proctor can offer every other week. How does that sound?"

"What do you know about making cider?"

"A little louder, dear?"

"I said," Chandra sputtered, turning to face her father, "what do you know about making cider?"

"That's what the machine is for. That's the beauty of it!"

"It is *not* beautiful," Chandra spat. "That thing is disgusting. What if the cider that comes out of that thing is just as disgusting? What if there's more to it than just smashing some apples or some pears and chucking them into one of your precious machines? How do you know it's going to be okay?"

"I'll get some help from the neighbors," Nitesh protested. "If I still need help after looking through the manual, I'll ask for help when the neighbors come down for the harvest celebration. I'm not above asking for help. You'll see."

"If you're so ready to ask for help, then why can't I be a Shikaree? Why can't I do something helpful for the family and not have to feel ashamed for it?"

"That's different," Nitesh replied with a dark shift in tone. The lines on his face creased with agitation, and the corners of his mouth reached for the dusty barn floor. "I'll not have another member of this family dying on some fool's errand for that blasted town."

"Mom was a Spellseeker!" Chandra shouted. "This is different. I'm not asking to die to protect a town that doesn't care for me. All I want is to help our family pull itself out of the gutter. The farm is ours, and I want to help keep it that way!"

"And you will. By helping around the farm and making sure our produce sells at market. When you're old enough to be a professional, we can talk—"

"That's three years, Father. *Three years.* I don't want us to get kicked out before I have a chance to make a difference around here. Please!"

Composure abandoned Chandra. Frustration and rage. Sorrow and grief. Everything came to a head all at once and shattered any suggestion that Chandra was okay. She fell forward into her father's chest and cried like a small child. Feeling her father's warm embrace as his arms gathered her up made the tears flow more furiously. There was no stopping the deluge. What had been bottled for years was being set free in a single moment.

Chandra clutched at her father's overalls as she allowed her pain and uncertainty to flow outward into the quiet barn.

5

Prayer

Night hung over Arnstead like an ancient woolen shawl. It was cozy and familiar, though not without its share of moth-eaten holes. Most respectable people went to sleep with the setting of the sun. Those who remained to walk the streets at such a desolate hour were either up to no good or, courtesy one too many drinks at the Creaky Board or Iron Goblet, did not know entirely what they were up to. Those latter folks tended to wake up in strange beds and notice a suspicious absence of their wallet in the morning.

Chandra was pleased to know that she fell squarely into the former camp. She had tied Alabaster to a post in the memory-glass quarry outside of town and continued her way on foot. It was a walk she had made a hundred times or more, though she never bothered to keep precise count.

Gravel shifted to packed earth as Chandra made her way from the quarry into Arnstead proper. A welcome change, as far as Chandra's ankles were concerned. The steady ground allowed her to make better time toward Oldstead and her ultimate destination: the House of Many. One of the few buildings in Arnstead that never locked the front door. Those who needed the guidance of the gods were never turned away.

The walk through Oldstead was quick. Dilapidated huts and squalid homes lined the narrow streets that led to the towering House. It loomed like an opaline monolith over the low buildings that surrounded it. There was no place in Oldstead from which the landmark could not be seen, so large was the House.

It all served as warning. The rundown homes. Beggars sleeping in makeshift tents down narrow alleyways. Oldstead was where those who did not have the resources to survive gathered. The bankrupt, victims of grand larceny, people whose image had been destroyed beyond social repair. Chandra felt closer to these people tonight than she had for years. The shadowy tendrils of Oldstead reached out and rested on her shoulders, sending shivers down the length of Chandra's spine.

Not if I have anything to say about it, Chandra thought as she approached the front doors of the House.

Chandra adjusted her backpack as she looked up at the large House doors. The immense portal was barely open. Left just enough ajar for a single person to squeeze through at a time. A stark contrast to how wide the doors hung open during the day. Starlight twinkled on the white stones of the House. The intricate symbols of the gods, crafted of iron and affixed to the doors, shimmered under the moon. Chandra took a deep breath, then crossed the holy threshold to reach the dark recesses of that place of prayer.

The entryway to the House was sparsely lit. Candles in silver sconces flickered above offering basins of generous size, which had been thoroughly cleaned of all dollars and pennies before sunset. Slits in the sconces fractured the already dim light. The sort of illumination that hindered nearly as much as it helped. Wooden pews and a long, wine-colored carpet offered a plethora of ways to trip on the way to the transept.

Chandra did her best to move in silence. The carpet stifled the noise of her boots, separating her footsteps from naked marble. The muffled footsteps, however, still carried throughout the empty main chamber of the House. Chandra simply sounded more like a shuffling old woman than a fit young girl charging down a football pitch. She hoped her presence would not disturb any who sought sleep beyond the main chamber.

When she neared the transept, Chandra slid sideways into a pew and knelt to assume the position for prayer. Hands knit together with palms facing the ceiling. Head bowed in a show of reverence. Backpack on the ground and out of the main walkway.

"Lucina, hear my prayer," Chandra began. "Please watch over the remainder of our harvest. Please ensure that our fruits sell without fail. We can't afford any losses, not with this new machine my father has purchased. I pray that your hand showed leniency when the Orlands built their contract for my father to sign, even though he knew we couldn't afford another contraption." Chandra exhaled a heavy sigh, one born more of shame than relief. "I am sorry to ask so much of you, Lucina, goddess of so much that our family holds dear. Blesser of harvests. Steward of commerce. Lucina, hear my prayer.

"Atherea, hear my prayer." Weakness left Chandra's voice with the new invocation. Confidence swelled in her chest at the mere utterance of Atherea's name. "Watch me as I descend into the World Below. I know that the Baylocke Battalion hunts me, and I ask for the strength to deal with any of their ilk who would seek to do me harm. I wish them no more ill will than they would wish upon me. Atherea, hear my prayer.

"Manus…" The conviction in Chandra's voice faltered. She struggled to find the right words to express her desire to the god of life and death, caretaker of souls. "Manus, please hear my prayer. Please continue to watch over my mother's soul. I know I don't need to ask every time, but I can't help myself. She worked hard to help as many folks as she could in life. I ask that it continues to shine favorably on her in death. That's all. I'm sorry to waste your time over something that sounds so trivial. On the grander scale, that is. Nothing that you do is trivial… and now I'm rambling. Apologies. Manus, please hear my prayer."

Chandra sighed and allowed her head to fall forward onto the next pew. The gentle thump of her skull knocking against wood echoed twice in the silent House. She gave the gods silent thanks that she was alone in the room.

"That was lovely. Very well said."

A well of shame rose to Chandra's cheeks. Fortunately, the voice was one that she recognized.

"Ryleah," Chandra hissed. She turned her head to look at the acolyte that stood beside her in the pew. "As quiet as ever, I see."

"Comes with the territory, moving about without disturbing those at prayer. The sandals help too," Ryleah added brightly, wiggling her exposed toes. "I figured you were done. Do I need to step away? I could make myself scarce if you have more prayers to make."

"Oh stop." Chandra chuckled through her embarrassment. "I'm not about to send you away. I've only one prayer left to make if you wish to join me. Some words to share with Hyperios."

"I would love to join you. Could you give me your hand?" Ryleah asked sheepishly, her hand extended vaguely in the direction of Chandra. Sightless eyes sat still in Ryleah's sockets as she waited. "Would hate to trip over your things, if you have anything with you."

Chandra moved her pack out of the way and took Ryleah Pembrooke by the hand. The young woman's skin was supple in comparison to Chandra's beaten hands. It felt like running rough sandpaper over a baby's cheek. A pang of jealousy reared its ugly head at the notion. Ryleah was of similar age to Chandra, yet the half-human half-kin's hands would suggest that Ryleah had never worked a day in her life. Not the sort of work that Chandra was used to, at any rate. Only some slight bruising around the wrists and forearms suggested work beyond sitting in a divulgence booth or collecting Sunday tithes from worshippers.

The thoughts were unwelcome, and they passed almost as soon as they had arisen. Ryleah was a friend. This was not a question in Chandra's mind. The acolyte's white robes rippled as Chandra helped ease her friend into place.

"Hyperios, hear our prayer," Ryleah requested in a warm, encouraging tone. She adopted the position of prayer and tilted her head slightly toward Chandra.

"Hyperios, hear our prayer." Chandra nodded. "Help the bookkeeper Olu in his study. Ensure he learns as much as possible about the map that I left in his care. I pray that it may lead to good fortune and a way for my family to escape the bootheel of the Orland Bank. Hyperios, hear our prayer."

"Hyperios, hear out prayer," Ryleah echoed with a sense of finality. She opened her eyes after the prayer had concluded and looked through Chandra. "That sounds exciting! The map, I mean. Something for your Shikaree work?"

"Nailed it, Ryleah. Clever as always." Chandra gave Ryleah a light punch on the shoulder and followed with a light chuckle. Ryleah returned the chuckle, covering her mouth as she did so. The bruising on her arms became more apparent as clouds parted to allow additional moonlight to flood the House. "You all right there? Those bruises on your arms, I mean. They look awful fresh."

Ryleah recoiled at the question. Embarrassed hands shot out to grab the ends of her sleeves, which she pulled down on to hide the bruising.

"Oh, no, I'm fine. Really," Ryleah assured. "We've just been short-handed lately when I have to make rounds in the catacombs. That's actually why I'm up right now. My turn to do night rounds, and I'd hate to wake anyone else on my account."

"How thoughtful. I imagine you wouldn't get more than a grumble if you asked another of the clergy for a hand, though, right?"

"Why bother waking another acolyte when I have a perfectly willing member of the congregation right here?" Ryleah asked with a wide smile. "Care to join me on my rounds tonight? I figure you'll be heading that way anyway."

"You act like it's not normal for folks to come knocking on the House doors at midnight to say a prayer or two. Sounds perfectly reasonable to me." Chandra paused for a moment. Long enough to let disbelief contort Ryleah's features. "Yeah, I guess not. Of course, I'll go with you. At least until we reach the passage. Time has never been on my side for these trips, you know."

"Of course." Ryleah nodded. "Of course."

The pair rose, Chandra shouldering her pack as she did so. Ryleah took Chandra's arm for guidance as they crossed the transept toward a door tucked into the back-left corner of the House.

It was more a doorway than an actual door. The oaken slab that once barred entry to the living quarters of the House had been removed ages ago. Ever since the catacombs below were expanded to service folk from outside the clergy. Chandra had never known the archway to hold an actual door, nor had her father.

There were other doors in the small antechamber. To the left was the office of the pontiff, Isaac Avendale. Straight to the back led to the House dining area, which connected to both the kitchen and larder. The door on the right led to the living and washing quarters of the clergy. None of these areas were particularly expansive. Each served its purpose with no extra room to spare. It made life for the clergy particularly cramped when a new acolyte joined the Arnstead House and the residing members had to push their double bunks closer together.

In the middle of the antechamber was another entryway. One that did not point to a cardinal direction like those that surrounded it. This portal led straight down a winding staircase of black iron. Down and down, it wound to the grand arch that marked the entrance to the Arnstead catacombs. Resting place for the dearly departed from all walks of life. Lit sconces dotted the walls of the descent like little stars.

"I'll go first then, yeah?" Chandra posited as more of a statement than a question. "Just in case you get tripped up. Easier to catch you from below than grab at you from above."

"How thoughtful," Ryleah replied with a wink in Chandra's direction. "My brave Keeper, here to protect my sorry and woefully inadequate ankles."

"I could give you a push if you prefer."

"I think not." Ryleah suppressed a chuckle. She brought a finger up to her lips as a tacit request for silence. "Until we're below and away from those who sleep."

Chandra nodded in compliance and took the first few steps down the iron staircase.

Metal groaned and creaked under each step. Chandra kept one hand on the railing for guidance. The steps were deep and narrow. One misstep would make for a nasty tumble and more than a few broken bones.

It was difficult to imagine what descending the steps must have been like for Ryleah, Chandra mused. Chandra was afforded the gift of sight. All she had to do was look down and not misjudge the depth of each step. Ryleah, on the other hand, had no such luck. Each step for the blind half-kin was made in pure darkness. Depth had to be judged by footfalls alone.

Despite her lack of sight, Ryleah offered no hint of struggle. Her grip on Chandra's shoulder was light. Her spare hand rested lightly on the iron rails that followed the staircase in its downward spiral. There was even a sliver of a smile on her face.

She doesn't need me, Chandra thought. *She makes these rounds alone all the time. I'm just here as company more than anything else.*

Chandra's foot slipped on a particularly worn step while her vigilance had waned. Both hands clamped onto the iron railing as her heart leaped out through her mouth in the form of an alarmed cry. Chandra felt each racing beat in her ears as she found herself planted on the unforgiving iron step.

"Oh, that's a nasty one, isn't it?" Ryleah inquired. "Everything all right? No sprains or scuffs that need a bandage or splint? A minor miracle perhaps?"

The sincerity with which Ryleah asked her questions shifted Chandra's excited energy into embarrassment. Chandra pulled herself back up and readjusted her pack. She was glad that her friend could not see the flustered look that hung on her features.

"No, I'm fine," Chandra grumbled as she placed Ryleah's hand back on her shoulder. "Just a minor trip was all. Nothing to worry about."

Chandra's tailbone disagreed.

"Good to hear," Ryleah replied. "On with the procession, then."

What remained of the descent was not plagued by further mishap. Methodical plodding down step after step brought Chandra and Ryleah at last to the stone floor of the catacombs. A great archway of polished black stone separated the stairwell from the catacombs proper. Inscribed in white on the impressive keystone was the symbol of Manus, god of life and death: a simple scale to weigh the merits of a soul. A message was carved into the stones that led from the floor up to the keystone on either side. On the left, it read "May you be weighed fairly." On the right, "Balance in all things."

Chandra knit her fingers together in the sign of prayer and bowed her head before passing through the archway. The grand nature of the passageway still carried emotional weight, even after years of crossing its threshold.

While Chandra had been consumed by minor awe under the archway, Ryleah had already made her way through the left side of the archway and found the wall with her hand.

"Come on, then," Ryleah muttered. "Neither of us has all night, you know."

Chandra joined Ryleah in the main corridor of the catacombs. She walked in reverent silence as she observed her surroundings.

The catacombs were not like the memory-glass quarry or the strata of the World Below. More love and effort were put into its construction than the odd support beam every ten to twenty feet. Walls were ground down and polished until they resembled the keystone of the entryway, black and glossy. The floor was paved with white brick that gripped at the soles of Chandra's feet. There was space enough overhead for the tallest katarl to stretch their arms high.

On either side of the main walkway yawned small archways. Some led to hallways that cut away from the main catacombs passage. Extensions necessitated by the endless flow of time and the fragile nature of mortal vessels. The older Arnstead grew, the more expansive and mazelike the passageways became. All of them with walls as black as death and floors whiter than fresh snow. A perpetual winter night that dug its claws deep into the cold ground.

Not all the archways led to further passages. Most from the main hallway led to small rooms. It was into one of these that Ryleah dipped.

The first room on the left just beyond the entryway to the catacombs. Chandra followed, shrouded in a veil of silent respect for the dead.

The room was small. Not so cramped for space that a handful of people would be unable to visit, but by no means would it fit the entirety of a Sunday congregation. It had the same polished walls and white stone floor of the main corridor. The ceiling of the room had been laid with white stone as well. A single lantern hung from the middle of the ceiling lit the room. The room was quite like the main corridor in almost every way with one exception: the receptacles.

Great basins of stone that stood three feet high surrounded the walls of the small room. Each receptacle was six feet wide and about two feet back to front. Piled up to the lip of the simple, rough-cut stone were the ashes of the dead. Small brass plaques were fastened to the basins, as well as to the wall above. They bore the names of the individuals who rested in each basin. Years were engraved along with the names.

Mass graves that housed hundreds of people lined the walls of that room. The same was true for most of the other rooms that Chandra and Ryleah visited that night. Places where miners and teachers were laid to rest. Soldiers basked in somber slumber next to Spellseekers and fisherfolk. Titles bore no importance in a public grave.

Ryleah walked into the center of the small room. She pulled a dash of salt from a pouch on her belt, plus a little dash of something Chandra did not recognize. Once the acolyte had tossed both substances over her shoulders she began to speak.

"Manus, hear our prayer. Watch over the immortal souls in the afterlife as we watch over their earthly remains. Protect them from decay as we here protect them from ravenous ashlings. We serve you in life as we shall serve you in death. Manus, hear our prayer."

The reagents Ryleah had tossed over her shoulder sparkled, then danced like firecrackers around her ankles.

"Manus, hear our prayer," echoed Chandra.

"That's one done. On to the next!" Ryleah declared in triumph as she raised a finger. "How about we work down the left side of the main corridor and get you to your passage faster? I can deal with the right side on my way back to the stairs. No problems there."

"That sounds lovely," Chandra replied with a playful curtsy, realizing too late that the gesture would be lost on her friend. Chandra settled for grabbing Ryleah carefully by the arm and guiding her to the next room.

The process was quick. Sprinkle some dust. Say a few words. Indulge in a bit of a light show. Everything was smooth and according to plan. It gave the girls time for some idle chatter between rooms.

"So," Ryleah began after the third room had been cleansed, "how's the farm?"

"Depends," Chandra said sheepishly. "How much of my prayer did you hear upstairs?"

"I heard you drop your pack and shuffle around the pew."

"Right, so all of it, then." Chandra sighed. "We *were* doing fine. Up until my dad bought another machine from those bastards at—"

"Language."

"Right, sorry. So, my dad bought another machine from the Westinghouse people. He knows we're hanging on by a thread as it is."

"And what's the machine for?" Ryleah asked with a placid expression.

"Something about making cider. I didn't ask for the details. It was all I could do to not hit the man."

"Sounds like a great way to make some money. Folks around here do love their booze. You'd be amazed by the things a person says while drunk in one of our divulgence booths. They confess to all manner of desires and tricks. The sort of stuff that turns your cheeks red."

"Yeah, well…" Chandra snickered. "I'm sure the idea has its merits. If we can figure out this whole cider-making thing. I'll have to dip into the taverns around town and see where they get booze from. Might offer a few leads on how to make the stuff before the competition realizes we're competition."

"I like the sound of that. Much better than this doom-and-gloom talk about losing the farm."

"It's not just doom and gloom. Either we need to make the best cider in the New World, or this map I've found needs to lead me somewhere worth my while."

The girls stopped to cleanse another room. Ryleah resumed the conversation with a question once she had finished.

"Where does the map lead?"

"Best guess," Chandra began with an exasperated huff, "it's a map to some kind of treasure stash. It's got markings from the ratfolk. Some notes scribbled in Federal common by someone from the Baylocke Battalion."

"That sounds serious. How did you get your hands on something like that? You didn't have to, uh…" Ryleah made a gesture to suggest a throat being cut.

"Oh, no! Of course not. No, the fellow I took it from was dead down in the World Below when I found him. No help needed from me."

"Good. Good." Ryleah sighed. "You think there will be a bunch of relics at the end of this map, then?"

"That's the hope." Chandra ran her fingers through her black hair, then gave her scalp a hearty scratch. "With any luck, I'll find enough down there to pay off some of the loans we have with the Orlands. Get some money to stash away rather than having to live month to month like we have since mom passed."

"May Manus shepherd her soul with care."

"Thank you, Ryleah. I mean that."

"Of course." The half-kin smiled.

The next room was different from those that had come before. Large basins of ash were nowhere to be seen. Instead, chest-high pillars cluttered the walls. More dotted the floor. The girls had to weave their way between these pillars to reach the center of the room. Atop most of these pillars rested an urn. The more reserved among the urns were decorated with bright paints. Others were inlaid with gold and silver. A handful were even encrusted with jewels.

What set the ostentatious urns apart from the ash basins most was that the urns were accompanied by singular names. The name of a mayor might rest beneath one urn on a plaque of gold. One particularly distasteful urn had the name Jeffry Orland bolted into place under its solid gold brilliance.

No matter how fanciful the container, however, the prayer remained the same.

"Manus, hear our prayer. Watch over the immortal souls in the afterlife as we watch over their earthly remains. Protect them from decay as we here protect them from ravenous ashlings. We serve you in life as we shall serve you in death. Manus, hear our prayer."

Neither of the girls lingered in this space to talk. Words that were spoken in such affluent, hollow company somehow felt tainted. There was enough waste in the room, Chandra felt, without her contributing wasted words.

The rooms rotated between decadence and communal burial. It was not a perfect pattern of alternation. Rooms that housed the poor outnumbered the places of wealth by a considerable margin. Arnstead was, by and large, a town of workers. It had not yet grown to match the splendor of Southport or New Haven. Some residents of Weststead were certainly trying to change that fact, but it was a slow and laborious process to garner so much opulence.

Eventually, the girls came to a room that was different from all the others. It had been hollowed out and laid with stone as had all the others. A few basins had been brought in and set next to the walls, but they were empty and did not cover all the available space that the walls had to offer.

A rope was hung over the doorway to bar entry. Ryleah, who had maintained contact with the left wall with her hand when traveling from room to room, recoiled when her hand touched the braid. A coy smile played across her features.

"Always brings back memories," Ryleah said. "When you found me, lost and alone, in a place I did not yet belong."

"You all right?" Chandra asked, squeezing the hand of her friend. "I don't have to go *right* now. Would hate for you to turn into a sobbing mess. Like old times, and all that."

"Oh stop, you villain. No, I'll be quite all right. I've walked these rooms alone more times than I can count since then. Go on ahead, and thank you for making the night shift a little less lonely."

"If you insist," Chandra added, squeezing Ryleah's hand one more time. "And thanks to you too. For listening, I mean. I needed somebody to talk to."

"I live to serve." Ryleah laughed as she knit her fingers together in the sign of prayer. "Go with the gods, Chandra."

"Same to you, Ryleah."

Warmth overcame Chandra as she watched her friend disappear into the next room. It felt good to speak to someone who Chandra knew she could trust. The divulgence booths offered a limited outlet for frustration, but this was more intimate. Chandra knew she could say anything exactly as she felt and not have to pick and choose her words.

The rapport was much better as well. Responses from the other side of the divulgence booth were always so sterile. The kind of responses that a mother and father make up when their four-year-old child asks where babies come from. Even if Ryleah did not know the correct answer for a question or the exact response for a given statement, Chandra knew that the acolyte would at least speak from her heart. That sort of relationship could not be bought with money or faith. Only with time were such friendships forged.

Chandra ducked under the rope and entered the vacant chamber of the catacombs. She moved to a specific basin that rested against the back wall. Digging her fingers between the wall and the basin, she began to pull with all her might.

The basin budged an inch.

Chandra took a deep breath, slid her fingers further behind the basin, and pulled again. This time, her efforts pulled the basin far enough to get her shoulder between the wall and the basin. Chandra utilized this space to push off the wall against the basin.

When Chandra was finished, a neat hole revealed itself where the basin had been resting. A rope, fixed to the back of the basin by a manarail spike, dangled down into the hole. Chandra dropped her pack into the hole and listened for the resulting thump. A familiar distance. Not so far that Chandra would die as a result of the fall, but far enough that a twisted or broken ankle was not out of the question. She grabbed the rope and slid herself into the hole. As Chandra worked her way down, her weight slid the basin noisily back into place over her personal entrance to the World Below.

6

—

Lost and Stolen

Tense stillness pervaded the musty air of a village of stone, the homes and shops carved out of the bare rock of the World Below. Their walls were smooth, without evidence of being tooled or chipped away by hand. Perfectly square windows and rectangular doorways that would cause a level to whistle aloud. These structures, like any others found in the World Below, were carved by channelers of the Flow.

Chandra stood in one of these houses. Her hand ran across the smooth surface of a wall carving at the back of the structure. Depictions of odd little people in what looked to Chandra like a family tree. Meticulous lines connected several families of Those Who Came Before until all hint of succession vanished.

Most murals in the homes of Those Who Came Before ended in similar fashion. Chandra could walk to the structure next door or the last house on the opposite end of the village, but where she went would make no difference. What remained the same were the handful of runes that every Shikaree could decipher blindfolded. One of these runes, common in the kitchens and smithies of Those Who Came Before, was the rune of fire. The other was more abstract: the rune of terror.

The village in which Chandra stood was known to her. There would be no fantastical finds. It had been picked clean by Shikaree who had explored the middle strata before her. If Chandra did manage to find something as she walked the halls of the long-dead civilization, it would be worth little more than pennies. Things like small fire starters or irons that pressed laundry. None of the flashy stuff like the sword Chandra had happened upon some days ago.

Chandra's aim on this trip below was not to accrue wealth. Not that it stopped her from pocketing the few minor trinkets that she found. No, Chandra had descended after her prayer in the House because she was restless. Full of that type of energy that keeps a person awake at night no matter how tired they might be. Chandra had rolled and rolled in half sleep until Omala, politely but without room for discussion, kicked her sister out of bed.

There was no better way to expel excess energy than a trip to the World Below. At least, that was how Chandra felt on the matter.

The ride into Arnstead burned away most of the nervous energy Chandra had pent up. Leaving Alabaster hitched just outside the memory-glass quarry, Chandra made the last leg of the trip to Oldstead at a jog. Prayer in the House and the company of Ryleah had calmed her mind. All that remained for her to do was whittle away the hours until she was ready to head back home.

Thinking about the World Below inevitably brought Chandra's mind back to Frontier Finds. To the proprietor, Olufemi, who could even now be poring over the details of her strange map of the World Below. Chandra felt her restlessness begin to rise once more.

It doesn't make him work faster, dwelling on it, Chandra reasoned to herself. *Doesn't make time move quicker either. A week is a week, and he's still got about four days to go.*

Chandra kicked a loose stone across the threshold and out into the perfectly even street. It plinked and skittered outside the familiar aura of Chandra's light spell.

"Hello?"

The single word crept through the village of stone. It sounded unsure, as if looking for someone it could not say for sure was there.

The same word crawled through the village once more with growing uncertainty.

"Hellooo?"

At first, Chandra had thought her ears played tricks on her. No Shikaree with their eyes on a prize would think to come to the bare bones of this village, not unless they were merely passing through to another area. It would not have been the first time that a shifting rock or crawling creature had made Chandra hear things in the dark places of the World Below. The second calling, however, guaranteed that someone was out there.

Chandra doused her light and took refuge deep in the recesses of a house. Which house in particular made no difference, so long as she was not in the middle of the street when the owner of the forlorn voice passed by.

Footsteps cut through the shadow. The sound of metal striking stone resounded with each step, echoing throughout the village. A light came into view as the footsteps grew louder. Soft light that flickered with each step. As the source drew near, Chandra crept up to a window and peeked around the wall to see who this voice belonged to.

The bearer of the light was a man of average height. Instead of producing light through the Flow, he carried what Chandra guessed was an oil lantern. The flickering nature of the light suggested as much. On the man's hip were a sword and a caster pistol. He was garbed in a blue coat with white piping on the breast and sleeves. Short brown hair framed a face that was fraught with distress and impatience.

"I said hello?" the man called again. Chandra pulled away from the open window as the man turned in her direction. His light just barely reached the house in which she lurked, and she was not prepared to reveal herself just yet. "Is there anyone out there?"

Something about the man's clothes looked familiar. The nature of the outfit was just on the tip of Chandra's tongue. They looked quite official, but Chandra could not imagine for her life who would be patrolling the depths of the middle strata. It was not a job for the 4th Federation Army. They kept to the upper stratum. Shikaree had no uniforms outside of maybe a marking or patch that identified their crew.

Wait a minute, Chandra realized. *I know that coat. It's like mom's coat. Is he a Spellseeker?*

Chandra poked her head up to the window to get a better look.

Definitely a Spellseeker! But what's he doing down here all by himself?

Before Chandra had a moment to ask her question to the stranger in a familiar uniform, there was a crash followed by a shift in light. The glass of the Spellseeker's lantern shattered into a thousand pieces and spilled flaming oil onto the stone street. Some of the flaming oil doused the Spellseeker's pants, which he patted out with the thick sleeve of his coat.

"Ack, gods damn it!" howled the Spellseeker as he finished smothering the fire on his pant leg.

An unnatural gust of wind whipped through the street. It pushed fast enough to whistle against stone and spread the oil for the lantern so thin that it went out. Darkness resumed. Darkness, but not silence. A chittering sound swirled amid the sounds of curses and crunching glass. Claws scraped and teeth gnashed.

Varmints, Chandra thought, frozen in place. *How long have they been watching this guy? Were they watching me too? No, I would have heard the buggers. They must have put an arrow through the lantern. Maybe a stone. Something to kill his light but keep the sport. Vicious little shits.*

A light cut through the darkness. It was small, like a match that burned with furious purpose. Chandra could now see the Spellseeker's torso again. In his hand was the caster pistol, which served as the source of light. A small gout of flame roared from the muzzle of the tool.

Enough to see by, Chandra reasoned, *but not enough to keep varmints at bay. This guy is gonna need some help.*

"Seeker!" Chandra called to the half-lit figure. The man whipped toward the sound of her voice and stared into the void with rapt attention. "Close your eyes!"

Chandra visualized her light spell as she stepped toward the Spellseeker. She saw the light grow and grow until the small orb was filled to the point of bursting with luminous brilliance, and burst it did. As Chandra drew close to the Spellseeker, who had gathered Chandra's intent and tucked his face into the crook of his elbow, the small orb of light popped in a brilliant splash of sparks. Chandra closed her eyes to the blast at the last possible second.

The spell had the desired effect. Chittering cries filled the darkened village, bringing it to life for what must have been the first time in centuries. Wood and iron clattered to the stone floor in an awful racket. Hands abandoned weapons to cover eyes seared by blinding light.

Chandra smirked at a job well done as she brought another, tamer spell of light to bear.

"You all right, Mr. Seeker?" Chandra asked, putting her back up against the Spellseeker's. She pulled her staff off her backpack and used the Flow to fit a manarail spike to one end. Another bit of channeling had the spike looking like a genuine spearhead. "No knives or arrows where they shouldn't be?"

"Nothing of the sort," the man replied. "Assuming that's thanks to you, Shikaree. You *are* a Shikaree, right?"

"Sure am."

"So," he started before a weighty pause, "what comes now?"

"We wait," Chandra said as flatly as possible. "Let the light grow a little more. See if there's anything left waiting in some nook or hole to grab us once we let our guard down."

"Out in the open like this?"

"I can't send the light too far away. I'll lose concentration if I do."

"Wouldn't want that," the Spellseeker conceded. Chandra felt his shoulders shrug in tangible resignation. "How long do you typically wait when something like this happens?"

"Honest answer?" Chandra probed.

"Please."

"About an hour." She sighed through her teeth. "I don't know about you, but I want to make damn sure those varmints are gone before I let my guard down."

Chandra felt the Spellseeker shuffle for a moment. The sound of a pocket watch flipping open and then clicking closed filled the cavernous space. Another bit of shuffling preceded the unsheathing of a sword. He drew in a deep breath and let it out slowly, shuddering a bit as he did so.

"Already been a day," the Spellseeker began. "Suppose another hour or two won't be the end of me. Not like running into a pack of varmints in pitch dark would."

"Wait, you've been down here a full day?"

"And some change, yeah."

"You don't even have a pack!" Chandra cried. "What have you been doing down here all by yourself for a day?"

"I hadn't planned on it, really."

"Ah, so you're lost."

"Honest answer?" the Spellseeker asked, his tone cheerful despite the dire nature of his predicament. A feeble attempt to bring some mirth to the situation. "About as lost as a sheep in a pack of wolves."

Chandra could not help but snort at the idea of a grown adult entering the World Below alone, much less without any apparent preparation. She was amazed that whoever guarded the checkpoint that day was lax enough to allow someone through. Further amazement came in the form of a Spellseeker being present at all in the World Below.

A careful shrug dropped Chandra's pack to the ground before she reasserted herself against the Spellseeker's back. She leaned some of her weight onto the improvised spear she gripped in her right hand. If Chandra was going to be stuck, she was going to be stuck in comfort.

"Owen, by the way," the Spellseeker said, breaking a few minutes' silence. He slotted his caster pistol into its holster and shifted his sword to his right hand. Chandra heard the metal swish through the air with a small flourish. "Third Seeker Owen Raulstone, of Lost and Stolen. Pleasure to make your acquaintance."

Owen hung on his last word, inflection making it clear that he expected a name in response. Chandra felt no need to make the situation awkward.

"Chandra Pattal. Novice Shikaree."

"Novice? Operating a bit deep for a novice, aren't you?"

"Operating a bit deep for a Spellseeker, aren't you?" Chandra snapped back.

"Most days, yes. There's been a rash of thefts lately that involve something burrowing into the claimant's home. A sort of smash and grab where the perpetrator takes anything it can find with memory glass and takes off as quickly as it came."

"Sounds like varmints."

"Indeed, it does," the Spellseeker confirmed. "That's where my mind went too. Not the first time I've seen something like this, but it's the first time I've seen it on this scale. It's normally a single house and the claims are spread out by weeks or months. The crawly little bastards seem to be getting bolder, though."

"Oh yeah?" Chandra encouraged. She even gave Owen a gentle prod in the back with her elbow. "Like how bold?"

"Like people seeing their possessions taken in broad daylight. The varmints tend to act at night. Not sure if the things are nocturnal or if they just want to operate when people are asleep. Could be both, I guess."

"That sounds nasty. Anybody hurt?"

"Not yet, thankfully. When confronted, the varmints seem to run off. Not sure how long that's going to last, though."

"So, what are you going to do about it? Like if you find where the varmints are holed up at. Ask them nicely to stop or something?"

"Hardly," Owen snorted. "No, right now my goal is reconnaissance. Find where they keep their loot. That or find where the varmints live, which should lead me to the loot in turn. Once I have that nailed down, I'll talk to my superior about getting some extra help. Maybe grab some folks from the Violent Offenses department if they can find the time to step off their pedestals. A squad or two from the 4th Federation Army wouldn't hurt either."

"Hey now," Chandra cut in. "My mother was a Seeker. She was on the Violent Offenses team. Worked hard to get there."

"Explains why you bothered to save my skin."

"What's that supposed to mean?"

Chandra had saved the man because he was in trouble, and felt comfortable doing so when she realized he was not a competing Shikaree. The act had come as natural as whisking a fly from her face.

"Well," Owen began, discomfort dripping from each word, "I think you're in a different position than most people in Arnstead. Haven't been here long, but most folks don't have a Seeker in their family to tint their glasses a bright, rosy red. I'm just a bluecoat to most of the folks around these parts. I think—"

"You talk too much," Chandra muttered intrusively. "You're welcome."

Chandra could feel Owen's frame shudder from barely contained laughter. He took another deep breath before he spoke.

"Yeah, I get that a lot. And thank you, Chandra."

Appreciative silence hung in the air for a time after the lengthy exchange. There was more the Spellseeker wanted to say. Chandra could feel it, but the man kept his words to himself for the time being. All she heard was the occasional shifting of feet and steady breathing. If she focused, Chandra could feel her pulse pound in her ears.

Part of Chandra wanted to ask more of the Spellseeker as well. She had never known any of the Pattal family's neighbors to hold a grudge against her mother. The woman did not spend much time on the farm, but she was a riot during festivals or when the neighbors dropped by for some fruit. The only time Chandra could recall having any bad blood for the Arnstead Arcanarium was when their people came around to remind Father to update his licenses for Westinghouse farming equipment. Even *that* disdain was directed more toward Westinghouse Industries.

Chandra shook the distractions from her head. She had a spell to focus on and shadowy nooks to reveal. The radius of her light had grown steadily since her time with Owen began. Now that they had grown quiet, Chandra focused her full attention on the spell. Its growth increased at a rapid pace.

"See anything?" Chandra asked once her light had fully lit the surrounding village of stone.

"No," Owen replied, turning his head from side to side to ensure he did not make himself a liar. "Haven't seen much of anything. Just more stone houses. That light spell of yours is pretty handy down here, huh?"

Chandra did not engage.

The new silence lasted for a swollen minute.

"So, your mother," Owen started, "you said she was a Spellseeker with Violent Offenses. What does she do now?"

Chandra's heart sank.

"Nothing," she said aloud.

"Ah, so she minds the house, then? An honorable post, taking care of a family."

"She didn't retire. She died," Chandra said softly. Without realizing it, her hand had wandered into her pocket. Fingertips absently rubbed the brass pocket watch that rested within. All its contours and scratches were familiar under her thumb. There was no inch of the object she did not recognize. Chandra pulled the watch out and handed it back over her shoulder to Owen, who took it without a word. The telltale click of the watch being opened confirmed the man's interest. "I overheard them talking to my father—the Spellseekers who came to tell him. They said my mother had been beaten. Couldn't recognize her just by looking. Her badge and that watch were the only reason they figured out who she was."

"I'm sorry," Owen said gently, closing the watch and handing back to Chandra. "I didn't realize."

"Nothing to apologize for. Was a long time ago, and it wasn't your fault."

Apologies had grown tiresome. Five years on and people still apologized when the subject came up. What happened had happened, and there was nothing to be done about it but move on. Wallowing in the misery that accompanied thoughts of her mother never served Chandra any good.

"Besides," Chandra added, "she died doing what she loved. That's what my father says, at any rate."

The suggestion of a nod worked its way through the Spellseeker's muscles to Chandra's back.

Chandra buried the watch in her pocket and looked around the village once more. Her light had reached its maximum brilliance. Any more of the Flow and the bubble would burst just like the one before. All that remained to be done was a quick check of the surroundings, which appeared to be varmint free.

Probing eyes scanned shadowed nooks. A few shrouded recesses gave Chandra a moment of pause, but there were no sharp claws to be seen. Any varmint that remained in the area had done a fantastic job of hiding itself. That was, of course, assuming there were any. Perhaps one or two dregs were left behind by the larger pack. Not something that would present a threat to a coordinated, well-lit pair of humans who were armed to the teeth.

Chandra pulled herself away from the Spellseeker. A thump of her spear against the stone floor cut through the silent village as she shouldered her bag. She opened her mouth wide and took a calming breath.

"All right then, we should be good."

"You sure?" Owen glanced over his shoulder as he spoke, getting his first good look at Chandra. She recognized the look on his face. It was the look of someone who was surprised by the age of their savior. "I thought you said an hour was best."

"We have enough light to see the whole village by," Chandra said, pointing to the orb that floated just above both their heads. "If there *are* any still lurking out there, I doubt they'd dare attack us in light this strong. I assume you're ready to get out of this place, right?"

"Oh, you have no idea," Owen blathered through a half-hearted chuckle. "Any chance you're headed the same way? I must admit—*again*—that I'm dreadfully lost."

"Guess it's your lucky day." Chandra grinned. "I was just about to finish up here and head for home. Enough excitement for one night and all that. Come on, then. Let's get out of here."

It did not take long to reach the checkpoint between the middle strata and the upper stratum. Chandra had poked through the village where she encountered Owen many times. Making her way back to the checkpoint was as familiar as the ride home to the farm, especially with a conjured light that burned like a small sun.

Chandra was pleasantly surprised by the Spellseeker's agility. The man was several years her senior, and the coat he wore as part of his uniform somewhat obscured his figure. Climbing up small rock walls and clambering through low passageways all seemed to agree with the man well enough. Chandra would not have left the man behind if he were slow. There was no doubt there. It was a pleasant thought, however, that he was not hindering Chandra from reaching the sleep she now desperately desired.

The most troublesome obstacle reared its head upon approaching the checkpoint. A familiar face manned the passageway that night, and it was not a face with which Chandra had built any rapport. It was the soldier who had confiscated her newfound sword just a few days prior.

"Gods above, you did it!" Owen cried. "Well done, Chandra. Couldn't have asked for a better guide."

What Chandra wanted to do at that moment was hide the scant few trinkets and baubles she had uncovered in the stone village. Unfortunately, the Spellseeker's cry and awfully loud footsteps drew the attention of the guard. There would be no time to shift articles from her pockets into secretive pouches within her backpack.

Chandra clicked her tongue as she followed Owen up to the soldier on duty.

"Yup," she mumbled. "Best guide you could ask for, all right."

The soldier looked over his shoulder to scan the approaching pair. A single, incredulous eyebrow craned upward. His focus was on the Spellseeker who had flung his arms wildly to either side.

"Heard they let a Seeker go down into the depths yesterday," the soldier grumbled in his gruff tone. "Didn't expect I'd be the one to see him come up. Get your fill of the caves, I imagine?"

"Oh, you have no idea," Owen sighed.

Good, Chandra thought. *He's distracted. If I can just keep the Spellseeker between me and the guard, I might get out of—*

"And where do you think you're going, Miss?"

Chandra winced at the question.

"Home, I reckon?"

"Not without a search you aren't. This is the second time I've caught you scurrying out from the middle strata in a week. I'm not about to let you slide on out of here without a thorough check. Let me see that bag there."

The demon of a man pointed a finger at Chandra's backpack. She grumbled to herself as she began to unshoulder the bag. Realization that the bag was about to grow lighter managed to make it feel twice as heavy.

"Excuse me?" Owen butted in. He took a step backward, placing himself once again between Chandra and the checkpoint guard. "What's the problem here?"

"This one's a novice, Seeker," the soldier replied. "Anything she pulls out of the middle strata is property of the Federation."

"That's great and all, but I'd appreciate it if you stopped harassing my guide."

"Excuse *me? Your* guide?"

"Yes." Owen smiled. "That's what I said. She was a vital resource for my work down here. Would have been at a complete loss without her. I can testify that she never had the time to search for any relics or the like."

It was the soldier's turn to grumble. He looked back and forth between Chandra and her bag before letting his hesitant grip go. The man was a wolf releasing a fresh kill from its jaws.

"That so?"

Chandra did not let the opportunity pass her by.

"You heard it from the Seeker himself," Chandra said with barely contained glee. "Last time you mentioned I wasn't allowed to hunt, but there wasn't any mention against helping a federal official in their line of duty."

"Come on, then," Owen said as he patted Chandra on the shoulder. "Time to finish the job and get us the rest of the way out of here."

"Yes, sir!" Chandra replied.

When they had passed out of earshot of the checkpoint, Chandra hissed a thank you to the Spellseeker. Owen whispered back a few thanks of his own before settling into a quiet that lasted until the pair reached the surface of the memory-glass quarry. They said their goodbyes under the moon as Chandra mounted Alabaster. The Spellseeker set off on foot for Arnstead.

7

Celebration

Chandra glowered at the Westinghouse Industries Express Cider Press and Fermenter, a look that combined molten contempt with frigid anguish. The craggy, igneous expression bored deep into the unwanted collection of gears, panels, and memory glass. Weaponized malice Chandra hoped might litter the machine with patches of rust. Perhaps dislodge a gear through sheer contempt. Any excuse to get the expensive pile of scrap out of the barn and back to the Westinghouse company.

The machine, lifeless though it was, stared back at Chandra with equal intensity.

In Chandra's hands was a basket of pears. They were handpicked from the orchards, both succulent and fresh. An excellent harvest without question. This basket was to serve as tribute to the monstrous Westinghouse machine. The first of many offerings Chandra expected to make. Blind, uncertain attempts at creating cider using the metallic abomination.

The machine had sat untouched since it arrived at the farm. A thick manual rested atop the monster's sleek frame, provided with the promise it held answers to all mechanical questions. Chandra had been too tired between working in the fields and her occasional night visits to the World Below. What her father's excuse was for leaving the sealed document untouched was beyond her ability to guess. If asked, Chandra was sure her father would provide a dozen different excuses. Some would make sense. Others would sound as if the man was simply trying to avoid a scolding from his eldest daughter.

Whatever the reason for leaving the machine be, Chandra was adamant that the device would rest no longer. She set the basket of pears down next to the piece of Westinghouse Industries technology and picked up the manual. The twine-bound paper wrapping came away with ease to reveal a cover populated by a colorful family. They surrounded a machine just like the one that cursed Chandra with its presence. Each member of the family laughed with joyous abandon as they worked collectively to operate the device.

Chandra was not convinced.

The first handful of pages were filled with legal nonsense well outside Chandra's comprehension. Language meant to prevent stealing the body of work or to claim ownership over this or that. A line about the manual not being for resale made sense but was of little use in understanding how the machine functioned.

After the spat of nonsense came a title page, which seemed redundant to Chandra given that the title of the work was already published on the front cover.

Finally, after sorting through what felt like a healthy portion of the book, Chandra came to the table of contents. A quick scan told her that the introduction came first and was over twenty pages of text. "Cider Made Easy" was the second section, which sounded an awful lot like a second introduction. The beginnings of a pattern that checked Chandra's already rock-bottom hopes.

A measure of luck might mean that reading half of the book could impart all its knowledge. It was a tantalizing prospect given that the manual contained over two hundred pages between its covers. Given that the machine was near her home at all, however, reminded Chandra of the poor nature of her luck.

"Cider made easy, my butt," Chandra murmured at the unfeeling passages as she tucked into the introduction. She took a derisive bite out of one of the pears that had been destined for the machine.

To the book's credit, the language was straightforward. Helpful diagrams straddled bricks of text where appropriate and made understanding said bricks a simpler task. The main problem that Chandra faced remained the girth of the manual. By the time she had finished reading the introductory section, she was a whole pear into the book.

Chandra was no fool. The proctor that serviced the Pattal farm and its neighbors, a Nirdac harn by the name of Wetherbee Jones, had taught Chandra how to read and taught her well. The problem here was not ability so much as pace. Chandra was confident in her ability to read the manual from front to back and comprehend its contents. Her fear was that the entire basket of pears might fall to her ire in the process.

About five pears into the manual, Chandra felt a tap on her shoulder. She turned to see the familiar smile of Jacob Hartsfield.

"To what do I owe this displeasure, Jacob?" Chandra asked. She had just been about to turn the machine on for the first time since cracking the manual and did not care for the distraction.

"A whole evening of displeasures, if that's your mood," the boy chuckled in response. "It's the day of the harvest celebration, my dear Chandra. Folks are getting set up on the lawn as we speak. I volunteered to come pull you out of the barn. Your father mentioned you'd been in here all day."

Between the rigors of the World Below and navigating the manual for the Westinghouse Industries Express Cider Press and Fermenter, Chandra had forgotten the date. Only now that she had been made aware of the festivities did she notice the hustle and noise coming from the lawn.

Celebratory robes served as an additional indicator of the day's coming festivities. It was not often that anyone neighboring the Pattals traipsed around in such dressy clothes. Dirt-caked pants and rolled-up sleeves were the order of most days. Robes fit for a party did not fare so well out in the fields.

Seeing the Hartsfield boy in finer attire was further confirmation that the festivities were, indeed, today. Not that the boy wore something particularly fancy. A red robe with yellow trim and a violet sash to serve as a belt. No fanciful embroidery or complex designs. Not a ring or pendant to speak of. Still, it was more than Chandra had to wear for the occasion.

"Right," Chandra sighed. She gave the manual one last look. A challenge to the book, defiant declaration that it best not leave the premises until she returned. The volume yelped as she snapped it closed and placed it back atop the Flow-infused mechanical abomination. "I'll be out in a minute. Consider your mission done."

"You sure you can manage on your own?" Jacob beseeched as he held his arm out to be taken. "Still got the look of work all over your face. Hate to see you get distracted and start picking apples until sundown."

The awkward display chiseled a smirk into Chandra's grumpy features. It mixed an even amount of desperation and confidence into something Chandra could not readily identify. She jammed a pear into Jacob Hartsfield's smiling gob and spun the boy about. A gentle kick in the rear got Jacob moving toward the lawn.

"I said give me a minute," Chandra replied. "I'm almost done in here."

That was a lie. Chandra would have eaten through the entire basket of pears or read the entire manual, whichever came first. She might have preferred a different messenger, but the distraction was a welcome one when all was said and done.

Jacob glanced over his shoulder with a wide grin, took a hearty bite out of the pear, then strolled out through the barn door.

The last thing Chandra wanted at that moment was to have it look like Jacob had done her a favor. To waste a few minutes, she hand-fed a pear to each of the Pattal family's horses. Mortimer first, then Alabaster, and Patra last. A short distraction that ensured Chandra would not be walking to the lawn right on Jacob's heels.

When Chandra finally set foot outside the barn, she was amazed at how many neighbors had arrived already. It felt so early in the day. At least that was the case until Chandra spied the evening sun. The manual had managed to jumble her internal clock more effectively than Chandra realized.

Each of the arrivals wasted no time in getting themselves to work. Mr. Hartsfield, Jacob's father, managed a roaring fire. Over the blaze was one of the Hartsfields' pigs. Chandra smelled the succulent meat well before drawing near. Mr. Hartsfield rotated the pig-laden spit with a practiced hand. It would have been quite the lie if Chandra said the pig was not one of her favorite parts of harvest festivities. Her brothers made a proper breakfast, but they lacked the wizened skill of the devout pig farmer.

The Okujayes, Zumbatran katarl who farmed mainly vegetables, were hard at work with their own smaller fire. Potatoes and carrots always rounded out the Hartsfield pig. A dense meal that left swollen bellies pitched to the night sky.

Obi, oldest among the Okujaye children, shaped and warped pieces of wood. He was in his early twenties and spent most of his time as a carpenter's apprentice in Arnstead. Golden hands traced intent over spare planks the family brought along for just such a purpose. When the stock proved insufficient, Chandra's father offered split firewood. Bark fell away from wood under Obi's Flow-infused touch as if he were whisking scum from a pond.

Mr. and Mrs. Okujaye beamed approval as their eldest contributed to the festivities in his way. Meanwhile, they and their two younger children, Dakarai and Taisha, set about preparing vegetables for the pot.

The Roebucks, a family of Nirdac harn, completed their preparations in advance. Cheeses and cream from the cattle farmers were laid out on the table even as Obi Okujaye was in the process of making it. Their two children, twin boys by the names of Arthur and Eric, busied themselves kicking a football around the crowded area and drawing the ire of those who had work to do. Their mischief was eventually exiled from the lawn. Both boys, freckled nightmares with curly coats of red fur, shrugged the matter off and resumed their festivities over by the barn.

Chandra's siblings found their way to the football one way or another. A game of keeping the ball away from Omala developed. Youngest of the bunch and not one to deny herself a challenge, Omala accepted the role of middle and skillfully stripped the ball away from her brother Najran. Part of Chandra wanted to hustle over to the ball and show the group what for. A less spirited part demanded that she go to her father and ask if there was anything she could do to help.

"Hello, Chandra!" Mr. Hartsfield called as Chandra cut across the lawn. "Good to see you, my dear."

"Hello, Mr. Hartsfield," she replied with cheer. Chandra's line across the lawn deviated somewhat toward Mr. Hartsfield to avoid shouting. "Always a pleasure."

"A shame I only get to see you when you come by for meat. You really should stay for dinner more often. Jacob has taken quite a liking to you, you know. I'm sure he would love to have you stay for a while."

"You don't say?" Chandra replied while stifling the urge to cringe. The wondrous smell of the pig roasting over an open fire helped keep her features in a more delighted visage. "I'll have to think that over, Mr. Hartsfield. Thank you for the invitation."

"Oh, no trouble at all."

The man gave a wink to Chandra. His earnest nature colored the gesture with an innocent hue. He seemed quite pleased with his attempt to play matchmaker. Chandra did not have the heart to smother the offer.

"How close are we?" Chandra asked while pointing at the pig. It continued to roll over and over as the pair talked, even though there was no crank handle on the spit. Chandra assumed the rotation was the result of a spell cast by the kindly Mr. Hartsfield. One of his hands waved leisurely at the pig while the other scratched at his salt-and-peppered beard.

"Oh, not long now. Not just yet, though," he added as he gave Chandra's creeping hand a light slap. "Can't go digging in until the Kumars arrive. Don't worry, there will be plenty for everyone."

Chandra shook her hand in mock pain, then laughed the moment away with a courteous nod toward Mr. Hartsfield.

"I'll hold you to that," Chandra said. "Now, if you'll excuse me, I need to bother my father. Feels wrong having idle hands, you know."

"Talk to you later," Mr. Hartsfield said with a wave before returning his focus to the sizzling hog. The intoxicating aroma continued to spread itself over the lawn. Even as Chandra left the site of the roast, she could feel the tantalizing odor like it was tapping her shoulder for attention. Her mouth was flooded with anticipation.

Passing each family was much like passing Mr. Hartsfield. Well-wishing and bright smiles that accompanied joyous waves. Chandra saw that she welcomed each family and turned no blind eyes. The warm atmosphere of celebration was busy at work melding the collection of families into a single, cohesive unit. Chandra knew there was no better time of the year than where she was at that very moment. Thoughts of caves and Westinghouse machinery would not ruin the love she harbored for this annual celebration.

Colors flourished about the gathering. Blues with yellows. A mix of green and purple. Robes of various hues and fashions twirled about to form a living tapestry among the guests. The sort of sight Chandra would expect to see in a busy tavern in Weststead, or hung on the wall of a wealthy merchant's home. It would have brought more of a smile to her face had her own family not stood in such stark contrast to the others. There was no room in the Pattal family budget for something so fanciful as a party robe. A dyed shirt was the closest Chandra might come to matching her guests, though she did not feel the need to blend in. To watch the colors swirl was enough for her, she convinced herself. A robe could wait.

"Father!" Chandra called as she approached. Nitesh was busy welcoming the latest arrival, the Kumar family. A large family of Bangeli katarl who farmed all manner of grains. "Father, do we need hands anywhere?"

"Oh, we're all right, Chandra, bless you!" interjected Mrs. Kumar before Nitesh had a chance to speak. "If we're short of anything, it's definitely not hands. Come on, you lot," Mrs. Kumar demanded with a clap. Her children, seven smartly striped katarl aged from seven all the way up to twenty-two, snapped to attention. "We've got loads to share. Unload the bread and corn to the table that young Obi is putting together. On the double!"

A chorus of affirmations preceded a flurry of hands that grabbed at baskets. Ears of corn and loaves of bread were shuffled over to the progressing dining table.

"Wonderful to see you, deary," Mrs. Kumar creaked as she flung her arms wide to Chandra. "Oh, you look more and more like your mother each year, gods bless her."

"Thank you, Mrs. Kumar," Chandra replied with a genuine smile. It was a comparison that she was always proud to receive. "It's good to see you, as well. Same to you, Mr. Kumar."

The thin-lipped katarl tipped his hat in response, giving something approximate to a smile in return before he joined the children in moving goods to a dining table that was now receiving its final flourishes. Obi next began work on simple benches to seat the small army. It was a spectacle that garnered adulations from some of the newly arrived katarl.

"Now then," Chandra said after having given Mrs. Kumar the third set of good wishes, "Father! Where am I needed?"

"Ah, my dearest Chandra." Nitesh chuckled. He gave his daughter a tough squeeze, enough to lift her feet from the ground. Chandra let out a playful squeal in response. "How far did you get into the cursed manual? The one for the new machine?"

If there was anyone who could darken this luminous day of celebration, it had to be Nitesh.

"Oh, come on," Chandra grumbled. "Can we not talk about that particularly poor decision? Just for today?"

"Chandra," Nitesh replied with sarcastic dour, "how far did you get?"

"Halfway-ish?" Chandra sighed. She had no will to fight the exasperation that she felt to her core. "I'll have it finished tomorrow with some luck. Day after at the latest, and then we can finally turn the thing on and get cracking with it."

"Well, then it sounds like you've done plenty of work today." There was mischief in Nitesh's smile as he continued. "I'd wager those young ones over there by the barn could do for some proper football lessons, if you've still got some energy under that gloom and doom of yours."

An eyebrow reached for the heavens as Chandra looked over to see that Omala was back in the center of the ring. Chandra sniffed. She wiped away something from under her nose that was not actually there to begin with.

"Football lessons, huh? I reckon these old bones might be able to teach a trick or two to the youngsters."

"There's my girl." Nitesh cackled. "Now get a move on, or dinner will be ready before you've done your job!"

Some of the freshly squeezed smile dripped away from Chandra when she looked past her father. Coming up the way was a familiar storm cloud. Nitesh, noticing the sudden change in his daughter's expression, turned to follow her gaze.

"Ah, hello, Victoria!" Nitesh called with a bright wave. "That's the Chandler clan for you, always last to arrive."

Seated at the head of a small cart was Victoria Chandler. The Orland collector had traded her smart uniform for an elaborate robe of glittering silver and amethyst. A robe that could have lit an entire village if it caught the moon just right. Fiery red hair had been tied back and fell over one shoulder like a shower of sparks. Around her neck was an emerald pendant. The sort of thing that might cover months of the Pattal family's payments to the Orland Bank.

"Nitesh," Victoria called back with a polite wave, "always a pleasure."

Children hopped from the cart when it came to a stop near the celebration area. All were clad in robes fine enough to match their mother's. Expensive clothes they would outgrow in a year or two. Each carried some sort of dish meant for the long table. They all offered Chandra a bright smile in turn as they passed.

"Where's Will?" Nitesh asked. "Haven't got him tucked in the back of the cart, have you?"

"No." Victoria chuckled as she dismounted and secured the cart. "My husband had a little business around the farm to get to yet. He'll be along by dinnertime, no worries. Chandra, a pleasure."

Hollow words from a hollow woman, Chandra thought. What pleasure could a monster find at a normal person's party? There was no way the woman wanted to be here among her neighbors. Constant reminders that Victoria was not so high above those she lived near as her attire might suggest.

"Vic," was all Chandra could say in reply. Nothing but ugly words would come from the thoughts that danced vile circles about her mind. Better to keep the venom to herself than to spoil the night. Chandra allowed herself to shoot Victoria a mean look as she passed to join Omala and the other children in their games. Once again, distraction was sorely needed.

* * *

Bright violin notes swept over the ravaged dining table. It was no particular song. Just a handful of notes to get the blood flowing through Mrs. Roebuck's delicate fingers. The party was only half done as far as the attendees were concerned. With the meal out of the way and a short rest in between, it was time to dance.

Accompanying Mrs. Roebuck's excellent violin was a pair of drums. A small drum tucked underneath one of Mr. Kumar's massive, striped arms, and a larger one cradled between Nitesh's legs. The men took turns pounding out a beat to be matched by the other. Mischievous smiles faded into concentration as the pair showed off their speed and accuracy in increasing amounts. The competition alone was enough to dance to without Mrs. Roebuck getting involved. Some of the younger children made good on that fact and began to flail about in the crimson firelight.

The sun had long since set. Multiple fires, maintained from cooking, kept the party illuminated as the moon rose to peek through packs of clouds. Patches of stars glinted like crystals where they had the chance.

While the younger children danced to the warm-up, the older ones kicked a football around the crackling fires. Their passes weaved around and between the stone rings that kept each fire from spreading wildly. It was a game that even some of the adults could not resist.

Passing the ball around was a way to stay active and awake without burning too much energy. Adults continued to talk to each other about their respective harvests as they passed the ball around. Chandra did not have an ear for the narrowly missed blight on the Kumar crops, nor did she pay attention to whispers of wolves near the Roebucks and their cattle. She was more interested in the chip shot she launched over the largest fire. It landed right at the feet of young Dakarai, who marveled at the precise maneuver.

Chandra took her father's playful command to heart. This night was one of revelry, she thought to herself. She could worry about her more adult troubles tomorrow. Chandra knew they would be waiting for her bright and early.

Out from amongst the chatter came three identical notes dragged across the strings of the lone violin. Mrs. Roebuck was ready.

A reply came in the form of matched drum beats from opposing drums. Both Nitesh and Mr. Kumar were ready.

It was time to dance.

Mrs. Roebuck began to shred her bow over the strings of her violin. Fierce movements produced a fountain of mirth. Underneath was a driving beat cut by Mr. Kumar. A thrum that drove the violin forward as much as it responded. Below all of that was the even pounding of Nitesh that kept everyone on the same page.

Those gathered around the fires knew the song. They knew its swells and its valleys, a traditional favorite to start the night off with vigor. A whoop here and a holler there punctuated musical phrases. Dancers and players all joined in the delighted cries. Those old enough to know that dance began in earnest, moving in rings around the fires.

The younger children scampered after their seniors and did their best to imitate the simple, flowing performance.

The crackle and pop of the fires were the dancers' instruments. They ebbed and flowed, becoming the glue that held everything together. New life had been injected into the party in the space of a breath. Full bellies were settled. The night was young. There was no longer a care in the world between them all.

For Chandra, it was like coming alive after a year of hibernation. Vibrant energy propelled her body. Each dip swelled into the next movement as she twirled around the fires. One moment she bounded hand in hand with Omala. In the next, Chandra was twirled by the Hartsfield boy or by Mrs. Okujayes. The who of it was not important. Bias had no place in the primal expression that engulfed the party.

The rage of passion could not last forever, though, and soon the drums slowed to a crawling pace. Quieter notes, both sweet and somber, rolled out from Mrs. Roebuck's violin. Everyone took a collective breath and allowed themselves a sigh of relief. Not all songs needed to be enjoyed at breakneck pace, and this was one of those songs.

Little Omala grabbed Nitesh by the hand and pulled him out to dance, a heartwarming gesture that reminded Chandra of her younger days. Stealing her father away from her mother when it was time to play. These days Chandra wished she would have stolen her mother away instead, but she did not linger on the thought. There was no use in the somber exercise.

Chandra found that her attention dwelt on the Chandlers. An uncomfortable habit that she struggled to break. Watching Victoria sweep about with her husband, carefree and full of joy, formed an ugly pit in Chandra's stomach.

Why does this woman deserve to be so happy, Chandra thought, *when all she does is bring pain and sorrow?*

The collector was swathed in mirth at the very doorstep of the house she so frequently robbed.

There was a certain strangeness to Victoria when seen next to her husband. Will was a man of the fields, just like his neighbors. Tanned skin and thick arms were clear markers of dedication to his family's land. He was a loud, boisterous man that brought smiles to anyone who lucked into crossing his path. An exact opposite to the mousy, reserved Victoria. How William had seen anything of worth in Victoria was beyond Chandra. Still, they danced and swayed and enjoyed the company of one another.

Shrewd observation kept Chandra busy. She could have taken to the floor and spent time with one of her brothers, or maybe one of the neighbor boys or girls. There was no shame in allowing a measure of fun. However, Victoria was too present for Chandra to disengage. She felt her attention locked on the Orland collector. The sheer audacity of Victoria to enjoy herself on Pattal land. Discontent soured the blueberry tart that Chandra munched on with intermittent enthusiasm. For now, she was nailed to one of the benches that surrounded the long table.

"May I?" Jacob Hartsfield asked of Chandra. He had approached quietly, adorned with a warm, unsure smile.

At first, Chandra was inclined to say no. She wiped a collection of blueberry crumbs from the side of her mouth and turned to examine Jacob in full. One hand was behind the boy's back, while the other was extended as a polite offer. His frame was tucked forward in a slight bow. Rather than gaze expectantly at Chandra, Jacob kept his eyes locked on the ground at her feet. Red robes waved a subtle welcome on the cool night breeze.

It's gotta be better than skulking on this bench all night, right? Chandra continued to look Jacob up and down while she mused. *I at least need to say something before the poor guy gets nervous and walks off.*

"You may," Chandra replied. Her words were hesitant. "I'll give you this one chance," she added before Jacob had his hands wrapped around Chandra's. There was a similar hesitancy to the boy's movements as there had been to Chandra's words.

"Thank you," Jacob whispered, not quite into Chandra's ear.

"Yeah, yeah," Chandra sighed. She wrapped her arms over the top of Jacob's shoulders, keeping a comfortable distance between the two of them while still allowing for the slow, meandering dance. Chandra played with her fingers behind blond curls. She was not quite sure what to do with her hands. "Just don't blow it, okay?"

"Wouldn't dream of it," Jacob replied through a nervous chuckle. In the same breath, he added, "I know you've got to be tired of it all. The double life, I mean."

"Excuse me?" Chandra was genuinely taken aback by the remark. Though she had been struggling to look anywhere near Jacob, the boy now garnered her full attention. "I have no idea what you're talking about."

"Those trips to the World Below," Jacob said innocently enough. "Omala talks about it when I help in the field. You go hunting for relics to scrounge up some money to keep the Orlands at bay. You didn't think it was a secret, did you?"

"Well, I—" Chandra was flabbergasted. Words did not come readily to her side as she froze in place, her face hot with discomfort. "I didn't think—how does—who? Does *everyone* know?"

"Your father tells my father. He tells the Okujayes." Jacob shrugged under the weight of Chandra's arms. "Not all of Arnstead knows, I'm sure, but out here? We're a small bunch of folks. Word gets round, you know?"

"I guess that makes sense, but... what does it matter if I'm tired or not? Someone's gotta pay for all the things my father buys. If it won't be him, I'm next in line to make up the difference."

"You don't have to be, Chandra."

"And what's that supposed to mean?" Chandra asked defensively. It felt like she was being eased into a small corner.

"I mean... you don't have to do it alone," Jacob began again after a healthy pause. "Make up the money, I mean. We're not rich, but we're not in debt to anyone. Why not join the families? Let us help you out? Let *me* help you out?"

"What?" Chandra asked. She had become still as a House bell at midnight. Her next words came out slowly. They more tumbled out of her mouth than rolled off her tongue. "You mean like… like marriage? Are you asking me to *marry* you?"

Jacob's sun-darkened skin turned red in embarrassment. He broke eye contact with Chandra, desperate to find reassurance somewhere.

"I mean… maybe?" he practically squeaked. "Two families would be better than one, I mean. Right?"

"Right," Chandra whispered to herself.

"And even if it's not right now, we could get the idea planted with our folks," Jacob continued. Evenness returned to his voice, but it sounded like the boy had begun to ramble. The quantity of speech spoke more to his discomfort than the quality of his voice. "That could get our families closer *now* if they knew for *later*. Wouldn't be a terrible surprise, then, either."

"I guess not," Chandra muttered. Infectious rambling spread from Jacob to Chandra. She felt her face grow hot with embarrassment. "But we hardly know each other! I mean, we grew up next to each other, and you get along with my brothers, and you help Omala in the field when I'm not around, and— wait. Just wait."

Chandra took a moment to collect herself. The pair had ceased their dance at the first mention of the word marriage. Their lack of movement in a crowd of neighbors that swayed away with their loved ones felt painfully awkward. Though she was too afraid to scan the guests, Chandra knew there had to be errant glances falling upon her and Jacob. She wrapped her arms a little tighter around Jacob's neck and resumed the dance. The boy was a little slow on the uptake but began to dance along with Chandra again before long.

There was some truth in what Jacob had said. They were young, but it was not unheard of for people of Chandra and Jacob's ages to promise themselves to each other. A sort of soft binding before a proper wedding. So long as the families did not object, they were more or less joined at that point. It was not a bad idea from a practical standpoint.

Another family to help pay the Orlands off would be a life-altering change.

Practicality aside, this was not an option Chandra had ever considered. Least of all with Jacob. Not that she had a particularly strong dislike for the boy, despite his constant pestering. He was kind enough, and he *did* offer his free time to the Pattals when it was available to be given. Jacob was a handsome boy, to boot.

None of that pushed Chandra over the line to desire marriage for such mundane reasons. Especially when she was so young. Just fifteen years old. Maybe given a few more pitiless years Chandra might change her mind, but right now?

When she spoke again, Chandra addressed Jacob with a mixture of finality and tenderness. Like the way she bid farewell to Omala on nights when Chandra was bound for the World Below. Sweet assurances with a bitter tinge of reality for good measure. Chandra could not look at Jacob while she spoke. Her gaze remained fixed on the great pyres that lit the night's festivities.

"That's very sweet of you, Jacob. I appreciate the offer," Chandra whispered. "I need to figure this problem out on my own, though. I don't wanna just trade one debt for another. Even if the new debt came with good intentions. Does that… make sense?"

Neither Chandra nor Jacob spoke for a time. It was a welcome break for Chandra while the boy processed her response. Chandra could not imagine what else to say. The reply was an honest one if a bit blunt. Softening the blow felt like it might have given the wrong impression. Jacob seemed to take it in stride while he thought. The pace of their dance had not faltered, nor had he turned away from Chandra in defeat. Careful spins carried the pair around the bonfire and amongst their neighbors in pensive silence.

"So that's a no, then?" Jacob asked in a sheepish tone after a time.

"For now, at least," Chandra smiled. A bittersweet gesture that formed on its own as Chandra fought to regain eye contact with the spurned youth. "It's just not a good time. I'm hoping to have everything sorted soon, but I have too much to focus on right now. Okay?"

"There's always next year, I suppose?"

"Sure," Chandra chuckled. "There's always next year."

Chandra held Jacob a little closer as the slow, meandering song came to a close.

8

Battalion

"Wait, wait, wait!" Chandra called out as she skidded to a halt on the dusty road outside Frontier Finds. Loose dirt slipped out from under her, which led to a graceless tumble. The abrupt conversation continued with Chandra seated on the dusty road. "Please, can I have a moment?"

A bemused Olufemi, key slotted into the gnarled door of his store, looked down at the crumpled heap that was Chandra. Amusement glittered in his eyes as he turned his key back the way it had come and pulled it from the lock. He pocketed the key and offered a withered hand to the splayed heap of limbs at his feet.

"I was beginning to wonder if I would see you again, my dear. How are you?"

Olufemi's words were gentle. They brushed across Chandra like a scholarly hand roving the pages of an ancient tome. She accepted the man's hand and stood. The dust of Arnstead was thick and took deep root, but Chandra attempted to brush it off her pants regardless.

"You asked that I gave you a week when I brought the, uh—" Chandra paused long enough to look both ways down the street. Her attention rested on shadowed alleyways, but noted nothing that might give merit to the pause. "When I brought you the map. You said you needed a week."

"Did I, now?" Olufemi asked himself as he clapped away the dust Chandra had parted onto his hand. "That's odd. I finished the translation days ago. Thought you might have decided to leave that little treasure to me."

"'Fraid not. Still need the little thing. Still need to know what it *said* too. Got a second to talk?"

"Inside?" Olufemi clarified with a gesture toward the door.

"Please, if you don't mind."

"Not at all. There are few things I love more than imparting knowledge upon those who seek it!"

Olufemi pointed a finger to the heavens as a bolt of excitement raced through his warm voice. Chandra was whisked across the threshold before she realized the door was open.

The sound of a bell above the doorway fell flat, dying against walls and shelves covered with books of all kinds. Not even motes of dust, of which there were many, seemed to move without the presence of the store owner. Footsteps creaked over flexible floorboards and cut through the silent air. Chandra could have been convinced, without much persuasion, that nothing had moved since the last time she visited Frontier Finds.

It was not until Olufemi had stepped inside and closed the door that the sense of mysticism receded. He made sure not to flip the small sign on his doorway from closed to open. The hustle and bustle of Eaststead might as well have been a whole world away.

"Come on, then," Olufemi said as he adopted a leisurely pace that matched his surroundings. For all the books that littered Frontier Finds, Chandra would have been amazed if a single volume among them mentioned the word haste. "I've got your map in the backroom. Some notes I took as well."

"So, you were able to figure the varmint words out?" Chandra asked, following after Olufemi.

She had to check her step every few paces. Nerves ached to know what the words on the map said, and having to wait a full week had further intensified the burn. A stash of goods, both relics and focuses, all ripe for the picking. Chandra had even devised a clever way to sneak the haul past her new best friend from the middle-strata checkpoint. An industrious use for the nervous energy that accumulated over the past week.

All her anxiety and mental preparation hinged on the outcome of Olufemi's studies. It was barely within Chandra's power to keep herself from hurrying the older man along.

Olufemi led Chandra to a small backroom. The sort of room that was secreted away from the prying eyes of the public. A place to store tomes that were not for sale; the kind of books a person thought they might need but were not yet sure why. A place to work out thoughts in unfamiliar languages and ancient script.

In the middle of the room was a small table. A single chair, simple and worn, sat on the far side. Olufemi made a kind offer of the chair to Chandra, but she shook her head politely. Anticipation continued to bound through each fiber of muscle in her body. Chandra focused on the mess of papers that half covered her prize: the map. There it was in the middle of the table. Surrounded by notes and ink pots, it called to Chandra with promises of opportunity.

Timid fingers touched the edge of the table. Energy whipped from the place of study, up Chandra's arm, and then throughout her entire body. She could bear the wait no longer.

"That's a lot of notes," Chandra said, desperate to shatter the silence before it could do the same to her. She bit her lip for a moment. Anxious energy tossed her gaze back and forth between Olufemi and his notes. "Anything worth the effort in there? Or did I just bring you a bunch of chicken scratch?"

"Useful to whom, I wonder?" Olufemi grunted.

The dark-skinned man eased himself down into the chair. He brushed a few loose sheets of paper aside. With his other hand, he removed an inkpot from a corner of the map. The map began to curl inward the moment it was freed from the improvised paperweight. Olufemi smoothed the map with both hands and looked over its entirety with a clinical gaze.

"It's been a while," he said, "since I have seen so much varmint text in a single sample. Full sentences, not just hairbrained notes jotted onto a loose scrap of paper. Actual writing meant to convey full messages to the next person who reads it. Clean lines of thought and purpose bound into one. For me, it is useful for understanding their sentence structure. Their way of communicating with written words. To me, this map of yours is nearly priceless."

"Marvelous," Chandra replied with an unintentionally curt tone. "Fantastic. What does it say, exactly?"

"Ah, yes," Olufemi continued. If he had noticed Chandra's tone, he made no show of it. "Straight to the meat of the matter, I see. I suppose a week *was* a long time to wait. Here, I've made a copy of my notes and cleaned them up. Should be easier to read than my original translation, what with trying to incorporate the bits of Federal common where it seemed appropriate."

The map rolled in on itself once more as Olufemi removed a hand from its crisp surface. He grabbed a few papers from the far end of the table and offered them to Chandra, who practically snatched the pages from his grasp.

None of the words took immediate root. Chandra scanned the pages so quickly that it all became a pool of beautifully inked gibberish. It was like those pages were her first meal after a week without food. Chandra made it to the end before realizing she had retained nothing of substance. She forced down the noise with a deep, calming breath and started again from the top. This time she read aloud to moderate her pace.

"'Start near the red lights where the soldier stands.' Well, that's easy enough, has to be the middle-strata checkpoint. 'Follow the left path. Path that leads to crescent moon chamber. From there climb down. As far down as the moon descends. At the bottom of the well is a fork.'"

Chandra paused. A droplet of water had fallen onto the pages from somewhere, soaking in and distorting the ink. Without realizing it, Chandra had begun to weep tears of joy. She put the pages down on the round table with a gentle hand before covering her face in her hands. A short sniff preceded the mopping of tears. Sheer relief consumed Chandra. An overwhelming tide of emotion she had not been prepared for.

"It's directions," Chandra croaked, wiping the last of her tears away. "It's directions, after all."

"Just what was expected, I assume?" Olufemi placed a reassuring hand on Chandra's shoulder.

"Just what I wanted, yes. With this, I should be able to get my family out of debt. I don't know how I'll be able to repay you."

"I was wondering about that myself," Olufemi pondered aloud.

It had been an honest statement, wanting to somehow repay the bookkeeper. Honest, but immediately regretted. The thought of having to split what she found in the World Below came to mind. That, or some definite sum. Another debt. The thought made Chandra's stomach curl.

"Well," Chandra began, belabored by expectation, "I am in your debt. The map made little sense before you came along. Name your price and I'll do my best to repay you in time."

Olufemi raised an eyebrow to the heavens. It seemed that the thought of payment was only just now crossing the man's mind.

Chandra made a mental note to kick herself square in the behind when she was well away from Frontier Finds. Surely the throngs of Main Street would see nothing odd about a random girl exacting reprimand upon herself.

The moment of self-reflection was cut short by the sound of crinkling paper. Chandra looked down to see that Olufemi was tapping the map with a gnarled finger, an easy smile resting on his face like a handkerchief billowing on a clothesline.

"When you're done with the map, I'd like to have it. If you don't mind, that is. It's quite the find."

Olufemi made that last note with a gesture of his hand that encompassed the whole of Frontier Finds.

"That's all?" Chandra asked. When Olufemi nodded, she felt another wave of relief wash over taut shoulders. Chandra spoke with a smile born of promise. "Consider it done. With any luck, I'll have it back in a week."

Olufemi returned Chandra's smile in kind.

"How about some tea, then?" Olufemi pointed to a kettle upon a small stove in the furthest corner of the backroom. "Nothing like a nice hot cup of tea to read through some notes. Maybe a bit of fresh lemon too. I managed to grab a few from the market before they were all gone."

"That's kind of you, but I should probably be going." Chandra thumbed the straps of her backpack. Manarail spikes jingled about her waist as she did so. "The sooner I get started, the sooner you'll have the map back for your collection."

"Yes, but—" Olufemi began in protest, but Chandra was already turning to leave.

"You really have no idea how thankful I am to you. My family is going to be living a new life thanks to you."

There was too much cheer in Chandra's voice for Olufemi to continue his protest. Instead, he caught Chandra by the hand as she went to open the backroom door and return to the floor of Frontier Finds.

"At least let me show you to the door, my dear."

The entrance to the store was obscured by shelf after oddly sized shelf. In her haste, Chandra failed to realize that if she sprinted toward the entrance, she would not have known where to go. The unwieldy bulk of Frontier Finds had swallowed her in a vast swath of literature. A maze of wood, leather, and pages upon pages upon pages.

"If you wouldn't mind," Chandra said through a nervous chuckle. "That would be lovely."

Returning to the entrance proved to be an odd series of twists and turns. The complexity of the route had been masked on the first passage by Chandra's anticipation. Curved shelves that formed into strange, nonuniform shapes had been little more than scenery. One particular shelf caught her eye for its resemblance to, the best Chandra could guess without a bird's eye view, a square knot.

Though the return was complicated, it was not particularly long. Olufemi knew which turns to take and which to avoid, like a fisherman returning to shore amid familiar shoals.

The bell tinkled its bright notes as Olufemi opened the door for Chandra. She was halfway across the threshold when she realized she had more to say.

"I really, really can't thank you enough, Olufemi. From the bottom of my heart, I know nothing I give you will compare to what you have done for me and my family." Chandra turned on her heels to face the man. His worn features had yet to abandon the smile they adopted in the backroom. Chandra stepped forward and embraced the wizened man. It was a tight squeeze filled with all the warmth that she could muster. She whispered, "Thank you so much," as she released Olufemi and stepped out into the street.

"Be safe," Olufemi said as Chandra began to cut a path through Eaststead toward the House of Many.

The day was growing old. Chandra had bought herself time by convincing her father that the cider contraption required some additional ingredients before it would yield results. Some added cane sugar was the first thing that came to mind. Another ingredient she specified was yeast. This one was a more genuine excuse, as the manual had specified its use. She had made a point to gather the ingredients and stow them on Alabaster before her visit to Frontier Finds. She saw no point in allowing a good half-truth to be discovered. Why not grab the goods and make the trip a legitimate one on all fronts?

Walks to and from Alabaster, who was tethered in the memory-glass quarry, had eaten a fair amount of daylight. Enough time that Olufemi had almost left Frontier Finds for the day's end. Time Chandra could have used for exploration, but it meant a lighter pack for when the time finally arrived to dive.

Waning daylight did not spell the day's end for all Eaststead. As Chandra moved north toward the Dawn Bridge over the River Ro, she could hear a blacksmith banging away. There was equal chance that they worked horseshoes or the home of a memory-glass crystal. The beginning stages in the creation of a focus. It was impossible to know without seeing the smith at work, but Chandra liked to imagine the extravagant option. She saw in her mind a smith toiling away at the blades of a plow that could push itself. Much like the one her father had purchased from the folks at Westinghouse Industries.

Before she realized it, Chandra had managed to spoil her fun with bitter thoughts of the problems at home. These thoughts would normally fester in clouds of gloom. They left sour little raindrops on all her thoughts for the remainder of the day. Today, however, was different. Tucked away in her backpack was the means to end her family's debt.

Halfway through Eaststead, shops began to thin and allow for homes and apartments to spring up. Bakeries mingled with houses shared by two or three families. General stores stood on corners surrounded by apartments and shacks. There was Parn's Apothecary that served those too poor to seek healing from the House of Many. Even now Chandra could see the sparkling pinnacle of the House as the sun crawled further and further over Weststead. It served as the main beacon for her northward travel. A landmark that was easy to spy from half of Arnstead.

The northern stretch of Eaststead, the area near the Dawn Bridge, was made up mostly of split houses and other similar dwellings. Traffic for the day was beginning to reach its end as daytalers found their way home for a warm meal with their families. Even the tariff guards on the Dawn Bridge had been released to return to the 4th Federation Army barracks over in Weststead.

Tucked into the sleepy lull of a day's end was a shuffling of footsteps. Not the typical kind of steps that carry a regular person about their business. It was the shuffle of unsavory individuals that Chandra had passed by an alley or two ago. Furtive movements that warranted a look over the shoulder. A look that Chandra offered too late.

A coil of rope slithered across the ground and wrapped itself around one of Chandra's ankles. There was no time to cry in distress as she felt her foot yanked from beneath her. Grimy fingers caught Chandra's face as it plummeted toward the ground. The rigid digits battered surprised screams down to muffled grunts. Another strong arm bound Chandra in place.

Chandra felt the animated rope slink around her other foot as she tried to wriggle away from her captor. Both her ankles were pulled together. The rope continued to wind tightly up to her shins, stopping just above her knees. Chandra had been bound and gagged in the span of a single breath. The as-yet-unseen captors pulled Chandra into the nearest alley away from any prying eyes that might decide to get involved.

"She's squirming something awful, Alyssa," grunted a voice next to Chandra's ear. "Have you got another rope for her arms? Something else to cast a spell on and keep her still?"

The voice was just on the cusp of familiarity. A faint suggestion of someone she might have heard before, though Chandra could not remember where. She might have been able to recall a face or place if not for the panic that paralyzed her mind. Thoughts scattered farther and farther apart as she was carried deeper into the darkened recess of the alleyway.

"Yeah, give me a second," came another voice. This one was female, as opposed to the gruff male that bound Chandra. "This one's got a length of rope dangling from her bag. Seems fitting to bind her hands with her own rope, doesn't it?"

An unfeeling cackle rose from the woman. Chandra felt unseen hands violate her backpack and undo the rope attached to it.

Hands!

Chandra realized that, though her legs and arms were bound in place, her hands were still somewhat unrestricted. There was enough play in the man's grasp to grab one of the manarail spikes that dangled from her waist. She wasted no time in ripping one from its housing and forming it into a crude blade. Chandra made her best guess as to where the man's leg must be and stabbed with all her might.

"Agh!" he cried in pain. "Hurry up, Alyssa! She's still got some teeth on her."

"Quit your whining!" the woman shushed.

Despite Chandra's best effort, the man maintained his hold. His arm slid down to keep Chandra's dagger in place. She twisted the improvised weapon in a last-ditch effort to cause as much pain as possible. A desperate hope that Chandra might be able to free her torso.

Energy crackled in response to Chandra's struggle. The man's grip tightened to the point that Chandra thought she heard her bones crack. Pressure grew on her face until it felt as if her jaw would crumble backward through her neck.

Another crack of Flow-infused energy permeated the air like muffled thunder. Chandra felt her rope wrap around her wrists even as it was yanked from her backpack. It was not long before the rope had similarly bound Chandra's arms. They were stuck in front of her torso and wrapped tight up to the elbows.

"Finally," the male voice gasped.

Now that Chandra had been properly bound, the man released his grip on her torso. The hand on her mouth remained firmly in place. Metal thumped to the ground. Chandra's only weapon had been taken from her and tossed to the dirt. A swift kick to the back of the legs put Chandra on the ground soon after.

"She got you pretty good, huh?" The female voice chuckled.

"Uh-huh," the male replied. "It's not funny. I'm really bleeding here."

"Then wrap it up. The little rat isn't going anywhere now."

"Yeah, yeah. Gimme a handkerchief or something."

"What do I look like?" sneered the female voice. "Your wife? See what she's got in her bag."

"You look!" the male whined. "I'm done touching this girl. Next thing you know she's gonna be biting me. One gash is enough for me, thank you!"

An opportunity presented itself. The man removed his hand from Chandra's mouth, leaving her face uncovered. A deep breath fueled a cry for help that caused Chandra's entire body to shudder. The word she chose was help, but it might as well have been murder so strong was the call.

Desperate eyes flew to the street from which Chandra had been dragged. A pleading gaze that spoke with the same volume as her cry for help. The alley was narrow. Narrow and dark. The sort of place desperate looks and cries went to die.

A single person stopped in their tracks. The hazy outline of a Nirdac harn, nose quivering at the shadowed suggestion of a person in distress. Another cry for help could set that person over the edge, Chandra realized in her state of frenzy. She sucked down as much air as she could in preparation to call out specifically to the harn.

Air rushed from Chandra, but not in the form of another cry for help. The toe of a booted foot dug deep into her stomach.

"Quiet down," hushed the male voice. "No more from you."

A second boot, propelled by unnatural strength, found the left side of Chandra's ribcage. She heard a sickening crack. It rode across her torso on fiery waves of pain.

"That's right," the woman said. "No more hollering. You sit tight while we take a peek through your bag. I'm thinking you've got something that we're looking for. She *is* the same one, isn't she?"

"What, the same girl from the day Hendricks died? The one who said she found him? It's definitely her. No mistake about that."

Chandra coughed and sputtered. The pair of assailants talked over the sounds of Chandra's suffering as if they had not just tied and beaten her. Spittle coated the side of her cheek. Dust greedily caked over the moisture. Chandra felt dirt line her lips as well, but was too stunned to care. What thoughts she was able to focus on went straight to the tugging sensation on her back. The sound of a sharp claw tearing through leather pack straps as the backpack was removed from Chandra's shoulders.

"There we are," the female voice cooed in sickening fashion. The voice carried the promise of further violence if expectations were not met. "Now, let's see if we have a bandage for poor old Tumwe."

"Names, Alyssa! No names!"

"Excuse me?"

"We don't need her asking around about us."

"Tumwe, Tumwe, Tumwe!" the woman cackled. "Like you haven't said my name ten times by now, already. *Oh...* I think we have a winner."

"A bandage?"

"No, you dolt. The map. It's right here in her bag."

"Then take it and let's get out of here! I need to get this cleaned and wrapped up. No telling where that dirty spike has been."

They might as well have kicked Chandra a third time. Names clicked into place. Voices came around to full recognition. She was able to turn her head through her daze to catch a glimpse of familiar yellow-and-black armbands. Their words sealed the final piece of the mystery into place. These were the members of the Baylocke Battalion Chandra had taunted the day she found the map.

Chandra felt the remnants of her backpack dash against her side. It crumpled in a formless way that suggested utter destruction. Another blow added to the mounting pile of mental and physical injury.

"C'mon," said the human through gritted teeth, "before anyone gets too curious."

"Yeah, yeah, all right. Let's get you to the apothecary so we can fix your boo-boo," the katarl said as if she were speaking to a toddler. Carefree footsteps carried the pair of Baylocke Battalion members down to the opposite end of the alley and out of earshot.

Defeat settled over Chandra like the tattered husk of her backpack. An errant cough reignited the pain in her back and stomach, a dull thrum that she could feel throughout her entire body. The urge to vomit welled up from deep within. Chandra choked the instinct down between labored grunts.

Forming a spell proved to be a challenge. Constant pain dominated Chandra's focus. A clean dagger, as Chandra was used to forming, was out of the question. Simplicity was called for. This implement had a different destiny. It was not to be used as a weapon. Instead, this improvised, toothy blade was used to saw through the rope that bound her arms in place. Tricky business. Chandra barely had use of her wrists. The brunt of the work was done with delicate fingertips.

The sun was low by the time Chandra had freed her arms. Light from streetlamps poured into the alleyway to fuel the unbinding of her legs. At first, Chandra tried pulling at the rope around her legs. There were no knots or lashings. Whatever spell the katarl used to animate the rope still lingered in the tightly coiled mass of threads. The rope resisted all attempts to yank or pull it away. Chandra was forced to cut each layer of the coil.

Freed completely from her bindings, Chandra rested against the alley wall. Sagging shoulders heaved with every breath. She looked down at the rags that were her leather backpack and the claw marks that gouged deep into its body. Supplies hung out from holes. Bits of food were scattered about the alley. Pieces of paper fluttered in the light breeze that trickled through the alleyway.

"Paper?" Chandra mumbled, wiping dirt and grime from her face.

Paper!

Olufemi's notes poked out of Chandra's bag, overlooked by those who did not know they existed. One final wave of relief for the day washed over Chandra. A wry smile cracked the pained expression on her face as she leaned out to grab her things.

"I'm gonna need a bodyguard."

9

Objection

Lightning crackled. Storm clouds raged. The bright sun mocked Chandra as fire and brimstone filled her lungs. Each breath fanned the inferno that raged in her side. A haphazard stumble through the alley where she had been assaulted was a battle. When she reached the main road through Eaststead to the Dawn Bridge, that battle exploded into outright war.

Twilight had not thinned the streets of Eaststead. Craftspeople were on their way home. Fisherfolk abandoned the riverbed for the day. Shops and stalls closed. Traffic carried all sorts over the Dawn Bridge into Oldstead. It was nearly as busy as the noonday rush when hungry tradespeople ran errands or roamed the streets for a quick bite to eat. This all translated to pain for Chandra. Busy streets meant a bump here or a shove there. No malice, just a road packed with people eager to be on their way. A gentle nudge would rip Chandra's breath from her chest. Misted eyes made it impossible to cut through the crowd with meaningful intent. Chandra felt like the smallest child in a schoolyard game.

Efforts to wipe away tears proved a mistake. Chandra had used her left hand. The same side where she had been kicked. Muscle fibers screamed in horrific chorus as they dragged over the site of the vicious attack. What started as an effort to clear away tears instead produced more.

"Gods dammit," Chandra gasped. Another mistake. One that Chandra was not keen to repeat without good reason.

The white, dust-covered steps of the House called to Chandra. Her pace quickened once the massive structure was in sight. A promise of relief. Grace from the gods that could take the pain away. Allow Chandra to take a full breath. Though pain did not subside as she climbed the steps, the promise was enough to propel her upward.

Open doors welcomed Chandra like a parent's embrace. The few people that milled about the entrance hallway steered clear of Chandra, who rocked and swayed. They must have thought Chandra to be drunk. Chandra paid them no mind. Judgment from strangers was the last of her worries. She was happy to have the extra room. More space meant less pain, and less pain was all Chandra could think about.

Surprise wormed its way to the front of Chandra's mind when she felt someone touch her arm. She did not expect to receive help from anyone. Not even on the steps of the gods. Their grip was firm and allowed Chandra to ease off some of her weight.

"Ma'am?" the stranger said. There was a hint of agitation. Chandra wondered if this was not the first time that the stranger called for her attention. "Ma'am, are you okay?"

Chandra looked at the furry hand that gripped her arm, then followed the arm up to the face of a young Zumbatran katarl. Golden furrows crinkled the boy's brow. He was so young that he showed no signs of a mane. White robes, free of any mark or symbol, covered the boy's trembling frame. His concerned gaze roved ceaselessly over Chandra to locate the source of her ails.

"N-no," Chandra struggled to say. Her grip on the poor acolyte's arm tightened as a new surge of pain wracked her body. A bit of spittle fought through her clenched jaw and trickled down to her chin.

"Oh, oh gods," the boy murmured. His free hand clapped over his mouth the moment he finished the utterance, embarrassed by the outburst. Muffled words clawed their way through his fingers. "I'll… I'll go get someone. Let me set you down."

"Bring Ryleah," Chandra sputtered.

"Of course, of course!"

The pair inched their way toward the closest pew. A journey made easier once the katarl boy offered his shoulder in support. Gentle hands eased Chandra down onto the padded seat. Velvet cushions stood in stark contrast to the wooden back of the pew. That Chandra no longer had to support her weight was enough. Breaths still caused agony, but it was easier to manage when all she had to focus on was the pain.

Sandaled feet thumped down the wine-colored rug that cut through the middle of the House. There was an eagerness about the young acolyte that brought a measure of reassurance. His frantic departure told Chandra that she would not have to wait long for Ryleah. She hoped that the boy would relay the situation well and that Ryleah would come prepared. Chandra was ready to be hauled from the soup of sweat and pain in which she stewed.

Comfort was difficult to find on the pew. While cushions provided a pleasant seat, the rigid wood protested contact. Chandra felt a jolt of pain radiate from her left side through her whole torso if she tried to lean back. Hunching forward was no better. She was forced to sit with a back as straight as a flagpole.

Several times Chandra heard footsteps and assumed her pain was near its end. Several times she was disappointed. As late as it was, other denizens of Arnstead still milled about the House. Making out who was who through clouded eyes proved difficult. Blurred shapes that sought a pew to offer prayer looked no different to Chandra than a member of the clergy that might approach to offer aid. The uncertain nature of the wait was unbearable. There was nothing to focus on to distract Chandra from the fire in her side. No string of thought lasted more than a few moments before being drowned in agony. All she could do was force herself to take shallow breaths until help arrived.

"This pew here?" The voice was familiar and brought with it a wave of comfort. Even through her trancelike state of pain, Chandra could not mistake Ryleah's voice. "Okay, sit me down next to her. Ma'am, help is on the way."

Chandra did not bother to look over. The act of twisting her torso to face her friend was not a pleasant thought to entertain. Instead, Chandra waited until the shuffle of leather sandals subsided. Velvet cushions shifted and bulged at the weight of another person. Chandra did not need to turn to know that Ryleah had been seated just a few inches away.

"All right, ma'am. I'm here to help," Ryleah said, now situated in place. The acolyte's voice was cool and pleasant. Like honey infused with mint. "Can you tell me what ails you?"

"Ribs," Chandra sputtered. "Ribs. Maybe… broken."

"Chandra? Is that you, Chandra? What happened? Never mind, show me where it hurts."

Tears were swept aside by the back of Chandra's hand. This time she made a conscious decision to use her right arm and spare herself some pain. Her vision somewhat cleared, Chandra was able to see the pale white hand Ryleah offered. The process was familiar. Chandra understood the request.

With her right hand, Chandra lifted the left side of her shirt. Just far enough to expose the site of pain on her ribs. Cotton felt like nails as it rose over Chandra's inflamed skin. A clear portent as to how dreadful examination would be, but Chandra snuffed the gripe. She took hold of the hand Ryleah offered and guided it to her injury. Soft finger-tips roved over ribs with a tentative touch. Still, it felt like Ryleah had rubbed a sheet of sandpaper over Chandra's skin. Chandra could not help but wince and suck air through her teeth.

"That's broken, for sure," Ryleah murmured. "You must be in a world of pain right now. I can get this fixed, but it's going to take a little while. Just try to stay still, okay?"

"Yeah." Chandra coughed. A new wave of pain radiated through her torso as a result.

"Badru, hand me the materials please." Chandra assumed Ryleah talked to the katarl acolyte. The one that had received Chandra and gone for help. Command had slipped into Ryleah's voice. She was telling the boy just as much as asking him. "And chew on the mint while I get this ready, please."

"Yes, ma'am," the boy replied.

Various sounds riddled the air. Objects, hard and soft, fell into what sounded like a metal basin. Small claws scraped on the same metal. A sudden squeak followed by a meaty squish. Chandra recognized the noises that accompanied the healing miracle. Life traded for life. Herbs and sands added to the blood of a freshly drained mouse.

With all her ingredients assembled, Ryleah took a deep breath. The next order was to recite the prayer.

"Manus, hear my prayer. I offer you these worldly goods that you might hear me. I offer you this lifeblood that you may empower me. Wield through me your power to knit flesh. Wield through me your power to mend bone. I am your servant and vessel. Manus, hear my prayer."

Warm light trickled into Chandra's periphery. Manus heard the prayer, and the ingredients merged into some kind of radiant salve. Chandra was not clear on the specifics of the ritual. All she knew was that the result should be able to fix her ribs with some help from Ryleah.

"Badru, the mint," Ryleah demanded.

"Yesh, ma'am," the boy slurred.

"Thank you, Badru. You can go now. Chandra, take my hand again. Guide me back to the injury."

Icy relief washed over Chandra's torso when Ryleah touched the broken rib. The constant pain that seemed to radiate with each heartbeat calmed to a manageable level. Instead of waves of fire, it felt more like Chandra had stumbled into the edge of a tall table. A dull inconvenience purged after by a stretch or two. Chandra was able to take her first full breath since she had been kicked.

"Oh gods," Chandra panted. "Thank you, Ryleah. You're a lifesaver."

"Don't thank me yet." Ryleah chuckled. Her professional tone had faded now that the other acolyte was gone. "Sage's mint works better on open wounds than when it's just applied to the skin, so I wouldn't move too much if I were you. Might bring the pain back."

"Noted." Chandra sighed as she eased herself back against the pew. "Need anything else from me, or can I close my eyes for a bit?"

"Go ahead, I've got my hands where they need to be. All we need now is time for the miracle to do its work. Wouldn't mind an explanation, though. You take a nasty fall again?"

"Something like that," Chandra grumbled. She did not want to alarm Ryleah with the truth. It was better that the acolyte thought Chandra hurt herself doing Shikaree work. That was a discussion Chandra was more prepared to have.

"I know your family needs the money, but there's gotta be a better way than beating yourself up down there. One of these days you're going to get yourself hurt so bad you won't be able to make it back to me."

"What? No, a little thing like this isn't going to— ah!" Chandra gasped and recoiled. Ryleah had poked the tip of a finger into the still inflamed skin near Chandra's broken rib. It startled Chandra how such a gentle gesture could reignite so much discomfort. Reflex told her to get away from the source of the pain, but that same source was also what promised a remedy. "Okay, I get it. Stop. Stop!"

The pressure abated.

"I don't have many friends, Chandra. I don't want any of them to disappear in the dark."

Chandra tilted her head to face Ryleah. The sudden softness of speech had caught Chandra by surprise. Soft words were the norm for the half-Deepkin girl, but these were vulnerable. A younger sister or brother wishing a war-bound sibling well. Moments like these made Chandra wish she could look Ryleah in the eyes and tell her everything was okay. Share a look of confidence that transcended words. Instead, she had to settle for placing a hand on the acolyte's shoulder. A kind smile was offered out of habit rather than for effect.

"Thanks, Ryleah," Chandra whispered. "I'll try to take better care of myself next time, okay?"

"Yeah," Ryleah offered through a feeble chuckle, "you'd better."

"If I'm lucky, I won't have to dive the World Below for much longer. Got something big lined up that should get us outta money trouble for good."

"Nothing that's going to break another couple of ribs, I hope?"

"I said I'll be more careful. Promise."

"Well, that's good news, then." Ryleah sighed. "Though I *will* miss your evening visits while I'm doing my rounds in the catacombs."

"What's that supposed to mean?"

"I figure I'd see you a lot less if you didn't need to go below, is all. The House is a bit out of your way, right?"

"Hmm," Chandra murmured.

Life without debt had always seemed like a fantasy. Thoughts of what would come after felt more like painful distractions rather than fruitful plans. There would be no need to venture into the World Below, to be sure. That would mean more time on the homestead. Less time in Arnstead. Chandra was sure she could conjure up reasons to visit, but the prospect of nights filled with sleep instead of danger was tantalizing. Embarrassment stabbed Chandra's heart when she realized she had never considered Ryleah in her thoughts of a life without debt.

Chandra knew how much she owed Ryleah. The secret path through the catacombs would have remained a mystery if not for the acolyte. Ryleah never mentioned the opening to any of the clergy, either. It would have been easy to discuss the hole and have it sealed without a second thought. This was nothing to say of all the minor miracles that Ryleah had performed for Chandra over the years. The current situation, a battered Chandra being attended by Ryleah, was more common than Chandra would have liked. How the acolyte managed to explain the missing reagents without giving up Chandra was a secret that Ryleah refused to discuss. The girl looked out for Chandra's wallet as well as her health.

"With all that time on my hands, I guess I'd have to visit mother in the catacombs more often," Chandra said. "Only seems right. I'm sure my father would understand."

"I suppose so," Ryleah said with a small, understanding smile.

* * *

The sun had long since vanished from the sky by the time Alabaster came plodding onto the Pattal family farm. An unfeeling moon looked down upon Chandra, who hung her head low in the saddle. Man-arail spikes clattered and clinked around her waist in time with slow hoofbeats.

Haste was not on the agenda. So much of the day had been spent in a rabid frenzy. Riding to town. Buying sugar and yeast. Riding back to the quarry to tie up Alabaster. Walking back into town to meet with Olufemi and learn the great news about the map. Her excited march to the House of Many was so viciously interrupted by the Baylocke Battalion. All of it was done so quickly that Chandra struggled to keep it all straight in her head.

Under the moon, everything changed. There were no prying eyes to gander at a girl whose clothes were two years too small. No officials telling her she was too young to help her family put food on the table. Chandra could let the sounds of the night envelop her. Cicadas cried out to one another in timeless ritual. The steady clip-clop of Alabaster's hooves over the packed earth of the Pattal family's lawn. Barn doors with hinges that needed fresh oil. Excited whinnies from Patra and Mortimer as Chandra returned with their missing friend.

The night was quiet amid the sounds of life echoing into eternity. With Alabaster tucked into his stable, Chandra felt like she was able to rest. She leaned against the stable door and slid down to the hay-strewn ground. Both her stomach and back protested the action. Chandra did not care. She took an even set of breaths and thumped her head against the stable door.

"I need to take off your saddle, don't I, boy?" Chandra muttered. She half chuckled the thought as she pushed herself off the inviting ground and raised a light spell to see by. "Didn't think I'd forget about you, did ya? No, course I wouldn't."

Chandra eased the stable door open and slipped into the space with Alabaster. She was too tired to parade the horse back out into the open barn. There was enough space in the stable to make do. It was a task that Chandra could do blindfolded with a hand behind her back. Tight space to perform the work was the last of her worries.

Most present among her worries was the sound of *another* door being opened and closed. Not one that was attached to the stables. Chandra pretended not to notice and went about the task at hand.

It was not long before the sound of human footsteps mingled with the occasional clomp of a restless horse.

"Long day to buy sugar, don't you think?"

Leaning against the barn door, haloed by Chandra's spell, was her father, Nitesh. He wore a look that told Chandra he was more disappointed than angry. It was a look she had grown accustomed to discerning in the dark hours of a late return. Chandra chose only to give the man a passing glance before she returned to her task of dressing down Alabaster. One of these tasks could wait. It was Chandra's decision which would be which. At least, that's what she thought at the time.

The charade continued for a few tense moments before Nitesh spoke again. He had drawn a few feet closer to the stables but did not make a show of hurrying to Chandra's side.

"Did you even do what you said you left for? I'd hate to imagine any of this family's hard-earned money going toward some escapade miles below the ground. Were you spending the day looking for dust-covered baubles again?"

"I got mugged," Chandra said flatly without looking away from her task. She made a show of tossing her shredded backpack onto the floor for her father to see. The bag cast a small, weary shadow as it flopped to the ground and splayed its meager contents for all to see. "Happy?"

Another half-truth. What damage could one more do at this point, Chandra wondered. It had the desired effect. Nitesh sniffed at the night air before he replied.

"No, of course not," he muttered, taking a few more steps closer to his daughter.

Chandra felt her movements speed up. Heat rose in her face as she pressed the matter.

"Not going to say 'I told you so'? Not going to tell me I should leave Arnstead to burn to the ground, along with all the miscreants that walk its streets? All the normal crap?"

"I did not come out to reprimand you, Chandra," her father said softly.

"Liar," Chandra spat. She turned and forced the stable door open, striding out to stand next to the remnants of her bag. "What was that about spending money, then? From *you*, of all people. Don't talk about wasting the family's money like you give a damn, while I'm out trying to do whatever I can to make sure this farm doesn't end up in Orland hands. I'm putting my body on the line to make sure that Omala gets fed every day."

"That's not fair, Chandra—"

"No, what's not fair is that Najran has shoes that fit because *I* almost died in the World Below. Kumail has an automatic plow from those Westinghouse bastards because of the blood and sweat from my *escapades* in that nightmare below the town."

"Can I talk—"

"No! No, you can't!" Chandra fumed. She was speaking with her hands as much as her voice, making wild and threatening gestures toward her father. "I'm tired of having to lie to you just so that we can have a meal every morning as a family. I'm tired of the lies I havta tell because of your thankless hatred for a town that's allowed me to support this family because you *know* that the money from the farm is not enough to feed those vampires at the bank. You *know* we wouldn't have a house to live in or land to work on if I didn't throw myself into some dark pit over and over again just to let us pretend that this is working. You know *all of this*. What do you have to say for yourself, Nitesh?"

"That you remind me so much of your mother."

This caught Chandra off guard. Both the calm way in which her father spoke, as well as what he had said. What she had expected was for Nitesh to join in the fray. Chandra hoped she could push her father over the edge, that she could get him to face all the truths she had espoused for fervently. She did not want a quiet reminder that she was her mother's daughter.

What Chandra wanted was a fight.

Her father refused.

"What… what does that even mean?" Chandra sputtered. She threw her hands up in confusion at the notion that her long-dead mother could be relevant at a time like this.

"It pains me to say," her father began slowly as if he had to hunt for each word in turn. "I don't mean how you look, dear. You have your mother's drive. Her unwillingness to leave any opportunity unexplored. You as a Shikaree, and your mother as a Spellseeker. Fighting the injustice of Arnstead one job at a time."

"Is that so?" Chandra's rage was somewhat quelled by the rare sliver of sincerity from her father. She looked down at her bag, then up to the horses, then up further to the beams that supported the barn. She wanted desperately not to look at her father, lest the rage inside be completely quieted. The fuel to fight was still so hot and near. "You think I'm going to end up like mom, then? That I'm going to get myself killed?"

"I know the farm cannot support itself," Nitesh dodged. "It never could. The money your mother earned from the Bureau of Arcane was always what propped this farm up. I knew it then, and I know that the farm is not more sustainable now. That's why I buy these machines—"

"That's why you find more debt to saddle us with? Because you want our failing farm to fail just a little bit less? Is that about the size of it?"

"I want this farm to make the kind of money that can keep you at home, Chandra," Nitesh whispered. He drew nearly within arms' reach of Chandra. Every small utterance of painful truth inched him closer and closer. "I want to do for you what I could never do for your mother. I want to be the one to keep the family safe. To keep the house and the farm safe. I want this to be a place where you and Omala and

Kumail and Najran can live long after I am gone. I want this place to be your *home.*"

Nitesh put out a tender hand. His palm faced upward, with fingers uncurling gently under the light of Chandra's spell. Soft eyes twinkled in that same light as any shred of condemnation melted from his uncreased brow.

There was nowhere else for Chandra to look but at her father.

She took a step back.

"If you want this to be *our* home," Chandra murmured, "then you need to do better. No more machines. I mean it this time. If you buy another machine, I move the family into Arnstead. You'll have this automated wonderland all to yourself before you can say mother's name."

Though her rage had simmered down to a manageable, intelligent temperature, Chandra was still prepared to fight her father on any point. This display of honesty did not have her fooled in the slightest. She was ready to draw lines of war across the barn floor if push came to shove. Tender embraces were not in the cards for this conversation, a notion Chandra cemented by withdrawing from yet another advance.

Nitesh sighed, realizing that the conversation had ended.

"Okay," he said. "I understand. Thank you for your honesty, my dear," Nitesh added as he turned and strode toward the barn doors.

The battle, bitterly fought, was over.

Light wavered in the barn as Chandra's concentration began to fade. Darkness enveloped the space. Night was allowed to creep back into where it belonged, to swallow Chandra whole.

If this was a victory, Chandra thought, she was afraid to know the feeling of defeat.

Chandra gathered the remains of her bag in the dark and set off across the lawn. Sleep called for her, and she did not have the strength to deny it any longer.

10

Proposal

It was an hour after sunrise when Chandra trotted into Arnstead atop Alabaster. She passed the memory-glass quarry by in favor of making better time toward the town. There was hope that she might beat the rush of bodies to the Arnstead Arcanarium if she woke with the sun and moved with purpose. No words were spoken as she passed her father to the barn, nor as she mounted Alabaster and took off for town.

Already the streets were choked with people going about their daily business. Chandra may have arrived at the beginning of the day, but she had not beaten Arnstead to rise.

"No big deal," Chandra said as she leaned down in the saddle to pat Alabaster's neck. "As long as we're at the Arcanarium before folks break for lunch, we should be able to beat the rush. No problem."

The Arcanarium, center for the Bureau of Arcane in the town of Arnstead, was a deceptively small building in Weststead. It stood one story tall and was just down the road from the local Orland Bank branch. Bodies swirled around the two pillars of organized society like bees in a busy hive.

Those outside the bank moved like a well-oiled machine. None waited outside under the sun but moved in and out freely.

Outside the Arcanarium was a different story.

If the Orland Bank was a well-oiled machine that spat out busy little bees with ease, then the Arcanarium was a hive that had fallen from a tree and exploded on the ground. The space in front of the Arcanarium was densely packed with a pocket of bodies that obstructed traffic on one side of Main Street. Carts were forced to make wide turns to avoid being sucked into the churning roil that blocked the Arcanarium's doorstep.

"Well, that's not the usual line, now, is it?" Chandra grumbled. She hopped down from the saddle and guided Alabaster to a hitching post in front of the Orland Bank. "Might be a while, friend. Let's keep you out of the mess. I'm sure there's a clause in our loan somewhere that covers borrowing a hitching post for"—Chandra looked at the throbbing mass of people outside the Arcanarium—"for a few hours, I'd guess."

Chandra tied Alabaster in place and, after another few pats on the neck, set off to join the crowd in front of the Arcanarium.

The walk was short. Only a few buildings separated the bank from the Arcanarium, both of which were located on prime real estate along Main Street. Halfway between the edge of town and the Bridge on Main that crossed the river Sisir's Run. There was no finer place in all Arnstead to conduct legitimate business if that was of particular concern. Even the 4th Federation Army barracks were nearby. It was about as physically safe and clean as Arnstead could get. The sort of place where people with fancy clothes felt comfortable holding their wallets and purses out for display.

This was the exact place in Arnstead where Chandra felt the most uncomfortable. She was certain that she could go to a hundred people before finding a single callus on someone's hands. There was plenty of work to be done in Weststead, but none of it was honest. The presence of the Orland Bank branch was testament enough to that in Chandra's mind.

Her misgivings of the area aside, Chandra found a spot at the edge of the crowd outside the Arcanarium. There were two reasons for her visit to Arnstead that day and both required attention from the Bureau of Arcane.

First, and simpler of the two matters, was that she needed to have her Shikaree license renewed. A task that required fifteen bitterly fought-for pennies to complete, which Chandra had put off as long as she could. It was one problem to have relics confiscated upon leaving the middle strata. To lose her license meant an entirely different problem. No buyer in Arnstead, or the entirety of the New World, would deal with an unlicensed Shikaree. That included Robin. Chandra could not risk the one source of moderately consistent income the Pattal family had to something so simple as an expired license. Not after the comments she let fly the night before at her father.

Second on the list was something less routine. Chandra had a hopeful question to ask the attendant at the desk. She had never asked after a Spellseeker by name before, but she had the sneaking suspicion that one by the name of Owen Raulstone might be interested to hear about a cache of relics and focuses. One secreted by varmints for some unknown purpose.

The idea came to her last night as she tossed and turned, trying to forget the events of the day and drift off into much-needed sleep. It was something that the Spellseeker had said when Chandra found him in the World Below. That he was searching for focuses stolen by varmints. Specifically, the varmints broke into people's houses through their basements and then scurried off with whatever Flow-infused objects they could find. Chandra figured that since most of the markings on the map were in varmint text, who was to say that her goal and the Spellseeker's were not the same?

Chandra mulled on the right words to get the job done. What she should tell the Spellseeker versus what information she should keep close to her chest. She knew that the Spellseekers were a driven and determined bunch, or at least her mother had been. Outside of her mother, though, Chandra had limited dealings with the Bureau of Arcane and its Spellseekers. Owen seemed kind enough, but she needed to make sure she could spin the story in a way that would still lead to a profit.

While Chandra ruminated on what to, and not to, say, the coiled-up mass of people outside the Arcanarium failed to shrink. There were quite a few new arrivals behind Chandra since she joined the mob. No longer was she at the back of the chaotic scramble. Chandra had been thoroughly enveloped as the group of humans, harn, and katarl continued to bloom across Main Street.

Chandra stood on her toes to see why the ungainly group of people had not coalesced into a seemlier line to conduct business. A couple of hops were in order. The average height of the crowd was taller than Chandra could manage to see over unassisted. She tugged on the sleeve of a particularly tall Bangeli katarl nearby.

"Excuse me," Chandra bid with honest yet firm conviction. "Excuse me, sir. Can you see why the line isn't moving? I'm a bit short to see."

The katarl looked around for a moment, his head stuck firmly in the clouds. He eventually realized that the request for attention was a little closer to ground level. When he noticed Chandra, who waved politely, the katarl smiled a sweet smile that was tempered by rampant annoyance.

"Morning, miss," the katarl rumbled. He looked from Chandra toward the Arcanarium and squinted. "Doors still aren't open."

"What do you mean, *not open?*" Chandra asked, unable to contain her disappointment. "But there's so many people out here. How could they not be open yet?"

"I don't like it any more than you do, miss," chimed a smartly dressed Zumbatran harn to Chandra's left. The harn peered at a pocket watch attached to her vest by a silver chain. "Shouldn't be long now. Another fifteen minutes. They always open the doors at nine on the dot."

"So much for being early," Chandra sighed.

"You have to beat the sun to get ahead of this crowd," chuckled the katarl. "Folks that can afford it line up before dawn if they want to get seen before noon. Just the way things are."

"Great. Thank you, by the way," said Chandra with a polite smile.

"Not a problem, miss. Might as well get along with the ones you're stuck next to, don't you think?"

"I suppose so," murmured the harn.

"Fair enough," Chandra agreed.

Idle chatter carried on for the better part of an hour. Discussions of the weather went hand in hand with talk of the decay of Oldstead, and how it was bleeding into Eaststead and Weststead. Chandra even went so far as bring up the mugging from the day prior. A topic that earned her quite a bit of sympathy.

By ten in the morning, the mob had formed into something much closer to a line that snaked westward down Main Street. Open doors, an event that happened at nine on the dot, aided in the process. Much of the main body of the crowd was able to file into the lobby of the Arcanarium. This boon was not afforded to Chandra until closer to noon. Her compatriots in line had fallen into the awkward silence that accompanies strangers who have run dry of small talk to share.

All Chandra could think about was how abysmally slow the line moved, even now that the doors were open and people were being attended to. At least, she assumed, people were being seen. Chandra supposed it was just as likely that people were fleeing the line in utter frustration.

Chandra bore with the frustration until she noticed something blue sneaking its way out of the alley next to the Arcanarium. It was a person, to be sure. They moved in a way that suggested they were trying, and miserably failing, to act as naturally possible.

The reason for stealth became clear when the person in front of Chandra began to holler at the sneaking individual.

"Hey, bluebell!" the man shouted as if he reprimanded a dog that snuck scraps from the dinner table. The furtive individual stopped and drew up straight, realizing they had been caught. "Yeah, you! How about you get inside and do something about this line, yeah? I've been out here for hours."

"Yeah, blue," joined in another individual from the line. Her voice was slick and greasy, like oil running over the top of water. "How about you go do something useful for a change."

When the made person dressed in blue turned to address the hecklers, Chandra recognized him. The Spellseeker coat had not been enough information to go on alone. Chandra was looking at a very embarrassed Owen Raulstone. He pointed to himself in the face of insults and chuckled nervously at accusations of laziness.

"Sorry, folks," Owen replied after a few more bouts of verbal abuse. He waved a clipboard toward the agitated Arcanarium line that threatened to return to its previous occupation as a mob. "Official Spellseeker business to attend to. I'm sure Sam will get to every one of you in turn. Just have to be patient!"

A communal groan rose from the crowd as they gave up on their too-willing target. There was no sport to be had from a person so ready to receive an array of personal abuses.

Chandra, against her better judgment, stepped out of line and toward Owen. There was no telling if or when she would ever see the man again. She had to strike while the chance presented itself.

"Mr. Raulstone?" Chandra asked. "Can I talk to you for a minute?"

Owen, who had already turned to leave by the time Chandra left the line, spun on his heels. He was surprised to be addressed by anything other than the color of his clothes. The look on his face was plain to see.

"Sorry, citizen," Owen said as he turned. "I'm on official business. Any complaints need to be raised with Sam at the front desk. I can't circumvent the process, or the folks in line over there will have a— wait a minute," he interrupted himself as Chandra stopped just outside arm's reach. A light came over his face, accompanied by a bright smile. "You're the girl from the other day. The one that fished me out of the World Below. It was, uh… Pattal, wasn't it?"

"Just Chandra is fine, thanks," Chandra replied as she returned Owen's smile. "Do you have a minute to talk?"

A pained expression cracked Owen's smile. He looked at the still-grumbling and sneering line of people outside the Arcanarium. Some of them cast hateful sidelong glances at Owen, the kind of venomous glare that made a viper coil into a protective knot. His internal struggle manifested words after a brief period of silence.

"I really can't be making exceptions," Owen grumbled, still looking at the line. "I do owe you a favor though. Can I ask what you want to talk about?"

Chandra grabbed the opportunity by the throat and gave it a solid punch in the face.

"A cache of relics and focuses that's been amassed by a pack of varmints somewhere in the World Below, and how we're gonna get it."

Owen's expression changed from one of indecision to the face of a person who had just discovered a corpse lying in the middle of the road. A dark and sudden change that startled Chandra.

"Walk with me," Owen said in a low, serious tone that matched his new expression.

The license would have to wait for another day.

* * *

"Say that one more time," asked a peeved Nirdac harn of Owen. "One more time, blue, but in a way that makes some lick of sense."

"Yes, sir." Owen nodded with the resoluteness of one performing an ingrained routine. "I can't certify when exactly your request will be completed. The purpose of my visit today is to verify the information from your Initial Complaint Form, or ICF, that you filed with the Bureau of Arcane's Lost and Stolen division. After having confirmed that the article in question—"

"The focus ring my wife uses to do her *job*!"

"Yes." Owen nodded again after a glance at his clipboard. "I appreciate you verifying the initial details. And confirming that the article is still missing, of course."

"Still *stolen*, you mean."

"As the case may be." Owen respectfully nodded a third time. "I will be able to pass this information on to my superiors for further investigation."

"So, what you're telling me," the plainly dressed harn spat, "is that you came all this way to waste my time? A whole *hour* of my day wasted because you wanted to make sure that an essential piece of technology that my wife uses to put food on the table for our four children is still, in fact, stolen?"

"I appreciate your cooperation, Mr...."

Owen paused to look at his clipboard with dead eyes.

"Fisbaine, you blue dolt. Our family name is Fisbaine. I can't believe our tax money goes to feeding useless wastes of space like you."

"Sorry you feel that way, sir."

"Unbelievable," the harn grumbled.

Mr. Fisbaine stepped back across the threshold of his Eaststead home and slammed the door in Owen Raulstone's face. An expected reaction that did not elicit so much as a flinch from the Spellseeker. Instead, the blue-clad official took a quiet step back and made a few scribbles on his clipboard.

Chandra stared open-mouthed at Owen during the entire exchange. It felt like watching a manarail engine collide with a helpless bystander, except that it happened over and over and the bystander was forced to smile the entire time. A display Chandra wished she could have looked away from. Morbid curiosity to see how a Spellseeker does business, however, denied her that comfort. This was the first time she had ever watched someone from her departed mother's place of work conduct business. Chandra found herself hoping that her mother, gods rest her, had not been forced to endure such abuse.

"Are they all like that, then?" Chandra could not help but ask.

"Hmm?" Owen turned his head to face his captive audience of one. His eyes flicked back to the door for a moment before making lasting contact with Chandra. "Well, sometimes they close the request on the spot. Those are my favorites. A lot less paperwork to be done in those cases. Anyways," he said as he casually waved, "that's one done, a dozen more to go. Start from where you left off as we walk to the next one."

"Sure," Chandra said hesitantly, unsure if she could endure the spectacle of another Lost and Stolen house visit. "Where was I, exactly?"

"Something about being mugged, which is reportable to Violent Offenses. You said they bound you with a spell over some rope, right?"

"Yeah."

It was Chandra's turn to nod.

"Well," Owen continued, "if you know their names and can give a decent description, I could help you get that request filed. Violent Offenses is a bit more agile with their headcount. Not months behind like we are over in Lost and—"

"That's all well and good," Chandra interrupted, "but I don't think we have the time to get distracted by going through your friends. They're members of the Baylocke Battalion. A really experienced and well-funded group of Shikaree, and they have the map I was talking about. I'm worried they might beat us to the punch if we give them too much of a head start."

"I'm not a part of Violent Offenses, but I don't like the idea of letting dangerous muggers walk the streets unpunished. We could at least get some of my people pointed in the right direction."

"Would you rather punish two people that beat up a young woman over a piece of paper, or get back potentially dozens of focuses before the Baylocke Battalion can get their hands on them for resale?"

"I see your point," Owen conceded with a click of his tongue.

The pair continued to weave in and out the streets of Eaststead in silence for a moment while the Spellseeker gestated everything he had heard. For ease of keeping her story straight, Chandra had decided to tell Owen everything about the matter. It felt better than potentially having to backtrack later over some small falsehood that did not matter in the grand scheme.

More importantly than keeping herself honest, it allowed Chandra to feel like she had a confidant. Someone who she could talk to and bounce ideas off. Someone as invested in the situation as she was and a lot less likely to just wave the talk off as a child's ramblings. The sort of quality that Chandra wished she could have in her father, but it was no time to get picky about who felt what and why. Owen was willing to listen and Chandra was willing to talk.

"How are we meant to beat the Battalion to the punch if they have your map?" Owen broke the silence with a poignant question, and then followed with another. "These Baylocke folks aren't the type to just sit on their heels while we go fumbling around in the dark, are they?"

"Oh," Chandra practically squeaked, "that's right! I forgot to tell you about Olufemi he—"

"Olufemi Bradly, by chance?" Owen asked. He gave Chandra a curious look over his shoulder. "The fellow over at Frontier Finds?"

"That's the one."

"There's a good man. Trusted friend. What's he got to do with us knowing how to find the focuses, though?"

"Well, he actually translated the map for me. There were bits around the edge that were written in varmint and—"

"In varmint?"

"Yeah, I was just as surprised as you." Chandra chuckled. "Anyways, the varmint writing. A friend of mine said that Olufemi was good with languages and sent me his way. He translated the whole thing for me and gave me notes. Translations that I still have, and that the folks at the Baylocke Battalion are none the wiser about."

"And that's why you think we can beat them to the cache? Olufemi's translation?"

"That, and the map was complete shit, to be honest."

"That so?" Owen asked through a chuckle of his own.

"Yeah, completely useless without the notes from your friend Olufemi."

"So, then." Owen came to an abrupt stop in the middle of a small Eaststead street. There was only a trickle of people that needed to cut around the slight obstruction formed by Chandra and Owen. Not enough of an inconvenience to feel guilty over. Especially not when the conversation was getting back into full stride. Chandra could not handle another interruption on the level of a Lost and Stolen house call. "What's the plan, Ms. Pattal? You strike me as the type that has a plan before she opens her mouth to what amounts to be a perfect stranger."

Chandra was aglow with pride at the notion. A professional finder of lost focuses was asking her for a plan to find focuses. Someone that her mother would have called a colleague.

"Well, first we need to get gear. I've got some stuff at home, but we'll need to get you some stuff as well. I'm not really accustomed to packing for two."

"And what kind of gear are we talking?"

"Oh, you know." Chandra shrugged. "Ropes. Some pitons. A harness or two. Grab some food that won't go bad in a day. A pack to put it all in."

"Quite the list, huh?"

"Oh, it's all simple Shikaree stuff. We might want to get you a different pair of boots if you haven't got something more suitable than those. I think I hear iron in those heels?" Chandra pointed at the pair of black, knee-high boots that Owen wore.

"That's a good ear you've got." Owen nodded. "Or eye, whatever the case may be."

"There *is* some metal, then? Yeah, that won't do. You'll be sliding all over the rocks down there. Slick as moss on a river rock sometimes. Can't have you breaking an ankle the second we get you down there, can we?"

"And, assuming I agree to your list, what's the plan after that? We go to the Shikaree emporium and plop our list down on the counter?"

"Not too far off the mark."

"Right." Owen laughed again. He scratched the back of his neck as a cloud of kicked-up dust fell and stuck to him. The sun was high in the sky and did neither of them any favors. "Well, I can't just abandon these forms to the roadside. How about I spend the rest of the day getting these squared away and we meet up tomorrow?"

"Tomorrow at noon, outside Robin's Field Goods? Gives me some time to get my Shikaree license renewed. Needed to do that anyways."

"Ah, I know Robin's place. Near my apartment. All right then, consider your plan accepted."

The unlikely pair shook on the deal and parted ways under the sweltering Arnstead sun, Chandra feeling considerably lighter than she had when she awoke that morning.

11

Goodbyes

"Don't forget the top row," Omala said on her tiptoes. The strain in her voice matched the stretch of her quivering arm. "I can't get that high yet. Still your job."

"It's all right," Chandra replied. "You're getting taller every time we come out here. A few days, and who knows? You might be putting me out of a job here soon."

Omala looked from the tips of her outstretched fingers to the top rung of the Pattal family's chicken coup. There were still a couple of inches yet before she would be touching that row. Another few inches after that before she would be able to stick her hand under the roosts of the chickens that sat there. Both Chandra and Omala knew that the words were a nicety and little more.

"Whatever you say," Omala replied with a heavy sigh. She resumed picking eggs from the lower rung of nests. The chickens fielded mild protest at the disturbance, clucking in response to Omala's small, probing hands. "Glad you're out here. Been a while since you've helped make breakfast."

A pang of guilt bit Chandra's heart. There was something about so tiny a voice airing a complaint of loneliness that grieved her sorely. Chandra covered the thought with a sisterly smile that dripped sarcasm.

"You've just gotten so big. You seemed like you could handle a little old thing like breakfast all on your own. Wouldn't want to go getting in your way."

"Oh, right." Omala chuckled. Some of Chandra's sarcasm rubbed off on her younger sister. "I guess you're just too busy chasing after Jacob Hartsfield to help your little sister."

"Stop," Chandra grumbled in protest.

"I saw the way you were holding onto him at the harvest festival," Omala pressed. Her tongue was keen like a silver dagger. "The way you two were swaying back and forth. Coulda swore I saw babies in your eyes."

"Stop, stop, stop," Chandra begged. "No… now it's stuck. You've got that dirty image stuck in my head."

"Serves you right, leaving me alone for all these breakfasts. Do you even realize how much the boys eat?"

"I get it." Chandra waved a fresh-plucked egg at the notion. There was a hint of bitter laughter in her voice as she continued. "I'm sorry, all right?"

"It's okay," Omala replied sweetly. "Just try to help more often, yeah?"

Another innocent sting. Chandra felt her heart skip a couple beats at the earnest words of her sister.

Not yet, Chandra told herself. *Wait until they're all together. It'll be hard enough to say it once. Don't know if I can do it twice, much less three times. Why does saying goodbye have to be so difficult if it's just for a few days?*

"All right," Chandra conceded. An act that brought a broad smile to Omala's slim face.

The pair finished their picking in relative quiet before returning to the house with their collection of fresh eggs for breakfast.

It was set to be another light meal. Eggs and flatbread formed the brunt of the menu, plus whatever chutneys could be prepared before the boys and father awoke. Chandra and Omala were not adventurous in their preparation. They stuck to the bare essentials that could be prepared in time. It would not be a veritable rainbow, but there would be some flavor beyond just egg and bread.

"It's a shame we can't afford a pig," Omala grumbled over the scrambling of eggs. "Would be so nice having some meat in the house."

Chandra tightened at the thought. She knew why there was no meat in the house. Money was too tight after Nitesh had purchased the cider machine on loan. Tighter than it already had been. The collective grip of Westinghouse Industries and the Orland Bank was merciless.

"I'll see what I can do about it," Chandra said after a heavy pause.

"Got something big in the works?" Omala asked in a hopeful tone.

"I'll talk about it when the boys are up and everyone has eaten."

"I bet it's a big sword, isn't it?" Omala prodded. "It's a relic sword that belonged to a giant, and it's so big that you can't even move it without your metal magic. It's been taking you a month to move it out of the caves. Once you get it out, though, we're all going to be rich!"

"Gonna be rich, huh?"

"That's right!"

"Well," Chandra mulled as she moved scrambled eggs back and forth over a hot skillet, "maybe you're right there. Not sure about that fairytale stuff about giants, though."

"You're no fun," Omala pouted.

The pair worked elbow to elbow in the small kitchen area of the Pattal house. Connected to the main dining and living area, there were no walls to obscure the girls as they cooked. Omala kept herself busy cracking and beating eggs. Chandra took the beaten eggs and cooked them over a firelit stove. Egg shells were tossed into a small drain in the sink, where Omala pressed a blue memory-glass button to make the refuse disappear.

The disposal unit was the only piece of memory-glass technology in the house. There was no faucet for running water. All the water used by the Pattal family had to be pulled from the well that sat between the house and the barn.

Omala, having cracked the last of the eggs into a bowl and transferred its beaten contents to the skillet, ran from the house to fetch a pail of water for washing up. Her feet thumped and thudded across the floorboards of the house.

The house began to stir, if not from the smells of breakfast, then certainly from the sounds of its preparation. Chandra could hear the boys begin to rise in their room. Sheets rustled and their mattress groaned. The Pattal house was coming to life at last.

Several minutes slogged by before the boys shuffled out in unison from their bedroom, the door creaking as it opened and closed. They were dressed for the day with overalls and work boots. Both had washed their faces. All this being true, neither Kumail nor Najran were truly awake. Not yet.

"Morning, Chandra," Kumail mumbled through the beginnings of a wide yawn. "Eggs and flatbread today?"

"You guessed it," Chandra replied, emptying the last of the skillet's scrambled contents onto a plate that she transported to the table. The skillet was set down in the sink to await a post-breakfast wash with the water that Omala went out to fetch.

"Smells good," Najran said through a yawn.

There was nothing to smell. The eggs were plain apart from a pinch of salt. Flatbread was a day old, at least, and so there was no scent of freshly baked bread. Even the sauces for dipping were tame by the family's usual standards. Breakfast was about as plain as could be. About as plain as *would be* for quite some time, Chandra thought to herself.

What the meal lacked in flavor or variety, it made up for in volume. The Pattal family would not go hungry. Not yet.

Omala returned with the pail of water as the boys were taking their seats. She greeted them through their continued yawns and poured glasses of water for the table from the pail. The rest of the water was stowed near the sink to facilitate eventual cleanup. Omala wiped her hands on her plain white shirt in satisfaction at yet another job done well.

"All right," Omala sighed, "that just leaves—"

"Morning, everyone," Nitesh cut in as if he had been summoned by his youngest daughter.

"Morning, Father," Omala, Najran, and Kumail all chimed in unison. Chandra bade her good morning with a nod.

"Nice of you to join us, Chandra," Nitesh added as he took his place at the table. Steam rose from the pile of eggs to obscure his expression.

"Yes, well," Chandra offered hesitantly, "I don't like to miss breakfast."

"A shame you don't feel the same way about lunch and dinner," Kumail jabbed as he craned a handful of eggs onto the plate Chandra had provided. He flicked scraps of steaming egg that clung to his fingers back into the pile, surprised by just how hot the mass of eggs was. A slab of flatbread followed the eggs to his plate.

"And how about a prayer, Kumail," said Nitesh, "since you seem so ready to be on with the meal."

"Yes, Father," Kumail replied with a bow of his head and a labored sigh. He wiped bits of sleep from his eyes with his egg-free hand before reciting the morning prayer. "Lucina, hear our prayer. We thank you for this breakfast. For blessing the chickens that lay our eggs and the pigs that... well, for the chickens and the eggs. For the grain in our bread and the spice that grants us flavor. Lucina, hear our prayer."

"*Now* you can eat," Nitesh said with a tired smile. "Wasn't so hard, was it?"

"No, Father."

Once the prayer had been said and Nitesh gave his blessing, hands scooped eggs to plates and grabbed scraps of flatbread. Dollops of red and green sauces added some color to the otherwise plain meal. Small islands of flavor on the wooden slabs that the family used as plates.

It was a quiet meal. Hands moved slowly to scrape at the scraps that stood in as seconds. Chutneys were drained, their remnants sopped up by bread like sponges clearing grease from a skillet.

Omala was first to finish. She had not yet swallowed the last bite before she was talking to the dreary table and its unenthused residents.

"So, Chandra," Omala said through a mouthful of egg before swallowing, "what's the big news? You said you were going to tell us something. I still think it's about a giant's sword."

The last bit was directed in a sweeping manner to the table as a whole. It was clear that Omala had shoveled through her breakfast like a starved pig to ask the question. Legs that could not quite reach the ground from her seat swung back and forth in the air, quivering with anticipation.

What innocence hung from Omala's words was lost on Nitesh. Their father knit his brow and turned a prying gaze toward Omala.

"What's this about a big sword? Are we talking about Shikaree business?" Nitesh panned his glare over to Chandra. "Shikaree business *at the table?*"

Chandra closed her eyes before she rolled them. It was too early for a fight. She summoned the most neutral tone she could muster before responding to the assertion. A deep, calming breath preceded her words.

"I'm going to be gone for a while. I met a Spellseeker in town who needs my help navigating the World Below. He's promised any relics we find along the way are mine to keep or sell as I please."

"Is that so?"

Further wrinkles crowded Nitesh's already full brow. It was as if he could smell the half-truth that Chandra baked under his nose. He leaned forward in fierce anticipation. Chandra took another breath and matched her father's intensity.

"It is."

Chandra let the words fall onto the dining table like an anvil.

Both Kumail and Najran stopped in the middle of mouthfuls, shocked by the flat defiance of their older sister. Kumail looked hesitantly over to Nitesh. The curiosity of Najran was more sly. He did not turn his head but perked his ears as high as they would rise. No word from this conversation would be missed.

Only the conversation did not continue. Not immediately. The weight of it hung around the neck of everyone in the room, save for Omala who still kicked her feet in the air. Everyone else at the table was just as busy digesting the conversation as they were with their meals.

Shikaree.

Spellseeker.

Significant words in the Pattal household. Words that Najran was afraid to speak around his father. That Kumail only whispered in passing to his older sister, and only when no other words would do. Even Omala typically knew better than to spout off about Chandra's side work, though Omala's excitement got the better of her on this day.

"What's this about a Spellseeker, then? I thought you went alone on your escapades to the deep places."

There was something about the way that Nitesh said the word Spellseeker. Never had a single word walked so tight a rope between the realms of reverence and disdain. Like a bittersweet memory that refused to be laid to rest.

Chandra swallowed air, words failing her for a moment.

Why am I so nervous? Chandra blinked at her hesitation. *I wasn't worried the night we fought. Why do I feel so weighed down? Is it because everyone is watching?*

"He owes me a favor," Chandra said at last. "I found him while he was lost in the World Below and got him back to the surface. Seeing what happened to me a few days ago— the *mugging* and all— I thought it might be better to find an extra set of hands. He offered his and I didn't say no."

"Is that so?" Nitesh asked again through withered patience. He did not wait for a reply before asking his next question. "And how long will you be away? I figure you wouldn't bother to tell me if it was just an afternoon or something like that. Days? A week?"

"No more than a week, I'm hoping," Chandra replied defensively. "We have some exploration to do, but I have it on good authority where our goal is resting. Just a matter of getting there and getting what we find out."

"Sounds easy enough," Kumail offered.

The speed at which Nitesh snapped over to his eldest son alarmed the table. Even Chandra started at the ferocious gesture.

"I am speaking with your sister," Nitesh said with unexpected calm. "Please wait until we have finished. So," he said turning back to Chandra, "how do you plan to get to town?"

It was Chandra's turn to knit her brow in confusion. She cocked her head to one side, an involuntary gesture she could not suppress. The answer to the question seemed so obvious that she was surprised it needed to be said at all.

"I'll ride Alabaster, of course."

"And where will he stay for a week?" Nitesh probed. "Have enough sock money tucked away to house a horse in Arnstead? I'm sure you won't be able to see him every day to feed and water him, after all."

"Well, I'm sure—"

"And besides, Alabaster is the *family's* horse, not just yours. What if the rest of us need to get something from town? We don't have saddles and the like for Patra or Mortimer. Are we supposed to hitch up the cart just to visit town?"

"So, I'm walking, then? Is that it?" Chandra asked as her shoulders sank. "You're forcing your own daughter to walk into town so she can feed her... no, you know what? That's fine. I'm sure I could use the exercise. For crawling around hellish places to pay off your debts. Why should I expect anything different?"

A fire rose in Chandra's stomach. All hint of hesitation vanished upon the realization that she would be forced to reach Arnstead on foot. She pushed away her plate, meal half-eaten, and stood from the table.

"I need to pack and get on my way," Chandra continued. Each word was laced with enough caustic venom to melt flesh. "I was expected at noon, not that I'll be making that appointment anymore. Not with this insanity."

"Enjoy your stay in town," Nitesh offered as parting.

It was too much. Chandra kicked a table leg in frustration as she left. True to her word, she had an appointment to attempt to keep. There was no time left to waste at the table with her family. Business was calling and she had to answer.

Chandra ducked into the room she shared with Omala and began furiously packing for the trip.

* * *

Twenty minutes on the road had the improvised bindle digging into Chandra's shoulder. With her backpack still in tatters from the mugging, and no saddle bags to fall back on, she was forced to come up with a new solution. A few moments' thought had Chandra throwing what could not be carried on her waist onto a spare sheet. Things like extra clothes and her mess kit. When the space was filled, she pulled the corners together and tied the best knot she knew how. Chandra carried the whole lot over her shoulder on the end of her staff.

For consisting of little more than sundries, the bindle felt heavy as it dangled over her shoulder. Each step caused the package to bounce and dug the staff further into her shoulder. It felt like quitting to move the bindle over to her other shoulder so soon, but there was nothing for it. Chandra listened to her body, knowing that she had a long trek ahead of her. Too long to ignore the occasional plea for comfort.

By the time she reached the main road to Arnstead, Chandra had moved the bindle a total of five times.

It was a demoralizing walk. The distance from her home to the main road should have taken no longer than an hour. On horseback, Chandra would have already made the turn from south to east to begin the long stretch of the journey. On foot, the sun was already high overhead when she made her eastward turn. There was no hope of meeting the Spellseeker at the appointed place by noon. Chandra could only hope that Owen did not take the delay as some kind of joke and dismiss the plan entirely.

As Chandra walked on and on along the dusty road, head hung low and swaying with the southerly breeze, she contemplated the feasibility of utilizing the Flow. Speed had never been an issue for Chandra before. Access to Alabaster and the draft horses always got her where she needed to go above ground. Below ground, she prioritized caution over haste. To move with quiet precision was a valued skill in the

World Below that had spared her many an unwanted encounter. With nothing to focus her thoughts on, however, she toyed with the idea of taking up a new skill.

It was a lost cause. Chandra knew from experience how long it took to cultivate a spell. The initial process of forming the Flow into what was needed was like learning to play a musical instrument without a tutor or instruction book. It was doable, but it would take months to get a general idea straight. Maybe weeks if she turned out to be some sort of prodigy in speed magic. All that with assuming she did not suffer friction burns from wading into untested waters. Then it would take years to dial the general sense of speed down to exactly what she wanted: to run at the speed of a horse.

No. Enhanced speed was the passing fancy of a girl who needed to be elsewhere, but was powerless to do so beyond the limits of her own two legs. Chandra knew better than to try and form a new spell in haste. Regardless, she gritted her teeth each time someone passed her by on horseback.

A distraction was needed. The road alone was not enough to keep her mind off the morning's events. Not enough to quell the silent rage that boiled in her stomach. Chandra needed something tangible. Something to do with her hands beyond holding the bindle steady. Her right hand, for it was her right hand that held the bindle in that moment, drummed fingers on the haft of her staff. Something to do, something to do. But what? The idle left hand readjusted the belt that was riding on her hips. Manarail spikes jingled like a wind chime.

Oh! Chandra realized. *That could do.*

Chandra unhooked one of the manarail spikes from her belt and held it up at chest height. She twirled it on her fingers for a moment and cracked a thin smile. Practice. What better time to get some practice done than right now? There was nothing better for her to do anyway.

It took no time at all for Chandra to dip herself into the Flow and gather energy. The process was no more difficult than cupping her hand in a stream to gather water. Warm and reassuring, the natural energy seeped into her left arm and gathered in the palm of her hand. She held her hand out flat with the spike balanced in the middle. A violet glow, almost imperceptible under the near-midday sun, coated the manarail spike. Chandra relished the sensation of the energy moving from her hand to the spike. It felt like washing her hand in hot, sandy water.

Metal softened. The spike creaked as it curled inward on itself into a small, uneven sphere. It rippled like liquid in response to each of Chandra's steps. Pockets of violet light escaped from the sphere where ripples ran deep. The once cold and rigid spike of iron was now under Chandra's complete control.

"Let's start with some utensils," Chandra muttered through her concentration. "Keep it simple."

The metal began to reform before Chandra finished speaking. It elongated into a handle with a large lump at the top. A measure of rigidity returned as the lump flattened out, then bent into the shape of a spoon. It was not a fancy tool by any stretch of the imagination. Unpolished and rough, it was more the suggestion of a spoon than something a person would want to stick in their mouth. That did not tarnish Chandra's smile. Function brought more delight to her craft than needlessly fanciful form. She twirled the spoon around her fingers as she had done with the spike. An unceremonious toss in the air, followed by swift snatch of the spoon, completed Chandra's celebration.

Let's do a fork next.

Chandra whiled away an hour bending the same spike into various utensils and crude tools. The fork and kitchen knife were simple exercises, as was forming a hook to secure rope, a crude dagger, and a small chisel for peeling away flakes of stone. After that, Chandra worked on forming the small mass of metal into chain links. It was a more difficult endeavor. Not so much from the act of separating and rejoining the metal, but more that it was an exercise she did not partake in often. This was where most of her time bending metal was spent. Chandra was unsure if the sweat on her brow formed due to the spells she wove or the heat of the autumn sun. Either was fine with Chandra. It felt good to stretch her magical muscle and push the world aside for a time.

It was a healthy and thorough distraction. Chandra paid no mind to the cart that slowly wheeled up behind her. The clatter of wheels on the uneven ground penetrated her mind only so far as to force her to one side of the road. She would have kept on with her metallurgic manipulations had the driver not called out to her.

"Well, well, if it isn't my favorite person from the Pattal household. What's got you on the road to Arnstead without a horse on this fine day?"

The spells continued for a moment before the driver used Chandra's given name.

"Hello? Chandra? You all right down there? Has the heat gotten to you?"

At the sound of her name, the spike snapped back into its original form. Chandra turned and walked sideways to allow a better view of the person addressing her. Much to her surprise, she saw that Jacob Hartsfield sat at the head of a cart with reins in hand. He waved to Chandra as she turned.

"Awake at last, I see," the boy said with a smile.

"Sorry." Chandra chuckled. She held the manarail spike up toward Jacob as a form of explanation. The boy cocked his head, which prompted Chandra to continue. "I was practicing my spells. Concentrating on the Flow and whatnot. Didn't even hear you at first."

"I could tell. So, like I said, what's got you on the road to Arnstead without Alabaster? With your whole world draped over your shoulder too."

Chandra felt her thin smile freeze and crack away. The question was expected, but it felt far too close for her liking. She had only just managed to distract herself from thoughts of home. Now they came crashing back to her at the whim of a young man Chandra had half a mind to spurn. She settled for clicking her tongue against her teeth and rolling her eyes.

What to say? There were all sorts of things she *could* say, Chandra knew. Jokes about running away from home. Half-truths about fighting with her father. Anything that would avoid discussing the whole and actual facts of the matter.

"That bad?" Jacob asked in response to the hesitation.

"It's a bit of a story." Chandra rolled her head from side to side a few times. It was a slow, uncertain gesture. More honest than Chandra expected of herself.

"Well… I've got extra space up here, if you're not too proud." Jacob freed a hand from the reins of his black-and-white horse and patted the bench of the cart twice. His gesture was confident. The boy knew what he was asking for and, this time, was not so shy about it. "If you're headed for Arnstead, then we're going the same way. I've got two pigs to deliver to one of the butchers in town. Probably faster than you walking the whole way by yourself."

"Probably," Chandra conceded as she sighed through her nose. Cautious eyes looked from Jacob to the vacant space next to him. A pig squealed as if in response to Jacob's offer, followed by the content snorts of a creature that did not know it traveled to its doom. Chandra noticed the pull of her bindle toward the ground once more. "No funny business, yeah?"

"Wouldn't dream of it," Jacob dismissed. His expectant smile broadened with glee. "Do you need me to stop the cart?"

"Hardly."

The opportunity was too good to pass up. Relenting, Chandra tossed her staff and bindle up to the seat before she clambered up to take the free space. The cart was moving slow enough at the time to have kept pace with Chandra. She was not concerned about making her way up to the promised comfort of still legs and a solid seat. The frame of the cart jostled a bit under her advance. One of the pigs turned its head to view the source of the commotion on the otherwise peaceful day.

It took a moment to get comfortable. There was a coordinated effort behind getting Chandra's things out of the way. The length of the staff made it cumbersome to work around the driver's legs. Chandra had to situate her bundle on the foot rest between her and Jacob, a buffer between her legs and the boy.

Jacob snapped the reins once Chandra was situated. The pair picked up speed and were back on the trail to Arnstead at a more respectable pace.

There was no back to the cart seat. It was just a slab of wood covered with a brown cloth. Nothing special. It did exactly what it needed to do and no more, though the lack of a back did make it difficult to find a comfortable position. Chandra experimented with resting her hands behind her on the cart and leaning back into the breeze, but the position did not last. It placed too much strain on her arms. She eventually settled for resting her elbows on her thighs and leaning forward.

The Hartsfield boy was patient while Chandra made herself comfortable. He did not press her for details. Instead, he kept his eyes on the road ahead, minding the horse as he did so. It was not until well after Chandra became situated that he spoke again with a gentle, probing tone.

"So, I hear you've got a long story for me. When you're ready, of course."

Chandra did not turn her head to Jacob. Her only acknowledgment that the boy spoke was a quick flit of her eyes before staring back out over the road ahead. A deep breath ended with Chandra resting her chin in her hands.

"It's not a secret that our family needs money," Chandra said. Unsure what to say next, she allowed a pause to fill the space between her and Jacob.

"I've heard bits and pieces," the boy offered. "I know you're a novice Shikaree too. Going into town to do some work?"

"Yeah. I think I've found something that can help turn our situation around. Get us out from under the bank's foot, you know?"

"Sounds fine to me so far," Jacob said with a casual shrug. "It's not the first time you've done Shikaree work, right? Why is it so different this time that you havta walk to town instead of ride?"

"Normally it's just the night I'm gone for. My dad doesn't know because I'm always back by morning, so there's never really any time for him to get upset about it. I just go on with the day like nothing had happened. This time, though… this time I'm gonna to be gone for a while. Long enough I needed to let him and the family know I'd be gone. Couldn't think of an excuse to explain why I'd be gone for a week, so I just settled on the truth. My dad went off about Alabaster belonging to the family, not just to me. Told me I couldn't take a horse for so long if it was for Shikaree work. Didn't feel like arguing."

"Nothing to say back?" Jacob asked, surprised. "Doesn't sound like the Chandra I know. You've always got something quick to whip back with."

"Well," Chandra began, giving Jacob the courtesy of a short, poignant glance, "we had it out a little while back. *I* had it out a little while back. Screamed and shouted at him. About the new focus he bought from Westinghouse. About how he doesn't do enough for the family. I really let him have it. Guess I was running on empty from that fit still. Didn't have it in me to fight back today."

There was no immediate response. Chandra stopped to allow for a reply but did not receive one. She let the silence hang while her company digested what had been said. It was only fair to give the boy a moment to think, Chandra felt.

"I guess I understand where your dad's coming from," Jacob said after an uncomfortable minute had passed. "I know I hate the idea of you going down into the World Below all by yourself, day after day, just to scrape together a few pennies here and there. Especially what with having lost someone to Arnstead. Can't imagine he wants to go through that again like he did with your mom."

"I'm not going alone this time. I think that might be part of the reason why he got so mad at me too. Met a Spellseeker that deals with stuff that's been lost. Focuses and what have ya. Said he's willing to help me find what I'm after down in the World Below. Lines up with his interests."

"Working with a Spellseeker, then?" Both of Jacob's eyebrows shot toward the heavens. He leaned forward to try and catch Chandra's gaze. "That probably hit him pretty close to home. Your dad, I mean."

"Probably."

Chandra sank her face into her hands for a moment. She felt an uncomfortable heat rising in her cheeks. This was more than she had intended to say, but it felt good to get her thoughts out of her head and into the open air. She ran her hands through her hair, tucked black strands behind her ears, and flung her gaze to the cloudless blue sky.

"I just want us to be comfortable," Chandra began again through a whisp of a sigh. "Like your family is. Like the Okujayes and the Roebucks. To be able to live off of what we make without cowering in the shadow of the Orlands. Is that so much to ask for?"

"No," Jacob replied without pause. "No, it's not."

Another silence enveloped the cart. This one was not so heavy as the others. A contented silence that did not suffocate Chandra with gnawing expectation. The sort of quiet that she could stew in for a moment without having to worry about what would come next. Chandra closed her eyes for a moment and allowed her face to bask in the warm light of the sun.

Chandra tilted her head to the left and cracked open an eye. Just enough to see Jacob without looking too conspicuous. His focus was on the road.

Bless him, Chandra thought. He had brought courtesy and kindness in full force that day. Nowhere was the prying boy who fought to garner Chandra's attention. This Jacob was attentive and thoughtful. This Jacob was exactly what Chandra needed after her tumultuous morning.

"Thank you, by the way," Chandra said. Her words were just loud enough to climb over the noise of horse and cart. "For listening, I mean. I needed that."

"Happy to help." Jacob smiled while returning the sideways glance. After a moment had passed, he added, "You ever thought of doing something more consistent?"

"What do you mean?"

"Like… you're good with metal, yeah? Ever thought about studying with a blacksmith in town? I'm sure you could find someone that would love to have you around. Who knows? You might even like it."

"Is that so?" Chandra snorted playfully. "What you mean is, I should be doing something safer."

"Not what I said," Jacob said, raising a single finger in protest.

"It's what you meant, though. You're going to give me a toothache if you keep trying to be so sweet, you know?"

Red flooded Jacob's cheeks. Chandra had hit home, and there was nothing that Jacob could do to hide his sentiments. The sincerity gave Chandra an honest chuckle as she turned her head away from the boy and back to the road.

Both Chandra and Jacob waved as they passed a wagon headed west. It was the first sign of life Chandra had spied since hopping onto the cart. A mother katarl held the reins of a roan horse that pulled the covered wagon along at a meandering pace. A father was visible within the wagon cradling a small child in his arms. Two more children poked their heads out over their mother's shoulders to give their hellos.

It was a heartwarming sight. A loving family headed out to face the unknowns of the western frontier together. Were they headed to the Great Expanse to settle away from Arnstead? Maybe out to the Gods' Reach to prospect for precious gems and minerals? There was no way to be sure, and the family had come and gone before Chandra could have asked the question.

The wagon family made Chandra think of home. Not in a way that caused anger to boil. No, Chandra remembered minding the fields with her siblings. Being shooed off to bed by a loving mother and father, then asking for just one last story before the candles were doused. Simple memories that faded almost as soon as they had welled up. A look of longing hung from Chandra's cheeks as she turned to watch the covered wagon disappear over the horizon.

"Can I ask you a favor?" Chandra said.

"What is it?"

"If I don't come back, will you help my family in my place? Help make sure they keep up payments to the bank and keep the farm?"

"Silly question," Jacob replied with an unsure half smile. "You always come back. Nothing to worry about there."

"I'm serious."

There was no humor in Chandra's voice. No room for a joke or space for a question. Reality, bitter and cold, had taken up residence in her tone and froze her words as they left her mouth. She felt the frigid nature of her speech clash with the heat of the overbearing sun. Part of her expected to see ice on her breath.

The same frost coated Chandra's eyes as she turned her head square to Jacob. She took the boy into full view and did not intend to let him go without an answer.

Jacob did not meet Chandra's gaze. His head rolled from side to side as he looked out over the road ahead. A few times he allowed his eyes to wander to the footrest of the cart seat. The boy looked like he was searching for the exact right thing to say, but was struggling to find it. Jacob looked up to Chandra only when he had found that answer.

"Okay."

12

Field Goods

"She did *not*," Jacob said, shaking his head. Incredulous laughter shook the words into a jumbled mess. "She chased you all the way around the house?"

"That's right." Chandra nodded with a guilt-ridden grin. "It was just after Najran had been born. I was maybe five or six, and I had a powerful sweet tooth. Crawled up onto the counter while mother was busy with the baby and fancied I'd dip my fingers into the sugar jar. Well, turns out it was a jar of flour. Found that out when I tipped the thing over and it spilled all over my face. Jar crashed on the ground and flour went *everywhere*."

"Gods above, you were a mad child."

"You have no idea. Anyways, mother hears the crash and comes to see what happened. She finds me covered in flour, just standing on the counter trying to figure out what I had just done. Next thing I know, she's got a wooden spoon in one hand and is chasing me out of the house, but she's still got little Najran under her arm. I'm screaming bloody murder the whole time."

"And did she get you? With the spoon, I mean?" Jacob asked as he wiped a joyous tear away from his cheek.

"Oh, boy, did she," Chandra exulted. "Third lap around the house, she finally gets me by the scruff of my collar. Pinned me to the ground and showed my backside a whole new world of pain. She was fierce, mother was. There was no stopping her once she got an idea into her head. Father used to say there was no better place for her than at the Arcanarium. That it was like she'd been born to be a Spellseeker."

Those last words left Chandra with an unfocused look. She looked through the dozens of people that crowded the streets of Weststead, but none caught her eye. Nor did the many businesses that lined Main Street. She had become entrenched in a long-forgotten past that Jacob had managed to worm out of her. A past Chandra kept locked away to cherish free of insight or judgement.

Chandra dug into her pocket and produced her mother's Spellseeker watch. Dull brass tried to glimmer in the unfettered sunlight. A harsh click cut through the break in conversation. Chandra had no desire to check the time. It was the name inside that she wanted to see. Her mother's name. Trayni Pattal. The only part of the whole watch that still caught the sunlight in a shower of brilliance.

"This is all I have left of her," Chandra mumbled. "Dad didn't keep anything of hers around. No clothes. No rings or tools. Nothing like that. Said it made him too sad. Reminded him that mom would never come back to wear those clothes again. Had to fight him to keep the watch. I still get a dirty look if I pull the thing out at home."

"I wish I had been old enough to know her," Jacob added with tenderness after a moment had passed. "Sounds like she was a fierce and respectable woman. A lot like somebody else I know."

"Oh, stop it, you silver-tongued snake." Chandra chuckled. She pushed an open palm against the boy's broad shoulder. A playful jest sprinkled with the lightest touch of sincerity. "But thank you, anyways. She was quite the woman. I'm sure she would have liked you, given some time."

Jacob did not respond in words. The red that clouded his tanned cheeks spoke enough for the boy to keep silent. He was pleased with himself, and Chandra was not about to take that away.

The moment did not last. Jacob's attention returned from Chandra to the myriad of people that clogged Main Street. He stood on the cart's footrest to tower over the crowd. Broad, sweeping gestures Jacob made with his arms did nothing to persuade the people to part. Harsh whistles lit no fires. Progress had slowed to a crawl for fear of trampling someone under hoof.

After a few minutes of wasted effort, the boy lowered himself back down to the driver seat with a huff. He sniffed and looked about the cart with an ugly expression.

"Hate to say it," Jacob began, "but I think you'll be even more late if you stick with me. You should probably go on foot if you're going to catch your Spellseeker in time."

The frown that blanketed his features made it clear that Jacob was loath to shoo Chandra away, even if done with the best intentions. He turned to Chandra in resignation as shoulders fell beneath imagined weight. Chandra might have thought a family pet had died if she had just found the boy in his current state. Unfortunately, that made the boy no less correct.

"I think you're right," Chandra replied. She pursed her lips as she did so, crinkling her nose at the shame of it. "It's Arnstead. Nothing to be done about it. Thanks for getting me this far, Jacob. I really appreciate it."

"Chandra!" Jacob said, catching Chandra's hand as she stood. "You make sure you come back in one piece, all right? I expect to hear everything about this mad adventure of yours. Full details."

Chandra gave the boy a sweet smile and a gentle squeeze. His words brought an odd sort of comfort. A manner of reassurance that made her conscious of the beat of her heart.

"Don't worry. It'll take more than a few varmints to knock me down for good. Come calling in a week and I'll have a story for you. Promise."

With that, Chandra hopped down from the cart. She grabbed her staff and bindle just as she hit the ground and slung them over her shoulder. The act almost clubbed more than a few passersby in the head. Chandra was still riding high from the exchange and did not notice the dirty looks thrown her way.

After a final wave and a few more pleasantries, Chandra turned and shoved her way into the dense crowd of Main Street. There was no more time to waste if she wanted to meet her new partner and body-guard. Chandra did not know the time until she heard the bell of the House pierce the din of the populace. A single note to tell her that she was already late. The sound forced out a careless pace as Chandra wove and pushed her way through the sea of unfamiliar faces. A shout or swear here or there was a small price to pay for speedy passage across town.

Chandra moved with admirable speed at first. Openings in the crowds were spied with ease, and she dipped through families and small groups without thinking much of it. It was around the time she reached the Bridge on Main that she felt a little off. Something different in the air. Tension that Chandra had never associated with Arnstead before. The gaps in the crowd became smaller and less clear. She grew hesitant to weave through groups of strangers.

There was nothing about the town of Arnstead itself that had changed. Instead, now alone and without the distraction of conver-sation, it felt like the mass of people was crowding in on her. They pressed against her and made it difficult to breathe. Chandra stopped for a moment in the middle of the hustle and bustle and allowed the flow of bodies to move around her. Her free hand clutched and pulled at her shirt. The light garment suddenly felt as if it would suffocate her just by resting on her shoulders.

An arm caught Chandra in the chest, knocking her from her unsure feet to the ground. Her staff clattered on the stone bridge while her bindle exploded. Clothes and tools scattered themselves without care. She was slow to gather her things in response. Hesitant hands dodged plodding, uncaring feet that threatened to grind Chandra's digits into the stone bridge. Nobody stopped to apologize. Help was not on offer. It was just Chandra, alone amidst the crowd, picking up her scant belongings before they were lost to the rush.

Why? Chandra asked herself. *Why is this happening?*

She knew the answer. It was not difficult to arrive on. No matter how many people surrounded her, no matter how familiar she had grown with the streets and places of Arnstead, nothing could ever change the fact that the town had almost swallowed her alive. Mugged. Left in the gutter. It had happened once. There was no way to know if it would happen again. Maybe that day, or the following day, or the day after that. The faces of strangers that towered above her no longer bore looks of indifference. Whether real or imagined, Chandra saw a measure of malice everywhere she looked.

Then Chandra began to breathe again. Slow, beleaguered breaths. Each new inhale smoothed her nerves until Chandra found a comfortable pace. A calm reclamation of agency despite the hectic environment. There was work to be done. People needed to be met and tasks lay unaccomplished. If progress was to be made, Chandra knew she had to pick herself up and go about her business.

A hand, wrenched from her bindle, wiped thick beads of sweat from Chandra's brow. She could feel her heart resume its regular cadence. No longer did she feel as if she were running in place. The moment had passed.

Chandra grabbed her staff with her free hand and used it to force herself up. She continued to use the staff as a walking stick rather than toss the bindle over her shoulder. Somehow it felt more comfortable to keep her belongings close to her chest and in plain view. The absolute last thing she needed in her life was to be robbed by some random passerby with light fingers. Her pace was slow, but the clack of her staff against the stone bridge kept Chandra grounded. A stalwart cadence by which to march. By the time the House bell tolled two in the afternoon, she had found her strength again and was approaching Robin's Field Goods.

Two cursory glances around the front of the shop revealed details both good and bad. Part of Chandra was worried that she might run into people from the Baylocke Battalion again. It would not have been the first time she encountered them at Robin's place, and there was no way to know if they still held some sort of grudge. She held vague rec-ollections that they blamed her for the death of a compatriot. The odds of her explaining that away in a rational conversation, she guessed, were slim to none.

The absence of the Baylocke Battalion served as the good news. As for the bad, she did not see anyone in Spellseeker blues standing out-side. No Spellseeker leaning against the support columns of the awning or loitering around in the neighboring alleyways. She double-checked to be sure that Owen was not standing around in plain clothes. Squint-ing against the afternoon sun revealed no further trace.

"Gods dammit," Chandra muttered to herself.

In truth, Chandra was not surprised by the Spellseeker's absence. Deep down the expectation had always been there. The back of her mind whispered the probable absence to her all the night before. A little nag that she had refused to acknowledge fully until now. Chandra did her best to stifle her disappointment and made her way toward Robin's store. There was no harm in poking around to see if the Spellseeker was waiting for her inside.

Dusty winds whipped through the streets. It caused the crowd to raise their arms in collective protection and forced Chandra quickly up the steps to Robin's porch. Weather-beaten floorboards creaked under the duress of her approach. Chandra tucked herself through the open doorway and into the relative safety of the shop.

No sooner had Chandra set foot into the store than did she hear her name, whispered as if carried on the wind outside.

"Chandra!"

Chandra turned her head to the source of the noise. What she saw was an agitated Robin standing behind the shop counter. Both of the harn's hands were planted on the counter as she leaned her whole body forward. Nostrils flared below wild eyes. Robin kept one of her hands rooted in place and summoned Chandra with a violent gesture.

"Get over here," she spat. "Now!"

Robin hopped down from her place behind the counter and bounded to the far side. She lifted the wooden divider that kept the space closed off to customers. Peeking her head around the counter, she made another swift set of beckoning motions.

Confused did not begin to describe how Chandra felt at that moment. She had expected to walk into Robin's Field Goods to find an empty counter, the eponymous Robin off somewhere in the store helping a customer. That seemed to be the default mode for the harn. Hopping and bounding all over the store to ensure that nobody left the place emptyhanded. Maybe, just maybe, Robin might have been leisurely kicking her feet in the air as she sat atop the counter. This ferocious intensity, however, was beyond unexpected.

Rather than try to parse the matter out in the doorway, Chandra followed Robin's request and walked over to the opening in the counter. Hesitant footsteps carried Chandra on a cautious path. She had her head on a swivel. Perhaps members of the Baylocke Battalion were somewhere in the store again and Robin was offering a haven?

There was no pause on the harn's behalf when Chandra reached the opening in the counter. Robin leaped into the air and grabbed Chandra by her collar. The harn, weighing more than Chandra guessed by sight alone, brought Chandra down into a crouch. Robin grunted as she hauled Chandra around and behind the counter. It was a graceless affair that ended with Chandra plummeting to her hands and knees. Staff and bindle crashed to the floor as Chandra caught herself with her hands. Another couple of tugs at Chandra's collar ensured that she pulled her feet out from the view of the shop floor.

Chandra was face to face with Robin. The width of a thumb separated their noses. Chandra could see each twitch of Robin's nose, and every subtle adjustment of her rigidly upright ears.

"What, Hyperios help me, have you done *this time?*" Robin whispered. "You didn't kill somebody *else*, did you?"

"Excuse me?" Chandra replied, matching Robin's whisper. She cocked her head to the side and furrowed her brow. "First of all, I've never killed *anybody.* Second, what are you going on about?"

"There's—"

Robin stopped midsentence and snapped her ears to the left. Both furry towers quivered in anticipation, then folded down slowly behind Robin's head. She raised herself until she was at eye level with the counter. It was like watching a prairie dog that had just spotted a hawk outlined by the sun. Robin did not wait for long, either. A few moments saw her lowered back into a crouch and glaring at Chandra. Robin squinted as she looked Chandra over from head to toe and back again.

"There's a *Spellseeker* here. Says he's looking for you. When I told him I haven't seen you in a while, he just shrugged and started wandering around the shop. He's been out there for *two hours*, Chandra. What did you do?"

"What? Is that it?"

Chandra fell from the precipice of worry and confusion to land in the boughs of sweet relief. Every muscle in her body went slack as Chandra let a sigh pass through lax lips. She leaned her head against the back of the counter with a gentle thunk.

The laughter was quiet at first. A slight rocking of Chandra's shoulders, and a change of breath that could have been mistaken for another sigh. It grew in volume with each breath until Chandra was cackling. She doubled over and clutched at her sides to quell the involuntary display.

Robin looked at Chandra with an expression of abject horror.

"What is so gods damn funny?" Robin asked. She dropped her whisper to climb over Chandra's raucous laughter. Robin prodded the shaking mass that was Chandra to garner attention. "Knock it off. If he hears you laughing like a madwoman, he might come over here. The last place I need him is close to the back room. Do you have any idea how busted I would be if—"

"I thought I recognized that voice. Glad you're finally here, Chandra," Owen said in a casual tone as he leaned over the countertop.

Robin, surprised by the appearance of the Spellseeker, jumped so high that her ears touched the low ceiling over the counter.

"Hello there, Mr. Seeker," Chandra struggled to say through her dying laughter.

"Just Owen is fine," Owen said with a polite smile. He returned his gaze from the explosive surprise of the harn back to Chandra. "Seems like you're having quite the party down there. What'd I miss?"

"Nothing!" Robin shouted. She had not yet regained what little composure she had shown that day. One of her feet tapped incessantly on the wooden floor. A rhythmic thump, thump, thump.

"Robin's just trying to look out for me, is all," Chandra said. She expelled the last of her laughter and stood to fully face Owen. "Last time someone came looking for me in her store, it was the Baylocke folks. You know how well that turned out for me."

"I have to admit, I was worried when you didn't show, at first. Especially with what you had told me about the mugging."

"The mugging?" Robin intruded. She flipped her gaze from Owen to Chandra. "What's this all about?"

"I guess I haven't seen you lately, have I?" Chandra asked with a deflated tone. She rustled around in her pants pockets until she found a small slip of folded paper. Unfurling the little square, she handed it to Owen over the counter. "I have some catching up to do with Robin, but this is a list of what we're going to need. Could you start getting everything together? I'll come find you once we're done."

Owen's smile thinned. A show of understanding, it seemed, as he took the note from Chandra and began to look it over. He spoke quietly to himself as he analyzed each line.

Chandra placed a hand on Robin's shoulder. The rhythmic tapping slowed, and then stopped altogether.

"Sure," Owen said after a moment of examination. "I can get started on this. I'll see you shortly, then."

The Spellseeker, dressed in the heavy-looking blue coat of his station, turned and wandered off. Iron-heeled boots projected each step he took as Owen disappeared behind a set of shelves to begin his newly appointed task.

Once Owen was gone, Chandra looked down at Robin and gave her a wink. The harn snorted at the gesture. Robin hopped up to the countertop to stand at a more conversational height. With immediate danger out of the way, there was no reason not to be civil.

"This is about that map business, isn't it?" Robin asked, speaking once again in a hushed tone. "What the Battalion was after you for the first time?"

"That's right," Chandra affirmed with a nod. "I took it to Olufemi like you suggested. Sure enough, he managed to get the thing translated. Turns out the map is to a cache of stolen focuses and relics that varmints have piled up down below."

"That sounds big."

"Real big."

"So, this mugging business," Robin said, pausing to look out at her shelves. She continued after confirming the Spellseeker was still nowhere to be seen. "Baylocke and her people got to you?"

"After I picked the map back up from Olufemi, yeah. Imagine they didn't want to let a big find like that go to some small fry. Lucky guess that I had the thing. Found me in Eaststead on a quiet road and boom, I was tied up and robbed faster than you can close a sale."

"Bad business." Robin frowned. She reached out and gave Chandra a tender touch on the arm. "I'll gouge the bastards every time they come to buy something. We'll get them back. Don't you worry."

"Well, it's not all lost," Chandra replied with a confident tone. She raised a finger to ask for a moment before diving into her bindle. After rooting around, Chandra came back with the translation notes provided by Olufemi. "They got the map, but I'm willing to bet they don't know what it says. Bet they had no idea what I was up to at Frontier Finds."

"That's my girl. What's the plan, then? Going to beat them to the punch?"

"Hopefully," Chandra said with no small amount of apprehension. "The notes are way better than the map, but I'd rather I had both, you know?"

"Ya work with what you have," Robin replied with a casual shrug. She hoisted a thumb over her shoulder and pointed toward the shop floor. "So, where does the blue boy come in?"

"Owen? He's my muscle. Pulled him out of the World Below when he got lost, so he owes me a favor. Turns out he was down there looking for the cache without knowing it. Says his people have been getting a bunch of reports of varmints making off with people's focuses. He keeps me safe, I serve as a guide, we split the pie. He takes the focuses for processing and I get the relics to sell as I please."

"And those relics… they're coming straight here, right?"

"Of course," Chandra conceded with a knowing smile.

"That's my girl," Robin replied with an avaricious smile of her own. She took Chandra by the shoulders and pressed their foreheads together. "You beat those Baylocke bastards before they even know they've been swindled, you got that?"

"That's the plan," Chandra whispered as her smile devolved into an impish grin. "I'll be back in a minute, okay? I need to make sure that Spellseeker doesn't get lost again."

With that, Chandra stepped away from the encouraging embrace of Robin, grabbed her staff and bindle, and sidled away from the counter to hunt for Owen. It was not a difficult venture. The telltale sound of iron heels clapping on the hardwood floor was a dead giveaway. Chandra pinpointed the Spellseeker's location without ever laying eyes on him.

Owen was looking quizzically at a shelf around eye level when Chandra found him. His attention was split between the shelf and the scrap of paper he had been provided. On his left arm were slung two leather backpacks, one for him and a new one for Chandra. Already burdened with part of the list, they hung tight on his arm. Fresh leather straps creaked under the strain. His right hand hovered with marked hesitation over something on the shelf. Twice he made as if to grab what was in front of him. Twice he squinted and withdrew his hand.

"How's the hunt?" Chandra asked, leaning around the corner of the shelf in question. "Find everything okay?"

"Ah." Owen shook away his concentrated glower and looked over to Chandra, donning a bemused smile in the process. It was an entertaining shift to watch. Chandra felt it a shame that Owen managed to compose himself as quickly as he did. "Well, I'm about halfway through your list here, but I have to ask"—he pointed to the shelf—"what in the world is… *pemmican?* And why do we need it?"

"Never had the pleasure? It's a mix of dried meat, berries, and some other goodies. Old Fieldkin recipe that never seems to go bad, least not for a long while. Perfect to bring along when you don't know how long you'll be gone for."

"Oh, is that so?"

Owen picked up one of the red-brown hunks of foodstuff and turned it over in his hand. His nose crinkled in an obvious sign of skepticism. He looked over to Chandra and raised the lump slightly as if seeking reassurance.

"Yep. We're going to need plenty, so no skimping on the portions."

As she spoke, Chandra grabbed a cloth from a nearby shelf and walked over to where Owen stood. She placed the cloth over her hand and presented it to Owen, who pursed his lips and placed the pemmican into Chandra's covered hand. A small smile of approval was followed by a nod as Chandra took the cloth and held it by two ends. The pemmican rested in the middle like a lonely red brick. Chandra raised the cloth in tacit encouragement. More was needed, and there was no time to spare.

"What does it taste like?" Owen asked as he shoveled more hunks of pemmican onto the cloth.

"Not important," Chandra replied with a curt nod. "It's got everything a growing Spellseeker needs to stay tough and strong. Couldn't ask for anything better."

"I'm not so sure." Owen chuckled, giving one of the hunks a whiff before placing it on the cloth. "Quite fond of bacon and toast, myself. Bit of strawberry jam. But that's just me, I suppose."

"Isn't much in the way of firewood down below. So, unless you're good with channeling the Flow for fire, we're just going to have to work with what we've got."

Chandra tied the cloth off and set it down in one of the packs with care. She then grabbed another cloth and presented it to Owen as she had done before, a sarcastic smile hanging from her ears. Owen rolled his eyes at the sight. Apprehension aside, the Spellseeker acquiesced to his guide's instructions and heaped another collection of pemmican onto the new cloth.

The Spellseeker had done quite well in regards to the list before he had stopped at the pemmican. Once they finished with the foodstuffs, Owen walked through what had already been collected and deposited into the backpacks. He displayed a thorough knowledge of the climbing equipment. All of the harnesses, ropes, and bits of gear had been squared away before anything else. First-aid supplies had been gathered, as well. All that remained after the pemmican was to grab pliable water skins, two for each of them, and the shopping would be done.

With all her list gathered and stowed into the backpacks, Chandra had one remaining question for Owen. She grabbed one of the Spellseeker's sleeves between her thumb and forefinger and clicked her tongue against her teeth. A gentle kick to one of Owen's boots followed before Chandra said what was on her mind.

"Some awful heavy clothes you got there, partner," Chandra murmured. She could not help but scan the entirety of the bulky blue coat. It looked comfortable, but there was just too much of it. All Chandra could imagine was the coat tangling between harness and rope. Though she was not afraid to try, it would be the first time Chandra had freed someone from their rigging while the person was still suspended in the air. "Those boots are pretty... sturdy too. You know I could hear you walking clear across the store?"

"Standard Spellseeker uniform," Owen said with a shrug. "It's what I wore to the Arcanarium today, same as always."

"You have anything else you could change into? We're probably going to end up in some tight places, and the quieter we move the better. I don't wanna fight anything if we don't have to, you know? All sorts of nasty stuff crawling around down there."

"Fair points," Owen said. He rocked back on his heels while taking a glance at his footwear. The iron heels made an awful grating sound as he swiveled in place. "Well, I'm just across the street. I live in the space above Kamotho Bakery."

"Really?" Chandra inquired as she beckoned Owen to follow her to the counter up front. "My family does business with Kamotho. Surprised I've never seen you around before now."

"Only been there a little less than a year, truth be told. I'm still fresh to Arnstead, *and* I'm an early riser. You'd have to get to the bakery pretty quick to catch me in the morning."

"Hmm." Chandra bent her lips into a sort of thoughtful frown. There was no displeasure at Owen's words, just a sense of surprise at having missed the path of such a standout figure over the last year. Not that she and her siblings ever arrived at the market near dawn. Chandra allowed the thought to pass and moved on. "Kamotho really is a sweet man. Does he treat you well?"

"Oh yes," Owen said with emphatic fervor. "Absolute gentleman. Always has my order ready for me before I've come down the stairs to leave. What sort of business does your family do with him?"

"I live on a farm, mostly apples and pears and the like. A bit of wheat for ourselves to make bread. Kamotho is one of our regulars. Buys fruit from us for his pies and pastries. A couple crates every time we visit."

"Fantastic! I might have indulged in some of your harvests myself."

"You just might have." Chandra chuckled.

A short pause preluded Owen's next question, which arrived just as the pair reached the front counter. They placed the stuffed packs onto the worn wooden surface for Robin to inspect.

"So, a farmer *and* a Shikaree? That sounds like an awful lot for one plate. How'd that combination come about?"

Robin froze in her inspection. A quick halt accompanied by a glance at Chandra before resuming the act of generating a total cost for the goods.

Questions about the job ahead were fine. If Owen had wanted to know about the Shikaree business, that would have been something else entirely. As to why Chandra was a Shikaree? That thought gave her pause. She had not anticipated the Spellseeker to be so inquisitive. Chandra expected that they would talk about the job, when necessary, but otherwise leave each other in respectful silence.

Chandra opened her mouth a few times to answer. Each time her jaw closed without a single utterance. The thoughts were there. She could talk about how money became tight after her mother passed, though it would not make for polite conversation with a practical stranger. The same could be said of the family debt to the Orlands, or her father's continual insistence that more technology would somehow make their problems vanish in a puff of smoke.

Indecision formed a tightness in Chandra's chest. The silence had dragged on too long for comfort, so long that it made her skin itch. She drummed her fingers on the counter a few times while she settled on some vague nothing to skirt around the unpleasant subject.

"Well," Chandra started, unsure where to go as she traveled. "That's the funny thing about money, isn't it? Just when you feel like you've got enough dollars in the bank, something else happens and you've got to start all over. Heard there was easy money in Shikaree work and didn't think twice."

"Fair enough," Owen replied after letting the answer simmer.

Chandra knew the man must have felt her discomfort. He *must* have. After giving her a light nod, he turned his attention to Robin and watched the woman go about her business. The process was carried out in awkward silence broken only by the coming of a new group of customers. Chandra feared that she had struck a sour chord that would infect all further interactions with Owen. A prospect that cast a grim shadow over the week or so to come.

Turning away from Robin and Owen, Chandra looked out over the store. The rows of shelves formed a simple yet effective labyrinth. Heads bobbed up and down as people searched for goods to match their needs. Some were bare, while others were wrapped in colorful scarves.

Others wore wide hats to fight the sunny day. Chandra wondered to herself what each person was looking for. What they planned on doing afterward. Maybe go home to their families? Back to whatever place of profession or business they had come from? Maybe some would leave Arnstead altogether, newly equipped with the finest goods that Robin had to offer. So many questions that Chandra had no way to discern answers for. The perfect distraction.

Tall ears shot up to the roof once Robin had completed her calculations. She wrapped her knuckles on the table to garner Chandra's attention and only spoke when Chandra had turned fully to face her.

"Fifteen dollars."

Chandra thought her jaw might strike the countertop. She felt as if she had just been run through at the hands of a friend. It was with eyes pried wide by disbelief that Chandra looked at Robin. The harn did not so much as twitch.

"Fifteen dollars for the whole lot?" Chandra asked.

"Fifteen each," came the harn's cold reply.

A low whistle escaped Owen. He reached into his pocket and produced a small leather purse. It looked to Chandra like a well-worn accessory. Stretch marks littered the plain brown surface like wrinkles on a bulldog's face. The Spellseeker wasted no time in digging around through the bag until he produced fifteen silver dollars and deposited them on the table. He did it like it was nothing. No complaint about the price. Not a single attempt to haggle Robin down to something more reasonable. Owen just slapped the money down like he was handing Robin a plate of toast.

Disgust and jealousy mixed into an ugly sneer that Chandra could not fight. Never before had she seen someone throw money around like that. Not so freely, at least. Chandra was lucky to see half as much money from her best, most profitable forays into the World Below. The family sold full crates of fruit for just a silver dollar each. Chandra had to turn her head before the rage in her cheeks manifested into regrettable words.

Chandra closed her eyes. Deep, calming breaths came up through her nose and filled her lungs. She allowed the unfair feelings to dissipate before she turned her attention, now cooled, back to Robin.

"Come on, Robin," Chandra said with as much dignity as she could find. "You know we don't have that kind of money just lying around. That *I* don't."

Robin's lips slid up and to one side as if contemplating what to say. The anticipation curled Chandra's hands into fists on the counter. Fingernails bit into her palms like rabid wolves tearing at a fresh kill. Chandra braced herself for whatever might come next.

"You know I love you, sweetheart," Robin said through ripe hesitation. "But that's a lot of goods you've got on the table, and this is still a business. I'm already rounding down for you."

"What about credit, then?" Chandra asked, biting her lip in frustration. "You know what we're after down there. I'll have plenty of money to sort all this out when I get back. Just this once?"

Robin looked over Chandra's shoulder. Chandra followed the woman's gaze to find that their discussion had garnered the attention of a few other curious customers. None made direct eye contact, but the occasional sidelong glance made it clear that people were listening to what transpired at the counter. Chandra clamped her eyes shut as she turned back to Robin. She wished she could unsee the onlookers. Wished that she was not some circus spectacle on display for the amusement of strangers.

"I can't set a precedent like that, honey," Robin said. There was a twinge of regret in her tone, but not enough to override a firm sense of business. "Especially not with other folks walking around the store. If word gets around that I'm taking credit, I'll have to fight for every sale."

The thump of Chandra's head on the hard countertop sounded her ultimate defeat. What else could she say? Robin was right and Chandra knew it full well. It was a stupid request from a desperate girl and nothing more. Another thump sounded on the counter, followed by a third. Another desperate attempt. This one to see if bouncing her head on the table could make the shame she felt come tumbling out and onto the floor. There was no such luck.

"I know," Chandra whispered. "Sorry I asked."

Another thump sounded on the counter. This one was metallic and fleshy at the same time. More importantly, Chandra thought, she was not the one to have made the sound. She turned her head toward the sound to find there were now thirty silver dollars on the table where once there had been fifteen. Chandra looked over just in time to watch Owen withdraw his hand from the counter.

"That should cover it," Owen said to Robin with a polite smile. He turned in complete innocence to a flabbergasted Chandra. "Sounds like you've got a healthy payday coming. You can just pay me back once we're done and you've got your relics sold."

Disgust. Relief. Rage. Thankfulness. A storm brewed within Chandra that she did not know how to process. The gross display of wealth was at odds with the kindness in the Spellseeker's words. Chandra found herself looking back and forth between Owen and the pile of coins that Robin was busy collecting. It was not until the payment had been squared away that Chandra realized her mouth was hanging open like a slack-jawed buffoon.

What do I say? Chandra asked herself. *What do I do?*

So accustomed she was to economic cruelty, Chandra was at a complete loss for how to respond. Her experience had always been to give. Whatever she received was immediately taken away by the Orlands and their bank. It didn't matter how little food was in the house or who was sick or what holiday it happened to be. The bootheel of the bank was always on her throat, an unrelenting force in a world where she had to fight tooth and nail for every penny.

Never before had Chandra experienced such generosity. There had never been enough to go around. That was just the world that Chandra knew, that she had struggled in since the passing of her mother. She barely even knew the man who just tossed her a small fortune like it was pocket change.

Chandra wanted to scream. She wanted to pound her fist on the counter, to cry in combined thankfulness and spite. So fierce was the inner conflict that it rendered Chandra numb. Words failed her.

Rather than speak, Chandra offered Owen a pitiful nod and began to put her newly acquired goods back into a smooth, unmarred backpack. She undid her bindle and stuffed its contents into the pack, as well. All without looking up to see that Owen was busy doing the same.

"Thank you for your patronage," Robin said to Owen with a shy expression. The woman seemed almost as stunned by the display as Chandra.

"Of course," Owen replied. "All right, Chandra, I'm going to hop across the street for a quick change, maybe grab some extra clothes while I'm at it. I'll meet you outside the bakery?"

"Yeah," Chandra nodded, still stuck in a daze.

Owen said a few more pleasantries to Robin before shouldering his pack and strolling out the front doors, down into Main Street. The telltale sound of his iron-heeled boots died when they met the packed dirt of the road. Just like that he was gone, leaving the two bewildered women standing stone still in his wake.

It was Robin who broke the silence. First with a tap of her knuckles on the counter, then with a proper question aimed at Chandra.

"Seems like you've made yourself quite the friend there, haven't you?"

"Yeah," Chandra mumbled. She looked out through the door at the dense traffic to try and spy the blue Spellseeker coat. "Yeah, I guess so."

13

Descent

"I still don't understand why we're going to the *House* of all places. I thought Shikaree entered the World Below through the memory-glass quarry outside of town, same as I did. Are we getting a blessing before we go or something like that?"

It was not the first time Owen had asked the question. Each time was a different permutation of the thought, but the brunt of it remained the same. He thought going to the House was a waste of time. Time being a factor in their race against the Baylocke Battalion, the notion of taking a detour seemed to irk the official. His right hand rubbed the pommel of his arming sword in agitation. Given a rag and some polish, the tick might have left a brilliant sheen on the scratched metal.

"I told you," Chandra replied with a wink, "it's a trade secret. You'll see when we get there."

"You keep saying that, but it doesn't really put me at ease."

"Well, if you stopped asking, you'd stop getting the same response over and over. Just trust me on this one. We're not that far now."

Uncomfortable resignation played across Owen's face. A smug smile dawned over Chandra's. Celebration of victory over the barrage of useless questions.

There was no malice in Chandra's avoidance. She spoke the truth when she mentioned protection of a trade secret. As far as Chandra was aware, she was the only person who knew of the entrance to the World Below through the catacombs of the House. At least she was the only Shikaree. That was how she hoped to keep the matter. There was no way for her to know who was listening on the crowded Dawn Road. Answers would be plain to see once the pair arrived at their destination.

Silence allowed Chandra to enjoy the walk. She was still hesitant to venture into the back alleys of Eaststead, but Owen's company put her at ease on the Dawn Road. The man carried a militant air even without his telltale blue coat. In addition to his sword, he carried a caster pistol on his left hip and a small dagger on his lower back. Iron-heeled boots were swapped with tall riding boots. A red linen shirt, sleeves rolled up above his elbows, replaced the iconic Spellseeker coat.

No longer wrapped up in pointless inquiry, Owen kept his head on a swivel. It made Chandra feel like she was walking in the company of a loyal mastiff. Someone observant and dependable that could be trusted to spot peril before it arrived. It did not keep Chandra from eyeing people who came a little too close for her liking, but there was only so much to be done about that on the second busiest street in Eaststead.

Each observation helped Chandra feel more at ease. She saw farmers riding in from the east on their carts. Acolytes of the House going from door to door to offer the services of their establishment. The occasional merchant behind a stand selling fruit or belts or whatever else. Regular people doing regular things. Life going about its business in the organized chaos of Arnstead.

There's nothing to fear here, Chandra told herself. Multiple times. In quick succession. *I am strong, and I walk with good company. There's nothing to fear here.*

Buildings shrank as the pair continued. Shops and hovels showed various states of disrepair. Broken and boarded windows became more common than whole ones with glass or shutters. All signs that Chandra and Owen approached the Dawn Bridge and the cancerous dilapidation of Oldstead. The gentle murmur of the River Ro grew into a roar that muffled the commotion of the crowd.

Lines of carts and coaches waiting to access the Dawn Bridge obfuscated the river from view. Soldiers of the 4th Federation Army stood at the mouth of the bridge to collect tolls from the drivers. Their long spears jostled as foot traffic flowed freely around them like water under the stone bridge. Chandra was just another drop in the deluge as she passed.

This was an area unfamiliar to Chandra. Her normal path took her from Weststead across the Dusk Bridge over the River Ra. Looking to her left as she crossed, Chandra could see the massive sandbar that split the River Ro in half just before it joined with the River Ra to form Sisir's Run. Ramshackle huts dotted the malleable surface of the island. The brave fisherman that called the island their home toiled away with rods and nets. Licks of white foam sprayed over rocks that broke up the river's flow.

No such sights marred the clear and calm path of the River Ra. The western river had always reminded Chandra of a sheet of brown-green glass. Uneven and ever shifting, but covered with a brilliant sheen that reflected the rays of the sun. A calmer river for a calmer part of town. The River Ro suited the bustle and clamor of Eaststead well.

Another pair of soldiers stood watch over the western mouth of the bridge, collecting tolls from those passing from Oldstead to Eaststead. The amount of vehicle traffic headed East was smaller but existed all the same. Money was money, Chandra knew. Every little bit helped to keep the bridges safe and secure. They had lasted for nearly a hundred years now. There was no sense in allowing them to erode like the surrounding homes. Chandra relished the stability that caressed each step, as well as the fact that she did not have to pay a ferryman for every trip across.

Despite the throng of people, the Dawn Bridge did not take long to cross. Chandra and Owen were across and into Oldstead with little fanfare. The belltower of the House loomed larger and larger overhead as they walked. The centerpiece of Oldstead could be seen from almost anywhere in Arnstead. A sparkling white beacon of hope to guide the faithful to their spiritual home.

For those who had abandoned prayer, it still served as a handy landmark while moving around the town.

Chandra had grown so accustomed to approaching the House after sunset that the belltower was quite the spectacle. Its white stone glistened in the afternoon sun of the cloudless day. She wondered at that moment if the tower served as a lightning rod to the silent gods, guiding their attention to the hub of prayers.

I should say a prayer or two next time I'm here, Chandra thought. *Maybe Lucina might hear me better if my prayers rose from the tower. Bless us with a harvest so plentiful that we might make a dent in our loans.*

Wishful thinking, Chandra knew, but what harm could come of such a minor indulgence?

The steps of the House were littered with the comings and goings of people from all walks. Soldiers in uniform strode side by side with those garbed in the colorful robes of affluence. Common humans, katarl, and harn all came and went in droves. Some sought the attention of the gods, while others came to pay respects to their dearly departed. Others may have arrived to expunge their sins in a divulgence booth. There was no way to know who came for what purpose at a glance, but these were the main reasons Chandra imagined people would visit the House outside of Sunday mass.

Acolytes and priests welcomed those who ascended and wished well to those departing. The acolytes, adorned in the plain white robes of their station, stood attentively by their masters' sides. Each of the three priests on the outside steps bore the iconography of a different god on the breast of their white robes, with extra trim in black to signify their station. One represented Manus, the judge of life and death, with the depictions of a set of scales. The priest of Lucina, the goddess Chandra knew and respected best, bore the silhouette of a hammer and chisel. An industrious symbol that spoke to all who worked with their hands for a living. Sisir, the navigator, was the last of the gods to be represented. An ornate compass rose adorned the chest of her priest.

At the base of the steps, out of the way of traffic but near enough to catch the eye, sat beggars. Some merely held their hands out in plight to those who passed nearby. Others tried to push small trinkets of dubious worth on anyone polite enough to stop and listen. They did no harm, and so were tolerated by the clergy who kept a close watch on all the proceedings before them.

Chandra knew better than to waste her time caught up by the stories of those who vied for her attention. She ascended the steps of the House determined not to look any beggar in the eye. It was too painful, for in them Chandra saw her own family should her expedition fail. Owen made a polite gesture of refusal to a frail Nirdac katarl who bore beaded cords in either hand, keeping as close to Chandra's heels as he could without tripping on her boots.

The clatter of coins dropped into collection basins poked out over the murmur from within the House as Chandra and Owen cut a path through the entry hallway. Dazzling light bathed in glorious color shone through the stained-glass windows in the western wall, projecting the stories of the gods and their champions onto the congregation below. Another sight that Chandra was unused to due to her nocturnal visits. She absorbed the majestic depictions in awed silence as she wove around passersby. Lucious red carpet led down the main walkway to the transept and muffled the sounds of feet on marble floors.

"So, we're here," Owen said. It was clear by his tone that he was still confused as to the nature of their visit to the House. He made a full turn to take in the entire building and its people. "What, exactly, is our plan now?"

"We're almost there," Chandra replied. "Just a little further and you'll see."

Chandra tugged at Owen's sleeve before resuming her march to the back of the House, cutting as straight a line as she could to the spiral staircase that led down into the catacombs. There were more people than she would have liked on a similar path. Chandra had hoped that the catacombs might be sparsely populated in the afternoon, her expectation that people would still be busy toiling away at their work for the day. The shuffle of footsteps on the metal stairway told Chandra otherwise.

A stray glance might catch her prying the ash basin away from her secret passage, but it could not be helped. This was the fastest way she knew to reach the World Below. Enough time had been wasted by her father's belligerence. If it saved her a few precious hours, raising a few eyebrows near her treasured secret was a trade that Chandra would begrudgingly accept.

The procession that led down the spiral steps was slow. All moved with care to avoid slipping on the well-worn metal steps. Chandra knew the risks of descending the staircase with reckless abandon, but the pace made her think of mud frozen over in the dead of winter. She grumbled to herself with each step. Nothing specific. Abstract interpretations of frustration rather than actual words. Chandra warded away inquisitive looks with the quick flash of a flawless smile before returning to her base state of dissatisfaction.

Light from above faded to be replaced by the torches of the catacombs. Chandra refrained from casting a light spell to supplement to flickering flames, despite her wish to see with unmarred clarity. She had garnered enough curious looks with her outward displays of impatience. Casting a spell on holy ground would only draw the ire of any of the clergy. Another obstacle that Chandra preferred to avoid.

Upon reaching the lower landing of the staircase, Chandra shot Owen a quick look before jerking her head toward the inner catacombs. She cut her way through the surprising number of people that lined the eternal resting place. It made for a tricky course. More than once did Chandra hear a yelp in response to a misstep.

The goal was within sight before long. Chandra could see the rope that blocked her destination off from those who might wander in.

Finally, Chandra thought to herself.

The real journey was about to begin. All her preparation and hardship had led to this moment. Chandra felt light as she approached the sagging rope barrier. Gone was the weight of her body and the pack on her back. Adrenaline surged through her excited frame as Chandra lifted the rope and began to duck under.

A gentle hand on Chandra's shoulder stopped her in her tracks. She turned expecting to see Owen with a dozen questions ready to fire. What greeted Chandra's attention was an acolyte hunched overhead. The Bangeli katarl had a perplexed look on his face.

"Excuse me," the acolyte said. His face was distorted with mild discomfort, as if the mere thought of confrontation put him ill at ease. "This space is off-limits to the public. It's still under construction. Wouldn't want you to get hurt."

The boy forced himself to chuckle as he stood back up to his full height. He knit his fingers together with his palms facing the ceiling, the traditional sign of prayer. Two steps back allowed room enough for Chandra to drop the rope and vacate the space. That seemed to be what the acolyte hoped for, at any rate. Chandra merely turned her head, slouched as she was, to look at the boy with a mixture of embarrassment and confusion.

It was another side effect of coming to the House during the day. Chandra was accustomed to entering the catacombs when most of the clergy was asleep and the general populace had gone home for the day. The only person she ever encountered was Ryleah making her rounds, who never so much as suggested that the area was off-limits.

"Oh," Chandra said vacantly. She was at a loss for how to recover from the situation and stumbled in her speech. "Umm, sorry. I—"

"No worries," Owen said as he placed a hand on Chandra's shoulder. The words were directed at the young acolyte. Owen slipped a brass badge off his belt with his free hand and presented it to the boy. Light glimmered on the polished metal surface. When Owen continued, he spoke with an unfamiliar sense of authority. "We're here on Spellseeker business. Investigating the reports of focuses having been stolen from the catacombs."

The acolyte's demeanor made an immediate shift. Uncertainty was replaced by a wash of cool relief. The katarl's whole body seemed to relax at once.

"Oh, yes," the acolyte said. "Caretaker Rajani has mentioned you and your people might be about from time to time. I'm sorry for intruding on your business. You didn't look like Spellseekers, is all. Sorry."

"Quite all right," Owen replied with a kind gaze. "My fault for not wearing the coat today. No need to apologize. It's all right if we poke around in here, then?"

The boy looked from Owen to Chandra, then leaned to peer into the unlit room ahead. A puzzled look crawled across his face. It lasted for a moment before disappearing under the guise of a welcoming smile. Rather than say yes, the acolyte gave an emphatic nod before stepping away to busy himself elsewhere.

Chandra eased away from the vacant doorway to watch the acolyte disappear amid the collection of people who came to wish their departed relatives well. When the boy had completely vanished from sight, Chandra allowed herself a slight grin.

"You come in handy, you know that?"

"Glad to be of service," Owen replied after a muffled snort. He pointed past Chandra into the dark, empty room. "We're going in here, then?"

"After you, Mr. Seeker."

Chandra lifted the rope as high as it would allow, making a sweeping gesture with her free hand to encourage passage. A grand motion of feigned elegance. One foot went behind the other as Chandra performed a shallow bow to her compatriot. Owen needed no further prompt. With a quiet, breathless laugh, he ducked under the rope and stepped into the segregated void of stillness. Chandra ducked under to follow and allowed the rope to drop behind her.

The shuffle of those in the main corridor died away like long-forgotten warnings. They failed to penetrate the gloom of the restricted chamber. Chandra, grateful for the respite, shrugged off her pack and set it on the ground.

Aimless steps from Owen were the only other sound in the room as he took the space in with curious intensity.

"So, how exactly does this room help us?" Owen asked. It was difficult to tell if he squinted against the darkness or his unanswered questions. "Do we have some tools stashed in here? Something that warranted such a massive detour?"

"Patience," Chandra said as she snaked her fingers between a specific ash basin and the wall. One last look through the doorway confirmed that nobody was spying on their business. Chandra placed one foot on the wall and pulled with all her might. The heavy vessel of stone inched away from the wall, grating against the floor as it did so. Another pull was followed by yet another. Chandra hated this process. It always sapped her arms before she had even begun to delve. An annoyance that was unavoidable if she wanted to enter the World Below undetected.

Owen turned to watch Chandra after the first yank of the vessel. He winced at the harsh noise that dug through his ears and burrowed into his brain. Against his better judgment, he drew closer to get a better look at what Chandra was doing.

"I'm not a godly man," Owen said between exertions, "but this seems awfully... sacrilegious? Maybe?"

"It's fine," Chandra grunted as she yanked on the basin again. "Thing's empty. Always has been. *There!*"

The final word came as a triumphant gasp. Chandra stood and worked out a fresh kink in her lower back, groaning all the while. She pointed to where the basin had been after her stretches were concluded. The gaping hole the basin had covered lay open like a shadowed maw, ready to devour any foolish enough to enter its depths. There would be no remorse for the unprepared.

Rope dangled from the manarail spike that Chandra had embedded in the ash basin over a year ago. A good sign that nobody had discovered her secret and tampered with the passage. Relief was a welcome sensation that Chandra did not turn away from.

Another look to the entryway of the room showed that the noise had not drawn any spectators. It also revealed a thoroughly confused

Spellseeker, who stood with one hand on his hip while the other scratched his head. Words formulated on his lips only to die in his throat. Squinted eyes narrowed still further.

"What... what, what is this?" he managed to voice at last. Owen drew closer to the hole and peered down into the abyss. "Where does this lead?"

"Straight to the middle strata of the World Below," Chandra replied, her chest puffed out with pride. "Found it while helping out an acolyte that managed to get herself stuck. It's my own personal passage."

"How does nobody else know about this?"

"Well, the acolyte knows. She keeps it to herself as a favor to me, though."

"Yeah, but..." Owen shook his head and trailed off. "Somebody else *has* to know about this. This might even be how the varmints have managed to steal offerings from the catacombs. I can't imagine there's no one else in the clergy that knows about this."

"Look, it's a gift I choose not to question. Okay? Now, are you ready to get started or not?"

Chandra shouldered her backpack and took hold of the rope that led down into nothingness. A quick thought and a small amount of channeling produced an orb of light that Chandra willed down into the passage, lighting the way for both her and Owen. She looked expectantly at her newfound partner.

"This really should be sealed up, you know?" Owen offered after a moment's hesitation.

"Yeah, yeah," Chandra replied, taking the rope in both hands. "We can discuss it after we get the cache out of here. I won't need the hole anymore if this pays off."

Loath to waste more time, Chandra stepped over the lip of the hole and began to work her way down the passage. Her search for the cache of focuses and relics and begun at last. A flash of excitement jolted through her body. At that moment, Chandra felt unstoppable.

* * *

A haze of red light marked the fringe of the middle-strata checkpoint. The faint suggestion of a body shimmered in the scarlet hue. Chandra would draw no closer for fear of interaction with whoever staffed the checkpoint that day. She saw no sense in hunting distractions where they could be avoided with ease. The knowledge that she was near the checkpoint was all that Chandra desired, as the notes from Olufemi prompted her journey to begin from there.

Wood scraped over the uneven stone floor of the cave system. The soldier appeared to be restless in the chair that was afforded to the station. Chandra gave Owen a tacit signal to follow before the 4th Federation Army soldier happened to notice their presence.

The directions were easy enough to follow at the start. From the checkpoint, Chandra walked down the main path until she reached the first left turn and took it. She was familiar with the terrain to this point and knew where the path led. It instilled a sense of confidence in Chandra as she traveled the still walkways. Each line of directions she read to that point was simple to parse out and understand.

At the end of the leftmost path was the Crescent Moon Hall. What had been a narrow, claustrophobic passage opened wide into a chamber that resembled the shape of a waxing moon. It was wide enough to accommodate twelve people abreast and had a ceiling so tall that it eluded the reach of Chandra's light. Tips of stalactites poked through the black veil that obscured the ceiling. The only sounds in the chamber were the footsteps of Chandra and Owen, along with the occasional drip of water from above. Sections of the floor glistened as Chandra willed her light about the room.

Chandra skirted the curved walls of the spacious chamber. She was familiar with two passages that left the Crescent Moon Hall. One was situated near the middle of the moon's crest. The other was at the far end of the room near the moon's tip. To Chandra's dismay, neither of these paths led downward. She dropped her pack in the room and gestured for Owen to wait. A cursory bit of exploration affirmed Chandra's memory of the place. There was no apparent way to travel down from the Crescent Moon Hall.

"Okay," Chandra whispered as she returned to Owen and collected her backpack, "we need to find a way down from here. Normal paths all lead up, so let's split up and check for something smaller."

"Something a varmint might be able to scurry through?"

"That's the idea." Chandra nodded. "I'll leave the light in the middle of the room. You might have to squint a bit, but we should be able to see the whole room."

"You go ahead and take the spell with you," Owen replied with a polite shake of his head. He slipped a small cylinder of metal out from his belt. It was small enough to disappear when clutched in the palm of his hand and had a memory-glass jewel fastened to one end. Owen placed his thumb on the jewel and, after a short pause, a pallid beam of yellow light shot out as if he were holding a covered lantern. Motes of silver glimmered in his eyes as he channeled the Flow. "Rummaged around in our Collections department before we met today. Grabbed a few focuses I thought might come in handy."

Along with the display came a wily smile. Owen raised his left hand to the level of his eye and thumbed a ring on his fourth finger. The piece of jewelry glittered like silver and was socketed with a purple stone. What the small focus could do was unclear, but the man seemed proud regardless.

"Well, all right then," Chandra said with no attempt to stifle her surprise. She allowed her light spell to hover just over her right shoulder. "I'll take the far half of the room. You take the side we came in from, and make sure you don't leave the room. Can't have you getting lost down here again, eh?"

"Yes, ma'am," Owen replied with a shallow bow. He turned on his heels and left to examine his assigned portion of the Crescent Moon Hall, his light cutting through the oppressive shadow of the World Below like a lighthouse guiding sailors to shore.

Chandra turned to her side of the room. It felt odd to think that another passage out of the Crescent Moon Hall existed. She had passed through the chamber more times than she could be bothered to remember on her way to explore some long-abandoned settlement or secret crevice. That there could have been some wretched, flea-infested creature watching her from the shadows sent a shiver down her spine.

Could be watching right now, Chandra thought.

Discomfort stood the hairs on Chandra's arm on end. She did not care for the thought of furtive eyes scanning each movement she made. It was a position that Chandra knew well from her time in the World Below. To watch strangers pass from a sheltered nook was her customary method to avoid encounters. Being on the other side of the coin felt wrong.

It was an unproductive line of thought. Questions that would only heighten the sense of unease that came with delving into the deep places of the world. Chandra focused herself back on the matter at hand. With a thought, she willed her orb of light to hover just above where the wall met the floor. The orb maintained the same height as Chandra walked it around her half of the room.

Small pockets of water pooled underneath stalactites that crept ever downward from the ceiling above. The occasional drip sounded like a drop of water striking an empty pail. Ripples disturbed the pools with each drop, their minor motions drawing Chandra's eye. The pools were otherwise stationary. None flowed toward the wall to suggest some crevice hidden from her light. It remained this way for her entire patrol around the chamber. No hint of a passageway that led to further depths, varmint-sized or otherwise.

Perhaps up in the wall? Chandra thought. *Nothing in the directions said the hole had to be in the floor.*

Chandra embraced the thought and raised her light to the level of her waist. On this patrol, she focused on the slick surface of the chamber walls. Much like the floor, the walls were a mottled collection of black-and-gray swirls with the occasional pocket of orange. Smooth surfaces that devoured whatever light was unfortunate enough to present itself. Chandra traced the wall with her fingertips to ensure she did not miss a single divot.

The walls proved as barren of secrets as the floor. Unless there was some button fixed into a fold in the rocks, or fashioned into the rock itself, there would be no passage through the walls. Not on Chandra's half of the room. She clicked her tongue against the back of her teeth and made another pass around the walls with her light at the level of her eyes. No stone would be left unexamined.

Another fruitless round of searching made Chandra question her memory. She set her pack down and pulled the directions from a side pocket. The light back over her shoulder, Chandra scanned the beginning of Olufemi's notes.

"Start near the red lights where the soldier stands," Chandra murmured. "Follow left path. Path that leads to crescent moon chamber. From there climb down. As far down as the moon descends. At the bottom of the well is a fork."

Yeah, Chandra confirmed to herself, *says down. Not up. I wonder if Owen is having any better luck than I am over here.*

Chandra allowed her frustration to get the better of her. She tossed the directions back into her pack, shouldered the pack, and then started over to the other half of the room. The beam of light from Owen's focus traced up and down the wall. His movements were slow and thorough, covering the floor to the space just above his head. Perhaps a little too thorough. He was only halfway through searching his portion of the room.

Rather than discuss matters of expedience, Chandra set to work on Owen's half of the wall. She started at what she assumed would be Owen's destination and emulated his process. The orb of light descended until it grazed the floor. As Chandra became satisfied that she had seen nothing, she raised the light up and slightly to the left. A pattern of narrow triangles traced on the wall continued to reveal nothing of importance.

"Nothing on your side of the room, I take it?"

Chandra turned her head to see that Owen was looking her way. He spoke at a conversational volume, which further unnerved Chandra.

She made a gesture as if to hush a rowdy child before she whispered in response.

"No, nothing. You?"

"Well," Owen began with a lowered voice, "I did find one crevice. Just over that way, tucked into the floor." He shined his light at a particular spot near where they had entered the chamber. Sure enough, there was an alcove cut into the floor just where the wall met the floor. "Not sure if that's what we're looking for, though. It's awfully small."

"And when did you plan on mentioning this?"

"Hoped I wouldn't have to, to be honest," Owen sighed. "Thought we might find something a little more suitable to… human passage."

A look crawled over Chandra's face that she hoped might be obscured by shadow. Disbelief tainted with a touch of disappointment. The sort of look she used to give Omala when the young girl first started making a mess of breakfast preparations. Chandra rolled her eyes and did her best to wipe the expression away.

"I'll take a look," Chandra whispered. "You keep making a pass around this half of the room until you hit the middle. See if you find something that I might have missed."

"Yes, ma'am," Owen replied with a nod.

If nothing else, Chandra mused, at least the Spellseeker was keen to follow directions.

Soft steps carried Owen away from the hole in the wall. It was not the sort of hole that extended a warm invitation. Chandra had to kneel and crane her head to see inside. The opening came up little more than a foot from the floor. Just enough room for Chandra to drop her pack, lie down on her stomach, and wedge herself into the mysterious crevice.

Chandra wondered how she had never noticed the hole before now. It stuck out like a sore thumb when she knew what she was looking for, but until now it had eluded sight. Perhaps she had overlooked the passage as a shadow on the wall? Whatever the case, the thought was not relevant now. Chandra pulled her light into the crevice to get a better view.

The space was barely wider than it was tall. It raised another foot or so in height as it went back and ended at an abrupt wall. Not enough room to stand in, though it did allow Chandra to twist and turn without fear of her hips or shoulders raking over the stone ceiling.

At the back of the tunnel was a hole in the floor. Unlike the mouth of the tunnel behind her, the lip of this new hole was smooth to the touch on the side nearest Chandra. She ran her fingers along the edge until the rim grew rough. A sign of use, Chandra thought. Stone passed over so frequently that it had been worn down. She ran her fingers along the smoothed side again. This time she moved her hand slowly and with greater care. Small ridges were gouged into the stone. Ridges that felt an awful lot to Chandra like claw marks.

"Definitely a rat hole," Chandra murmured to herself. "No doubts there."

Light poured over the smoothed lip of the new hole as Chandra moved her spell forward. She took hold of the lip and pulled herself near to the edge. The manarail spikes on Chandra's belt clicked and clattered on the stone surface as she inched her face over the hole and peered downward. Much like the ceiling of the Crescent Moon Chamber, the bottom of the hole escaped the reach of the light orb.

Chandra willed her spell down the hole at a slow, consistent pace. It allowed her to get a good look at the walls of the crooked shaft. With the proper illumination, Chandra could see that it was not a straight shot to the bottom. The shaft was comprised of what almost looked like natural stone steps. They alternated positions on the wall. One would be on the left side, and the next on the right. Their configuration made it impossible to see to the bottom of the shaft.

The makeshift steps were smooth to the touch, just like the lip of the hole. It was close enough for Chandra to reach down and get a firm grip. The step did not move despite Chandra's best attempt to dislodge it. She tested moving it in all directions until she was satisfied that the stone was well and truly stuck.

"Guess we've got our way down. No ropes needed," Chandra whispered as she began to wriggle her way back through the tunnel and into the Crescent Moon Chamber. The orb of light whizzed back up and followed Chandra out.

Owen was still making his diligent rounds when Chandra emerged from the squat tunnel. His free hand rubbed the stubble on his chin and cheek as his cone of light wove up, down, and around the wall. It was good to see that he had not slacked off the moment Chandra left him to his own devices. She approached with quiet steps so as not to shout across the room.

"Looks like you found our way down," Chandra said as she placed a hand on Owen's shoulder. "Good job."

"You absolutely sure?" Owen asked without looking away from his examination. "That hole was *really* small."

"Widens up a bit as it goes back. Not by much, but you'll get a little wiggle room before you get to the drop at the back."

"Hmm. And how's the climb down?"

"Well, it doesn't look like we'll be needing ropes just yet. Shaft has outcroppings as far down as I could see. They make for sturdy handholds. I'll check them as we go down to make sure we don't get surprised by something shifty."

"Rubbish," Owen said. He looked away from the wall and leveled his gaze at Chandra. "I'll go down first. Not about to let a civilian come to harm on my watch, and especially not for my sake."

"How noble," Chandra managed to get out through a stifled snort. "I'm the guide. I'll go first. Besides, I'm smaller than you. Makes sense for me to get in there and wriggle around first."

The Spellseeker's face darkened and contorted into a thoughtful frown. It was a sudden shift that caught Chandra by surprise. She wondered if something she said might have insulted Owen, though she wasn't sure how proclaiming herself the smaller of the pair could be offensive. His hesitation to speak further heightened the discomfort that gnawed at Chandra's stomach.

Whatever had bothered Owen relented. The frown melted into a more inviting look that softened the creases around his eyes. Owen seemed to grow ten years younger in the span of a single breath.

"All right," he whispered, "but just because I know first aid doesn't mean I want to use it. Don't press your luck if you feel unsure about something. Even if it's just for a moment."

"I'll be fine," Chandra replied. Her words were stiff as a brick. The sudden change in Owen's mood left Chandra struggling to acclimate. "No need to worry. Now, let's get going. You'll need to take your pack off and push it in front of you as you crawl. Not enough space to wear it on your back."

"Oh, great," Owen sighed. He arched his brows in mock anticipation. "Even smaller than I'd thought."

14

Making Sense

"Slip the slot... avoid the path...?"

"Why does it sound like this is your first time reading that?" Owen asked in a hushed tone that mirrored Chandra's. There was no need to turn her head and meet the Spellseeker's gaze. Chandra heard the hints of incredulous disappointment clear enough.

"Busy past few days," Chandra murmured in reply. "Besides, what good would reading lines of text do me without something to look at? The directions were never gonna make sense until we got down here."

"Still, it would have been prudent to sift through the whole thing before we left. What if Olufemi made a mistake and we didn't find out until it was too late?"

"No sense in dwelling on might have and maybe. We'll deal with problems as they come, not before."

Owen grumbled but kept further opinions to himself.

They had come to the bottom of the well after what felt like an hour of shimmying and scraping down the uneven shaft. Owen produced a brass pocket watch once they reached the bottom and advised that the descent had been closer to twenty minutes in length. The assessment did not convince Chandra. She was certain they had been stuck in the bump-covered pathway for at least twice as long as the watch indicated.

It had been easy going at first. Though they were required to bend into unnatural shapes to proceed, there was space enough to navigate the shaft for the first half of the journey. Chandra imagined she would have had to liquify herself had the passage been any narrower. Fortunately, the walls never grew so close together that navigation was impossible. What provided further challenge was when the walls began to grow farther apart.

The change was subtle. Positions required of Chandra and Owen became more and more manageable. Traversal was even comfortable for a brief period. There was no need to bend and crinkle in ways that would make a contortionist wretch. Both Chandra and Owen had room to extend their limbs and could press against the wall when rest was needed.

If the passage had remained so hospitable, there would have been no problems. The shaft, however, had other ideas. It did not stay the same comfortable size or shrink to its previous size. Walls continued to move further apart. Chandra had to fully extend her legs just to get a toe onto the next foothold. By the time they reached the bottom, both Chandra and Owen were leaping downward to catch outcroppings. Fortune held in that the shaft dried out as it pressed further and further down. If not for that blessing, Chandra feared she might have slipped and fallen into the expanding abyss.

At the bottom of the shaft, or "well" as the directions called it, was a roughly circular chamber a bit narrower than the shaft itself. Owen could nearly touch both walls when standing with both arms outstretched. An obvious and inviting path was carved out of the wall. They had to duck to press through it, but it was a much more enticing prospect than the recent descent.

Chandra looked again at the directions.

"Slip the slot. Avoid the path."

Chandra swung her orb of light around the circular chamber to examine its walls. Inviting as it was, the crawlspace that promised easy passage did not fit the directions. It was not until Chandra's inspection reached the opposite of the wall that she located what she might refer to as a slot.

A jagged fissure erupted from the otherwise smooth walls of the chamber. It resembled a bolt of lightning that ripped through the clouded stone surface. The opening began a foot or so off the ground and reached up well over Chandra's head but was too narrow to traverse head on. She would have to turn sideways and enter shoulder first.

Curious fingers reached out to touch the black stone. Ridges within the fissure proved more fine than expected. They drew blood as Chandra dragged her finger along the rim. She withdrew her hand from the fissure in surprise and looked at the crimson bead that pooled on her fingertip. A small but clear warning that this new passage must be traversed with care.

"This way," Chandra whispered, beckoning to Owen as she did so. She sucked on her wounded finger between words. "Be careful. The stone is sharp."

"Might be missing that thick coat of mine about now." The words were glib rather accusatory. Owen approached and shined his light through the fissure. An edge was visible on the other side. "Doesn't look too long. We'll just have to mind ourselves, I guess. Any suggestions?"

Chandra paused, then nodded at Owen.

"Don't slide."

"You don't say?" Owen replied with a marked drop in enthusiasm.

If there was some kind of secret technique he was expecting, Chandra had not provided it. This type of terrain was new to Chandra herself. She did not have a wealth of experience from which to create an informed opinion. The inside of the fissure itself looked foreign. Sleek and black, light shimmered across its surface like the moon over a placid lake. There were no deviations in color like the surrounding walls, either. It was that same glossy black from one side to the other.

Not gonna get anywhere waiting around, Chandra told herself. With a deep, preparatory breath and a light shrug, Chandra eased herself up off the ground and into the foreboding clutches of the black fissure.

The inside of the passage proved to be just as sharp as the edge of the entryway. Chandra could feel the hungry ridges the moment she raised her weight onto her hands. It was a struggle to follow her own advice and not slide in. She had to anchor herself with hand and foot, raise her torso, and edge her way inside. A task that proved too difficult to accomplish with a single hand while the other held her pack. Chandra eased her weight back out of the hole to find crimson droplets dotted her palm.

"Something wrong?" Owen asked, craning his head over Chandra's shoulder. He winced when he caught sight of her hand. "Ouch."

"Yeah, ouch," Chandra replied as she sucked a breath through her teeth. "Not a one-handed job, I'm thinking."

"So it seems. Here, let's get that wrapped up before you try again."

Owen unshouldered his bag as he spoke. His hands rifled around until they got a hold of a bandage, which he produced and unwrapped with care. A drizzle of water from his canteen washed away the droplets of blood that had accumulated in Chandra's palm. Freshly cleaned, Owen set about bandaging Chandra's palm with a practiced hand. The fluidity of the whole operation left Chandra impressed.

"Not your first time patching somebody up, I'm guessing?" Chandra asked.

"Unfortunately," Owen replied without taking his eyes off Chandra's hand. "They gave us extensive first-aid training at Eastpointe, but I can tell you that I didn't expect to use it as much as I have. Rough town, Arnstead."

"No argument there. Handy skill to have, though."

"It has proven to be, yes," Owen nodded.

"What's the worst you've ever seen?"

"Well," Owen started before he fell into a thoughtful pause. The moment of hesitation lasted until he cinched the bandage into a knot over the back of Chandra's hand. An action that caused Chandra to wince. She shook her hand as she pulled it away. "I saw a woman fall off a cliff once. One of her bones was sticking out of her leg. That was a rough one."

"Oh, gods," Chandra spoke louder than she had intended, her eyes wide at the thought of a bone protruding from someone's body. "Did she live?"

"Yeah. She wasn't happy about it, I think, but she lived."

"Glad to know I'm in good hands, then. Thanks."

Chandra ran her other hand over the bandage. Dots of red bloomed like roses on her palm as she traced her fingers over the thin cuts. She shook her hand to put the minor injury out of her mind, flexing her fingers as she did so.

"So, how do we deal with... this?" Owen asked, pointing a limp finger at the fissure. "Doesn't seem hospitable to people. Are you *sure* there aren't any mistakes in those directions?"

"It's the best we've got." Chandra sighed. "Everything has lined up so far. The last thing we want to do is get ourselves lost in an unfamiliar stretch of the World Below. We just have to be *extra* careful with this bit. Here, hand me your pack."

Chandra held out an expectant hand to Owen. The Spellseeker cocked his head but did not linger in thought for long before handing his pack to Chandra. She set Owen's pack next to the fissure and placed her own at the bottom of the sleek passageway. There was a plan forming in her head to free their hands from the packs.

Leather straps crinkled and groaned as Chandra detached her staff from her pack. Holding the staff by the end with her good hand, she pushed the pack through the fissure. She bet on the cured leather holding up to the sharp surface better than her bare hands. Much to her satisfaction, the pack did not burst or turn to ribbons as it slid along the glossy black rock. The pack was nearly through at the end of Chandra's reach. She pulled the staff back in preparation. Using the staff like a pool cue, she pushed the pack the rest of the way across the fissure. The leather pack disappeared to land on unseen ground with a cluttered thump.

A simple yet effective plan to free their hands. Chandra replicated the actions for Owen's pack, then slid the staff across the fissure. The sanded stick glided across the fissure like butter over a hot pan and clattered down onto the stone floor that awaited Chandra and Owen on the other side.

"No going back now, huh?" Owen murmured.

"We'll be fine. Just remember," Chandra said as she held her hand aloft, "don't slide."

Chandra tested the waters once more. This time she dispersed her weight over both hands and was able to hike herself up into the fissure with a measure of grace. Though it was cramped and movement was slow, Chandra was able to press her way through the fissure inch by inch. The occasional rip and tear of her shirt or trousers caught her ear. A not-so-subtle reminder of the hazardous nature of the terrain.

A few minutes saw the small distance crossed with minimal damage to Chandra's body or clothing. By the time she stepped out of the fissure and back onto safe ground, she heard the clatter of metal dragging on stone. Chandra did not dare to turn her head while still in the fissure. She waited until both feet were planted firm to look back through the hole.

There was little surprise when Chandra turned to the source of the noise. Though he had surrendered his pack to Chandra, a fair number of large tools still hung from the man's belt. Most notable among them was the arming sword. The hilt of the weapon dragged mercilessly along the sharpened edges of the fissure. It seemed to snag on everything and anything that it could. Owen was forced to fight not just the passage, but the items he still carried with him.

In the back of her mind, a small voice shouted at Chandra to instruct the Spellseeker to be quiet. That voice was suppressed by the overwhelming urge to laugh at the man's comical struggle. The troubled grunts put Chandra over the edge. She indulged in a quiet snicker and looked away before the crack in her seam became a proper explosion.

It was not long before the racket concluded and Owen reached the other side of the fissure. Just like Chandra, he was mostly in one piece apart from some superficial cuts in his clothing. The bit of red on his knuckles did not seem to trouble him in the slightest. He did not speak or focus on what had just transpired behind him. Instead, he dusted himself off, readjusted his belt, then bent down and picked up his pack. The noise of him clearing his throat filled the new chamber as Owen shouldered his pack and looked to Chandra with an eager expression.

"Right, then," he said in a high-pitched tone. "What's next?"

"We've only got the one path," Chandra said, her words laced with mirth that she could not hide. "I'll read while we walk."

Chandra swung her pack from her back to her chest. She flipped the top open and peered inside, spying for the directions that had brought her and Owen to where they now walked. The paper seemed to have a mind of its own. It flitted about inside the pack as Chandra rummaged. She could see the damned thing, but it refused to let her get a hand on it. Chandra stuck her tongue out to one side, turned her head, and reached deep into the bag. Fingers slipped over the crinkled paper. Once it had been felt, Chandra snatched the directions like a pickpocket at market and pulled them out to read.

Let's see what we've got next, Chandra thought as she unfolded the battered and crinkled paper. She skimmed through what had already been traversed until she reached a new section. Curious eyes flitted up from the page to the path ahead to be sure that the passage remained straight and free of obstacles or turns. The new directions read:

"Follow the fissure path to the sharp drop. Throw a rope and slide down. Don't trust the shimmer. Mind the danglers."

That all sounded clear to Chandra. There was only one path to follow at present, so no chance of diverting on accident. It sounded like no other option would present itself, either. The mention of a rope in the directions did catch Chandra by surprise. What little she knew of the varmints included the fact that they were excellent climbers. How smooth must a sheer drop be that their claws could not find gaps and ridges to grasp? Not that it would present any issue to Owen or herself. They had brought plenty of rope and the means to secure it.

The note about the shimmer was another matter. It was all Chandra could do to guess that line. She recalled several encounters with pools of water in the World Below that glowed without an apparent source of light. Maybe the notes were talking of a pool like this? A warning to not just jump from the mentioned drop and trust the water to catch her? The idea sounded plausible, but she had no way to be sure until she reached the drop in question. It could be a warning against something that lurked near the drop. Something that waited for little rat people to scurry along and present themselves as a meal.

The end of the passage was just as puzzling to Chandra as the mention of a shimmer. *What, gods tell me, is a dangler?* The thought bounced around in her head without purchase. Chandra had been able to make some kind of educated guess about the shimmer, whether she was right or wrong. Danglers? It brought nothing to mind. No experience down below made Chandra think of something that dangled.

It bothered Chandra that she hit a blank spot in her knowledge. There had been no complete surprises so far. She might have been caught off guard by what she saw, but Chandra could tie the likes of the well and the fissure to memories from past exploration. The notion of something so alien that it did not brush a single memory was more troubling.

We'll just have to be extra extra *careful, then,* Chandra thought as she folded the directions back into a neat square and tucked them into her pack.

Just as she slid her pack around to her back and turned her attention to the path, Chandra stopped in her tracks. So sudden was the stop that Owen barreled right into Chandra. Both stumbled forward a step or two. Chandra wheeled her arms in the air to regain balance. Her desire to remain in place was fueled by what hung mere inches from her nose.

"What's the matter?" Owen whispered.

"Don't move," Chandra whispered back.

In poor light, the object that dangled before Chandra could have been mistaken for a rope. It was thin and corded. Small protrusions that looked like frayed hairs poked out here and there from its surface. A gentle sway suggested that it had been agitated by some other traveler in the not-so-distant past.

That was with poor light. With the help of her light spell, Chandra was able to see that the dangling thing was no rope. Not in the traditional sense. It *was* thin and seemed to be comprised of several cords. The part that troubled Chandra was not the cords or the gentle sway of the thing. What caused Chandra's stomach to half turn in place was the fact that the cords were made of what looked like flesh. The thing pulsated with a steady rhythm as if it were alive.

Chandra put a hand over her mouth and took two steps back. Disgusted as she was, curiosity got the better of her. She willed her light spell to follow the pulsating rope of flesh up toward the ceiling. Up it went for six feet or more. When the ceiling came into view, Chandra saw a mass of something attached to the stone. Its nature was beyond foreign. The only feature she could put a name to was the area where the rope disappeared into... whatever the thing was. It looked like a giant beak.

"I guess that's a dangler," Chandra murmured.

"A what?"

"The directions mentioned them." Chandra turned her head toward Owen as she spoke. She did not, however, take her eyes off the thing affixed to the ceiling. "Said we need to watch out for them."

"It certainly doesn't look friendly, does it? Directions say how we're supposed to get around them?"

The Spellseeker raised a good point. Though the fleshy cord from the dangler was no wider around than the rope in Chandra's bag, the passage in which the cord hung was narrow. Chandra's immediate thought was to just press against the wall, time the sway of the creature's appendage, then slip past when the opportunity presented itself. Made sense enough to Chandra.

What happens if it touches us?

Before Chandra tempted fate and cross the path of the dangler, she wanted to know the consequence of being found. Did it emit some kind of ear-shattering screech and drop from the ceiling to gather its prey? Was the dangling appendage covered in some kind of caustic slime that would turn Chandra to jelly? Not knowing was too great a discomfort.

Chandra pulled one of the manarail spikes from her belt. Holding the bit of metal by the tip, Chandra extended her arm as far as she could and inched toward the dangler until she made contact.

The fleshy cord moved faster than Chandra could track. No sooner had the manarail spike touched the dangler than the creature wrapped around the metal object. So startled was Chandra by the reaction speed that she released the manarail spike from her grasp. A hushed gasp of surprise escaped Chandra as she took a step back.

By the time Chandra had a solid grasp of what was happening, the dangler had already wrapped itself three times around the manarail spike. Each new coil was accompanied by a horrid slosh. The sound was like a slab of meat being tenderized on a butcher's block. As the cords of pulsating flesh wrapped themselves around the spike, they were hauled upward toward the base of the creature. Toward the black beak that began to click with anticipation. Up and up the spike was carried until it disappeared inside the quivering maw of the creature. That there was no trace of the retracted chord once the beak had closed made Chandra wonder just how big the creature was.

"Absolutely horrific," came Owen's muffled reply once the dangler had fully retracted its lure. A hand held over his mouth muffled his words. "Why? Why does thing exist?"

"Best not think about it," Chandra replied, still caught in the struggle of tearing her eyes away from the gnashing beak. "All sorts of horrors down here looking for their next meal. Let's keep going before it drops that… whatever that meat rope was."

"Agreed."

Owen did not have to be told twice. He followed close at Chandra's heels as they pressed onward down the narrow passage.

The walk proved to be an uncomfortable one. There was space enough to navigate with ease, and the tunnel did not whip or wind about. It was remarkably straight for a natural passageway cut into the stone. The floor remained quite dry, as well, allowing for solid purchase as the pair continued on their way.

What made the walk unbearable was the constant fear that a cord of meat might fall from the ceiling and wrap Chandra up before she could react. Six feet was as close to one of those beaks as she would ever like to have come. The mere thought of one of those things tearing into her flesh while she struggled to get away was sickening enough. On top of that, Chandra had no idea just how strong one of those danglers was. She had released her manarail spike without struggle. A nagging voice in the back of Chandra's mind warned her that the dangler could have lifted a teenage girl off the ground with ease. Chandra did not care for that voice, but she found herself hard-pressed to disagree with it.

Another of the danglers presented itself before long. It lured with that same cord of flesh, a patient fisherman on the banks of Sisir's Run. The cord swayed as if a gentle breeze rolled through the narrow corridor of stone. Time meant nothing to the creature that clutched at the ceiling. An opportunity for food would present itself when fate allowed. There was no rush for the dangler.

Chandra raised a hand in warning to Owen as she approached the dangler's reach. Her other hand moved with quiet precision to grab another manarail spike from her belt. Could the creature even hear her approach, Chandra wondered? Was silence necessary to trick a dangler? Without a way to be certain, Chandra chose silence over brash expedience. Once again, she tapped the cord of flesh with a metal spike. Once again, the creature coiled with lightning speed around its perceived prey. The cord moved upward in a series of violent lurches. Waiting above was the gnashing beak attached to the beast's core.

The hand of warning flipped round and beckoned Owen to follow. To pass under the dangler while it was distracted with the slender piece of metal. How long it would take for the creature to learn it had been deceived was another mystery. One that Chandra was not keen on researching further than required.

This series of actions was repeated three times. Chandra hated to sacrifice her manarail spikes to the danglers. Each offering left her with a grimace that she struggled to wipe from her face. A new dangler meant the loss of another core to Chandra's metal spells. Those spikes would not be pitons or hooks that helped traverse the World Below. They could never be used to craft a dagger for self-defense. They were just gone, never to be retrieved for a future purpose.

The fifth and final dangler stood guard over the passageway's exit. Beyond the creature's area of control was a sharp drop. Walls and floor simply stopped, while the ceiling went on into the silent void. Poor light would have allowed the sudden stop in footing to catch a traveler by surprise. A fall of untold depth awaited those unfortunate enough to step over the ledge.

Strong sources of light did not completely preclude an adventurer's fall. The pure light from Chandra's spell illuminated something else. Almost like a cloud of vapor that hung in the air where ground should have been. Pushing her light closer to the cloud further increased the suggestion of solid ground. By the time Chandra's orb of light was inside the vapor, she might have sworn that the space ahead was a wet stone surface that glistened in the light.

"Don't trust the shimmer," Chandra mumbled. A nasty trick of light that could claim anyone not expecting the fall. She clicked her tongue against the back of her teeth at the thought of the sudden plummet.

"What now?" Owen asked, shinning his light over Chandra's shoulders. He bobbed back and forth between her shoulders to see what Chandra had mumbled about. "Some other beastie from the directions? What has old Olufemi got to say about this next monstrosity of the deep?"

"Just thinking about what might have been," Chandra said as she pointed a finger at the ledge. "We climb down here. Look around for a divot or slot in the rock, somewhere I can dig a piton into."

Chandra had no intention of using the pitons obtained from Robin's Field Goods. Not yet, at least. The manarail spikes around her waist were more substantial and offered more material to manipulate with her spells. She would rather mold one of her spikes to a perfect fit for some hole or slot than jam a rigid piton into place. The pitons could be used once the meatier spikes had been used up.

"Need an anchor for a rope, is it?" Owen asked.

"That's about the size of it," Chandra replied.

"Right, I've got a quicker idea. Give me a bit of room around the ledge, yeah?"

Curious, Chandra took a couple of steps back from the ledge to make room for Owen. The Spellseeker stepped forward and unholstered the caster pistol from his right hip. Metal ground against metal as he opened the chamber and removed some kind of cartridge, which he slotted into his belt. Another cartridge was removed and took the place of the original one in the tool. A harsh clink echoed out into the open chamber when Owen jammed the weapon closed.

"You're not going to try and blow up the cave, are you?" Chandra asked. One of her hands wandered behind her head and scratched at her scalp.

Chandra had heard of caster pistols and rifles, stories of the weapons being used to clear swaths of foes. Sometimes to subdue ferocious creatures that could not be approached on foot, a common tactic for the 4th Federation Army units that operated beyond the frontier. But this was her first time seeing one put to use. It unnerved Chandra to see something so devastating be implemented so near to her person.

A faint glimmer of light shone out from the cartridge chamber. Owen seemed to be about done channeling Flow for the focus. He took a breath of concentration in through his nose. When Owen snapped his eyes open, a loud plink pierced the silence of the chamber. It was magnitudes louder than when the Spellseeker closed the pistol. Like a blacksmith had struck an anvil with a hammer in the marble hall of the House. The noise was powerful enough to demand that Chandra place her hands over her ears to stifle the echo.

Chandra could see Owen mouth the word *sorry* as he turned his head over his shoulder. All she could hear, however, was the steady, metallic ringing in her ears. The noise took more time to subside than Chandra would have liked.

Eyes no longer crossed by the sheer volume of the activity, Chandra was able to see what Owen proudly presented. A metal spike driven into the smoothed stone floor of the corridor. Small cracks surrounded the spike in suggestion of the force required to bite into the stone. Owen had angled the spike so that the top faced away from the ledge.

Chandra knelt next to the Spellseeker's handiwork. She was unable to dislodge the spike with a single hand. It did not so much as budge in response to her attempts. The bit of metal appeared to be securely anchored in place. Though Chandra would have appreciated some kind of warning, she was certain that the spike would hold her weight as she rappelled over the ledge and down into shadow. She added one final touch to be safe. Channeling the Flow, Chandra formed the top of the spike into a closed loop to prevent any unwanted slippage.

"Neat trick," Owen said in response to the magical display.

"I could say the same," Chandra replied. She dug one of her little fingers into her ear and twisted it about. "Maybe give a warning next time, though?"

"Right, right. Been a while since I've driven one of those into the ground. Didn't think about how loud it would be in an enclosed space. Apologies."

"What's done is done. If it's done well, I won't complain too much."

Chandra spared no time in putting the fresh anchor to good use. She dropped her bag on the stone floor and unhitched a length of rope bound to the side. The neatly coiled rope splayed over the ground as Chandra unfastened the hitch that kept the rope in a neat bundle. She grabbed the end of the rope that had been used as a hitch and pushed it through the eye of the anchor. Deft hands worked to tie the rope steadfastly in place. A few tugs at the knot gave Chandra the confidence she needed in the job.

Next came the harness. That piece of gear was buried deep inside the pack. Though some might think its use would go without saying, there had been no clear indicator to Chandra that a descent of un-determined length would be required. A lucky trek might have been completed without the use of a single rope. Never mind that reading the translated directions beforehand would have given her a clue.

The harness was a light, well-crafted bit of technology. Something that Robin imported from the eastern coast. The webbing was made of completely synthetic materials put together using the Flow. What exact methods went into making the material was kept a secret, or so Robin had once told Chandra. Supposedly to ensure that competitors could not replicate the nature of the material. How it was put together was less of a concern to Chandra than how the material performed. It was comfortable, sturdy, went on easy, and had just enough give to allow her room to work. She wished she had had the money to acquire one sooner.

A few metal clips at the front and back completed the assembly of the harness. It was into these that Chandra slipped the rope. They were cleverly designed to fold in on themselves, allowing Chandra to push the rope into the device without having to loop the entire length of rope through. Chandra made a show of the effort to ensure that Owen could replicate the actions and descend on his own. As she started to explain the process of controlling the speed of descent, Owen raised a kind hand.

"No need to worry about me," he said with a smile. "Done it hundreds of times at the academy. You just focus on getting yourself down in one piece, trailblazer."

"You sure?" Chandra asked.

"Positive. Go on."

Chandra acquiesced without another complaint. *Worse comes to worst, he calls down asking for help,* Chandra thought. *Or he plummets to his death.* The notion drew out one final look of concern from Chandra before she whisked the thought away. Owen had not given Chandra a reason to distrust him yet. Rooting around for a reason to doubt him would only lead to trouble. Chandra assured herself the man would be fine and kicked the length of rope over the ledge.

Silence reigned for the span of a breath or two. The muffled unfurling of the rope was lost to the undefined reaches of the shimmering void that stretched out forever before Chandra. Then, once those breaths had come and gone, a distinct thwack rose from below. It sounded like the rope had reached the bottom with length to spare. A good sign. There would be no need to plant another spike and dangle a fresh rope while clinging to the stone precipice. Though Chandra was confident in her skills, it was still reassuring to know that there was a definite bottom to the chamber.

The ledge beckoned. Chandra turned her back to the open chamber. She took the rope in both hands and configured it like a lever to manage her speed. Her left hand held the rope steady before her, while her right held the rope behind. To go faster she would move the rope away from her body. To slow herself, Chandra would draw the rope behind her back. It was a routine that she knew well.

As always, the hardest part was getting started. A pit weighed Chandra's stomach down as she eased the arches of her feet over the ledge. The balls of her feet curled to grip the floor, while her heels dangled over nothing at all. She had to ease herself back into a seated position that allowed both the rope and the harness to do their work. A slip here might cause Chandra to scramble and panic, to reach for something solid. It would spell a long fall toward whatever waited below.

Chandra steadied herself against her nerves.

You've done this a hundred times, Chandra told herself. *And you'll live to do it a hundred more. Easy does it, now.*

Rope whined as it slid over metal and harness. A subdued hiss like the beginning of a kettle coming to boil. Chandra felt the harness take her weight as she eased herself down. The transition was perfect, just as Chandra reassured herself it would be. There was no cause for alarm.

Chandra allowed herself to look from the illuminated wall of rock before her back up over the ledge. There was just enough clearance to get a good look at Owen. True to his word, the Spellseeker was already halfway into his harness by the time Chandra was ready to descend. He had managed to get the webbing around all the various tools fixed to his belt without a hand to help. Another reassurance that their journey would continue to go as planned.

If that was all Chandra had seen, she would have been able to rappel with peace of mind.

Some trick of light caught Chandra's eye before she began her descent. An odd glistening behind Owen. Not like the luminescent vapors that clouded the open chamber at Chandra's back. This was different. Whatever it was looked slick, like a fresh slab of meat that still oozed blood. Chandra felt her face grow numb with horror as she raised her light spell to get a better view.

"Owen, move!" Chandra shouted.

The sheer volume of the cry caught Owen by surprise. Accustomed to the near silence that had pervaded the day, the distressed command snapped his attention to Chandra. Confusion furrowed his brow. The harness fell from his grasp as Owen reached to rip his arming sword from its sheath. He wheeled around too late to face whatever had come up behind him. Owen was slapped to the ground before he had a chance to arm himself, one of his legs pulled high into the air.

It was clear to see now that Owen no longer obstructed the light. The dangler above had finished with its manarail spike and sent its lure down to continue the hunt. Unfeeling silence shrouded the creature as it moved to catch both Chandra and Owen by surprise. Its fleshy appendage was wrapped tight around Owen's ankle. The full strength of the dangler was on display as it wrenched Owen from an upright position to suspend the man in the air.

Owen did not react to the ambush. The sudden fall had dashed his head against the stone floor. Arms hung limp as the creature lurched Owen upward. A slow, inexorable crawl toward the beak that awaited above. The sword on Owen's belt slid from its sheath and clattered to the ground. His pack followed soon after, jostled by the determined motions of the dangler. Momentum swung Owen from side to side like a macabre windchime in a bitter winter breeze.

Continued horror clutched Chandra by the shoulders. Frozen just below the ledge, she watched the creature yank Owen up and up.

"Oh gods," Chandra cursed in a brief fit of panic.

Chandra allowed her legs to fall. A shot of adrenaline coursed through her veins at the realization that help would not come from outside at this moment. It was up to Chandra to find help from within, to resolve this situation. She dug her toes into whatever poor excuse for a foothold she could find and propelled herself upward. She was able to get the first knuckles of her right hand up and over the ledge. A tenuous hold that did not promise to last for long. Determination roared up from the soles of Chandra's feet to her throat. Her cry filled the empty chamber at her back as she slung her weight onto her left hand to find better purchase.

Strained grunts spilled from Chandra as she worked her way upward. First a better grip for her right hand, then slinging up the elbow from her left arm. Her right leg was on top of the ledge. The left leg followed as Chandra rolled away from the open chamber and onto her back. She did not remain on the ground long. Chandra ripped a man-arail spike from her waist as she unfastened her staff from her pack. At the same time, she willed her light to rise to the ceiling and illuminate her target.

The Flow came to Chandra with tremendous speed. Channeling in such reckless haste sent a wave of fire through her arm. Invisible pins and needles born from the friction between muscle and Flow. A temporary pain to resolve a problem that might end a life.

Armed with a crude spear, Chandra looked to the ceiling. A quick extension of her arm, holding the spear by its end, told Chandra that the dangler was out of her immediate reach. She would not be able to jab at the creature to free Owen. Thoughts raced through her mind. What was the best option? Try and scale the corridor walls to get within reach? Throw the spear and pray she did not strike her companion?

Another lurch of the dangler's lure told Chandra she did not have time to debate with herself. Owen was already two-thirds the way up to the beak that gnashed with impatience.

One last, crazed look around the immediate area sealed Chandra's course of action. She gripped her spear like a javelin and locked eyes on the exposed flesh around the dangler's beak. All her strength and coordination poured into her right arm. With a desperate cry, Chandra wound up and launched her missile at the ravenous beast.

She missed.

The tip of the spear struck solid stone next to the rooted dangler. It made a hollow sound that pierced Chandra's soul before it fell back toward the floor. Chandra fumbled to catch the weapon, but it slipped her grasp and clattered at her feet. Failure continued to vibrate through the spear as Chandra picked it up and prepared herself for a second attempt. With no time to waste, she reared back and launched the spear again. Her cry followed the wooden shaft and sent the spearhead into the dangler's exposed flesh.

There was no reaction. Chandra stood locked in place as she watched her spear quiver, stuck deep into the dangler. Another lurch pulled Owen further upward. That was followed by another. Chandra could feel the weight of failure bearing down on her from all sides. Her eyes grew wide in terrified anticipation of what she was about to witness.

Then the strained motions of the dangler stopped. Owen hung in place, a ragged shirt swaying on a taut clothesline. A lifetime passed as Chandra watched events transpire just out of her reach.

The next lurch from the dangler moved Owen down rather than up. It was followed by another before the whole cord that suspended Owen went slack. He tumbled down to Chandra. Her trembling, outstretched arms did not have the strength to stop the Spellseeker's plummet. Instead, the weight of Owen brought both him and Chandra crashing to the floor. Chandra did her best to keep Owen's head from striking the ground a second time but lost track of her goal in the flurry of limbs.

Chaos faded into ragged stillness. Heavy breaths fought against the weight of Owen, who lay splayed atop of Chandra. She did not have the energy to push his body away. Instead, she allowed her head to rest on the cool stone floor as she took solace in Owen's regular breathing. Her partner was alive. The man might have an atrocious headache when he finally awoke, but it beat the alternative without contest.

Adrenaline drained from Chandra as her heat diffused into the floor. Both her arms felt like limp noodles stuck to a cutting board. Her efforts to move them were quickly abandoned. Friction burn still cut into her right arm. The result of her hurried spell to graft a manarail spike onto her staff. A necessary sacrifice, but Chandra did not look forward to an hour of minuscule nails driving into her flesh. It was that same sensation she got if she slept on her arm funny, only the intensity refused to subside.

Light flickered in the corridor. Owen's focus went out long ago when it stopped receiving the Flow through its bearer. The spell Chandra cast continued to burn bright throughout her struggle, but her focus waned. As her concentration dissolved in favor of rest, the last light source in the corridor readied itself to go out.

The sound of wood striking stone ripped the breath from Chandra's chest. Her natural reaction to sit straight up was foiled by the man still draped over her. A quick look toward the ledge confirmed what Chandra knew in the back of her mind, that it was just the spear falling from the dangler.

An odd gurgle filled the void once the spear had settled. It sounded like a slimy rock pulled from a riverbed against its will. Suction that had lasted untold years put to an end. Except there were no rivers nearby. No loose stones to be ripped from sand. Chandra looked up at the ceiling of the corridor just in time to let out a surprised yelp. She moved the bare inches she was afforded by the dead weight on her chest, narrowly avoiding the body of the dangler as it came crashing down to the floor like a thick slab of meat.

There Chandra lay. Stuck under an unconscious Spellseeker, with some ancient horror plopped mere inches from her head. It was with great relief that Chandra noticed the creature was not moving. The closest thing to a blessing Chandra expected she would receive. She closed her eyes, allowed her spell to fade, and let the darkness embrace her with open arms.

15

Ash and Stone

"Scale the wall and you are home."

"That's the last line, then?" Owen panted. The Spellseeker was doubled over with both his hands on his knees. His tired gaze was bolted to the stone floor.

"Sure is," Chandra whispered back.

The rigors of the day had worn on Chandra, but not to the extent that they had affected Owen. It took the better part of an hour for the Spellseeker to regain consciousness after falling from the dangler's grasp. Between the blow to his head, rappelling down the rock face, and the strenuous clambering through uneven tunnels that followed, the man looked to be in sore need of rest.

Chandra, on the other hand, was able to breathe deep and keep an eye on their surroundings. A light shift of the pack on her shoulders was all the relief needed to press onward. She knew better than to take her pack off before a planned rest. The burden would feel twice as heavy once it went back on. Not an ordeal that Chandra wanted to square with so close to her goal.

They stood at the base of a wall, sheer and narrow at the end of a tunnel. It was unlike most walls of the World Below. This one was smooth to the touch. Not a bump to be found anywhere that Chandra allowed her hand to wander. The uniformity was complete and unnatural. Another sign that Chandra and Owen were close to their goal. Chandra knew walls like these must have been tooled by someone, likely hundreds or thousands of years ago. Those who had shaped the wall were long gone. What lay beyond must be a village or town that once housed Those Who Came Before.

Excitement at the prospect of a target almost found pumped new strength into Chandra's limbs. She strode from one side of the wall to the other, dragging her hand along its cool surface. An earnest grin dawned on her face with the coming of the new day. Her two-day trek was near its end.

Chandra sent her light up the side of the wall. Though the smooth nature of the stone was an excellent sign of spoils to come, it also presented a challenge. A uniformly flat surface meant no cracks or crevices into which to stick a hand or foot. No holds meant that an honest climb to the top was out of the question. As the light climbed, it became evident that a jump was out of the question. Chandra guessed the distance between the bottom of the wall and the corridor above to be fifteen feet or more.

At the very top of the wall, protruding from the center of the even ledge, was an object that caught Chandra's attention. It looked like metal the way it gleamed under Chandra's light. Rust was absent from the silvery surface. Chandra wondered if it was newly placed or an alloy used by the previous inhabitants that resisted the rigors of time.

Whatever the case was, the opportunity presented by the rectangular beam of metal turned Chandra's grin into a full-blown smile.

"Hand me one of the ropes in your bag," Chandra whispered to Owen. She thrust out a grasping hand, eager to test the new idea. "I'm out."

"Sure, sure," Owen wheezed back. He shrugged off his pack, delighted to do so, and rooted around the bag for a rope. The search did not take long. Owen produced a rope and held it out to Chandra. "There you are. What's the plan, then?"

"You'll see."

Chandra took the rope by one end and allowed the coil to flop down to the ground. Once every couple of feet, she tied an overhand knot into the rope. Hand and footholds for the ascent to come. Owen, catching on to Chandra's intent, took the other end of the rope without question and began to emulate the process. The rope was fully prepared for a pack-laden climb and was ready for use. All that remained was to get the rope up to the metal beam.

A manarail spike was taken in either of Chandra's hands. She placed them end to end and channeled the Flow at a calm and casual pace. The tingling in her right arm had at last subsided from the day before, and she was not eager to invite the painful sensation for another stay. Instead, she took her time to fuse both spikes. The result was seamless. No mark or deformity was there to suggest the single piece of metal had ever been anything else.

On one end of the doubled spike, Chandra shaped a loop. Its eye was large enough to accommodate the rope on her shoulder with ease. The familiar action took mere moments to perform. Energy, primed and coursing through Chandra, formed the metal as desired in an effortless display.

The other end was a more complicated matter. Chandra had something in mind that she had never thought to do before. With such ideas came the trepidation of potential injury. Her plan remained to shape the metal. Its intended shape, however, brought an ounce of hesitation to her fingertips. The briefest pause before Chandra charged headlong into action.

Chandra placed a finger on the tip of the combined spike. Rather than imagine a bend or twist, she saw a cut in her mind. The spike broke into four equal segments as if cloven by a knife. Chandra focused hard on this intent as she fueled energy into the spike. Under her fingertip, she felt the metal become malleable. She opened her eyes to see that the tip of the spike had bloomed like an iron rose. One rough tip was split into four.

A shift in thought followed the bloom. Chandra willed the metal to bend under her command. As the thought consumed her, Chandra pinched one of the four metallic tips between two fingers and pulled. It was a slow and careful motion. The metal responded to Chandra and curled, peeling away from the other three tips to form into a large hook. Metal creaked and groaned as it was manipulated. Despite the reluctant noise, the iron offered no meaningful resistance.

The rest of the three tips moved with ease after the success of the first. Chandra had the feel of it in both hand and mind. It was as easy to form the bits of metal into hooks as it was to peel a banana. When she had finished the task, Chandra was left with an improvised grappling hook.

"Impressive," Owen remarked. The man had found most of his breath and spoke at a more even clip. "Spearheads, knives, loopholes. And now a whole grappling hook. You have quite the affinity for metal."

"Thank you," Chandra replied. "Took me years, but I can make just about anything I could need at this point. Give me a minute or two and I'll have it done."

"So, the plan is for another climb, it looks like?"

"That's the idea."

Chandra busied herself tying the rope to the hook as she bantered with Owen. It was nice to have another person to chat with down in the dark places of the world, but she did not let it distract her from her purpose. They had not reached their goal. There was work yet to be done and Chandra was not about to wait.

The plan was a solid one. Preparation was flawless. Where Chandra ran into a hitch was the execution. Her first throw of the grappling hook was far too low. Metal came crashing down to the stone floor with an awful clatter that echoed throughout the small chamber. It was as if the cave system laughed at Chandra's feeble attempt to overcome the final obstacle.

Another throw followed the first. Then another. Each failure resulted in that same metallic cackle. Chandra's smile eroded into a blatant sneer. She tried throwing the hook itself. She tried to swing it by the rope and launching the hook at the right moment. Neither brought any greater degree of success. Her throws were either too short or far to the side of her mark. The continued failures piled on Chandra's shoulders until her frustration overflowed into a kick that dashed the hook against the smooth wall.

"Mind if I take a shot?" Owen asked.

Chandra did not speak her reply. Instead, she flung her arms up and slapped them down against her thighs. She pointed to the grappling hook with a noncommittal wave of her hand and stepped away from the wall. The idea had seemed so perfect in her mind. It *was* perfect, she thought. The problem was her. A thought that just made Chandra more furious.

The scuffle of boots and leather on stone told Chandra that Owen had set his pack on the ground. There was a slight but coarse grate of metal as he retrieved the grappling hook. A couple shuffled steps to get into position.

"Huh-yup!"

A quiet snort escaped Chandra. She hadn't expected a circus act when Owen went to throw the hook. It was a comical noise that could conjure no other kind of reaction. Chandra was powerless despite her rage to chuckle a little on the inside.

Can't wait to hear that one again, Chandra thought.

Except she did not.

What Chandra did hear was the distinct sound of metal striking metal. She expected to hear the hook strike the stone soon after, that Owen had merely bashed the hook against the rectangular beam of ancient metal. All she heard was the jubilant thwack of two hands meeting after success. Chandra arched an eyebrow and whirled to face the scene.

Owen stood beneath the beam with the rope in his hands. Not only had the man managed to get the hook over the beam, but the rope had wound in such a way that bound the whole mess in place. A couple tugs on the dangled rope demonstrated a firm attachment. After his first attempt at launching the grappling hook. The smile of success that Owen turned toward Chandra somehow disheartened her further.

"I think we're good to climb," Owen said. He tugged the rope with one hand and pointed up to the ledge with the other.

Chandra rolled her eyes and stalked her way over to the beaming Spellseeker.

"Yeah, I see that," she grumbled. "Well done."

"You want to, uh… to scurry up first?"

"No, no. Please, you first," Chandra replied with a shallow bow. It felt to her like she was surrendering the stage to a lesser performer. Couldn't he have failed at least once? Just the one time so as not to rub her failures further into her nose? "You're doing so well. I'd hate to stop you now."

Owen blinked twice at the thinly veiled bitterness and recoiled. Rather than stop to address the matter, he chose instead to shoulder his pack with a nod and start his way up the rope.

That was rude, Chandra acknowledged. She let some of her discontent slide away on a heavy sigh. *Apologize to him when you get up there. Bad blood over something petty like that would be stupid. Have to keep up the trust, or we won't get out of this in one piece.*

Deep breaths rolled in through Chandra's nose. She held them, allowed them to calm her, then slid each breath out between her lips. This cycle repeated itself until she heard Owen call down.

"All right, you're up," he said. "Steady as she goes."

Chandra raised a hand in affirmation and forced a smile from nothing.

The ascent was no challenge. Traversing bare ropes, whether up or down, was just another skill she had picked up as a Shikaree. There was no way to delve deep into the World Below without cultivating such skills. Chandra made her nimble way up the rope. It was not the same brutish display that Owen had provided. Where the Spellseeker focused more on the use of his arms to wrench himself upward, Chandra wielded all her limbs in concert to glide up the rope. The pack on her back might well have not been there at all.

Near the top, Chandra saw a hand infiltrate her peripheral vision. Owen had taken a knee to help in the last hurdle. Chandra clapped one of her hands into his. If Owen was willing to assist after her childish display below, Chandra was not about to spurn the gesture.

"Thanks," Chandra whispered as Owen hauled her upward. There was a well of physical strength to the man that Chandra had not expected. Her effort played almost no role in seeing her up and over the ledge of the wall. Should could not help but say, "Oh!"

"No problem," Owen grunted in reply.

Though the climb was routine, Chandra's arms still trembled a bit from the exertion. She did her best to shake away the tenderness she felt in her hands. Such a sensation had no business settling among the callouses on her palms and fingers. The feeling made its best attempt to linger as long as possible despite Chandra's wishes. She pushed the throb from the front of her mind and stood herself up. It was time to face what the varmints had called home.

A wall of darkness receded as Chandra raised her light above the ledge. The stone on either side of her was tooled in the same way as the wall below. Surfaces devoid of deviation, unmarred by the passage of time and the trickle of water. Those walls continued a dozen paces until they formed sharp corners and pulled away from the corridor. What light Chandra could produce did not show the distance that the opened walls traveled. The chamber she had stepped into could have been fifty feet wide or a thousand.

What the light was able to catch, at the very rim of its reach, was a road. Not dirt, like the ones in Arnstead above. This road more resembled those of the eastern coast or the megacity that was the Old World. Bricks of stone were woven together to form a straight and sturdy path.

On either side of the road were faint traces of windowed walls. A few steps forward allowed light to pour over the stone buildings. The structures were small, and their construction was immaculate. Each wall had the same smooth texture as the chamber walls that trailed off into the abyss. What could have been razor-sharp corners were rounded down. It gave the angular structures a measure of softness despite their solid composition.

Cautious steps bounced off the faces of ancient homes and stores as Chandra and Owen walked deeper into the settlement. Echoes of a civilization long past, given a voice once more by those who dared to enter. Each building, though made of the same black-gray stone, had its own personality. Some were narrow and tall. Other spanned twice as wide like squat boulders. A few had great pillars out front to support awnings. Windows were carved into all manner of shapes: squares, triangles, stars, crosses. Entryways into the houses showed no signs of traditional doors. No hinges or slots for locks. Just an open passage for whoever might need to enter.

Runic symbols were carved into the archways above open door-ways. Chandra recognized some of the markings from her time with relics. Simple words like *fire* or *hearth*. The word *home* made a sensible appearance. Other runes were either too complex to decipher or com-pletely unfamiliar to Chandra. Her meager knowledge of the language of Those Who Came Before was limited to what she might find on a sword or candlestick. Simple inscriptions. The writing on some of the buildings conveyed complex messages to those who could read them.

Small roads diverged from the main thoroughfare at regular inter-vals. Where they led was a mystery kept by the dark. Street signs were present at each junction, but the names were too complex for Chandra to decipher. They passed several of these smaller roads before Owen voiced a concern.

"So," he whispered, "where do we go, exactly?"

There was no veil to cover the trepidation with which Owen spoke. Chandra turned her head to see that the man was awestruck. He was too distracted by the seemingly endless sprawl of buildings and homes. There was no way to know how far the road they followed might stretch. It was the first time that Chandra regretted not having the map of the World Below at her disposal. The detail was not stellar, but it might have offered more direction than what was available to her now.

Chandra stopped for a moment to ponder their options. A stream of thought wormed its way from her mind and out through her mouth in an absent whisper.

"Well, we've seen a few side roads. Can't tell what they are or where they go. Could leave some chalk signs to mark where we turn, but there's no telling how many turns we might take. Follow this road until we cross a bigger one, maybe?"

"Sure, that sounds fine."

Chandra had not expected a response to her rambling but nodded at the decisive choice all the same. The one thing she remembered about the depiction of the city on the map was that the cache appeared to be in the center. It made sense to follow the largest roads until they brought her and Owen to the city center. Some kind of plaza or market. An open area where items could be stored with easy access for all. The notion made sense in Chandra's head, but another part of her reasoned that the depiction of the cache on the map could have just been a label without navigational merit. Chandra chose to ignore that thought with all her willpower as she started down the road once more.

An hour at a casual pace brought Chandra and Owen to a road that dwarfed the one they had traveled. Two carts could have comfortably fit on the first road and allowed some room for pedestrians. This new road, made with the same stone and techniques, was wider than Chandra's light could reach. It took a fair few steps into the street to determine that it could accommodate half a dozen carts or more.

This new road also showed the first signs of wear that Chandra had spied in the settlement. Faint ruts in the stone showed consistent lanes of traffic. A few paving stones had lost a corner from constant abuse. It got Chandra wondering just how big this place below the earth was. Arnstead had no roads this size. Certainly, none as well crafted. Chandra had never visited the cities of the east coast or Orlena on the southern coast, but she imagined this ancient corner of the world must give them a run for their money.

In the center of the crossroads was a large statue. It climbed over twice Chandra's height and was surrounded by an empty basin. The thought that the thing might have been a fountain long ago flickered through Chandra's mind, only to be replaced by her marvel at the statue itself. Both the figure and stance of the statue were humanoid. The subject of the carving stood on two legs. Around its two arms and shoulders was wrapped an ornate scarf. One hand was raised as if to receive a gift.

It was the head that bothered Chandra. Its face was long and narrow with gaunt cheeks. Four eyes rested where human, katarl, or harn would have two. Two on either side, stacked atop one another. The eyes were sunk far back below the substantial brow like narrow pits of fire. Holes in the side of its head shared the approximate placement of ears, and there was no hair to shroud the unsettling visage. Most unsettling of all, Chandra thought, was the lack of a perceptible mouth. No thin line or suggestion of teeth. No lips or anything of the sort. Just a blank sheet of expressionless skin.

Sleek and slender, a tail protruded from the lower back and wound its way down near the left leg. At the tip of the tail was a vicious barb. The carefree wind and wrap of the tail gave the impression that it might flick to life at any moment. A fifth limb to help inflict additional terrors upon any who might cross the creature.

"It's hard to imagine that there used to be demons on this side of the ocean as well," Owen whispered. The words seemed to be as much to himself as to Chandra, as the man was fixated on the statue.

"Those Who Came Before," Chandra corrected.

This garnered a fraction of Owen's attention. Enough to cause him to turn his head.

"Excuse me?" he asked.

"Those Who Came Before," Chandra said again with emphasis. "The *d* word is bad luck. We have enough to worry about without summoning their kind to rip our souls apart."

"Didn't take you for the superstitious type."

"It's not a superstition. Those Who Came Before are real and—"

"*Were* real," Owen cut in. "Now they're dead and gone. The gods saw to that, back when they were a bit more talkative. So the stories go, at least. Lot of good they did in the end."

"They're still listening," Chandra retorted at the notes of sarcasm in Owen's last remark. "Just because you can't hear them doesn't mean they're not there. And it doesn't mean they can't hear *you*. You should be more respectful."

"So I've been told," Owen replied with a shrug. "Are they all this big, by the way?"

"What, Those Who Came Before?"

Chandra pointed a confused finger at the statue before them. She was by no means an expert on the subject. Her knowledge did not extend beyond the stories from her father and the rare sermon she might be able to attend at the House.

"No." Owen chuckled. "I mean this... place."

Owen spun on his heels and made a sweeping gesture to encompass all that surrounded him. When the slow turn came to a halt, he rested an expectant gaze on Chandra.

"No. I mean, I don't know," Chandra said. Her speech faltered as she sought the right words to share. She made a quick turn of her own to take in what her light could share. "I've never seen a settlement this large before. They're usually small. Like the size of a village or something. Not... not like this."

"Interesting," Owen murmured. He started to shine his personal light up and down the roads that comprised the intersection. The cone reached farther than Chandra's spell, picking up dormant storefronts and imposing homes. "Which way do we go, then?"

An excellent question, Chandra thought. Her gaze followed the cone of light that Owen shone on their surroundings. Though the buildings varied in construction to some degree, there was no clear direction where the structures grew notably taller. Her own experience with these settlements had taught her to look for the largest buildings if she wished to find the center. It was one of the few rules that Those Who Came Before followed without deviation.

Two options presented themselves: either direction of the largest road. The way behind was not the solution. While following the smaller road might lead to one that was even greater than those at the intersection, there was no promise that would be the case. Chandra left the statue at the center of the intersection to examine the street signs at each corner. Her small orb of light bobbed after her as she walked.

Chandra's expectation was not to get the full name of a street. Her goal was to find a word or two she recognized. Words like *square* might suggest a town square or the more blatant option that was *center*.

The first sign bore no fruit. It was an incomprehensible jumble of runes that Chandra had never encountered. Not only were they new, but they bore no similarity to any with which she was familiar. There was no opportunity to puzzle the meaning of a word through the utilization of the base symbols. All Chandra saw when examining the sign was a single word spelled out in her mind: *inadequate.* She clicked her tongue against the back of her teeth and moved on to another sign, only to achieve the same results.

A surge of pride rushed through Chandra's frame when she reached the third sign. The words *square* or *center* were nowhere to be found. What Chandra did recognize was the runic symbol for *core.* It was not so great a leap to Chandra that this could mean the core of the settlement. Perhaps terminology was different for larger settlements, she thought. Why not?

The corner in question connected to the road Chandra and Owen had walked. A boon, Chandra thought, as it would make the creation of a marker a straightforward task. She swung her backpack over her chest and dug through the contents. After a few moments of excited rummaging, Chandra produced a piece of white chalk. Her practiced hand outlined an arrow that bent around the corner and pointed back the way she and Owen had come. The white chalk popped on the black-gray stone. An impossible marker to miss, though she filled the outline in just to be safe.

Chandra took a step back to admire her handiwork as she replaced the chalk into her pack. She felt a touch less lost than she had mere minutes ago. The sensation further enhanced the excitement from reading part of the nearby street sign.

"I've found it," Chandra called toward Owen. She raised a chalk-dusted hand to her mouth to help focus the quiet words. It seemed to do the trick. Though Chandra was too far away to see Owen himself, she saw his cone of light swivel toward her.

"Think I found something too," Owen replied. He flicked his light from Chandra and back to his feet several times. "Come here."

"We don't have time to waste. We've got a battalion to beat, in case you've forgotten."

"Come here," Owen repeated. His voice was stern and rigid as if encased in ice. The request had become a command. This was a new side to the Spellseeker for Chandra. She would not have gone so far as to describe Owen as carefree, but intimidation had not seemed to be a part of his repertoire. Not the type who could have shaken Chandra with two small words.

This newfound chill piqued Chandra's interest as much as it perturbed her. Perhaps more so. She found herself unable to resist the pull to investigate whatever Owen had found. Her muffled steps were the only sound to be heard.

"What is it?" Chandra whispered as she drew near.

Owen stood in front of one of the stone buildings. The light from Chandra's spell revealed a concern-ridden face as she approached. Owen's gaze was locked on the building. On whatever was past the open doorway and crosshatch window slits. He was as rigid as the building itself.

"Look inside," Owen murmured.

Compliance was not a choice. Chandra had to look inside. Curiosity at the sudden change in Owen's demeanor demanded it. Chandra turned from Owen to face whatever was inside, her mind prepared to witness some unknown horror the likes of which she could not imagine.

"It's empty," Chandra said with a frown.

Tension deflated from Chandra like a ragged balloon. Her shoulders sagged, the taut wire that held them in place cut without warning or cause. Tired eyes scanned the inside of the building to ensure that nothing was missed. Chandra took a step forward through the open doorway, her light taking position in the center of the room that she might get a better view.

It was a single room with what looked like a counter at the back wall. Slots carved into the stone walls reminded Chandra of shelves. The building must have been some kind of store. Chandra kicked her way through detritus on the floor and approached the counter. A dilapidated table and chairs were pushed aside as she cut through the center of the room. More shelving space was available along the back wall. Space was hollowed out into another doorway. Chandra slid over the counter to inspect the next room, assuming whatever Owen had seen must have scurried back there.

Emptiness. Vacancy utterly devoid of life. Nothing but a ring of stones in the center of the room and a black patch in the middle. Chandra wheeled an aggravated glare back at Owen.

"There's nobody here," Chandra said. She did not bother to whisper. "Nothing."

"Nobody, yes," Owen replied, "but not nothing. Look at the floor in the main room."

Chandra hung her head. Things had been quiet since their encounter with the dangler. Neither skitter nor scratch to break monotonous footfalls. It was an uncomfortable silence. The encounter with the dangler had set Chandra's mind to wondering what other abominations might be sequestered in these deep places. Deeper than Chandra had ever managed to delve before. That she was being instructed to look at the floor felt like intentional misdirection. Owen could have led with that part, Chandra thought. Could have kept the tension to a minimum. There was enough stress to go around without manufacturing more.

On the floor were rags scattered about the room. Some burlap sacks with bits of cotton and stray feathers protruding through rips and tears.

When Chandra strained her eyes, she saw filthy pieces of clothing in drab, neutral colors.

Clothes?

The thought crested Chandra's mind like the first rays of dawn. Sudden enlightenment struck her with complete understanding. She swiveled around and poked her head into the back room. When she sent her light into the middle of the room, she saw the glint of metal tucked into the corners. There were pots and pans, bits of cutlery, a spit with crusted flecks of meat. Chandra stepped into the middle of the room and ran her finger along the blackened floor in the circle of stones. The substance gave way to her touch, blackening her fingertip.

"This is soot," Chandra whispered. "Someone's been living here."

"Or something," Owen offered. "Maybe the varmints that detailed your map? The neighboring buildings are like this too."

"Seems strange that they'd abandon all this stuff. They're notorious scavengers."

"And they're also skittish if I'm not mistaken."

"You think something scared them off?" Chandra asked.

"Would explain why we haven't seen hide or tail of the pests since we started our trek. Makes sense in my book."

But what scared them all away? Chandra thought. *What scared them so badly they just dropped everything and ran?*

Chandra did not want to say the thought aloud. Fear that mentions of some unseen terror might cause it to materialize took root in Chandra's heart. The tension she unceremoniously discarded now crawled back under her skin, ratcheting her muscles tight as a coiled viper. A hand wandered down to one of her manarail spikes in preparation to strike.

"We should keep moving," Chandra said as she turned back to Owen. She strode through the door, past Owen, and toward the street corner she had chalked.

"Was thinking the same thing," Owen muttered in reply. He followed close at Chandra's heels. His left hand clutched his light focus, while his right hovered near the grip of his caster pistol. Both Owen and Chandra were primed to encounter some veiled horror that lurked just beyond the reach of light. Primed, yet somehow unready.

Imagined eyes peered through each door and every window. Chandra could not shake the feeling of being watched. It quickened her pace. What had been a calm and measured stride throughout the settlement toed the line between walk and run. Her pack groaned and bounced with each step, smacking her back in time with her stride.

A look over her shoulder confirmed for Chandra that Owen was keeping pace. She had been worried, given the apparent exhaustion he showed near the entrance to the settlement. All evidence of fatigue had been cast aside. The man's head remained on a swivel as the pair blazed a trail through the forgotten street, winding and weaving around divots in the road. Owen looked for the same creatures that Chandra swore she could sense. That must be tucked behind walls or secreted into obscure crevices.

Footsteps echoed as feet slapped against the cobbled stone. The faster pace increased noise in kind. It gave Chandra the impression that something was running in tandem with her when the footsteps bounced back. An irrational notion fueled by her search for observers. She hungered for water droplets smacking stone, for the slide of rubble, or the groan of an ancient wall ready to tumble down into the street. Something to break the oppressive, monotonous patter of her own footsteps.

New roads were the best distraction Chandra could find. They were more frequent now, thanks to both the increased pace and the greater road they followed. She zipped her light across intersections to confirm the size of adjoined streets. In those moments of inspection, Owen kept his focus trained ahead to light the way. A silent swap of duties developed as the pair pushed further and further down the road.

Litter in the street grew more common as Chandra and Owen progressed. Bits of cloth that lay dormant in the vast, windless chamber. Light glared off pieces of discarded metal. Further down the road, abandoned carts cobbled together from warped and rotten wood sat unattended. Blankets covered what had been abandoned. Perhaps in the hope that the owners might someday be able to return to claim their belongings.

Chandra was able to smell those owners before she saw them. It was a thick, offensive odor that clung to her nostrils. Putrescent and persistent. It slowed Chandra's pace as she coughed against the assault on her senses.

Bodies came into view not long after the smell asserted its dominant presence. Varmint bodies. One or two at first, with considerable space between. The numbers and density grew as Chandra and Owen pressed forward. Some were missing arms. Others had severed legs. Gashes ran from shoulder to hip, some straight down while some crossed the torso. Ruptured organs and sinew spilled from the unfortunate corpses in a morbid display.

Those that had been cloven in half bothered Chandra the most. Ragged bits of flesh dangled from the separated halves. It looked more like the creatures had been ripped or torn rather than cut. Mouths were frozen in eternal screams. Some had closed their eyes to the horror. Others bore the sight with fragile eyes flung wide, shattered by the sight of their neighbors being rent asunder.

Patches of the road were too thick with corpses to walk. Chandra was forced to tiptoe around small mounds of bodies to find open patches of stone. The occasional misstep resulted in a sickening squelch of flesh underfoot. Compounded with the wretched smell in the air, it was enough to make Chandra gag. She did not have the presence of mind to turn and check on Owen. All Chandra's efforts were focused on pressing forward. Fighting the urge to turn and flee from whatever had caused carnage on such a massive scale.

The smell overpowered Chandra. She had to stop, to do something about the assault on her sanity. Desperate hands swung her backpack off her shoulders. Something in there would be useful. Had to be useful. Probing hands passed over metal and food to clutch the first piece of fabric touched. A spare shirt. It didn't matter that it had already been worn. All that mattered to Chandra was that she could use it to cover her face and stop her nose. The smell of her sweat was sweet by comparison.

"Good idea," Owen gasped.

A glance back at Owen showed him rifle through his pockets to retrieve a handkerchief. It was a bright yellow piece that almost glowed with a light of its own. Floral patterns fell from Owen's nose as he plugged his nostrils.

"Okay?" Chandra asked.

"Yeah," Owen replied as quickly as possible. "Keep moving."

Cotton did little to stifle the putrid stench, but it was better than nothing at all. It allowed Chandra to pay more attention to where she placed her feet. Small gaps between bits and bodies were still present. Chandra hoped to avoid further crunches and squelches underfoot for fear of further upsetting her stomach.

Close attention to the varmint corpses brought a thought to the forefront of Chandra's mind. In a welcome distraction, she realized this was the closest she had ever been to a varmint. Their usual disposition sent them away like cockroaches whenever Chandra flared her light spell. She was well accustomed to the scurry and scratch that accompanied a varmint presence. Teeth gnashed and makeshift weapons rattled, but they were gone as soon as their faces were revealed.

The varmints were not cute. Not by any stretch of the imagination. To Chandra, they looked like twisted and grotesque harn. That, though, kindled a sense of familiarity. Most of these varmints appeared to be unarmed, as well. The creatures must have been going about their daily lives when catastrophe struck in earnest. Chandra was surprised by the mote of pity that manifested for the vicious scavengers.

Of course, this carnage was a blessing for Chandra. She realized that the odds of sneaking through so many varmints would have been slim to none. The need for light would have been a dead giveaway. Though they always fled closer to the surface, Chandra imagined that trickery and light would not have dissuaded so many varmints in the heart of their den. She and Owen would have been overrun if they tried to battle their way to the cache.

Such thoughts further seeded wonder at what might have caused so many varmints to flee in abject terror. What could have cloven through so many bodies? What monster could slay with such ferocious speed that bodies lay piled atop one another? Was it a single entity? An army of some unknown monstrosities?

"Do you think the Baylocke Battalion beat us here? Did this?" Chandra found herself asking aloud.

"Doubtful," Owen replied. "I checked the Shikaree registry at the Bureau of Arcane before we left. Despite the name, there's only ten or so of them. Well, that are registered, anyway. Can't imagine a small retinue like that doing this much damage without military-grade focuses and some serious spellcraft. And even then—"

"Got it," Chandra cut in with a wave of her hand. "Wish it could have been them. Then at least we'd know what we're up against."

Silence overtook the pair once more. The less noise they made in the face of an unknown terror, the better.

The road widened as Chandra and Owen continued their way. It was a subtle change. Barely noticeable at first, it might have gone unseen altogether if Chandra had not continued to send her light out to the mouth of side streets. She felt the distance to the side streets increase. Her will had to push the orb of light further and further to illuminate street corners and their signs.

As the street widened, the number of bodies seemed to decrease. Chandra first attributed this to there being more road onto which the bodies could fall. There was less likelihood that the varmints might pile atop one another. That notion was pushed aside when the number of bodies had reduced so drastically that the street almost appeared clean. Sacks of belongings and improvised weapons littered the ground, but there were no more corpses to speak of. The wretched smell had even begun to clear. Enough so that Chandra felt comfortable removing the soiled shirt that covered her face.

There were no bodies to be found by the time the road made a sharp expansion on either side. The sides of the street rounded and peeled away from the center. Cobblestones no longer followed the same pattern, changing from a uniform path into a circular torrent. Swirls of stone meandered as far as Chandra's light could reach. The cone of light from Owen's focus revealed nothing more.

Chandra pierced the new terrain with a sure step and pressed forward. The change suggested some kind of plaza, though Chandra could not be sure without walking the perimeter. She followed her gut. It *felt* like she had reached the core.

Continued steps brought Chandra to another statue in what she assumed was the middle of the plaza. The figure was another of Those Who Came Before. It bore the notable tail and a face that did not seem quite right. The face was framed by what looked like a helmet this time. Intricate plate armor covered the torso. Individually carved chain links hung from the subject's arms and waist. A glorious cape, stitched with all manner of unrecognizable runes, flowed in a magnificent wind that did not exist.

Battledress was not the only difference between this statue and the one Chandra had encountered earlier. This one was colossal. It towered over the buildings that had led to it. There was no fountain at the feet of this statue. The space required to encircle the figure's spread feet would have been enormous.

Approaching one of the feet, Chandra noticed the ground around it twinkled. It was like the cobblestones on which the statue had been erected were little stars in a vast sea of black. Except the glimmer did not come from stones. The glint was metallic. Something surrounded the foot of the statue and the space underneath it.

Swords and axes. Mirrors. Calipers and hammers. Rings slotted with memory-glass stones that cast colorful refractions over the bleak surface. Chandra saw wooden tools as she drew closer. Some fitted with memory glass while others bore the runes of Those Who Came Before. There were objects Chandra could not even begin to guess the purpose of. All of this and more lay scattered about and between the feet of the statue. Breath abandoned Chandra as she realized where she stood.

"This is it," Chandra whispered. She whipped around to look at Owen, who also appeared spellbound by the discovery. "This is the cache. We found it!"

"So we did," Owen replied with the hint of a smirk.

Elation quelled a measure of the terror spawned by the carnage at their backs. Both Chandra and Owen knelt near the statue and began to examine the objects that lay on the cobblestones.

Chandra hefted a metal bracelet. The thing was large. Large enough to accommodate one of Those Who Came Before. Chandra would have had to wear it just below her shoulder to stand a chance at keeping it on. It was some kind of silver or white gold, Chandra guessed. She was no expert on the matter. What she could do was decipher a handful of the runes etched into the exterior. The words *speed* and *water* jumped out to her, among others. Possibilities for what the relic might be used began to filter into Chandra's thoughts.

Next to where the bracelet had rested was a single earring. This one appeared to be made of gold as well, but it was of Federation make. The memory-glass jewel facetted into the piece of jewelry served as a telltale sign. Chandra had no way of knowing what the focus might do without channeling the Flow through the device. Her curiosity was torn between testing the earring and further investigation of all the other finds that were strewn about.

The more Chandra moved her light, the more treasures she found. She placed a hand on the giant statue and traced a line with her fingers as she circled the stone foot. Careful steps landed between swords and hiked over shields. Each piece called to Chandra. The trove was a chorus of whispers that begged to be explored.

"Do you think they worshipped it?" Owen called out.

It took a moment for the words to penetrate the film of excitement that wrapped around Chandra's head. She had forgotten that another person was with her.

"Sorry?" Chandra replied. She had heard the words, but not listened. Their meaning was lost on her and necessitated repetition. Chandra turned her head to see that Owen stood near the other foot of the statue. He shone his light up the leg of the figure and craned his neck to follow the brilliant cone.

"The varmints. Do you think they worshipped the demon?"

"The One Who Came Before," Chandra corrected.

"Right, sure." Owen sounded just as distracted as Chandra, though she could not begin to guess what among the plethora of sights had captured the Spellseeker's imagination. "Would explain why they've been stealing so many focuses. To put them together with demonic relics and present them as offerings. I wonder if they think this demon is some kind of god?"

"One Who Came Before," Chandra snapped.

"Right, right," came the distant concession from Owen. An abrupt shake of his head seemed to pull Owen back from wherever his mind had wandered. "Anyways… what's the plan, Shikaree? There's way too much here for us to take in one go."

Chandra did not require a pause to craft her answer. It rested at the front of her mind and flew down to the tip of her tongue in haste.

"We jam as much into our packs as we can, stash it above ground, and then come back for more. The faster we move, the more trips we can make. We'll get this place emptied out before the Baylocke folks ever set foot down here if we're lucky."

"That's going to be a rough operation for just the two of us," Owen sighed.

"Well, if you don't have an army in your pocket or a better idea, better start picking. I'll grab relics. You concentrate on gathering focuses. We'll take care of ourselves and dip out together once we're stuffed."

"Sure, I guess—wait. What was that?" Owen asked. He flicked his light toward the edge of the plaza, the opposite side from which they had entered. "I think I heard something."

All movement came to an abrupt halt. Chandra locked herself in place and strained her ears against the quiet of the settlement, doing her best not to pollute the silence. Even breath ceased as Chandra focused her attention on sounds she could not hear. There was nothing. No subtle scrape or flap of cloth. No boots on stone or the swish of varmint tails as they sized up their prey. There was nothing but a tenuous silence that weighed on Chandra's nerves.

"You're hearing things," Chandra dismissed offhandedly, agitated that valuable time was squandered. "There's nothing out the—"

"Shh!" Owen commanded. He raised a single finger to point at Chandra in emphasis of his demand for continued silence. His light scoured the edge of the plaza like a watchman in the night.

Then Chandra heard a sound.

Hollow. Like a canoe dragged down a gravel road. It bore a rhythmic cadence that suggested no arbitrary sound caused by the slip of a stone or the collapse of an ancient structure. Whatever made the noise sounded large. It projected its grating rattle across the whole of the street from which it originated. With each subsequent shuffle over the stone road, the noise grew in volume. Something approached the plaza from deep within the gloom.

Another sound emerged amid the scrape and scratch of stone. This sound was familiar. A wet crunch turned Chandra's stomach when it reached her ears. The same sound that assaulted Chandra when she misstepped on one of the varmint corpses scattered about the road at her back.

A figure emerged into Owen's cone of light as the noises became unbearable. To Chandra, it looked like the head of a katarl. It bore the same shape and dimensions. Fine hairs on its cheek swayed as the head bobbed from side to side. Jet black fur glistened in the hollow light. Though the head had the typical snout of a larger katarl, a Bangeli or a Zumbatran, its mouth was closed fast and did not move.

Comfortable similarity ended at the basic construction of the face. A normal katarl had two eyes, front-facing and stuck into their head. The creature that presented itself now had far more than two eyes. Not all of them were attached to its head. A torso as black as the head forced its way into the light and revealed a dozen or more catlike eyes that flickered in response to Owen's focus. They moved independently of one another. Some scanned the great statue as they trembled amidst the creature's rippling muscles. Others took in the plaza.

One single eye fixed onto Chandra.

An immediate chill crackled through Chandra's body that she felt bite into her bones. The eye seemed to look into both of Chandra's at the same time. Though she was locked in place by the piercing gaze, Chandra could feel herself shrink. She felt so very small, so vulnerable as the rest of the creature slid into view.

Scrapes and scratches made sense when the creature was fully visible. The katarl-like torso was attached to a massive, chitinous body that slithered and slunk. Some horrific cross between the movements of a snake and the armor of a lobster. Its reflective, gray-black surface wound and coiled as the creature made its way closer and closer to the statue. Six arms, three on either side, protruded from near where the torso connected to the extensive tail. Four of the spindly, meandering arms reached out to clutch at the air with their scythe-like fingers. The remaining two hands held the corpse of a varmint. Those two hands pushed the corpse against the abdomen of the torso. The stomach split into a vertical mouth that housed rows of jagged teeth, which ripped a chunk off the varmint and began to chew.

Run!

Chandra could not run.

Run, you idiot!

Legs turned to lead. Fingernails dug into the palms of fists clenched in terror. Chandra had to fight her lungs to accept the short breaths she could manage. It felt as if her heart was tearing its way through her chest so that it might fall to the floor and find its way home. A visceral scream charged out into the darkness when she felt a hand on her shoulder.

"Don't look into its eyes!" Owen shouted into Chandra's ear. "Don't look. Just run!"

Chandra felt her body be forcibly turned. Her head remained locked onto the monolithic horror until it became physically impossible to do so. It felt wrong to turn her back. Like she was leaving herself vulnerable to attack by those wretched hands of scythes. She tried to snap her head back around to see the creature. Owen would not let her. He grabbed Chandra by the chin and rooted her head in place.

"It wants you to look, Chandra. Don't look!" Owen howled into Chandra's face. He spoke as if to a child frozen in a burning building. The intensity rattled Chandra somewhat from her fixation on the creature at her back. "Get to a building and hide. Douse your light. I'll lead this thing away and meet you where we entered the city."

"That's insane!" Chandra protested. "What are you going to—"

"I said move, soldier!"

With that, Owen released Chandra's chin, took hold of her shoulders, and shoved her away from the statue. Chandra struggled to maintain her balance as she stumbled away from the Spellseeker. She watched Owen draw the caster pistol from his hip and point it at the lumbering behemoth. He offered one final shout before firing a volley of metal spikes at the creature.

"Run!"

The spikes bounced and splintered off the creature's solid body with a sound like hammers pummeling an anvil. Not a single missile bit into the target. Every one clattered to the stone road and disappeared under the winding tail of the approaching monstrosity. Though it could not have been harmed by the assault, the sheer audacity of the attempt forced a wail from the creature in response. A noise like tortured cries mixed with sour church bells flooded the plaza and tainted the air.

Chandra dared not look back. If she did, Chandra knew she would not be able to look away. Her legs felt lighter now that her attention was no longer fixed on the creature. They moved, hesitantly at first, toward the edge of the plaza. She felt like a manarail engine. A slow crawl of a start that built speed with each unsure step.

More spikes smashed into the impervious frame of the creature as Chandra threw herself through a square window and crashed down onto a dilapidated wooden table. Pain sheered through her spine as she met the cold, stone floor shoulder first. Chandra did not remain on the ground for long. She doused her light spell and pulled herself up to the window she had jumped through. Owen's light had already begun to fade as he lured the beast away down a different street.

Tears of rage formed a boiling mist in Chandra's eyes. A primal cry from the depths of her soul spewed forth in a mix of fear and hate.

"Don't die!"

16

A Measure of Faith

Darkness settled over the ancient plaza well before silence. The horrid scratch and scrape of shell across stone persisted. A constant reminder of the ragged being that had so enthralled Chandra moments before. Though she wanted to move, to flee the plaza, the constant rasp of movement kept her legs locked firm. Not until the only sound on the frozen air of the city was the distant, pained moan of the monster did Chandra allow herself to move.

Light came first. Still reeling from the terror, it took more time to summon her spell than Chandra would have cared to admit. It was difficult to pull a fraction of her mind away from the visual of what she had been forced to witness. The light was unsteady and flickered like a firefly in twilit gloom.

Cautious first steps pulled Chandra from the stone structure in which she had taken refuge. Nervous hands patted down her person to ensure her pack and all her tools were in place. Another excuse to keep Chandra from venturing out into the plaza. If she had been of sound mind, Chandra would have strutted her way back to the monolithic statue of the One Who Came Before and gathered as much loot as she could cram in her pack. This was not the case. That Chandra could still hear the monster at all meant the creature was far too near to waste time. She kept herself to the edge of the plaza, following homes and storefronts back to the street from which she had come.

Chandra kept herself to the generous sidewalks. No longer did she feel comfortable enough to wander in the middle of the street. There was a sense of security in keeping one hand on the stone buildings she passed. The knowledge that Chandra did not walk in the middle of a black expanse that carried on forever in all directions, though each alley she passed heightened her unease. Fretful imaginings of what else lurked just out of reach of her light plagued each hurried crossing.

Such thoughts gnawed at Chandra until the putrid smell of dead varmints returned to assault her nostrils. Chandra once again pulled a dirty shirt from her bag and jammed it against her nose. The stench was somehow thicker on the second passing. Chandra knew what had killed the creatures splayed over the stone road. She had seen scythe-like hands that ripped and sliced through varmints' furry torsos. That cut legs from hips and arms from shoulders. Knowing what painted the street with gore forced the horror to burrow deep. Chandra could not help but wretch into an open alleyway.

Lightheaded, Chandra sent her light forward to illuminate the dense swath of bodies. To be stuck amidst the mire of death was not an enticing prospect. It had been a rough walk before Chandra was scared out of her wits with the taste of vomit in her mouth. Now? Chandra was not sure how she was going to make it.

Another soul-piercing wail tore through the quiet air to invade Chandra's ears. At least, she thought she heard another cry. It was so faint that she could not be sure if she had genuinely heard the sound or just imagined it.

Something snapped in that moment of fetid isolation. Chandra pulled her light back and took off at a run through the field of death. She did not pay attention to where her feet landed. Some steps found the road, while others met with the crunch of bone. Flesh squelched under heel. Chandra vaulted over bodies that had fallen atop one another. It didn't matter what she saw or smelled. All that mattered was getting to the other side as fast as possible.

A tail rolled under Chandra's foot and sent her tumbling down to the street. Hands desperate to break the fall abandoned the shirt that masked her face. Her fingers were met with wet fur as Chandra failed to keep herself from rolling over the nearest shredded remains. Reflex demanded that she pull away. Primal desire to put all of this behind her forced Chandra's hands deeper into the mess, to push herself off the ground and back up to her feet. Her pant legs, damp with varmint viscera, slapped at her calves as Chandra resumed her flight.

Death. Chandra was covered in it. She could feel it soak through her pants and drip from her fingers. The faint cries of the monstrous creature somewhere out in the city brought the sound of death back to Chandra's ears. Death surrounded her. It clotted her eyes and clambered with clammy hands up her nose. There was no escape. No matter how fast Chandra pushed herself, death hung about her shoulders and crawled into her mouth. A bit and bridle that suffocated without relent.

Hollow words dribbled out between ragged breaths of tainted air. Chandra was not sure what she said, only that she spoke. All sense of control abandoned her as she cut through the marsh of limbs and entrails. What remained was fear in its purest form. A fear that quelled reason and time. Forward was all that Chandra knew.

Chandra followed the momentum of her body as it tilted forward. To slow down meant to fall to the ground in heap. Her knees called out for her to stop. They trembled and quaked with each step. Chandra's body cried out in pain, screaming for her to slow the untenable pace. Visions of reaping scythes rending through flesh and bone forced her onward. She could feel the horrid appendages at her back. Knew that they must be mere inches behind her, clawing and grasping for her unguarded flesh.

It was not until Chandra reached the white chalk marker that she allowed her body to rest. Knees crashed sharply into unflinching stone and sent a painful shiver up through her already burning thighs. The bulk of her weight was caught on her hands. Cool rock drank the heat that radiated from Chandra's trembling body. It felt like splinters lined the insides of her lungs.

Pained though she was, Chandra did not allow herself to linger for long. Legs screamed for rest as she pushed herself up and away from the inviting slabs of stone. Arms refused to pump any longer. The rest of Chandra's trek back to her rope and grappling hook was made in a haggard stumble. Each moment felt like it might end with her aching frame crashing to the ground. Step after step became a tiresome war fought against her body, but Chandra would not relent. Not until she had reached the relative safety of a sharp drop into a narrow corridor.

Chandra's scrambled mind did not think to use her harness to descend. It was a short drop, Chandra told herself. Sheer, but short. She could handle the climb down with her arms alone. Numb hands gripped the rope like a lifeline at sea. Chandra certainly felt as if she had been cast adrift in an inky-black ocean of madness. Her grip held, hand under hand, until she neared the bottom. Chandra did not feel her hands release the rope. All she felt was a short fall followed by a hard thump.

The pack ate most of the impact. It kept Chandra's head high enough off the stone floor to avoid a cracked skull, though the whiplash made her regret life itself. Another instrument of pain to join the unharmonious symphony her body had become. Chandra uttered no cries of pain. She did not swear. After the surprised grunt when she contacted the ground, she lay in silence. Arms hung limp from her raised torso. The muscles in her legs contracted almost in rhythm with her erratic heartbeat. Light flickered for a time before finally sputtering out into a blanket of darkness. Chandra allowed her eyes to close as she wrangled her wild breathing. It was a short battle that she gave up after little effort. Rather than fight, Chandra allowed her body to recover on its own. It was like her whole being worked toward a single harmonious breath.

Chandra felt her fists unclench. Felt her toes uncurl. Breaths slowed and adopted a regular pattern. The sound of her heart receded from her ears. Relaxation came along at its own measured pace until it coated Chandra like a soothing balm. She slipped her arms out from her pack straps and flopped over onto the stone floor. Once more she felt excess heat being sucked out of her body. This time Chandra was able to relish the sensation. A reward for a mad dash run through a tangible rung of the hells.

Something much like sleep came over Chandra. Muscular tension broke down and crumbled. A small puddle of drool formed underneath her cheek. Her lungs had calmed enough to allow Chandra to breathe through her nose again rather than suck down massive gulps of air. She felt the world begin to slip away in her moment of comfort.

Chandra was unsure how much time had passed when she heard a gentle, metallic tinkle. The sound of the grappling hook jostling against the metal beam from which it hung. It sounded a world away to Chandra's exhausted ears. A few moments passed while her tattered brain processed the noise. When Chandra realized the noise meant movement above, she flipped over and bolted upright. The sudden action reminded Chandra just how sore her entire body was. A few simple motions made her muscles groan and her joints creak.

There was a desire for light. Chandra dialed in on the thought and tapped into the Flow, only to find that her body was unwilling to receive the energy. The simple burden was too much for her to bear in her exhaustion. Instead, Chandra was forced to see by a cone of light that bobbed every which way in the dark. It highlighted the metal beam, then the rope down, then one of the nearby walls. The light inched its way down the rope amid a series of grunts and swears. A jerking, uneven motion that started and stopped several times before reaching the bottom of the rope.

Once the light reached the bottom, it shone around the floor and walls. There was a grating sound. Like metal on bone or teeth. Then the light made its way across the floor until it found Chandra, who sat blinking against the brilliant glare forced upon her.

"Oh, thank the gods, you're alive," Owen panted, still obscured within darkness. He sounded just as exhausted as Chandra felt. Maybe more so. It was difficult for Chandra to tell.

"Same," Chandra sighed in reply. "All in one piece?"

"Mostly."

"Mostly?" Chandra felt her ears prick up at the odd choice of word. "Here, give me your light."

Chandra held out her hand. There was a brief pause, which elicited a beckoning motion from Chandra's fingers. Something like she might do to invite a timid child. Her insistence won out. The light bobbed closer to Chandra until she felt a metal cylinder placed in her hand. She manipulated the focus to point toward Owen with stiff fingers. Chandra felt her eyes widen with a new terror.

"Hyperios help me," Chandra gasped. "That's a lot of blood."

"It's fine, really. Not that deep," Owen reassured. "I just let the thing get a little too close for a moment, and he took a chunk. I'm fine."

Owen flexed his left arm and displayed a full range of motion as a sign of reassurance. Chandra was not convinced.

The sleeve over Owen's left arm was damp from the cuff to just above the elbow. Scarlet lines traced the back of his hand and dripped, dripped, dripped from the tips of his middle and index fingers. The injury itself was obscured by the shifting sleeve, but the cloth had a jagged tear along the upper arm that wrapped almost halfway around the arm. Weight from the blood-soaked cotton caused the whole sleeve to sag. Threads popped with each subtle movement of the arm.

"Come here," Chandra demanded, already rummaging around in her bag for the scant medical supplies she had. "Help me fix you."

"It's really not that bad, we just need to wrap it. Tie a knot over the cut."

"Uh-huh."

Chandra set a clean bandage on top of her pack and reached out for Owen's arm. He hefted the limb up into Chandra's grasp. The wound was still obscured by the sleeve. Bending and twisting the arm made the cut no more visible, though Chandra did hear Owen suck air through his teeth with each motion.

"All right, this needs to go," Chandra said. She took the cuff of Owen's left sleeve in one hand and braced his shoulder with the other. A quick jerk ended the sleeve's tenuous hold on life. Threads popped and the blood-soaked fabric hit the floor with a hefty squish.

"Ah, I really liked this shirt," Owen said through a wince and a chuckle.

"Yeah, well, now I can see the thing," Chandra muttered.

Without the sleeve in the way, Chandra was able to see the cut. It was smaller than the tear in the shirt sleeve had suggested. Blood did not spurt or gush from the injury. The red liquid just oozed out at a regular interval in consistently small amounts. Must have caught just the end of one of those nasty fingers, Chandra thought. The situation could have been much worse. Owen could have come toppling down the ledge minus an arm and most of his blood. What Chandra saw before her was manageable.

The fresh bandage crinkled as Chandra unrolled it for the first time. There was some give to the fabric. Enough to make the small bandage go a long way. Owen held his arm up and away from his torso to make the process as easy for Chandra as possible, a gesture she appreciated. She wasn't accustomed to patching up wounds. Rubbing some soap on Najran or Omala's scraped knee was one thing. An arm slick with blood from a wound caused by a walking nightmare? A whole different and unnerving process. Chandra could not tell if the tremor in her hands was from her previous exertions or the amount of blood on Owen's arm.

Whatever the case, the job needed to be done. Owen was not about to wrap his damaged arm with his one good one. Chandra bit down on the light focus to maintain vision and placed the bandage on Owen's cut skin with both hands. Immediately, she felt the blood ooze through the bandage and soak into her thumbs. A thought that Chandra shouldered past as she began to wrap the bandage around and around Owen's arm. The more times she wrapped the bandage, the less blood she felt under her fingers.

"Yeah, perfect," Owen said as Chandra neared the end of the bandage. "Now tie a knot over the wound. Helps keep pressure on the cut. Make it bleed less."

"So," Chandra began, cinching the bandage down onto the cut, "do you know what that thing was? I've never seen anything like it before."

"Ashling," Owen said without hesitation. "At least, I think that's what it is."

"You're worse than my sister," Chandra said and rolled her eyes. "Talking fairytale nonsense. Ashlings are stories to keep kids in bed at night."

"I can think of a Keeper that would disagree with you," Owen said. Levity returned to his voice now that he no longer felt the need to reassure Chandra. The tone stood at odds with his words. "The second one of these I've seen. They're not exactly the same, but there's enough overlap that I'm sure. Had to be an ashling."

"Second one, huh?" Chandra murmured. She was not convinced, but Chandra decided to entertain the suggestion regardless. "That how you knew about the eyes?"

"Yeah," Owen nodded. "Got me the first time too. Sucked me right in. Made it feel like the world was collapsing around me, and that there was nothing I could do to stop it."

"Sounds right," Chandra conceded. "How'd you deal with it? The first one, I mean. Didn't seem like the spikes from your pistol bothered it much."

"I didn't."

"What?" Chandra snapped back with a furrowed brow.

"I didn't deal with the first one. A Keeper I was with pulled me out of the trance and sent me away. Dealt with the thing on his own."

"So, you don't know how to deal with one of these... things? You just wrangled it off into the dark without a plan in mind?"

"Well," Owen grunted as he shifted into a more comfortable position, "if one of us had to die, it was going to be me. Just because I'm not wearing the whole uniform doesn't make me any less of a Spellseeker."

Chandra was about to protest but found the words caught in her throat. An image of her mother flickered through her mind. A stalwart figure that cut a proud silhouette before the terrors of the world. The pillar of support for her family. A Spellseeker. Though he was hunched over and covered in blood, Chandra saw a sliver of her mother in Owen. Defiance made manifest. She could not bring herself to berate that.

"Thank you for the distraction," Chandra said.

Medical treatment completed, she removed the light focus from between her teeth and handed it back to Owen. He gave the device an understandable wipe or two on his remaining sleeve and set it down between himself and Chandra. The light climbed upward and lit a portion of each of their faces. Enough illumination to carry out a civilized conversation.

"Well," Chandra began, "that thing— whatever it is— isn't going to let us just pick up focuses and relics at our leisure. Do we wait for it to wander off and find more food, then strike while it's away? If you're in a daring mood, you could try and lead it away again and I could grab two packs' worth of treasure at a time. Get the goods back here and out of the way."

"However delightful that sounds, I don't think its sustainable," Owen said through a cough. He patted his chest with a fist and cleared his throat. "I got lucky once. Would rather not test that luck again."

"Yeah, that's fair. I guess we're in for the hiding option, then."

"No, I don't think so."

"What?" Chandra asked in surprise. "You don't mean... we're not going to just leave this stuff here. Not while it's so close. My family *needs* this find, or we'll be homeless before the year is out."

"I don't want to abandon the mission, no," Owen replied with the shake of a hand. His head bobbed from side to side as he wrestled with some notion or other. "No... this thing needs to be dealt with."

"Dealt with? You mean like... kill it?" Chandra's incredulity grew with each subsequent question. "The monster that just deflected the spikes from your pistol, spikes that pierced *solid stone*, like it was nothing? You want to *kill* that?"

"It can't be left alone. The first ashling I encountered was on the surface, crawled out from the World Below. It was in a secluded forest and had little that it could damage. This one, though? Deep below Arnstead? If that thing got a whim to creep out of this city and up to the town above… well, I don't really want to picture it. I have a responsibility to the people of Arnstead. To keep the peace."

"I think an ashling is maybe outside your jurisdiction, don't you think? Let a Keeper deal with the monster. It's what they do. Fight monsters."

"Yeah, maybe," Owen mumbled. "We'd be lucky to get anyone to listen if I'm involved. The House doesn't much care for Spellseekers. Too much taint from the Flow and all that nonsense."

"Well, we won't know if we don't ask, will we?" Chandra offered with a meager smile.

Owen was not wrong. She had been young, but Chandra remembered the struggle involved just to get her mother into the House for prayer. It had just been heated words and aggravated insults at the time. Prayers of forgiveness for tapping into the Flow were just a matter of course. Not until she was older did the interaction between Spellseeker and the House click for Chandra. The bitter disdain the House held for those who steeped themselves in the goddess Damarae's gift. The lost goddess of monsters. Power so likened to that wielded by Those Who Came Before.

All of that was irrelevant. Chandra saw Owen's point. Whatever that creature was, it could pose a threat to the town above. To innocent people like Robin and her store, or gentle Kamotho and his bakery. The savvy yet fair people of the Arnstead markets to which she sold her family's produce. More people than she could ever hope to count stood to benefit from erasing this creature's existence. A sense of obligation rose within Chandra. She had sworn no oath or pledge, but she lived and drew breath. That was enough. She had to help.

Besides, Chandra had a friend in the House who might be able to help. A little light that might be able to bear some knowledge in this time of need.

* * *

A full day was required to evacuate from the World Below. Half the time it had taken to reach the city of Those Who Came Before.

Chandra attributed the speed to her newly acquired knowledge of the proper path. They exited the World Below through the memory-glass quarry with half the day left to burn, though it felt as if it were time to go to bed. The lack of sun for a full three days had distorted Chandra's internal clock and left her body in a state of confusion.

Though she was quite tired, Chandra seized the time she had been afforded for the blessing that it was. She sent Owen back to his apartment to clean up and repack his things. Maybe switch out his tattered shirt for some new ones. The plan was to meet back at the House at sunset. Chandra would use the window of time to learn all she could about ashlings and Keepers and anything else without the clouded presence of a Spellseeker in the House.

First, Chandra visited a bathhouse in Eaststead. She had changed her clothes, but still felt the grime and gore of dead varmints caked into her skin. A sensation she was eager to be rid of before engaging in conversation. The quick stop also gave Chandra the chance to cleanse her soiled clothes. Both the shirt and pants that had rolled in the field of death were a lost cause, but Chandra felt compelled to wash what remained as best as she could. Clean clothes went a long way to settling nerves that remained taut. Hot water and soap on her beleaguered frame extracted morsels of primal fear embedded in her muscles. A chance to release her hair from a tightly knotted bun and allow it to tumble over her back and shoulders into the water. She chose not to notice the concern on her bath mates' faces when she turned the water into a murky red-brown cloud.

Chandra made for the House after she had soaked up enough peace to approach a sense of comfort. Wet shirts and pants hung from her pack as she walked and caught the warm rays of the afternoon sun. Her clothes were almost dry by the time Chandra made it to the white steps of the House. As always, the doors were wide open and ready to receive any who sought the guidance of the gods. Chandra ascended the steps with a sense of purpose greater than she had ever known. A pair of cardinals flitted up from the vacant stairway as she passed.

The entry hall was populated by a handful of well-wishers. Coins clinked and clattered into metal basins as they spoke quick prayers and turned to exit the House. Words of haste spoken by those who felt their time could be spent elsewhere, and that money would make up for a lack of sincere intent. Portraits of the gods watched in their typical silence.

Members of the clergy glided about the House on their leather sandals. Acolytes followed at the heels of priests or made themselves busy with menial tasks such as scrubbing the marble floors or polishing pews. A trio of acolytes worked in tandem, along with a lift and pullies, to wipe tall, stained-glass windows clean. There seemed to be no corner or crevice that was spared the intrusive red-orange dust of Arnstead. The acolytes' battle was both endless and fruitless, but they carried on nonetheless.

Chandra approached the nearest acolyte, a young Nirdac katarl busy scraping scuff marks from the floor, and gave the girl a tap on the shoulder.

"Excuse me," Chandra said with all the politeness she had at her command. Perhaps too much courtesy. The katarl did not make any sign that she had heard Chandra or felt the tap. Chandra raised her voice and gave the acolyte's robes a gentle tug. "Excuse me, miss?"

"Hmm?" The katarl swiveled her head in a slow, deliberate manner. Her eyes widened. "Oh, hello there! Sorry. I was lost in my work. How can I help you?"

Though the acolyte's attention had been redirected, she still scraped away at the floor. The katarl displayed remarkable accuracy in her efforts despite not being able to see her work. Chandra blinked twice at the impressive display.

"Yes… I was hoping you might know if Ryleah is around? I'd like to see her if she's not busy."

"Oh, the half-kin?" the acolyte asked as she cocked her head. The motion was followed by a series of nods toward the pews ahead. "She's out on the benches. A boy fell from a barn and snapped his arm, so she's giving him the fix. Imagine she's about finished by now."

"Excellent," Chandra beamed. "Thank you!"

"Oh, not at all. Gods bless you."

"And you, as well."

Chandra straightened herself up and peered out over the rows of pews that covered the floor of the House. Sure enough, she saw a pair of pointed ears poking out through familiar white hair. Chandra wondered why she had even bothered to ask for Ryleah's whereabouts. To pick the girl from a Federation crowd was easier than spying a black sheep amongst a snow-white flock. It did not matter that Ryleah was half the House away from Chandra. There was no mistaking the distinctive girl.

The wine-colored carpet was free of traffic. Chandra was able to stroll toward her friend with ease. As Chandra approached, she saw the top of a scruffy head next to Ryleah. The boy that the acolyte had mentioned. He sat between Ryleah and another human who twiddled loose ends of an abused straw hat. Must be the boy's father or some-thing similar, Chandra assumed. The way the man craned over Ryleah's work suggested he was intent on scouring every detail of the process. A faint glow was discernable if Chandra squinted. It arose from the space between Ryleah and the boy.

Must still be working, Chandra thought. Rather than interrupt the process to announce her presence, Chandra took a seat two pews behind Ryleah and waited for the minor miracle to be completed. She thought it best not to stick her foot into the middle of a god's work. There was plenty of time before sunset.

Chandra allowed her attention to wander up the walls of the House and fall onto one of the stained-glass windows. She was familiar with the story that it told. Ibattua and his legendary voyage across the open ocean. The first person from the Federation to set foot on the New World after months of exploration over unforgiving waters. A cham-pion of Sisir who allowed the overcrowded islands of the Old World to bleed its burgeoning populace onto new shores.

The window was dominated by various shades of blue. Cerulean waters rolled beneath an azure sky. High above, garbed in a violet shroud of stars, was the goddess Sisir. A delicate hand emerged from the celestial veil to point west. Directions followed by Ibattua and his noble crew. The dark wood of the boat matched the Zumbatran complexion of its master as it cut through white waves and red-green serpents. Determination exuded from the great explorer's stance over the bow of his ship. Danger birthed a wily smile on his handsome face.

Ibattua and his stalwart crew always managed to impart their defiant smile upon Chandra. A group of men and women from all the Federation races working together in a time of turmoil. Trusted hands that stood side by side in the face of great unknowns. The world had been laid bare by their shared bravery and sheer force of will.

I need your strength, Ibattua, Chandra thought to herself as she relished the dazzle of sunlit colors. *Walk with me into the depths of the world as Sisir flew with you over the open sea. Guide my hands as she guided your sail. Help me face the terrors of the world as you did with your crew. Please.*

Without realizing it, Chandra had formed her hands into the sign of prayer. Her fingers knit together with open palms facing the high ceiling. Old habits. Chandra smirked at her tendencies and closed her eyes as she inhaled a deep breath.

Ibattua. Sisir. Mother... watch over me as I carve my story into the stony heart of this world.

The sound of bodies shuffling pulled Chandra from her prayers. Both the young boy and his father stood as they sputtered words of gratitude. A hesitant bow snuck from the farmer's rigid frame. He placed a hand on his son's head and forced the child into a low bow of respect. The farmer shoved a trembling hand into his pocket and retrieved a scant offering of pennies, which he dropped next to Ryleah. They clattered against metal. The boy and his father remained in their bows until the sound of coins exploring a metal bowl had died.

Chandra could imagine Ryleah's reaction. That the girl would smile like she had met a long-lost relative and bob her head in understanding. Clouded pupils wreathed in brilliant pink would stare at where Ryleah guessed the boy and his father to be. Little pleasantries would escape her lips, just loud enough for those in her immediate vicinity to hear.

Once the boy and his father had disappeared down the aisle, Chandra stood and approached her friend. She placed a gentle hand on Ryleah's shoulder and spoke with a kindness reserved for a select few.

"Pretty sure they didn't foot the full bill," Chandra whispered into her friend's ear. "Not by a long shot."

A small grin lifted one of Ryleah's cheeks as she recognized the voice at her back.

"Was anyone watching?" Ryleah asked.

"I was hardly paying attention, to be honest."

"Well, I guess it doesn't matter then, does it?"

Chandra chuckled at the notion. The glib defiance Ryleah offered when possible was always a delight to behold.

"I guess not," Chandra replied through her laughter. She allowed her hand to slide off Ryleah's shoulder as she stepped in front of her friend, then took a seat to the acolyte's right. The red velvet that cushioned the pew was a relief. Wood groaned in time with Chandra as she eased herself against the high-backed seat. "Do you have a few minutes, Ryleah? I was hoping I could run something by you."

"You're not hurt again, are you?" One of Ryleah's hands patted the bench until it found Chandra's leg. The acolyte began to probe various parts of Chandra. Whatever she could get her hand on. "It's awful early. I don't normally hear from you until well after sunset."

"I'm fine," Chandra laughed. She took hold of Ryleah's soft hand and gave it a gentle squeeze. "I'm fine. Promise. I just wanted to ask a few questions. House stuff."

"Oh! That's much better than patching you up. Ask away!"

"Right," Chandra said before an awkward pause roosted on her shoulders.

What needed to be asked, in a general sense, was clear enough. The specifics of how to ask were what evaded Chandra. To ask outright if she knew ashlings were running amuck in the World Below felt too direct. Chandra did not want to instill any unnecessary panic in her friend. After all, Chandra was still not wholly convinced that what she had seen was an ashling. There could be an untold number of monstrosities lurking in the deep places of the world that the Federation had yet to encounter or name.

"Well?" Ryleah asked. She returned the gentle squeeze initiated by Chandra.

"Right," Chandra stammered, a sigh of embarrassment stuck to the word. "So, I've spent the last few days in the World Below with a friend—"

"Oh, look at you!" Ryleah smirked. "Making friends!"

"Stop it!" Chandra gave Ryleah a light shove, enough to force a snort from the acolyte's nose. "So, we've been exploring. Looking for something big. When we finally find the thing, there's some kind of creature guarding the stash. Massive black bastard with fingers like scythes. My friend thinks it's an ashling, but I told him that's nonsense. Fairytale talk."

Chandra stopped. The gentle squeeze on her hand solidified into an iron-fisted grip. When Chandra looked up at Ryleah's face, she saw that all traces of mirth had vanished. A dour complexion replaced what had always been a wellspring of soothing kindness. Jaw muscles clenched and blind eyes narrowed. Deep furrows cut across Ryleah's pale brow. Spidery traces of purple and blue on the back of her hand bulged with prominence.

"Tell me more," Ryleah growled through gritted teeth. "More features. What did it look like in full?"

"Well..." Chandra paused. The vision of the creature had been branded into Chandra's mind. Recollection of what it looked like was not an issue. Her trouble lay in deciding what to describe first. "Most of it was like a long snake's tail. Except it looked armored. Like it was wearing plates. It had a small torso that looked like a katarl. Either Zumbatran or Bangeli, but I couldn't tell. It was all the same grayish-black sort of color. Mentioned the bunch of arms... oh, the eyes! It had a dozen of them. All over its torso, looking every way at once."

"Did you make eye contact?" Ryleah asked with a breathless voice.

"I did."

"And did anything happen?"

"When I looked at it?" Chandra asked. She continued without waiting for affirmation. "Yeah, it... it felt like the world was closing around me. Like I wanted to run but there was nowhere to go. I felt like I was being crushed. Couldn't move a muscle until my friend whipped me around and broke my eye contact with the... thing."

"Gods dammit!"

"Ryleah!" Chandra cried, more in surprise than admonition.

Ryleah threw her hand over her mouth. Rather than look about the House, the girl's ears perked. She listened for any response to her sudden blasphemy. Nervous teeth bit down on skin stretched thin over pearly knuckles. When no response came, Ryleah drew in a long, steady breath and released it through pursed lips.

"Sorry," Ryleah murmured. "It's just... that *sounds* like an ashling."

"Come on," Chandra whispered. She also perked up and looked around for any others that might be listening to the conversation between friends. "Come on, Ryleah. Ashlings aren't real. It's gotta be something else."

"Do you think I perform those rites on the ashes of the dead for fun, then? Or for people's entertainment?" Ryleah allowed her questions a moment to sink in before she continued. "Tortured souls bound to the ashes of the dead. Made flesh through rage and anguish. I say those prayers and perform those rites to *make sure* an ashling is never born from those who rest in the catacombs. They may start small and insignificant, but, given time, they are true monsters. Impervious to steel and spell alike."

"Well, how do Keeper's kill them?" Chandra asked, reeling. "That's what Keepers do, right? Kill monsters?"

"A different set of incantations and materials. One of Atherea's miracles. The goddess blesses their weapons, then the Keepers engage in combat to release the tortured souls from their binding."

"That's... a lot to take all at once."

"I know," Ryleah murmured. The explanation seemed to have vented some of the acolyte's frustration. Her grip loosened and her jaw eased into practical motion. "If a Keeper does their job, then most people should never have to meet an ashling. And if the clergy does their job, then, frankly, a Keeper should have no job to do. This is all my fault."

"No!" Chandra snapped. "It is not."

"Of course, it is," Ryleah countered with a roll of her head. "I perform the nightly rites. This House has the largest concentration of ash remains for miles. *Miles.* If the ashling came from somewhere, it must have been here."

"What if it was before your time?" Chandra asked. "You said they start small. This thing was massive. *Huge!* Maybe it's been growing since before you started, and somebody else let it through. It's not fair to rest the blame on your shoulders. And even if it did happen on your watch—which I'm not saying it did—we can just get a Keeper to come along with us, right? My friend and I know the way. If we get the Keeper to the ashling, then we can solve this problem before it becomes a bigger one."

Ryleah chewed on one of her nails. She turned her head this way and that as if looking for something to say. What she found brought Chandra no joy.

"We don't have any Keepers."

"What?" Chandra asked. Her head dropped a few inches, weighted down by incredulity. "How... how do you have no Keepers? This is a *House.*"

"We're always short on Keepers," Ryleah replied as she continued to chew on her nail. "Always. The Arnstead House of Many is the hub for the whole frontier. If there's a monster sighting somewhere out west, it's one of ours that's gotta make the trek. Our last Keeper set out a couple of days ago. No telling when any of them will be back."

"Is that like a few days 'no telling' or a few weeks 'no telling'?"

A snap came as Ryleah's reply. Chandra looked at her friend's hand and saw the nail that Ryleah chewed bore fractures. The jagged line ran all the way down to the girl's cuticle. Ryleah pulled her hand away from her mouth and shook the pain away, sucking air through her teeth as she did so. Chandra flinched at the whole episode. She felt her thumb cover the corresponding finger on her hand. A phantom pain covered her nail.

Chandra sank further into her wooden seat. It was apparent that Ryleah did not know when a Keeper would return. Asking again would not change the fact. Chandra wondered if asking another member of the clergy, maybe someone with more seniority, might yield a different result. A priest, or maybe even the pontiff if he had a moment to spare. One last look at Ryleah put the thought out of Chandra's mind. The acolyte looked disparaged enough without trying to go over her head. Chandra did not have the heart to bring her friend any lower.

Patience would be the key. A notion with which Chandra struggled to grapple. There would be no safe way to extract the focuses and relics from the cache without risking injury or death at the scythe-like hands of what was confirmed to be an ashling. Without a Keeper, combating the monster was out of the question. Chandra had to hope that the Baylocke Battalion would feel the same way if they managed to reach the cache. Hopefully, they might get cocky with their numbers and throw themselves at the monster.

A pang of guilt thumped Chandra square in the chest. She realized she had just wished a handful of people would walk into their deaths for her benefit. There was no more room on the pew to sink into. Her head had nearly reached the velvet seat by the time she stopped. It didn't matter if the Battalion had wronged her, Chandra told herself. Nobody deserved to die at the hands of that waking nightmare.

Chandra felt one of her hands rise. When she looked over to her left, she saw that Ryleah stood. The acolyte dropped her friend's hand when she reached her full height. Ryleah placed a hand on the end of the pew to gain her bearings, drummed her fingers on the dark wood, then set off toward the back of the House. Chandra followed the events in mild confusion.

"Sorry. Was I keeping you, Ryleah?" Chandra asked. This was the first time she had ever seen the acolyte storm off. It did not sit right with Chandra, especially knowing that she had a hand in ruining her friend's disposition.

"I'm going to fetch some reagents," Ryleah said, coming to an abrupt stop. She turned her head back toward Chandra as she spoke. "And to change my clothes. I'm going with you."

"Excuse me?"

"You're going back, aren't you?"

"I thought you said we need a Keeper?" Chandra sprang up from her slump and walked over to Ryleah, placing a hand on the acolyte's shoulder. Chandra's gentle grip was met by a resolute and rigid frame. "We need a Keeper, right?"

"I know the rites. I can ask the gods for the miracle that will let you and your friend's weapons pierce the ashling's armor."

"Well, just, uh…" Chandra's mind went blank. She looked for a way to say anything but what she was thinking. "Can you do it here? The rites, I mean. Do it here, and my friend and I can go deal with the ashling for you. No need to drag you down into the World Below for nothing."

"The rites don't last long. The Keeper who taught me said it would only last for a couple of hours at most, and I'm guessing the ashling is far below if we're just now hearing about it."

"Ryleah, you're *blind*!"

The word echoed throughout the calm chamber. Blind. What little movement there was in the House came to an abrupt stop. Heads turned toward the sound of commotion. Chandra had spoken far louder than intended. The words had burst from her chest with surprising desperation. She felt her cheeks sink as they flushed with shameful hues. Reflex pulled Chandra's hand away from her friend's shoulder, but not fast enough. Ryleah's hand leaped up in time before Chandra was able to pull away. The acolyte's grip was firm, but also gentle. She kept Chandra in place without discomfort.

Ryleah turned. She took Chandra by the arms and worked her hands up to her friend's shoulders. Chandra felt those white hands give her shoulders a tight squeeze. There was no malice in the action. No admonition or disappointment. A thin smile formed on Ryleah's face. Sadness pulled at the corners of her cheeks as she spoke.

"Chandra," Ryleah whispered with a voice like a feather on the wind. A hand crept up Chandra's neck to cup her cheek. "Chandra, I trust you. If you can get me there, I can give you what you need. This is for your family, right?"

"Yeah." Chandra nodded, her voice meek.

"Then we'll make it work. I know we will."

Words failed Chandra. She stepped forward and threw her arms around Ryleah in a tight embrace. Hands gripped tight at the acolyte's robes. Perhaps a bit sudden, as she heard Ryleah lose her breath. A quiet chuckle followed. Chandra felt Ryleah reciprocate the embrace. Warmth and understanding flowed from one into the other.

Chandra struggled to recall the last time she felt so much sincerity. Rather than puzzle over it, she pushed the thought from her mind and allowed herself to become lost in Ryleah's arms.

17

First Steps

Soft rays of dusk bathed the outer steps of the House when Chandra and Ryleah emerged. Hues of orange and purple intertwined over the rooves of dilapidated homes. Clouds devoured the color and twisted it into magnificent shapes. Those colorful rays painted natural murals over the white walls of the House. Sun-warmed steps glowed in the last light of day.

Traffic was thin. With the day near its end, most people had found their way home for an evening meal. Those without homes found sheltered alleyways in which to huddle through the cruel night. The dust of a day's worth of feet settled. A gentle breeze cut through the clear air that surrounded the House. Peace hung about Oldstead like a warm, if a bit moth-eaten, shawl.

Chandra sat a couple of steps up from and behind Ryleah and kept herself busy with her friend's hair. Ryleah's long, white swaths of dense hair could flow freely while she wandered about the House. Down in the World Below was a different story. There were too many snags and crevices that could grab a free lock of hair. At best, it would mean a short stop to untangle Ryleah from whatever managed to grapple her. At worst, it meant the girl might leave a part of her scalp dangling from an outcrop of rock. Neither outcome was desirable.

With the free time afforded her while waiting for Owen to arrive, Chandra set about confining Ryleah's hair into a tight braid. It felt to Chandra like she had another sister to care for. A thought she welcomed with a bright smile.

Hair was not the only transformation Ryleah underwent. Acolyte robes were traded for a white button-up shirt and a pair of brown trousers. On the right shoulder of the shirt, stitched in black, were the scales of Manus. It was the first time Chandra had ever seen her friend in something other than robes, though Ryleah's feet were still wrapped in leather sandals. No amount of protest from Chandra changed the fact that they were the only shoes Ryleah had to her name.

Gone was the plain belt of rope that Ryleah wore with her robes. A sturdy leather belt accommodated all the reagents she requested from the House storage. When she asked what each pouch and bag contained, Ryleah merely offered a knowing grin. An occasional squeak from one of the bags suggested there was something alive. Ryleah occasionally dropped a bit of cheese or rice into that noisy bag, but the others remained silent secrets.

Chandra touched a few fingers to one of her manarail spikes and pulled away a small sliver of metal. She pinched the end of Ryleah's braided hair with one hand and formed the metal sliver into a clasp with the other. The braid nearly touched the steps when Chandra let it go. A gentle thump died in the open air as Ryleah's hair plopped against her back.

"All done, then?" Ryleah asked. The snake of a braid climbed up Ryleah's back as she turned her head to Chandra.

"All done," Chandra confirmed. She patted her friend on the shoulders and slid down to sit next to Ryleah. "Should help a bit. Better than just letting it all flop around, at least."

"Much appreciated," Ryleah replied with a chuckle.

"So, what did you tell the caretaker? Isn't she going to wonder why you're away for so long?"

"Told her someone was sick on a farmstead outside of town. Too sick to make it to town on their own. Since I knew the family, and there was someone here to take me, I offered to be the one to go. Rajani said no at first, but she came 'round in the end."

"Sounds a bit too easy," Chandra probed.

"I wouldn't worry about the specifics. She said yes. That's all that matters."

Chandra's lips thinned. She squinted at her friend. It felt like there were some details her grinning counterpart failed to mention. Whatever it was, Ryleah did have a point. Clearance to depart was clearance. There was no need to overanalyze specifics. They had gotten what they wanted, what they needed, and that was that.

"Fine," Chandra grumbled. "Oh, speaking of leaving, there's our man."

A lone, familiar figure approached the House from the direction of Eaststead. It was impossible to mistake Owen, even at a distance. The man was a walking armory. With his pack slung over his shoulder, the man walked as if he had nowhere to be anytime soon. His head swiveled back and forth to take in either side of the street. A mixture of nonchalance and devil-may-care that chafed Chandra.

"Get the lead out, Seeker!" Chandra called. "We've got places to be!"

The call snapped Owen's attention over to Chandra. He offered a guilt-ridden wave and upped his pace to a jog. Tools and packs bounced comically about his person from the increased pace.

"Seeker?" Ryleah asked.

"Yeah," Chandra murmured in reply. "My friend is a Spellseeker. Had him run some errands around town while I saw you. Didn't want any problems in the House that could be avoided."

"I suppose that's fair."

"Chandra," Owen said in greeting as he drew near. "Ryleah."

"Ryleah?" Chandra mimicked. She cocked her head and turned to look at Ryleah.

"Is that Mr. Raulstone I hear?"

"Wait," Chandra said in deeper confusion. "What, you know him? Well enough to recognize his voice?"

"He gets hurt a lot," Ryleah whispered into Chandra's ear. She smiled and waved in Owen's general direction as he climbed the stairs to meet the girls. It seemed that Ryleah's words had missed the man. That, or his sunny disposition was simply unphased by the remark.

"So," Owen began with a winded voice, "what's the word, Chandra? Do we have a Keeper?"

"Nope," Chandra replied as matter-of-factly as possible.

"Wha—nope? That's it?"

"They're all out of town at the moment," Ryleah added. "No idea when a Keeper might be back, and the most recent departure was a couple days ago."

"Well… shit." Owen sighed. "I guess we're waiting, then."

"Nope," Chandra said again. She stood and dusted her pants off with a few forceful pats, then tapped Ryleah on the shoulder. The acolyte stood took Chandra's arm. The pair began to walk up the steps toward the doors of the House. Chandra looked over her shoulder and said, "Come on!"

"What do you mean, 'come on'?" Owen bounded up several steps at a time to close distance. "We don't have a Keeper. Where are we going?"

"You know where we're going," Chandra replied.

"It's okay, Mr. Raulstone," Ryleah added. "I know the rites. Between the three of us, that ashling is as good as dead."

Owen bounded further up the steps until he was ahead of Chandra and Ryleah. He stopped before the pair and raised a hand in protest. Rather than stop, Chandra walked Ryleah around Owen and continued up the steps.

"Hey," Owen snapped. "What do you mean 'I know the rites'?"

"It means she's standing in while the Keepers are away," Chandra said. Her tone remained cool and measured. That did little to reassure Owen, who Chandra saw was growing flustered.

"Oh no. No, no, no. She's not coming wi—"

"Yes, she is," Chandra said gently.

"Chandra she's… she's—"

"Blind," Ryleah interrupted. "Yes, we know."

Neither Chandra nor Ryleah broke stride as they cut Owen down.

"Chandra," Owen sighed, "I get we're in a hurry, but how could you ask—"

"I didn't," Chandra interjected.

"I volunteered," Ryleah added.

"Look, Owen," Chandra started again before Owen could get a word in, "I've already argued with her. Same points. Came from the same place as you. She's not gonna have it. Now that she's got my arm, Ryleah's not letting me go without her. I trust her. She trusts me. We'll make it work."

"What she said," Ryleah concluded, giving Chandra a gentle pat on the arm.

Owen remained unconvinced.

"Come on, girls," he pleaded. "I'm serious."

"So are we," Chandra and Ryleah replied in near unison. A display that elicited a bout of shared laughter between the girls as they reached the top of the steps.

Further protests from Owen fell on deaf ears. Halfway down the wine-colored carpet of the main aisle, Owen accepted that his words would be ignored.

Enough time was spent on the steps of the House that most of the clergy were nowhere to be seen. A couple of acolytes remained in pews to give nightly prayers. One unfortunate acolyte, a particularly young child, still slaved with bucket and brush to clean the floors. The marble would be spotless and glimmer with the sunrise by the next day. He showed no signs of slowing down as Chandra and company passed him and took the spiral staircase down into the catacombs.

The catacombs were just as sparse as the House above. Of the resting chambers Chandra and her companions passed, most were empty. Only a few dedicated well-wishers remained at so late an hour. Not a single acolyte remained to monitor the comings and goings of those who sought the counsel of family and friends long passed. A fact that Chandra relished as she made her way toward the secret entrance into the World Below. No acolytes meant no confrontation. No confrontation meant a smooth transition into the days of toil yet to come. The later that obstacles began to rear their ugly heads, the better.

Chandra pulled Ryleah into the unused resting chamber. Owen tucked in behind them just after. A final glance up and down the length of the hallway convinced Chandra that she had not been observed. She set her things down next to the specific ash basin and gestured for Owen to join her.

"Come on, Owen," Chandra grunted as she wrapped her fingers around the top of the basin. "Give me a hand."

"Sure," Owen replied. He set his things down and joined Chandra without question.

The pair had the basin pulled away from the wall in no time at all, though with a great deal of noise. There was no way to diminish the racket caused by the basin grating across the stone floor. Each yank of the basin sent a new shock of suspicion through Chandra. Concern that some curious buffoon might come to investigate the strange noises.

No such stranger came. Ryleah stood by the entrance to the resting chamber while Chandra and Owen worked. Out of the way and quieter than a House mouse. Another pinch of cheese made its way into a noisy pouch, accompanied by a shushing noise.

Chandra stretched her arms out to her full wingspan after the basin had been pulled far enough back. She let out a satisfied grunt, then looked back and forth between Owen and Ryleah.

"Hey, Owen," Chandra said, "you go ahead and go first. I'll get Ryleah squared away, and you can catch her if she slips. It's a long fall."

The words became progressively quieter as Chandra spoke. She realized that mentioning a fall so casually, and within earshot of Ryleah, might not be the best way to begin their journey. Chandra needed to instill as much confidence into her friend as she could muster. Guiding Ryleah down from above, and making sure that she was prepared to descend, seemed like the best way to start.

Owen nodded and shouldered his pack without a word. The rope attached to the back of the ash basin was in his hands and he was down into the darkness before Chandra had the chance to blink. There was barely enough time to grab the basin before the man's weight pulled it back into its rightful place. That was the sort of enthusiasm Chandra hoped the whole group could maintain on their journey down. It felt like a fool's hope, but some hope was better than none. Chandra sniffed the last whiff of somewhat fresh air she might get for the next few days before sauntering over to Ryleah.

Confidence, Chandra repeated on end. When she felt the pull of Owen's weight on the ash basin ease, she bolstered herself one last time before turning to Ryleah. *Confidence!*

Solutions rolled around in Chandra's head as she approached her friend. No level of confidence, however sincere, would resolve the situation on its own. The problem being how to get Ryleah down that first descent. It felt irresponsible to just hand Ryleah a rope and tell her to have at it. Chandra had not bothered to ask, but she felt safe in assuming that most of the House clergy did not have extensive climbing experience.

Carrying Ryleah down the hole would solve a handful of problems. Inexperience would no longer be a part of the equation, nor would Ryleah's lack of sight. Surely the girl had enough strength to cling to Chandra's waist or neck and ride her way to the bottom. Chandra even thought she herself might have enough strength to see the plan through. It would only serve as a first step, though, and would not resolve any of the greater descents and scrambles that were to come. This method was a plan to delay the inevitable struggle of guiding an inexperienced blind woman down the side of a sheer rock face.

How does a problem like this get solved, Chandra wondered? The short walk over to Ryleah did not offer sufficient time to plan. Chandra found herself with more questions than answers. Ryleah turned to the sound of shuffling steps and smiled her warm smile.

"All right, then," Ryleah whispered. "We're in the catacombs. We're at the secret hole. What do you need me to do?"

The mixture of innocence and eagerness on display further deepened the guilt Chandra felt through indecision. A nervous chuckle bought a few more seconds before awkward silence begged for Chandra to reply. Discomfort nudged and nudged until Chandra was compelled to speak.

"Well," Chandra sighed, "I'm not sure, if I'm completely honest. You're, uh… a bit of a tough nut to crack."

"Yeah, I was afraid of that," Ryleah replied. A sour note tinged her rampant optimism. Something that caught Chandra off guard, further seeding the pit of guilt that took root in her stomach. The rain cloud dispersed almost as quickly as it had formed, however, and Ryleah spoke again with a renewed hope. "How do you normally go down? Without… someone like me?"

Guilt was in full bloom. A sickly green rose that fed on Ryleah putting herself down. Chandra took some solace in the fact that Ryleah could not see the twisted expression on her face, but that was soon replaced by even deeper guilt.

"Just… hand over hand," Chandra murmured in reply. "I just get the rope in my hands and go down bit by bit."

"And what do you do when it's too hard to go bit by bit?"

"I throw on a harness that holds the rope. It's more complicated, but it gets me down in one piece."

"That!" Ryleah said with a little jump. "Slow and steady. That's the one for me. Can you teach me how to use the harness with the rope?"

Chandra blinked a handful of times and rolled her head at the thought. It made far too much sense. The lesson would be necessary at some point down the line regardless of how the current problem was solved. To teach Ryleah about the harness so soon had not come to mind. The first descent was so short, a matter of routine to Chandra, that the harness seemed like over precaution. That was how she needed to consider Ryleah: with *every* precaution.

"Right," Chandra said as she shouldered her pack onto the ground. She rummaged through clothes and food and tools as she continued to speak. "Bit of an involved process, the harness. But I guess I'd've had to teach you eventually anyways."

"We'll make it work," Ryleah beamed.

"Yeah." Chandra chuckled. "You bet we will."

To call the process involved was an understatement. Once Chandra fished the harness from her bag, she had to orient it correctly for Ryleah and feed her legs into the device. It felt like dressing Omala when the young girl was learning to walk. Straps had to be cinched into place. Belts clasped and tightened. The rope was the most difficult. What little Chandra knew of knots had to be reversed and applied to another person. Though she had helped all her siblings tie their shoes at some point, this felt much more difficult. Tying a shoe wrong would not drop a friend down a hole and to potential injury.

The tedious process of securing equipment accomplished, all that remained was to educate Ryleah on how to utilize rope to control her descent. Chandra walked through the process like she was speaking to an unusually attentive toddler. Each detail was explained in full without room for guesswork. Twice. The whole time she spoke, Chandra guided Ryleah's hands through the motions needed to safely control a descent. Each movement, no matter how subtle, was demonstrated three times over. Spare rope from Chandra's bag had been fed through the harness to allow for a close approximation to the real thing.

When Chandra felt comfortable with her explanations, and after Ryleah had assured her that the lessons were understood, the pair moved over to the hole. It was a bit trickier to get Ryleah attached to the rope in place than to the free-floating rope Chandra used as an example. Tricky, but not a genuine obstacle. A few more minutes were required to get Ryleah safely into place was all.

"Everything okay up there?" Owen called up from the bottom of the hole. He shined his light focus up at Chandra and Ryleah, causing Chandra to blink and swat at the intense beam.

"Yeah, we're fine," Chandra grumbled. "Get that thing out of my eyes. We just had a bunch to go over, is all. Ryleah's going to come down on the harness. Get some practice for the longer drops."

"Sure, sure," Owen replied. "Makes sense to me. I'm ready down here if she slips."

"Much appreciated!" Ryleah called out in response.

"You won't slip," Chandra said. She did another pass over the various sections of the complicated harness to make sure no connection was missed. Satisfied, she took Ryleah by the shoulders and gave her a tight squeeze. "You're gonna be fine. Just ease back like you're sitting in a chair like I told you. That's the hardest part. Everything after that is lemon cake."

"Oh, that sounds lovely."

"Focus, Ryleah." Chandra sighed.

"Yup, that's me," Ryleah managed through an embarrassed chuckle. "Completely focused."

"I'm going to ease you back to the ledge. When you feel your heels go out over the ledge—"

"Stop!"

"Yeah." Chandra nodded. "Just like that. Now, just like I showed you. Take a seat."

A vigorous nod was Ryleah's response. The girl hesitated to act on the command, but not for long. After a steadying breath, Chandra saw Ryleah's shoulders sag. The girl lowered herself inch by unsure inch until she was in a seated position. All the while she held fast to the rope. One hand kept Ryleah centered, while the other used the rope behind like a lever to control her speed.

It was quite the sight. Chandra had half expected to see a foot slip and carry Ryleah right into the rock wall. Not that Chandra desired to see her friend fail, rather Chandra recalled how long it had taken her to master the basics of climbing and rappelling on her own. A painful process that left her with a veritable museum of tiny scars.

I guess I'm a pretty good teacher, Chandra thought to herself. *Who would have guessed?*

"And... down."

As Ryleah spoke, she whipped her hand from back to front. The hand that gauged the speed at which she would descent. She had thrown the throttle from naught to full in a second. Chandra felt her eyes widen into saucers as Ryleah suddenly plummeted down from the ledge of the hole. A piercing cry followed the girl downward as she fell.

Chandra threw a hand out to catch her friend, but the reaction was too slow. Ryleah was far beyond Chandra's reach by the time her hand was extended to offer aid. Highlighted for a moment by Owen's focus, Ryleah was soon engulfed by shadow.

"Ryleah!" Chandra shouted down after her friend.

Sounds of effort and leather shuffling over stone rose from the hole. There were no cries of pain. No more ear rattling shouts of distress.

"Ryleah?" Chandra inquired. Her volume had dropped as a modicum of concern drifted away.

"We're fine!" Owen called up from the gloom.

"Yup!" came Ryleah's disheveled affirmation. "All good. Mr. Raulstone broke my fall."

"Please, just Owen."

"Right, right," Ryleah replied through a nervous chuckle. "Sorry."

Though unnerved by the experience, it sounded like Ryleah was fine. Chandra found herself glad that they had agreed to test the harness before the group reached a significant drop. A stern talking to about the control of descent was in order.

Relief shifted to purpose as Chandra shouldered her bag and took hold of the rope. She needed no harness for the short trip down. From a seated position with her legs dangling over the ledge of the hole, Chandra twisted so that her feet were against the wall and her body was in the center of the small shaft. The first few feet down came courtesy of her weight pulling the ash basin back into place. Once the awful grinding noise ceased, hand over careful hand brought Chandra down the hole to the cold stone floor below. Another successful, albeit more eventful than normal, descent into the World Below.

When Chandra reached the bottom, Owen was looking over a seated Ryleah to check for any signs of injury. He recognized that no direct contact with the floor did not mean that Ryleah had missed the walls on the way down. The light focus weaved around Ryleah's head and arms. A tedious task, Chandra thought from the looks of things. Such a small bit of light to search by. Chandra dipped into the Flow to summon her light spell. Time was against them once more, and Chandra thought it might speed along the process of inspecting her friend.

"Let's get a bit more light, yeah?" Chandra murmured as she knelt next to Ryleah. Two pairs of eyes would move the examination along faster than one.

There were no rips or tears in Ryleah's clothing. No reactions when Chandra poked at key joints like elbows and knees. When Chandra rolled up Ryleah's sleeves, there was no hint of bruise or blemish. Just pure white skin traced by faint spiderwebs of blue and purple. All was normal when it came to Ryleah. The acolyte seemed too preoccupied staring at her hands to pay Chandra or Owen any attention.

Chandra paused. Ryleah? Looking at her hands? Chandra looked from Ryleah's face to her hands and back again. There could be no mistake. The acolyte's pink eyes twitched and roved as if she were examining the slender digits. Ryleah even turned her hands over and back to see both sides.

"Hey, Ryleah, what are you—"

Words died in Chandra's throat as Ryleah's head wandered up in fascination. Eye contact. For the first time, Chandra felt Ryleah's eyes meet her own.

A smile broke through the astonishment and wonder that blanketed Ryleah's face. With tentative hands, she reached out slowly to Chandra. Ryleah cupped the face of her friend in her hands. Thumbs gently stroked Chandra's cheeks. Tears began to well and trickle down the sides of Ryleah's face. She sniffled and laughed at the same time. All confusion melted to make way for the purest joy Chandra had ever witnessed.

"Is that... is that you, Chandra?" Ryleah asked with a tremulous voice. Chandra nodded, a slow, dumbfounded gesture. She felt her mouth fall agape. "Oh my, I— you nodded? I *saw* you nod?"

"Yeah," Chandra replied. Her reply was soft, breathless. A whisp of a word adrift in a sea of awe. She felt one of her hands rise to take of Ryleah's. "Yeah, I nodded."

"I met a Fieldkin once," Owen cut in. His speech was flawless and resolute. He was the least affected of the three by what was transpiring between them. Owen leaned over to Ryleah and waved a hand in front of her face. Ryleah tracked the movement with perfect accuracy and followed the hand back to Owen. She cupped his face just as she had done for Chandra. Owen continued to speak while all this played out. "He mentioned something to me… while we were tracking a rogue mage. Said that he could see disturbances in the Flow. Like… whenever someone from the Federation would cast a spell, he could see traces of it weeks after the fact. You're half-kin, right, Ryleah?"

"Yeah," Ryleah said as she fought a joyous sob. "Deepkin on my mother's side."

"You think if I…?" Chandra asked, then doused her light before a reply could be made.

Ryleah shuddered, made visible by the light of Owen's focus. Her head snapped back and forth on a swivel as if looking for someone she had just lost in a crowd. Panic mingled with the pure joy that had dominated her expression.

"What… where did you both go?" Ryleah asked.

"We're right here," Chandra said sweetly. She reached out and put a hand on Ryleah's shoulder. A warm hand, trembling with a torrent of muddied emotions, rested atop Chandra's. "You don't see anything right now?"

"No," Ryleah replied.

Odd. The one word that came to Chandra's mind. While her light spell hung in the air, Ryleah was able to see. The acolyte's vision was clear enough to distinguish body parts and their associated motions. When the light from Owen's focus shone brightly in her face? Nothing. No hint of recognition. Ryleah appeared to be back in the darkness she had known her whole life.

Chandra tapped into the Flow once more. A bloom of light bathed the stone walls in a golden hue. Once again, Ryleah's head whipped to the source of the light and then back to Chandra. Eye contact had been reestablished.

"And now you see again?" Owen asked.

"Yes," Ryleah replied.

"So, I guess it's just raw spells she can see?" Owen asked, this time directed at Chandra. One of his brows was raised as he spoke. He seemed to be just as curious about the situation as Chandra was.

"Yeah," Chandra nodded. "And I wouldn't expect anybody to be casting spells in the House."

"No," Ryleah added with an emphatic shake of her head. "No, strictly forbidden. Channeling the Flow in a House would be sacrilege."

"This is probably the first spell you've ever seen, then?" Owen asked.

"A fair guess." Ryleah nodded. "I don't really get out of the House too often. It's always been easier to just keep me inside and bring those that need to help to me, instead of the other way around. Can you teach me?"

Ryleah's attention snapped to Chandra with an unexpected intensity. The acolyte edged her way over to Chandra and took one of her hands in her own. Desperation and longing hung from the acolyte's cheeks as sailors clung to flotsam. There was nowhere for Chandra to look but at Ryleah. Her request demanded attention that Chandra did not have the heart to deny.

"Didn't you just say that casting spells in the House is sacrilege?" Chandra asked.

"Does she look like she cares?" Owen interjected.

"Please?" Ryleah asked once more.

"Well," Chandra sighed, "it's not something you're going to learn overnight. It'll take time—"

Joyous squeals drowned out whatever else Chandra had to say. Ecstatic arms were flung around her shoulders as Ryleah tackled Chandra to the ground in excitement. Not a single word escaped the acolyte. So overcome by happiness, Ryleah's gratitude took the form of shapeless syllables and incoherent, sob-fueled babble.

Chandra could not help but smile. She wrapped her hands around her friend. A sense of wholeness engulfed Chandra as she grappled with the notion that she had just changed Ryleah's life forever.

18

Rites of Passage

"Once we get you used to contacting the Flow, we'll start working on how to channel," Chandra elaborated. "It's pretty straightforward. If you've got the Flow visualized in your head, you just imagine you're reaching your arm out to touch it. At first, I used to reach my actual hand out and feel around for the Flow. You don't *need* to, but it helped me focus on the act of channeling the energy into my body. Might help you out if you give it a shot. Just because it's straightforward doesn't mean it's easy, though. Learning how to channel safely without getting a friction burn in the process was probably the hardest part of spell casting. For me, at least. Any questions so far?"

"How... are you still... talking?" Ryleah asked.

"What do you mean?"

"I can... barely breathe. You're... wearing a *pack*... and talking like... it's nothing."

Chandra turned her head back to peer at Ryleah. Though she bore no pack or any other great weight, the acolyte was hunched over as she walked. Each haggard breath came as a struggle. Footsteps were heavy and imprecise. If not for the even terrain just outside the city of Those Who Came Before, Ryleah might have toppled over and crashed on the stone floor.

By stark contrast, Chandra walked and talked with ease. She had even slowed her normal pace to allow Ryleah to keep up. There was no way that such mild strain would exhaust Chandra. The mere thought of it made her chuckle.

"Well," Chandra began, "not all of us sit around the House all day. Healing the sick, listening in a divulgence booth, performing rites in the catacombs... not exactly an active lifestyle."

"I'm not... lazy," Ryleah replied.

"No, of course not. Just outta of shape, is all."

The comment elicited something like a laugh from Ryleah. In practice, it was more of a wheeze. A few strained coughs followed the gesture to hammer home that Ryleah was the farthest removed from her element she had ever been.

"It's all right," Owen cut in. He was in better shape than Ryleah without a doubt, but his breaths still came in heaves. His aptitude for spelunking fell somewhere between Ryleah and Chandra. A wide margin of operation. "We're just about to the city. Not far from the last climb."

"*Climb?*" Ryleah whined.

"Oh, come on," Chandra tittered. "It's a short one. We can take a short rest before we climb. Once we're up, we're in the monster's den. Won't be any time or place for breaks."

"Thank... the gods," Ryleah coughed.

It was no more than a few minutes to the promised area of the climb. The grappling hook and rope still hung from the ancient metal beam where Chandra left it. All the climbing gear that could be spared had been left in place. Both for ease of return, as well as to help mark their passage.

To leave their gear in place had been a gamble. Time and speed gained at the cost of a visible trail. If the Baylocke Battalion was able to puzzle their way through the first handful of chambers, they would stumble upon ropes and pitons. Helpful markers that led the way to the ancient city. Chandra knew the risk. She bet that the Battalion would spend so much time lost in search of the right way, the whole city would be looted before they ever arrived. Chandra gave a prayer to the twin gods, Manjayra and Manjayro, that a little luck might keep the Battalion at bay.

As soon as rest was called at the foot of the final climb, Ryleah collapsed to the cool floor. A few mild sobs of dismay punctuated her return to a normal breathing pattern. Owen followed suit and dropped his pack next to the dangling rope. He took a seat and rested his back against the wall.

Chandra was less inclined to have a seat. She dropped her pack but remained standing. Slow paces carried her back and forth down the narrow corridor that led to the climb. Thoughts of what to come began to rear their horrid visages. The memories of her first visit were still near, vivid in her mind. Rivers of blood and gore. Statues and halls of Those Who Came Before. Some hulking monstrosity… an ashling. Chandra had to remind herself that ashlings were no longer a thing of myth and fairytale. Not one of Omala's fanciful stories.

The armed and armored creature was very much real, and Chandra was sure it had no better place to be. Not with so many corpses around to feed on. Part of Chandra wanted to wait the ashling out. Give it time to feast on the carnage it had wrought and let it pass on elsewhere. Somewhere far and away from the cache of relics and focuses. It was not a realistic hope, Chandra knew. She was already locked in a race against time. The absolute worst scenario would be to meet the ashling with the Baylocke Battalion blocking any chance of retreat. Chandra had half a mind as to what that bunch of brigands might do if they caught her on the trail to riches. No, there was no time to spend in idle hope.

Thoughts of time brought about other memories. How long had she been away from home? A day for travel. Two days to the ancient city, and then one day back. Another day or day and a half to get Ryleah through the World Below and reach the city. Almost a week. The longest Chandra had ever been away from home. She wondered how the family was holding up. If the other children were managing to keep their father in line. Was everybody eating well and avoiding trouble?

Darker thoughts surfaced. What if the bank came by while she was away? There was no way Nitesh could be trusted to remain civil. He was likely to make their situation worse rather than better. None of the other children had experience dealing with the Orland Bank either. Chandra had shouldered those interactions ever since her father was forbidden from entering the Arnstead branch.

There's nothing I can do about it now, Chandra told herself. *Best I can do is get in quick and get out quicker. The sooner I'm home, the better.*

Chandra ceased her pacing. She stood still in the narrow corridor and inhaled a breath of calm through her nose, held the air in her lungs for a moment, and then a moment more. Shoulders eased as the breath was forced out through pursed lips. The process was repeated a half-dozen times. Each breath brought tranquility closer to the surface. Dark omens and ill notions were pushed into the shadowed recesses of her mind. Chandra brought herself to the moment in which she stood. A certain lightness trickled like warm rain from her head down to her toes. Fleeting peace meant to be savored.

"So," Ryleah began, "do I need to start performing rites now, or…?"

That acolyte still spoke with a winded voice, but she managed to raise herself to a seated position. Chandra could see Ryleah's shoulders rise and fall with each deep breath. Even at the precipice of exhaustion, Ryleah had a mind for helpfulness. Her hands wandered over the various pouches and bags that adorned her leather belt.

"I don't think so," Owen replied.

Both Chandra and Ryleah looked over to the Spellseeker.

"Why not?" Chandra probed.

"Well, there was talk of the resulting miracles from the rites only lasting for an hour or so. Isn't that right, Ryleah?"

"That's what I've been told, yes," Ryleah confirmed. "Maybe a little more, maybe a little less. Depends on how busy the gods are when we call to them."

"Right, and we still need to climb the rope and make our way to the stash of goods. Would be an awful waste if we used all your materials now and the miracles expired before we found the ashling."

"Yeah." Chandra sighed. "I was hoping to keep Ryleah away from the action, though. If we both go down, there's nothing to stop the ashling from tearing Ryleah apart."

"To be fair," Ryleah interjected, "if you both die and Chandra's spell ends, I'm probably not making it out of here anyway."

Ryleah tapped a finger next to one of her eyes. Though she had been able to follow unassisted while Chandra's light was in the air, the fact remained that Ryleah's sight would vanish if Chandra died. Another morbid thought to join the collection that Chandra just managed to quell. Chandra clicked her tongue against the back of her teeth in frustration. She wanted to argue. To find a counterpoint that would let Ryleah remain in the relative safety of the corridor.

Nothing came to mind. There was no way to be sure that the miracles lasted unless they were performed while the ashling was in sight. A dangerous dance at the fringe of death's reach. To perform the rites at any other time would be a gamble. One that could result in the loss of days. Time spent returning to the House for more reagents, and then the return to the ancient city. Wasted efforts followed by wasted hours. That was if the group could manage to escape the ashling for a second time. There were too many variables. Too many junctions where the whole plan could crumble to dust and float away into darkness.

"You're right," Chandra conceded after her fruitless rumination. "Both of you. Five more minutes, then we all go up and get this over with. Agreed?"

"Yeah," Owen nodded. "Sounds good."

"Maybe ten minutes?" Ryleah asked sheepishly.

"Sure," Chandra snorted, "ten minutes, then."

Ten minutes passed in a flash. Uneven breaths became steady and quiet. Chandra gave up her paces to gather what rest she could. There would be no peace after the group ascended the rope and plunged into the dark, death-ridden city of Those Who Came Before. The final span of stillness was relished for all its worth.

The only sound was an occasional click. A mechanical noise of metal brushed against metal. Its source was a mystery on the first occurrence.

When it happened a second time, Chandra happened to notice Owen with a pocket watch in hand. The same sort of watch her mother had owned. The one in Chandra's pocket. She slipped a hand into her pocket to feel the familiar scratches of the once-polished surface. It brought Chandra an extra layer of comfort.

A third click heralded Owen rising from his seat. He peered at the watch after he stood as if to be certain of the time twice over. Another click echoed in the narrow passage when he closed the watch and placed it back in his pocket.

"All right," Owen sighed, "that's ten. Up and at 'em, folks."

"You sure that was ten?" Ryleah moaned, cracking an eye to gaze quizzically up at Owen. A suggestion of enthusiasm remained in her voice, but it was wearing thin.

"Yes," Chandra answered, "he's triple sure. Been eyeing his watch like a toddler at a sweets stall."

"That's… a way of putting it." Owen chuckled. "So, who's first, then?"

"That'll be me." Chandra grunted as she shouldered her pack. "I want you down here in case Ryleah can't make it up. You've got a better chance of breaking her fall than I do."

"Your confidence is overwhelming," Ryleah chided over mock laughter. "I've only fallen twice."

"Three times," Owen corrected.

Ryleah glared at Owen but did not respond.

The matter decided, Chandra shouldered her bag and approached the rope. She spent a few moments playing with the position of her light. An effort to ensure she could see what she was doing close to the top, while also allowing Ryleah the best vision possible. A few experiments over the past day informed the group that Ryleah could see the light and anything it touched. Beyond that sphere of influence, Ryleah remained blind to the world.

Chandra began her climb once she was satisfied with the position of the light. It was not an effortless ascent, but Chandra made her way up without much concern. The strain of the climb lingered in her arms for only a moment or two after she reached the top. Minor aches fell away with a vigorous shake as Chandra set her pack down. Then she took a knee next to the ledge and lowered her hand.

"Okay, Ryleah," Chandra said as she caught her breath. "Your turn. I'll haul you up when you can reach my hand."

"Excellent," Ryleah grunted as she stood. The acolyte knit her hands into the sign of prayer before she began her ascent. A delay that lasted a few short moments before Ryleah took hold of the rope and began to climb.

Despite her hesitancy, Ryleah also made short work of the climb. Chandra caught her by the hand, as promised, and lifted her friend to the ledge for a better grip. Their combined struggle saw Ryleah up and over the ledge without mishap. Owen shouldered his pack and made a similarly uneventful ascent. The trio had risen and was ready to delve into the city.

Chandra walked at the fore with Owen at the rear. The two insisted on keeping Ryleah in the middle, the safest place there was in the black well of uncertainty. Flow-infused light bobbed over their heads as they walked.

A confident stride carried Chandra forward. The immediate path was both familiar and simple. One turn awaited them down the cobblestone road. Quite a way off, but Chandra knew to look for the chalk marker she left on the previous visit. Follow those simple instructions and she would lead Ryleah and Owen to the field of impending battle.

Who knows? Chandra thought to herself. *Maybe we'll catch the ashling asleep? Assuming the thing sleeps at all.*

Confidence bred speed. Knowledge of the route allowed Chandra to move at a faster clip than on her first visit. No longer did she need to peer at each street sign or investigate every corner. If she did not hear the telltale sound of the ashling dragging itself over stone, she felt comfortable pressing onward. They must be the only other people in the city, after all. Chandra's sense of superiority over the Baylocke Battalion had swelled on her return to the city. There had not been a single sign of their passage. Neither sight nor sound. The varmints seemed to have cleaned out, as well. It was just her, her companions, and the tortured carrion feeder that lurked somewhere in the darkness.

Carrion.

Varmints.

Thoughts of the field of corpses resurfaced when Chandra reached the chalk marker. She paused for a moment at the street corner. Long enough to reach into her pack for a pair of handkerchiefs. Lack of haste allowed Chandra to find something more suitable than a dirty shirt this time. She handed one of the cloths to Ryleah, then waved her own at Owen. A friendly reminder to prepare himself for the visceral stench that approached.

Ryleah accepted the handkerchief with a cross face. Before she could speak, Chandra placed a finger over Ryleah's mouth. Chandra shook her head in favor of silence. She placed the cloth over her nose and mouth and motioned for Ryleah to do the same. The acolyte, confused though she was, obeyed and mimicked her friend.

Chandra had not thought how to broach the subject of the bodies. It was something that the group would encounter unless they decided to explore unfamiliar streets for unclogged passageways. Chandra did not care for the idea of wasted time. In quick and out quick. The mantra bounced in her head with each step that brought her close to the varmints. At the same time, it felt wrong to surprise Ryleah with the horrid sight.

Sight, Chandra thought. She let the word linger on her mind as a plan formed.

When the first hint of foul air reached Chandra's nostrils, she doused her light. All that remained was the beam of light cast from Owen's focus. Enough to light the way for Chandra and Owen, though it would necessitate a slower pace. The Spellseeker's light was a poor substitute for the brilliant lantern that was Chandra's spell. Still, she felt better about this idea than allowing Ryleah to witness the horror ahead. Sight was still so new to her. It would have been wrong to show Ryleah something so gruesome. At least, that was how Chandra felt.

Fingers cut through the gloom and latched onto Chandra's shoulder. She felt Ryleah draw herself close. One of the acolyte's arms entwined with one of Chandra's.

"What's wrong?" Ryleah whispered into Chandra's ear.

"Nothing," Chandra replied in kind. "Just stay close to me. I'll guide you. Owen, keep that light up front."

"Yes, ma'am," came the hushed reply from the rear.

The smell worsened as the group drew near. Even when expecting the foul stench, Chandra was not fully prepared. Thin cotton rags did little to suppress the smell. It was all she could do to keep herself from gagging. Chandra heard Ryleah fight against the same urge, and she fought well. Ryleah had quelled her cough before the first bodies appeared under Owen's light.

Blood no longer lingered in pools on the road. Whatever fluids had been dumped onto the road were dried and caked to the stones. Open wounds and severed limbs no longer glistened where raw flesh was visible. The way appeared less treacherous than it had two days ago. One thing for Chandra to be thankful for amid the macabre display.

Chandra picked her way carefully. She gestured for Owen to shine his light closer to the side of the road. The middle of the road was thick with bits and chunks of varmint, but the side of the road was somewhat sparser. That meant by no means that the way was clear. As Chandra walked, she kicked arms and legs out of her path. Larger chunks, like dismembered torsos, required more than a simple kick. Chandra was forced to dig her foot under the deceased creature and lift the thing away.

The work was revolting. Bits of flesh and entrails clung to Chandra's boots, just visible with Owen's light. Limbs fell away from torsos to splatter on the stone. A wretched, squelching noise that reignited her reflex to gag. Each instance strengthened the putrescence that lingered in the air and clung to her lungs. All to ensure that Ryleah did not trip and fall. If she could help it, Chandra would not allow her companions to wallow in the river of death as she had just days before.

Trembling fingers served as a reminder to press onward. Not Chandra's own, but those of Ryleah. The acolyte clung tight to Chandra. Though she could not see what surrounded her, the powers of sound and smell had not abandoned Ryleah. The grip of terror Chandra felt around her arm told her as much. Chandra found her friend's hand with her own and gave it a tight squeeze. Tacit support as they both fought to carry on.

An eternity passed as Chandra picked her way through the mire. At a slower pace, there seemed to be more bodies than ever before. There was time to examine each corpse that she passed. Some of the faces still bore their dying emotions. Panic. Terror. Defiant rage, often accompanied by a crude weapon in hand. Their stricken faces wove together into a tapestry of brutal sorrow. The utter annihilation of a civilization preserved on a twisted canvas of stone.

There's an end, Chandra struggled to remind herself.

Despite the carnage laid out before her, Chandra knew the bodies would not go on forever. They began to thin. A sign that the desired end drew near. Chandra was close to the statue now, close to the cache of relics and focuses. Close to her treasure. Her prize. It would not be long before they stood beneath the monolithic statue of Those Who Came Before.

Squelch.

Chandra froze. She felt Ryleah crash into her back, a soft thump of cotton and flesh. The acolyte's hand tightened around Chandra's. A death grip that was sure to crush bones if left unattended.

"Why did we stop?" Ryleah whispered.

Chandra whirled about and placed her free hand over Ryleah's mouth without warning. Ryleah started but retained what little composure she still clung to. The tremor in Ryleah's hand spread to her whole body. Chandra felt her friend quake in her arms.

Snap.

Another sound. One that Chandra had not created, neither by step nor by shuffling varmint corpses. The noise did not come from Ryleah.

It did not come from Owen. What Chandra heard came from down the road. Ahead. Near the center of the street, she guessed.

Slosh.

Unable to contain her sudden distress, Chandra peered over Ryleah's shoulder to look at Owen. He was mostly obscured in shadow. The light he carried shone forward and only revealed the hand that bore the focus. It was enough for Chandra to guess where the man's face was. With teeth clenched tight, she stared toward Owen's face and jerked her head back and to the left. Toward the center of the street. The light flicked onto the street and returned to Chandra in the same instant. Chandra could almost hear the implied question: Check the street? She responded with a slow, deliberate nod and turned her head to follow the beam of light.

The light chopped through shadow like a dull machete. It moved slowly, prodding over the fallen varmints in search of a source. Whatever caused the familiar crunch of bone and tear of flesh. Sounds Chandra had only heard so viscerally in one place before. Made by one horror.

Rip.

Black plates loomed over the bodies strewn about the street. Arms the color of wet ash raked scythe-like fingers over the fetid banquet. A varmint was plucked from the ground, pinched between two fingers, and tossed into a cavernous well of pointed teeth. The light wound its way up and up to reveal the head of a katarl mounted atop the ghastly abomination. It was here. Right in front of them. The ashling.

Crunch.

With that last bite, an eye opened in the side of the ashling's torso. Just above where the katarl's hip met the snakelike tail. The eye, a vertical black slit surrounded by fields of blazing orange, flicked to the varmints near its tail, then across the street. Another flick brought the eye to rest on Owen's light. It followed the beam until it rested on Owen. The black slit of a pupil narrowed as the ashling gazed into the light.

A dozen more eyes opened as the ashling shifted its bulk to face Chandra and her friends. Hellish fireflies floating through a bleak night of regret.

"Move," Chandra gasped. The cold knives that accompanied the ashling's gaze had already begun to dig into her skin. It felt as if she had been pushed into an ice bath. Invisible hands wrapped around her neck and forced her head below the surface. An attempt to drown her in fear. Chandra ripped her head away from the ashling with all the will she possessed. A painful action that felt like tearing the skin from her face. "Move!"

The first test was passed. Chandra could speak. She still had control of her legs and arms. Now she needed to use them. Purpose flooded into her hand as Chandra plunged into the Flow and tore her light spell from its crackling depths. New knives pierced her hands. These were hot and persistent. Friction burn. Chandra knew the pain would linger for some time, but she could not afford to focus on the sensation. She heard the armored plates of the ashling scrape stone and crunch bone. The monster approached.

Chandra made a frenzied scan of the illuminated street. There had to be some kind of cover. A haven or a wall. She locked onto the closest open door, some kind of storefront from years past, and cut long strides to reach the entrance.

Sudden resistance kept Chandra from moving more than a couple of steps. She felt one of her hands sink toward the ground. The hand that had been clutched so desperately by Ryleah, and was clutched still. Sensory overload had immobilized the acolyte. Rather than run after Chandra, her knees buckled and sent Ryleah crashing to the floor. Her head was on a swivel. From the bodies, to the blood, to the looming atrocity that approached from the middle of the road, Ryleah did not know where to look first. The handkerchief fell from her numb hand. Ryleah's mouth hung agape at what lay before her.

"Come on!" Chandra howled. A forceful tug on Ryleah's arm did not rouse the acolyte from her stupor. Ill-formed words tumbled from the girl's mouth as incoherent babble. "Ryleah!"

Owen swooped past Chandra and took hold of one of Ryleah's arms. With a few swift motions, he had Ryleah draped over his shoulder and was ready to run. The expression on his face drove Chandra faster than any word ever could. Terror had no place on his face. Strained but steady determination commanded retreat. Chandra complied without hesitation.

The pair plunged into the nearest stone building, varmint bodies causing them to trip and stumble. Owen was barely past the threshold when he lost his footing and crashed. Ryleah came down with him and hit the ground. Hard. Hard enough to knock some of the terror from her limbs, it seemed, as she forced herself up and scrambled toward the back of the store. Leather sandals scratched the floor in search of traction to propel Ryleah forward.

Chandra risked a glance behind as she vaulted the ancient counter-top that bisected the room. Four sharp hands clutched at the door and surrounding windows. The fifth and sixth hands wormed their way through the door and slithered toward Owen.

"Move it!" Chandra shouted.

The fall hand not treated Owen well either. One hand pushed the man off the floor while the other cradled his head. Awkward steps carried him toward the counter as scythes nipped at his heels. He stumbled forward, hand outstretched. Chandra caught the hand with a vice grip and yanked Owen over the counter. The horrid sound of claws raking stone assaulted Chandra's ears just as Owen cleared the danger. Both Chandra and Owen threw themselves to the back wall of the store to join Ryleah.

"We need those rites," Owen panted as he felt his head for injury. His free hand ripped his sword from its sheath and placed the weapon at Ryleah's feet. "Chandra, give her your spikes."

Chandra complied without a word. Trembling hands fumbled with the manarail spikes on her waist. She was able to get two of them off her belt and dropped them before Ryleah.

Stone squealed. Scythe-like fingers probed the counter for flesh to bite. Each movement was agony to hear. Chandra smashed her hands against her ears and grit her teeth at the aural assault. She felt a growl well in her chest, then climb up through her throat. The ashling's hands roved closer and closer all the while.

When Chandra looked back to Ryleah, she saw panicked hands jammed into pouches and satchels. Fingers flitted from one container to the next. Ryleah did not look into the bags for inspection. Her gaze remained locked on the encroaching threat while she felt for whatever she sought. Delicate fingers poked and prodded until recognition flashed across her face. From one of the pouches, she produced a handful of sand. Grains dripped between clenched fingers as her free hand fumbled for one of the manarail spikes at her knees. Words poured from her mouth the moment a finger touched one of the spikes.

"Guide us, Sisir, through this blackest night. That we might find those who cry for help in the darkness and banish the evils that beset us. Sisir, hear my prayer!"

White light exploded from the manarail spike and filled the stone chamber. The purest, most brilliant light Chandra had ever witnessed. Its intensity brought tears and forced Chandra to shield her eyes. Light forked and split as Ryleah wrapped a hand around the spike and launched it over the counter. Metal plinked on stone, the spike bouncing its way across the room and toward the ashling.

Sour notes filled the shop. A metallic cry that curdled Chandra's blood. It was the ashling, crying out in response to the divine light pitched its way. Winding arms retreated from the counter. The ashling pulled itself into the street and away from the light. Back and back, the monster moved until it had become a silhouette of death. A shadowed presence that skirted the edge of Ryleah's miracle.

The ashling slithered back and forth in search of a path through the light so that it might reach its fresh prey. Its cries subsided. Feral hunger dripped from roving eyes that peered in every direction, accented only by the grinding of its armored plates over stone and flesh.

Chandra, Ryleah, and Owen let out a collective sigh. The trio had held their breath in horror at how near the ashling had drawn, and the wretched screech that followed did them no favors. They did not look at each other. All three had eyes for the creature that stalked just outside the reach of light.

"Good thinking," Owen murmured.

The sudden words caused Chandra to flinch. In her mind, she had been alone in those moments. Each scythe-like finger was probing for her and her alone. The others were washed away under the tide of fear that licked at Chandra's boots. She threw a few glances around the shop. Thankfully, her friends were all in one piece. There were a few scrapes and bruises from trips and falls, but nothing that would prevent either Owen or Ryleah from moving about.

Weak legs lifted Chandra. She stumbled toward the counter and hunched over its cool surface. The cold stone felt wonderful on her burning hand. That was until she noticed the deep gouges cut into the stone by the ashling's fingers. Chandra recoiled from the counter and took a couple of hurried steps back.

Though the ashling had fled beyond the reach of the light, one part of its anatomy was still discernable: its eyes. Chandra found herself gazing into the glowing slits before she realized it had happened. Unlike mere moments before, however, she felt no swell of cold fall over her body. There was no invisible force that demanded eye contact either. Chandra was able to freely look away from the ashling without effort or pain.

Maybe that's the light? Chandra wondered to herself. She turned to ask Ryleah if that was the case but found the acolyte was already searching her belt for new reagents. Ryleah still had her mind set on casting the promised rites. Even after such an awful experience. The show of determination brought a wisp of a smile to Chandra's lips.

Ryleah produced a handful of blue and red petals. In the middle of the petals was a glimmering white pearl. She clutched all her ingredients in one hand and lay her free hand on Owen's sword.

"Guide this blade, Atherea, that it might strike swift and true. Embolden the bearer that they might stand fast in the face of terror. Be the edge that sunders stone and shears metal. Atherea, hear my prayer!"

Warm light radiated from Ryleah's fingertips to cover the blade in golden film. Each pulse of light further wrapped the blade in shimmering gold. It was not a piercing light like what shone from the manarail spike in the street. This light was calm, almost soothing. Merely looking at the blade made Chandra feel like she was wrapped in a woolen blanket next to a roaring hearth. To look at the blade was to feel at home.

The same rite was performed on the remaining manarail spike near Ryleah's feet. Golden light enveloped the small hunk of iron. When the miracle had been completed and Chandra set her hand to the spike, the feeling of comfort increased twice over. It was like being tucked into the combined embrace of her mother and father. Absolute tranquility for the space of a breath. When the initial sensation passed, subtle confidence remained. Gentle words of encouragement hung at the edge of perception in a voice Chandra had not heard in years.

Fear remained. When Chandra looked at the ashling that lurked outside the building, she still saw an avatar of death and terror. However, the panic had subsided. Chandra could look at the unholy monstrosity and see a foe rather than an impossible obstacle. Shaken nerves became rigid. Confidence welled in her chest. The ashling was just another hurdle, dangerous as it might be. One that could be overcome.

"This is amazing," Chandra murmured as her gaze fell back to the glowing spike in her hand. She looked down at Ryleah, who was beginning to stand, with a face full of wonder. "Thank you."

"That feeling is all you," Ryleah replied. "Atherea just knows what a warrior needs to hear, and when they need to hear it."

Ryleah pressed both of her thumbs into another of her pouches. When she pulled them out, they were covered in some kind of soot or powder. She placed a thumb on Chandra's forehead and the other on Owen's. A line was drawn across their brows. Ryleah placed her fingertips along the lines and began to recite a new rite.

"Be my shield, Atherea, so that I might protect the weak and helpless. Allow me to become the bastion that stands firm against cruelty and pain. Atherea, hear my prayer."

Chandra felt a slight vibration. It originated at Ryleah's finger-tips, but slowly spread to envelop Chandra's entire body. Warm light trickled behind the vibrations like a sheet of honey. She could feel every inch of skin tremble with newfound power. Chandra looked at her hands and turned them over. The sensation was odd. It took a moment to acclimate to but was not unwelcome. Somehow Chandra felt sturdier than she had moments before. She looked for words to describe how she felt, but all explanations she found failed to do the sensation justice.

Owen bore a similar reaction. Chandra saw the confusion on his face as he examined his hands, then lifted his shirt to feel his ribs. The same thoughts must have gone through the Spellseeker's head. The same thoughts, resulting in the same loss of words.

"I don't know how strong that armor is, if I'm honest," Ryleah said. Her hands fell from Chandra and Owen's heads to rest on their shoulders. "You might be impervious, or it might shatter the first time that thing hits you. Don't just run at that monster like you're made of steel, okay?"

"Don't havta tell me twice," Chandra replied.

Chandra clapped a hand onto Ryleah's shoulder. When she let go, she concentrated her attention on the Flow. The light from Ryleah's first rite had afforded Chandra time. There was no need to rip energy from the Flow without care. Energy meandered through Chandra's unburnt arm and down into the manarail spike. Metal flattened and sharpened. A fine point developed at the end of the short spearhead. Its thin surface was broad and shaped like a leaf.

Metal sang through the air as Owen flourished his weapon. He gave his sword a few gentle practice swings as if he searched for some change in the weapon he knew. A slight nod conveyed his satisfaction.

"Ready?" Owen asked.

Chandra did not allow herself time to ponder the question. There was too much weight to the word. It was burdened by her own life, by the future of her family. Ryleah's safety. She dared not give herself time to think. Time to reconsider the next few minutes of her life. Instead, she dropped her pack next to Ryleah and approached the counter. One hand gripped the haft of her spear. The other was planted on the counter as Chandra vaulted its gouged surface.

There was no spoken acceptance. No gesture of summons. All the acknowledgment Chandra gave Owen and his question was a steeled look over her shoulder. It was enough to get her point across. Owen nodded and slid himself over the counter after Chandra. The two walked out of the store and into the street.

The ashling continued to pace its way around the brilliant semicircle that illuminated the street. Pointed fingertips were visible at the frayed hem of the light. A low rumble disturbed the air and grew in intensity as Chandra and Owen drew near. Anticipation. Frustration. Whatever a monster like an ashling was capable of feeling. Perhaps it was the growl of a stomach that yearned for human flesh. There was no way to know. No reason to be derived from the gray-black coalescence of ash and hate.

Chandra shuffled bits of varmint aside as she walked, gripping her spear in both hands. The fetid stench of the massacre at her feet had not lessened. It mingled with the latent fear that surrounded the ashling as the smell permeated Chandra's senses. Her eyes began to water. Being immersed in the stench for so long had done nothing to protect Chandra from its influence.

Both Chandra and Owen stopped a few feet short of the light's edge. Chandra's light mingled with the light of the miracle and put the ashling's bulk on full display. The creature did not seem to care about Chandra's spell. It was not perturbed about being revealed.

"Last chance, Chandra," Owen said. His voice was low, but he did not speak in fear. A gentle calm kept his speech steady in the face of death. "No one will think less of you if you leave. You can take Ryleah and get yourselves out of here. Walk away from this nightmare and back to your family."

I'll think less of me, Chandra thought. *I didn't come this far to go home empty-handed. I won't allow my home to be taken.*

"I'm not the type that walks into a fight head on," Chandra said. Despite all the blessings and confidence, there was still a slight tremor in her voice. She did her best to push past all signs of warning and danger. To ignore what her body told her was a horrific mistake. She would not allow those seeds of doubt to sprout again. "Any advice?"

"Spread out," Owen replied in that same even tone. "Try to keep its attention on one person at a time. If one of us gets behind it, I bet we can strike without having to worry about those eyes. I'll try and get its attention first."

"Okay," Chandra nodded.

Owen was on the move before Chandra managed to reply. He bent low for a moment, then dashed sharp to the right. The light of his focus flicked on as he moved. It marked his path as he left the radiance of the circle and plunged headfirst back into darkness. Precise steps carried him over and around the bodies that littered his path. He moved in silence. No battle cry or fanfare. One moment he was right at Chandra's side, and he was gone the next.

Cobblestones cried out in earthen agony as the ashling shifted its weight to track Owen. Most of the eyes followed, as well. The ashling was transfixed by the new morsel of prey that had presented itself for annihilation. Chandra moved left along the edge of the divine light. A pair of eyes followed her for a few steps before they turned to Owen. Air rushed about in the darkness. One of the ashling's great hands appeared in Chandra's light, then came crashing down toward Owen. The walls of nearby buildings screamed as they were raked by the ashling's claws.

Now was the time. The ashling had placed all its attention on the exposed target. Owen was fully immersed in the dangers offered by the monster. This was the time for Chandra to make a move. She would deliver the first blow against the horror that beset her and her friends.

The first step was the hardest. Walking along the edge of Ryleah's divine light was one thing. There was a sense of security as if she stood behind dense walls of solid stone. Across that line was danger. Death. The zone of control was surrendered to the ashling. Safety may return if she stepped back into the light, but there was no way to be certain. An errant swing of the ashling's mighty hands might follow back into the refuge of light.

Another strike of claw against stone screamed in the darkness. There was no time to deliberate. Chandra slammed her right foot across the line of safety and took off like a spring swell down a mountain stream.

Targets were plentiful. The ashling was impressive in size and presented a bounty of points to attack. Chandra chose to keep clear of the arms and charge for the monster's tail. Its movements were slow and slight. Just enough motion to allow the ashling to redirect its continued assault on Owen. There was no way to miss it. All Chandra had to do was lower the tip of her spear and charge straight into the beast.

The eventual strike came as Chandra leaped over a pair of varmint bodies. Momentum from the jump carried her right into the ashling's flank. Chandra expected some manner of resistance from the plated body. Much to her surprise, however, the tip of the spear slid through the ashling as if the creature was adorned with nothing more than a moth-eaten bedsheet. Chandra struck with enough force to bury the spear up to her forward hand. Far enough that Chandra could feel the sleek, hard plates of the ashling's armor.

A brief sense of triumph was quelled by the cry that followed. It sounded as if a hundred bells crashed into each other all at once. Wrapped inside each bell was the wail of dozen lost souls crying out in pain.

Though the cry stabbed at her ears, it pushed a new wave of confidence through Chandra's limbs. Pain. There was no doubt that the ashling suffered from her blow. Black ooze seeped from the wound and coated Chandra's forward hand. It must have been whatever the ashling had for blood. Chandra had made the monster bleed. If the monster could be injured, it could be killed. Chandra gripped her spear tight and pulled it back to deliver another strike.

The spear did not come out.

Another pull was followed by another. Followed by a desperate yank. Despite her best efforts, Chandra's spear was lodged deep into the ashling. Attempts to remove it did not make the shaft so much as budge.

Movement above caught Chandra's attention. The ashling swung on its hips. Its full torso now faced Chandra. All eyes were brought to bear upon her, and Chandra felt the weight of their frigid gaze. Chandra continued to heave her spear backward to no effect. One of the ashling's arms rumbled out of view into the darkness. The lowest arm on its right side. Realization struck Chandra like a dizzying blow to the head: the ashling was winding up to strike her. Chandra placed a foot against the side of the ashling to increase her strength and pulled with all her might. The spear moved. A slight twitch. Not enough. The ashling's great hand was already on its way back into view. Chandra braced herself for the blow to come.

Metal crashing against metal pierced the air. The stump of an arm whisked past Chandra, causing her clothes to billow in the resulting breeze. Confusion came and went in a flash. Chandra saw that Owen had positioned himself between her and the ashling's strike. One of the monster's great hands twitched on a pile of varmint bodies. Owen had severed the hand before it could strike Chandra.

As the ashling cried out in pain, another pair of hands came crashing down from the left. They bore down on Owen with alarming speed. He was able to avoid the first attack, but not the second. The ashling's palm caught Owen and forced him to the ground. A winded gasp escaped the man as he was pinned. The ashling twisted its wrist, maliciously grinding Owen against stone and gore. Owen did not cry in pain.

The armor, Chandra realized. *The rite.* She felt the slight vibrations of her suit of divine armor. A gentle reminder that there was some manner of protection between her and the ashling.

What Chandra saw was a desperate struggle to strike the ashling's great hand. Pinned as he was, Owen was unable to land a blow. He was trapped in place while the ashling steadily ground away the armor that Ryleah had bestowed.

Chandra turned her attention from Owen back to her spear. The only way she could help was to strike the ashling again. To garner the ashling's ire that it might release Owen and focus instead on her. Chandra replanted her foot on the thick plates of armor and pulled with renewed vigor. Another slight movement. She heard flesh release its suction on the spear. The next pull wrenched the spear from the ashling and sent Chandra tumbling backward through bodies and sludge.

There was no consideration for the thick layer of fetid muck that dripped from her body. Chandra planted a hand atop a severed leg at her feet and forced herself up. She began her next charge the moment she was upright. This time she would aim for the torso. Just below the armpit of the lowest arm on the left. The arm that bound Owen in place.

The gap was short. Chandra was still close to the ashling from her first assault. A powerful step launched her forward. She needed to strike before Owen was reduced to pulp. Though the arm was several feet above her head, Chandra could still reach with her spear. It would not be as deep a wound as her first strike. The head of the spear might just pass through the armor and reach whatever soft tissue lay beneath. All thoughts vanished as quick as they rose.

Spite and rage boiled in Chandra's chest. Vitriolic fervor climbed up and spewed forth as a titanic roar. Hands shifted to the base of the spear shaft. One swift jab carried the glowing point of metal up and under the ashling's arm. Black ichor welled around the spear as it pierced the monster. Another blow had been struck! This time, Chandra was able to rip her weapon out from the ashling and deliver a second and third upward thrust.

The first stab wrung a cry of agony from the ashling. The second forced the monster to move its arm, releasing Owen from the confines of its razor grip. The third and final strike drew the ashling's attention right to Chandra.

Retribution was swift. Speed hitherto unseen from the creature, perhaps born from pain or desperation, carried an elastic arm right to Chandra. She raised her spear to defend herself against the blow but was no match for the ashling's strength. The back of the ashling's hand connected with Chandra and lifted her from the ground. There was force enough to carry Chandra away from the ashling, tumbling through the air. Her light spell vanished. Darkness enveloped Chandra as divine light wheeled away from her.

Dizzy peace lasted for a breath. The blow itself had caused no pain, only ripped the air from Chandra's lungs. Peace ended when Chandra met the stone road. One bounce carried her back into the air. The next ended in a tumble that slapped limbs on cobblestone. Bits of varmint helped to cushion the wicked fall. Still, by the time Chandra had rolled to a stop, she could not tell which way was up or down. Any attempt to find footing resulted in a slip that brought her low once more.

Nothing *felt* broken. Her head spun and she wanted to vomit, but there was no great pain that wracked her body. Both arms could support her weight until shattered balance brought her back to the ground. Neither leg groaned when Chandra bent her knees or rolled her ankles. Chandra was surprised that she could feel anything at all.

What she could not feel was the gentle vibration that had caressed her body. Between the strike from the ashling and the resulting crash, the armor bestowed by Ryleah had been depleted. The warm kiss of light that had glistened upon her skin was gone. There would be no surviving a second strike of that magnitude.

Rising from the ground was an unstable battle. The adrenaline that coursed through Chandra's veins began to thin. She could feel her legs quake and her knees begin wobble. Felt a slight tremor in her hands. *Empty* hands. Chandra flexed her grip in search of a spear that was not there. Blinking through the darkness, she scanned what she believed was the road. Tried to locate her weapon so that she might stumble back into the fight.

A golden shimmer poked out through the field of black. It lay between Chandra and the ashling, on her path back to the fight. Chandra willed herself forward on shaken limbs. Twice she tripped and fell to the ground before reaching the glowing spearhead. Her head still spun as Chandra wrapped her fingers around the haft of the weapon. Though her right hand found purchase near the spearhead, Chandra's left hand found no wood to grasp. Fingers crept over gore and blood-caked stone where the rest of her spear should be. Nothing. Chandra felt down the haft of the spear with her right hand until she was met with a grip of splinters.

When Chandra had attempted to block the ashling's strike, the blow had shattered the spear. Where the rest of the weapon ended up was a mystery left to the veiled road. What mattered was that Chandra had the spearhead. That the weapon had been reduced to little more than a foot in length was not important. Blows could still be struck. *Would* still be struck.

Chandra forced herself up. Her left hand pushed off a bent knee for support, while she held the spear in her right. A wave of steadiness washed over Chandra as she gripped the spear. Confidence returned to her desperate legs. Strength surged through arms that felt spent. The Flow entered her body and produced a small orb of light to lead her next charge. Sounds of battle bristled the hairs on the back of her neck. The fight was not over, and Owen was alone. A fact that Chandra meant to correct.

The chitinous bulk of the ashling's tail called to Chandra. Now that she was behind the creature, the slow-moving thing appeared to her as a ramp that led straight the torso. Chandra was in motion before the plan had been fully formulated. Her eyes scanned the segmented plates of the tail with vicious interest. Before she realized it, Chandra had a manarail spike in her left hand. The Flow moved through her and bent the spike into a savage hook with a barbed prong. Like a giant fishing hook meant to wrangle a shark or a whale.

Deadly purpose pushed Chandra forward in silence. Not one of the eyes on the ashling's torso had detected her. She wanted to keep her stealth for as long as possible. There was no battle cry to accompany this charge. No hailing for the ashling's attention or wild gestures meant to distract from Owen. That the battle raged on meant Owen was still fending for himself. Something that Chandra was keen to take advantage of.

The first few steps up the ashling were no more difficult to tackle than a flight of steps. Steps that shook a little and wobbled about, but steps nonetheless. Chandra was able to press several strides forward before the methodical movement of the tail forced her to lower her body. The motion of the tail was slow but powerful. Slick plates also afforded little in the way of traction for Chandra's boots. None of this stopped Chandra. It merely slowed her progress. With the hook, she was able to snag the lipped connections between armor plants. Chandra used her weight to find balance as she pressed forward.

It was not long before the armored plates grew wide. Too wide for Chandra to reach from one to the next without taking a step or two. A casual look to the left and right told Chandra that she did not want to fall. The gap from where she stood to the road might be able to fit a small house. Not something Chandra was keen to tumble down. Especially now that she was without armor of her own.

Flailing arms were close ahead. The torso was nearby. Just a few large plates away. Chandra eyed her target, just out of reach, with murderous intent. A few long strides would carry her unnoticed up the ashling's back and directly to its head. Unless there was a sudden turn, some shift of weight that might buck Chandra from her perch and throw her down to the stone below. The spear could be used as another hold if Chandra jabbed it into the armor. A sure way to garner the ashling's attention, but it would also ensure that Chandra had a sure path up.

Strained grunts penetrated Chandra's lethal focus. She leaned her weight to the right as she clutched the hook with her left hand. An attempt to monitor the state of the battle and the condition of her partner. Chandra was nearly falling from the ashling's back before she could get a sliver of a glimpse at Owen.

The Spellseeker looked ragged. His shoulders sagged and his legs almost bowed inward. A battle stance that was about to crumble. Surrounding him were the five hands that remained connected to the ashling. Three fingers had been clipped away, but the hands remained mostly intact. The ashling changed its approach. Rather than swing an arm or two at a time, it formed a deadly cage of fingers around Owen. To strike at one finger meant to leave himself open to others. Owen was reduced to fending off the fingers that drew nearest. Though purple light bloomed from a ring on his left hand in the shape of a shield, rips and tears in his clothing suggested that Owen would not win the battle of attrition. For all its lumbering might and feral howls, the ashling did seem to have a measure of sadistic cleverness.

He needs help, Chandra realized. *He needs it now.*

Concealment was no longer an option. Chandra flipped the spear-head to an underhand grip and jammed it into the plate ahead of her.

The reaction was immediate. Another of those piercing roars barreled out from the ashling to fill the black void of the ancient city. Chandra felt the tail move beneath her with new vigor. An attempt to dislodge her from her vantage point. Chandra did not waver. She pulled the hook free, lifted herself across the armor plate, and slotted it into the top of the plate segment. The spear slid freely from the ashling's flesh when Chandra beckoned. Hand over hand, she violently crawled her way up the thrashing monster.

Violent wind buffeted Chandra as a razor-sharp hand whipped past her. The ashling was keen to squash the ant that crawled up its back. Elastic arms flailed fanned-out fingers like a barrage of swords. Most passed Chandra by. Some tore at her clothes and left thin knicks and cuts on her flesh, but none came close enough to sever a limb or create a deep gash. There was relative safety so close to the ashling's back. Chandra was almost out of its reach.

Her path of destruction brought Chandra right to the katarl-like torso of the ashling. It rocked from side to side. Desperate moves to find some angle that would allow the ashling to rip Chandra from its body. Chandra slung her hook around the ashling's neck and drew herself as close to the torso as possible. What should have felt like flesh was just as cold and hard as the plates Chandra had just scaled. Pressed against the torso, Chandra felt the beat of mimicked life. Some approximation of a heart that forced black ichor throughout the whole of the ashling. To Chandra, it was little more than a target.

Wild stabs into the ashling drew further cries of anguish. Again. Again. Again. Chandra drove her spear into the side of the ashling's torso. The skin gave no resistance. Spearhead slid in and out with ferocious ease, ripping a gaping hole into the monster. Black liquid gushed from the wound and coated Chandra's hand. It was cold and greasy. The liquid congealed on her hand, between her fingers, almost as soon as it touched Chandra's skin. A thick coat of gore developed. It bound Chandra's weapon to her hand as her assault raged on.

The ashling did not sit idly by while it was viciously stabbed. Erratic movements of the torso sought to buck Chandra from her position, to throw her down to the ground so that the ashling might crush her like a bug. A series of sickening snaps overpowered the anguished cries of the ashling. Whatever bones the monster had in its arms shattered to allow greater flexibility. The chance for scythe-like fingers to bite further into Chandra.

Chandra paid the blades no mind. Deathly focus drove her exhausted arm like a piston. In and out. In and out. Over and over and over she stabbed the ashling. Chandra stabbed until writhing, bladed arms sunk and flopped onto the stone road. She stabbed until the metallic cacophony that erupted from the ashling's mouths ceased. Still, she stabbed as the torso went limp and tumbled down to the ground. The force of the fall ripped the spear from Chandra's grasp and sent her sprawling over the field of varmint bodies.

The ashling moved no more.

Quiet. It enveloped Chandra as she lay heaving on the corpse-cluttered road. The last time she had heard silence felt so long ago. As if the battle had raged on for days and days. A calm stillness accompanied the silence like a soft pillow. Chandra felt all her muscles relax. Her whole body accepted rest without hesitation or thought of further danger.

"Chandra?"

It was a short-lived silence.

"Chandra?"

Short and sweet.

"Chandra?!" Owen called for a third time.

"I'm over here," Chandra croaked in reply. She raised a limp hand so that she might stand out from the bed of corpses. Footsteps gushed and squished as Owen approached her. His light shone directly into Chandra's face, forcing her to blink at the brilliance that assaulted her.

"All in one piece?" he asked. Owen took hold of Chandra's extended hand and pulled her up to her feet.

"Yeah," Chandra gulped. Her knees knocked as her full weight came to bear on her legs. One knee was forced to the ground. Much to Chandra's surprise, she was not ready to stand. "Maybe? I think so."

"Oh," Owen gasped. "Oh, wow. Looks like it got you pretty good."

"What?" Chandra asked in a haze.

"Your back," Owen muttered. "Come on, let's go have Ryleah take a look."

"What do you mean?"

As Owen threw one of Chandra's arms over his neck and hoisted her upward a second time, Chandra knew exactly what Owen meant. It felt as if a searing blaze engulfed her back. Any movement, no matter how small, ratcheted the pain to an unbearable level. Chandra felt the wind escape her lungs as she took her first step. Adrenaline must have masked the pain while she battled. Now that the fight was over, Chandra could feel each cut and slash the ashling had delivered to her back.

"It's all right." Owen grunted as he took on the bulk of Chandra's weight. "One step at a time. We're there before you know it."

They did not arrive before Chandra knew it. Haggard steps jabbed searing knives into her shoulder blades. Dragging her feet while Owen bore her weight brought no better result. Bodies and severed limbs that were strewn about the road made the task no simpler. Whenever Chandra raised a leg over some piece of a varmint, it felt like a razor blade being dragged across her lower back. Chandra clenched her jaw so tightly that it felt like her teeth might shatter.

"Chandra?" came a squeak from ahead. "Owen? Is that you?"

"Yeah, it's us, Ryleah," Owen replied. "We're going to need some help. Chandra is cut up pretty bad."

"Oh gods, lead me to her."

Why can't you see? Chandra wondered. Blinded by pain, Chandra had not realized that her light spell dissipated. Whether it vanished as a result of the pain or when Chandra was bucked from atop the ashling was unclear. Ryleah must have been tucked in the back of the store, oblivious to the struggle in the road.

The cool stone floor was a welcome reprieve when Owen set Chandra down. He was gentle and did his best to ensure that Chandra was jostled as little as possible. Chandra did not protest. Fight had left her. The burning fury that drove her up the ashling was snuffed in favor of casual indifference. Even the wounds on her back started to fade into the back of her mind.

"It's not that bad," Chandra mumbled. She planted her hands on the shop floor, intending to push herself up and follow the sound of Owen's footsteps. A mistake. Chandra crumpled back to the floor the moment she pushed. Renewed fire blazed across her back. A grunt pushed out as Chandra tried to suck air in. An odd combination that rumbled in her throat before it died an embarrassed death.

"Keep still!" Owen called back in response. His tone was stern. A sergeant reprimanding a fresh recruit.

"Yeah," Chandra sighed. "Okay."

Leather and cloth scuffled over stone. Ryleah slid over the shop counter with Owen's assistance. Hurried steps carried the pair to Chandra.

"Sorry in advance," Ryleah uttered. Her gentle voice was like a silk scarf carried on a warm breeze. It soothed Chandra before any miracle had even been administered. "Guide my hands, Owen."

"Yeah," he muttered. "On it."

More shuffling. Hands grabbing wrists. Loose sleeves swished over Chandra's exposed back. She had expected them to lift the back of her shirt, but it was not necessary. So little fabric remained from the tattered garment that Owen could guide Ryleah straight to the wounds.

There was no level of delicacy that could have prepared Chandra. No warning would have sufficed. As gentle as Ryleah was, her probing fingers felt like knives to the open wounds. Chandra grumbled in distress. It was all she could do to keep herself from smacking Ryleah's hands away. Her body wanted desperately to do something to offset the new agonies.

Words tapped at Chandra's ear. It was Ryleah. The words themselves were lost in a mist of pain, but Chandra could feel their intent. Gentle reassurance that the pain would not last. Owen spoke here and there, though his tone was more difficult to decipher than Ryleah's. Some mixture of empathy and concern. Possibly a smack of sarcasm.

A high-pitched squeak cut through pain and reassurance. It sounded like a mouse or a rat. The small creature that Ryleah had carried in a pouch on her belt. This was the first sign of improvement. She could not feel the reprieve yet, but Chandra knew what was on the way.

Ryleah placed her hand, open palmed with fingers splayed, on Chandra's back. Another round of winces and jerks accompanied the gesture. Chandra struggled to control herself. *Just a second,* she pleaded to her body. *Let her work.*

Fingernails dug into palms. Toes curled. Chandra fought to maintain some semblance of composure while she waited for Ryleah to begin a rite.

Then it happened. Though she had not heard the words of the rite, Chandra recognized the sensation. Like an icy cold rag had been laid out over her wounds. Muscles tensed as they began to knit themselves back together. The smell of mint and lemon was strong. So strong that Chandra might have sworn in her delirium that she ground actual lemon mint leaves between her teeth. That same sense of cool refreshment radiated from her injuries. Where Chandra had felt pain, she now felt a kiss of winter.

The process was too intense to relax entirely. Though the pain was gone, the activity in her muscles prevented Chandra from drifting off into listless slumber. Voices began to take on the shape of words again. Owen and Ryleah conversed as if Ryleah were idly twiddling her thumbs for amusement.

"You're sure you can handle your own injuries?" Ryleah asked.

"Yes, it's fine," Owen replied. "Just a few shallow cuts. Some bruises that I'm sure will grow by tomorrow. Put all of that to use on Chandra. She's the one that needs it."

"You're sure? Once I get Chandra's wounds closed, they should be able to heal on their own. Given some time, of course. There'd be enough balm to at least help get you started."

"No, it's fine," Owen grunted. The sound of cloth sliding over cloth suggested a knot being tied. Owen continued after a few more knots and another handful of grunts. "Already done. No need to worry about me."

"You sure?" Chandra groaned.

"Yeah." Owen chuckled. Chandra felt him pat one of her boots twice. "Yeah, I'm all good. You rest up while you can."

"Don't you leave without us," Chandra demanded with the authority of a teetering drunk. "We're leaving together. No solo stuff."

"Yes, ma'am," Owen replied, his smile evident in his voice.

19

Staking Claim

Fresh skin crinkled as Chandra cut a slow path down the stone street. Every time she moved her arms, she felt the new skin stretch and groan. Bits of scab where the wounds had not fully healed cracked and crumbled under the slightest strain.

There had been more to heal than just her back. The palm of Chandra's right hand had been rubbed raw and was covered with popped and torn blisters. Reckless channeling had created a more severe friction burn than Chandra realized. Coupled with the frantic attack to the ashling's torso, it made for a mess of a hand. Ryleah was forced to dedicate some of the healing salve to the hand to avoid infection. That same fresh-skin feeling covered Chandra's palm and fingers as if she had just peeled away a layer of hot wax.

What bothered Chandra the most was her shirt. The old one, blood soaked and shredded, had to be discarded. Little remained of the garment by the time Ryleah was done. A new shirt meant fabric where there had been spacious holes to let her skin breathe. Fabric that brushed and grazed Chandra's back whenever she moved. It served as a constant and uncomfortable reminder of how close Chandra had come to a burial in the World Below. She would not have been walking without the aid from Ryleah.

Kindness stretched beyond the act of a minor miracle. Ryleah now carried Chandra's pack. While the scratch of a shirt was merely hindrance, the weight of the pack brought genuine pain. Chandra had made an earnest effort to bear the load. A vain effort that ended with Chandra on her knees sucking air between gritted teeth. Ryleah had been quick to offer a hand and refused to take no for an answer.

"I can make myself useful," Ryleah had said. "Don't you worry."

There was no doubt in Chandra's mind that Ryleah had made herself useful. She could not imagine a scenario where their operation succeeded without the powers Ryleah brought to bear. That the acolyte seemed to consider herself useless bordered on insult. If not to Chandra, then certainly to Ryleah herself. Those thoughts remained silent. Chandra merely nodded her acceptance at the time and summoned a light to walk by.

The trio was back on track. They had passed the thickest patch of varmint corpses on their way to the monolithic statue. All was quiet save for their cautious footsteps. There was no high from the previous victory that caused the group to walk tall. The event left them feeling smaller and more vulnerable. At least, that was how Chandra felt. This was her first proper brush with death that she could remember. She could feel her mind engrave the events in memory, a sculptor slashing away at marble to commemorate some terrible achievement.

At the back was Owen. He spent as much time walking forward as he did backward, on a constant swivel. Light from his focus sliced through the dark in search of whatever might lurk in murky alleyways or inside ancient buildings. The smattering of bandages around his arms and torso did not seem to hinder his movement. If he was in pain, he did an excellent job of smothering it.

Chandra walked at the front. Her light spell hovered several feet in front of her, revealing the path forward. In her tender right hand was her last manarail spike. The one buried in the ashling had been given up for lost, and the one blessed by Ryleah was hidden among varmint torsos and limbs. Light from the miracle had withered long before Chandra was healed.

Around Chandra's left arm was Ryleah. The acolyte clung to Chandra with both hands. Fingers trembled as they clutched Chandra's limb. Fear, all-consuming and terrible, had become real for Ryleah, as well.

Idle banter was abandoned for vigilant observation. Owen was not alone in his scan of the street. Chandra, too, peered this way and that once the path ahead was free of obstructions. Ears strained for sounds that refused to echo. There had to be some other noise in the oppressive void. The trickle of water or shuffle of loose rock. Some ancient breed of lizard evolved to live in the dark places of the world.

Anything.

"What's that?" Ryleah asked.

Shattered silence caused Chandra to jump. Her head snapped from side to side of the street, to edges of where her light could reveal. Nothing moved in the field of view afforded to Ryleah by the spell. The light from Owen's focus whipped forward to skirt the sides of the street.

"What's what?" Chandra asked. "I don't see anything."

"That!" Ryleah whispered. She released a hand from Chandra's arm and flung a finger forward. The trembling digit pointed straight down the street. "There's something moving out there, past your light."

"Someone's channeling the Flow," Owen hissed. A swift hand snagged Chandra by the shoulder. She felt Owen yank her toward the side of the street. "Douse your light. We're not alone."

Action fired before thought. Both lights flickered out. Darkness fell upon Chandra and her companions in a fretful instant. Chandra felt her heart sink to her boots and hammer at the cobblestones below. It sought to burrow away from where she was. Anywhere had become better than there.

Baylocke.

The name rang in Chandra's mind like a sour bell. Baylocke Battalion. Competitors out to steal her livelihood. They were ahead. While she and Owen had been battling for their lives against a mythic menace, those vultures were busy picking over the cache of focuses and relics. Chandra and Owen were a distraction. Live bait. She shook her head, trying to dislodge the notion with violent refusal.

It could be anyone, Chandra told herself. *Could be some random Shikaree that lucked out and found my stuff. It doesn't have to be the Baylocke people. Maybe a varmint survived? A varmint that can channel the Flow...?*

Desperate thoughts for the dark. A solution that did not end with having to fight an army of hostile Shikaree with years of combined experience and determination. Chandra had already fought her battle. The hard part was supposed to be over. Curse after curse after curse formed in her head, too fearful to pass her lips lest they be heard by whatever lurked beyond.

Chandra swatted at Owen's hand. They had cleared the street and were pressed against the nearest stone building. Pushing and prodding now smushed Chandra and Ryleah against the cold stone wall.

Pressure alleviated in response to the silent demand. With Chandra at the front and Owen at the back, the group began to feel their way forward. No lights. Hands on walls. Faltered steps at every door frame and open window while Chandra sought for the next piece of wall.

Progress was slow. Chandra moved at a painful crawl, doing her best to silence her footsteps. No noise could be surrendered. Surprise was on her side and she intended to keep it that way. Patience would carry her forward. Calm would ensure victory. She was so close to her prize, to the stability of her family. Nothing would deprive Chandra of her future. Not now. Not ever.

A timid hand at Chandra's back posed the greatest test to her silence. Ryleah kept one hand on the smooth stone walls, while the other rested on Chandra's freshly sealed wounds. The light touch forced Chandra's shirt to grind harder than before. She bit her lip against the discomfort and pressed onward.

Metallic noises pierced the silence as Chandra drew near to where the great statue would be. Metal striking metal, or clattering over stone. Someone manipulating the focuses and relics beneath the statue. It had to be someone. A few steps later, the hint of a voice crept into perception. Two voices. Three distinct voices. Chandra lost count after four. In part because the voices melded together. They overlapped and pushed each other around the blank darkness. Another part of Chandra refused to determine just how outnumbered she was. The notion of running into a dozen or more psychopaths made her sick.

Clarity came to the voices as Chandra and company continued to inch forward. Words formed where before there had just been noise. An abstract drone became coherent conversation.

"Hey, how much do you reckon this bracelet is worth? Got a bit of memory glass, some studs go all the way around. Bet it can do all sorts of stuff!"

The voice was familiar. Chandra had heard it twice before. On the day she found the map, and again on the day she was mugged in Eaststead. It belonged to a male human. His name was—

"Tumwe!" an unfamiliar voice snapped. It sounded female. Somewhat wispy, in contrast to the aggressive manner with which it spoke. "How many times do I have to tell you? If you don't know how much something is worth, ask Genevieve. That's literally what she's here for!"

"Yeah, but V's busy," Tumwe complained.

"Don't call me that," interjected a third voice. This one was unfamiliar as well, probably the Genevieve that was mentioned. There was a certain focus in her tone. Like she heard and responded to Tumwe without thinking about it while her attention was diverted elsewhere. "Bring whatever it is over here. I'll look at it next."

"Yeah, all right," Tumwe grumbled.

"How's it looking people?" a fourth voice boomed. This voice, another female, wielded command like a hammer. Chandra almost felt compelled to voice a reply to the question. "We're on the clock here. That ashling could be done with those people any minute, and I don't want to be here when it comes back. I want everything sorted and ready for transport in the next fifteen minutes. Got it?"

A chorus of responses chimed from various points in the darkness. *Yes, ma'am. On it. Right away, ma'am. Will do.* All manner of affirmations from a collection of Shikaree that remained cloaked in darkness. How they worked without light was a mystery, but it was not the most pressing issue. A clock had been started. Fifteen minutes began to tick in Chandra's head like a malicious stopwatch.

Fifteen minutes. Chandra had to come up with a plan to distract the Baylocke Battalion and execute it in a short window of time. Something that could get a whole collection of dangerous strangers away from the prize and busy with gods know what.

That's not enough time, Chandra reeled. *I need more time. I need to think! How do I fix this? How do I make them go away? How do I—*

"Ashling's dead, boss. The amateur and her lackeys are right here."

Chandra froze. Her heart turned to a block of ice in her throat. It felt like her skin was about to slide off her face. Panic and confusion jockeyed for first place as Chandra looked upward. This new voice came from right above where she stood.

"What do you mean 'right here,' Harish?" the commanding voice asked.

"Look down," Harish responded.

"Oh. Oh! Wow, if they were a snake. Hey there, amateur!"

Before Chandra had the chance to act, there was a dull pop. Brilliant red light, accompanied by a prolonged sizzle, flashed next to one of the statue's great feet. The source was a flare held by a tall Deepkin, whose pallid skin turned crimson under the glare. From her hips dangled a pair of hand axes that clattered against her thighs as she approached. Brown leather boots kicked focuses and relics aside. Short, asymmetrical white hair, highlighted with a shock of vibrant blue, swished about the woman's face without obscuring ruby-red eyes. She wore a padded gambeson, military style, that was flat black.

The woman's path was a direct course to Chandra and her companions.

Chandra drew herself up to her full height. At least one question was answered. A Deepkin could see well enough in the dark. Red light from the flare was nothing more than a threat. It was a way for the Deepkin to present herself without having to rely on Chandra to make a light. Confidence manifested across the woman's face as a wide grin.

The Deepkin stopped an arm's length away from Chandra. Chandra felt Owen place himself between her and the Deepkin as the woman extended an open hand.

"You'll get your turn, Seeker," the Deepkin snorted. "Step aside. I'm talking to the Shikaree girl. Olivia Baylocke, at your service."

Light from the flare made it clear that Olivia was intent on Chandra. The introduction was to Chandra and Chandra alone. Olivia even gave Owen a couple of gentle taps on his forearm to drive the point home. Confidence on this level was disarming. Chandra was not sure whether she should feel welcomed or afraid. She squinted against the piercing light as she looked Olivia up and down a second time.

"Chandra," she said as an introduction. A timid hand bent around Owen to take the Deepkin's. "Chandra Pattal, novice Shikaree."

Olivia grabbed Chandra's hand with enough speed and force to make Chandra flinch. A single, vigorous shake reminded Chandra just how fresh the skin on her hand was. She made a concerted effort to save face. There would be no grunts of pain or expletives uttered. This felt like a professional introduction, however odd that seemed. Olivia's smirk widened into a glorious smile as she released Chandra. Straight rows of pearly teeth glistened in the pulsing light of the flare.

"Excellent work with that ashling, Chandra," Olivia beamed. She looked beyond Chandra, down the road Chandra had just traveled. A brief distraction. The woman's gaze was back on Chandra when she spoke again. "*Very* nice work. Almost lost a few of my people to that thing when we first stumbled on it. Was worried I'd have to wait for a Keeper to hit town so I could pay 'em off, drag 'em down here. How'd you manage?"

Instinct caused Chandra's head to turn before she realized. Enough to let Olivia know that Chandra was about to look at Ryleah, who still stood just behind Chandra.

"Oh," Olivia cooed as she looked over Chandra's shoulder. "That wouldn't happen to be the half-breed that lives at the House, would it? What's your name, dear? Jamayla, wasn't it?"

"Ryleah," was the half-whispered response from the girl. Chandra felt Ryleah's grip tighten on a patch of her shirt. It pulled the collar of the shirt up to Chandra's throat.

"Leave her be," Chandra demanded in an even tone. She stepped to the side to fully obscure Ryleah from Olivia's view. "Harass me if you want, but leave her out of this. She hasn't done anything to you."

"Hasn't done… oh. Oh, you're talking about the map business!" Olivia waved a dismissive hand at Chandra. A bright chuckle attempted to sever the tension that Chandra had forged. "Forgiven, and almost forgotten. If Hendricks didn't want to wind up dead, then he shouldn't have been delving by himself on the side. Doesn't really matter if you twisted the knife or if it was somebody else. What's important is that you gave the map back, *and* you got paid for it. A win for both sides!"

"Pai… paid? Paid!" Chandra spat. "I got paid in kicks to the ribs while I was tied up on the ground. Your people ripped the map from my bag and left me to stew in my own blood!"

A curtain of visible confusion fell over Olivia's face. She cocked her head and bit her lower lip. Red eyes shone with an eerie glimmer in the light of the flare. She narrowed those eyes to slits and crinkled the bridge of her nose. Her right index finger tapped an unpredictable rhythm on the head of an axe.

Twice Olivia attempted to speak. Both times the words died in her throat, and she lowered her gaze away from Chandra. Olivia turned on her left heel with a decisive sniff and peered back from whence she had come.

"Tumwe! Alyssa!" Olivia barked. "A word!"

No reply came from the direction of the statue. At least, not in words. There was the unmistakable sound of bootheels grinding on stone. Steps cut through the metallic shuffle of relics and focuses, growing louder as they drew near. Their pace was steady at first. More hesitant as they approached Olivia. They stopped just outside the reach of the red flare. Tips of their boots were just visible at the edge of light.

Not that Chandra needed light to know who approached. The name and voice that belonged to Tumwe were familiar. Details of his face were vague, but Chandra remembered the powerful arms that had held her in place. Long enough to allow this Alyssa, assuming it was the same person, to bind Chanda's legs and arms. Who had kicked her was a blur. Maybe it was one of them. Could have been both. What had not faded was the memory of pain. Chandra's left hand wandered up to her ribs. Bones that had been cracked and broken with brutal disregard. There would be no mistake of that memory.

All the same, Chandra wanted to see their faces. What stupid expression might be on their arrogant faces this time? She intended to wipe away any smirks that the dark might hide. Energy from the Flow dripped into Chandra's arms and coursed down to her hand. Nice and slow, so as not to upset her freshly healed hand. Warm light blossomed from her palm in direct combat with the red of Olivia's flare.

There were no smirks on the faces of her attackers. Just grim recognition, and the answer to another question. Both Tumwe and Alyssa wore some kind of goggles. They were keen to lift them from their eyes once exposed by Chandra's light. A pained squint was soon alleviated by the action.

Focuses, Chandra realized. *Something that lets them see in the dark. Probably expensive too. Makes sense.*

"One more time," Olivia said softly to Tumwe and Alyssa. Chandra could only see the woman's face in profile, but it was evident that Olivia's expression had hardened. Cordial grace was replaced by stony disappointment. The look a teacher reserves for their most troublesome student. "Tell me how you got the map back. I'd love to hear that story again. In *great* detail."

Neither Tumwe nor Alyssa looked Olivia in the face. They both cast nervous glances between themselves. Slight gestures of their hands spoke the words they were afraid to utter. Small hand signs evolved into gentle taps against each other's arms, which evolved further into knuckled strikes. The meatiest strike was landed by Alyssa.

The discussion ended. Tumwe shuffled in place and wrung his hands, uneager to shoulder his newly acquired responsibility as story-teller. A pathetic look overcame his features as he raised a hesitant gaze to Chandra. Tacit cries for help echoed from his clenched jaw and raised eyebrows. Cries that died a swift death when met by the revulsion that seeped from every one of Chandra's pores.

"W-well," Tumwe stuttered. He had begun the unenviable task that was walking the tightrope between truth and lie. A few timid steps carried Tumwe closer to his boss as he spoke. "We got a tip that she was seen at that musty old bookshop. The one Olufemi runs. So, we posted up outside a few days in a row and, sure enough, the girl came back. Turns out she had the map on her, and we got it back."

"I feel like we're missing a few key details here, Tumwe." Olivia sighed. "If I recall, your instructions were to find the girl, ask for the map back, and pay her for her troubles. Does that sound familiar?"

"Uh, yeah," Tumwe mumbled. "And that's what we did...?"

Olivia struck like a falcon: swift and without warning. She swept Tumwe's leg and forced him hard to the ground before he could cry out. Her right hand clutched Tumwe by the neck with a white-knuckle grip. The breath in Tumwe's lungs made an audible exit from his body. A mixture of pain and surprise.

Alyssa showed no desire to aid her compatriot. Rather than kneel by Tumwe's side, she took a quick pair of steps backward. Enough space to escape the reach of Olivia without her actions being considered flight.

"I don't like being lied to, Tumwe," Olivia growled. "You were supposed to pay the girl, not *beat* her. Do you know how poorly that reflects on the company? On *me*?"

Sputtered attempts at a reply crawled through Tumwe's desperate lips. There was not enough air in his lungs to utter a proper sentence, whether it was a cry for help or an answer to his superior's questions. Despite this, he did not resist. Neither of his free hands reached up to claw at Olivia's arm. Tumwe neither kicked his legs nor rocked his torso in a struggle. All Tumwe did was gaze intently up at Olivia while the light began to fade from his eyes.

A rush of air roared into Tumwe's lungs. Olivia had snapped her hand away from Tumwe's neck as quickly as it struck. As Olivia stood and regained her composure, Tumwe dragged himself across the cobblestones until he bumped into Alyssa's shins. He remained on the ground, gasping, as Olivia turned back to Chandra.

"I would like to express my most heartfelt apologies," Olivia began. The confident mask slid back over her face as if it had never left. Smile and all. "Those two are still pretty new to the company. Haven't quite gotten our operation under their belts yet."

"Uh-huh," Chandra sneered.

"Look," Olivia sighed, "I don't blame you for the attempted genocide of my people just because you're Federation. You weren't at the Kastkills. Too young. Not your fault. I'm just asking for the same courtesy."

Even if the violence perpetrated against her had been a misunderstanding, it did not change the fact that Chandra experienced it. She did not trust the image that Olivia was putting on. The woman was *too* cordial. *Too* understanding. None of this felt right.

"So, where do we go from here?" Chandra asked.

Chandra made a half-hearted gesture toward the statue. If this Olivia woman was going to put on an affable show, it felt right to press a few buttons. See where the Deepkin's air of generosity ended and where her true intentions began.

Olivia raised an eyebrow. She glanced over her shoulder to follow Chandra's gesture. Her head was bowed when she turned back. Both shoulders rose and fell in time with quiet laughter.

"You *are* a bold one, aren't you?" Olivia said as she raised her gaze.

There was no warmth in the stare. Cold calculation stepped in to replace the front of hospitality and concern. It was enough to make Chandra shudder in response, though she maintained a firm footing. A display of weakness was out of the question. Not when Chandra was so close to her goal that she could taste it. Some kind of pittance would be enough. Better than leaving this place with nothing to show for her hardships.

It hurt to think as much, but Chandra knew there would be no standing against this woman and her whole contingent. Their number remained a mystery. Worse still was that they were equipped to operate in total darkness. Chandra might be able to blind them if she burst her light spell, but how much time would that buy? A few seconds? Maybe a minute if she was beyond lucky? And there was still Ryleah to think about.

"*We* keep looting," Alyssa cut in. "You and your friends turn around and get out of here."

"Hey!" Olivia snapped, turning renewed ire onto Alyssa. "The more you talk, the worse it's going to be for you later. Got it?"

Alyssa wrinkled her nose in protest but did not voice her displeasure. She cast her gaze aside and replied with a curt nod. A response that proved sufficient. Olivia turned her head from Alyssa to look at Chandra once more. The speed at which the woman could suppress her rage was alarming.

"I tell you what," Olivia began. "How about I make you an offer?"

"Offer?" was the single incredulous word Chandra gave in reply.

"Five percent. You sign on with me and join the Baylocke Battalion, and I'll cut you in for five percent of the profits. Out of these idiots' shares."

"What?" Alyssa groaned.

"I said quiet!" Olivia howled upward. She did not dignify Alyssa's outburst with a glare. An even tone of business returned when Olivia began again. "Five percent. This whole debacle has been as good an interview as I could ask for. You found your way here, dealt with an ashling, and survived these two idiots. Imagine how well you could do for yourself if you had someone to mentor you. Someone that can show you how a *real* Shikaree makes their money."

"Someone who can beat me if I make a mistake?" Chandra asked. She gestured toward Tumwe with an open hand. The man had not yet regained his footing. Alyssa had knelt to examine his neck, while Tumwe continued to cough. "I don't think so."

"Oh, no, no, no," Olivia replied with a shake of her head. "Those two are placeholders while I look for talent. And I *know* when real talent is staring me in the face."

There had to be more to say. Something Olivia was keeping quiet about. Chandra refused to believe this woman would offer genuine employment at the drop of a hat. Even if Olivia was telling the truth, Chandra could not imagine working for someone that might snap her neck at a moment's notice. The speed and precision with which Olivia moved were unreal. Escape would not be an option if Chandra managed to anger the woman.

You killed an ashling. What's one Deepkin?

The voice was small. Nestled somewhere deep beneath the distrust and caution was a thought that fought for attention. It burrowed like a tick through reason. Grew in size until it dominated Chandra.

Five percent is more than a pittance, the voice said. *How were you even going to get the whole cache out anyways? Even if five percent doesn't pay off the debt, it should cut out a big chunk. Enough to keep the collectors off our backs for months. Years, even!*

Greater and greater the voice grew in Chandra's mind. It unclenched her jaw and softened her adamant gaze. Fingertips tapped against palms in anticipation. *Why make this harder than it needs to be?* Chandra asked herself. *Why not take the money now and just quit later?* Run off back to where she belonged with money in hand, ready and able to support her family for years to come.

The weight of rewards to be tugged at her shoulders and weakened her thoughts. This option, to join with the Baylocke Battalion and reap the immediate benefit, began to ring more and more true. It meant greater security on the trip back to the surface. More eyes than Chandra's alone to watch out for Ryleah. People to make sure that her friend made it out alive if Chandra herself perished. A wall of bodies to put between herself and any other Shikaree that might view Chandra as an easy mark.

Chandra turned her head enough to see Ryleah. The fear that was evident on the acolyte's face pained Chandra to her core. Ryleah would not be here in this situation if Chandra had not asked. Further unnecessary risk would only jeopardize Ryleah's safety. Her life.

When Chandra looked back at Olivia, Chandra forced herself to look past the veneer of confidence the woman touted. Beyond the display of violence and the uncertain future that might follow an agreement of service. Whatever loopholes might bind her to service and cage her in place, were they not worth it for a guarantee of safety? What would happen if Chandra said no? Would Baylocke and her people let Chandra walk away in peace?

Reason wormed its way back into the conversation with heavy questions. The sort of questions for which Chandra held no answer. There were too many unknowns to allow her to make the best choice. Even so, Chandra had to make *some* kind of choice. To stand silent forever in the ancient city of Those Who Came Before was not an option.

"Go with them, Chandra," Owen muttered. A harsh metallic ping sheared through the air. Chandra looked down to see that Owen had drawn his caster pistol and opened the breach. Nimble fingers replaced the cartridge within with another he held in his hand. "I'm sure five percent should take care of any money troubles you have. It'll be safer than sticking with me."

"Wait, what?" Chandra snapped. Her gaze rose from the pistol and up to Owen's face as her brow knit into a web of confusion. Grim purpose dawned on Owen's features. Familiar kindness was a distant memory. Reassurance was nowhere to be found. All that remained was a dour frost as he slid the chamber of his caster pistol back into place.

"Oh, wow," Olivia chuckled. "You are just *chomping* at the bit, aren't you, Seeker? All right. Go on. Say your lines."

"I am Third Seeker Owen Raulstone," Owen began, "and I represent the Lost and Stolen Division of the Arnstead Arcanarium. I have reason to believe that some or all of the focuses located near the statue are stolen. In accordance with Federal law, you must surrender all such focuses to the Bureau of Arcane for investigation. You will be fairly compensated for all focuses that have not been claimed by their original owners within ninety days. Your cooperation with this investigation is appreciated in advance."

These were not the ardent words of a Spellseeker about to claim a massive prize. They were hollow, wooden words spoken as a matter of course. Owen did not expect cooperation. Chandra could hear it in his tone. As if to further cement the notion as fact, Owen reached behind his back with his left hand and drew the dagger he kept on his belt. Sapphire light shone from the castor pistol. He was already channeling the Flow into the focus, readying it for use.

"Owen, what's going on?" Chandra asked.

"Aha, there it is!" Olivia laughed. With a snap of her fingers, she rolled her head to look at Tumwe and Alyssa. "You two are on Seeker duty. Harish!" she shouted upward. "We've got goodies to sort through. You too, amateur. Let's move!"

The scout from the building above fell into the light. A Bangeli katarl who wore a gambeson like Olivia's. The man did not make a single sound when he connected with the stone road. Familiar goggles hid his eyes from view. In his hands were a bow and an arrow nocked and ready to fire.

Olivia turned and walked toward the statue of Those Who Came Before. She tossed the red flare aside, narrowly missing Tumwe and Alyssa. The pair flinched as the pulse of light flew past them. Olivia raised a hand and beckoned with two fingers. A gesture Chandra assumed was meant for her.

"Owen!" Chandra barked.

The confusion began to dissipate as Alyssa and Tumwe walked forward and squared themselves before Owen. Alyssa drew a concealed knife with her right hand. Her left hand ran across a length of rope that dangled from her hip. Tumwe's preparations were simple. From his pockets, he pulled a polished pair of metal knuckle-dusters that gleamed in the light.

"I'm a Spellseeker," Owen said. There was steel in his voice, cold and lethal. "I've seen these people looting stolen focuses, and they've refused to surrender those focuses. There won't be anyone to file a report if I die down here."

"No," Chandra sputtered. "No, that's not okay—"

"It's all right, Chandra," Owen interrupted. For the briefest moment, there was a trace of warmth in his voice again. "I knew the risks when I agreed to help you. Go on and follow them, and take Ryleah with you. You'll be safe that way."

Full realization smacked Chandra in the face like a broken tree limb hurtling through a hurricane. Painful truth that dredged up haunting memories. Spellseekers standing resolute in their line of duty, death just an arm's length away. Irate crowds with weapons in their hands. Murder etched into the eyes of a mob.

This was it. This was what it must have looked like when her mother died. Breath failed Chandra. Her body forgot how to function. She blinked at hostile steel before turning her gaze back to Owen. Jagged disbelief severed tendons that fought to move. Words failed to form in her mouth. A cold fire burned in her stomach. A sickening fire that brought the taste of bile to Chandra's mouth. She wanted to double over and pass out on the stone road, anything that could silence her mind.

A hand clutched at Chandra's back. Another hand. Imagined pain was replaced by the real. Chandra felt Ryleah pull herself close. So close that Chandra felt the two of them might merge. Her tender back burned.

"Chandra," Ryleah whispered into Chandra's ear, "this is wrong."

There was no doubt about that. All of this felt wrong. That Chandra had convinced these people, Owen and Ryleah, to join her on her quest for treasure. That the people in front of her were ready to callously toss a life aside for being an inconvenience. That there were people in the world that could drive someone like Chandra to these lengths in good conscience. None of it made sense. All of it was wrong.

Through it all, Chandra felt a small weight in her pocket. A familiar sensation. Something she had not bothered to pay attention to for quite some time. Chandra could almost hear the tick of the pocket watch through its case. The sound reverberated in her mind, imagined though it was. Like the steady voice of her mother long past. Tick, tick, tick morphed into two repeated words. Chandra heard those words as if her mother whispered them into her ear.

Stand. Fight. Stand. Fight.

Chandra clicked her tongue against the back of her teeth and sneered at the Baylocke Battalion. Her left hand pointed toward the nearest unoccupied building. Chandra's right channeled the Flow into her last manarail spike.

"Go inside, Ryleah," Chandra said between gnashed teeth. "Don't come out until we're done."

After another tight squeeze, Ryleah released Chandra's shirt and stepped through the magical light. The girl disappeared into the shadow of a rigid home without a word.

"Chandra, I said—"

"Shut up!" Chandra snapped, cutting off Owen as he spoke. "I dragged you down here. I'm dragging you out. Alive."

A slight hint of motion in the corner of her eye told Chandra that Owen had turned to look her way. She did not acknowledge him. All her attention was focused on forming a dagger as safely as possible. Thanks could wait until the job was done. Now was not the time for celebration.

The two members of the Baylocke Battalion cocked their heads. Alyssa sniffed with her short snout. Tumwe squinted through the bright light, eyes fixed on Chandra. Alyssa and Tumwe gave each other a glance. Tacit communication to decide who would speak first. This time it was Alyssa's turn.

"Hey, boss," Alyssa hollered over her shoulder, "looks like your new pet doesn't want to come along. What should we do?"

Brief silence was quenched by an icy reply.

"Try not to kill her, if you can help it."

Olivia's voice seemed to hang in the air. A graceful prelude to the violence that would soon commence. Both Alyssa and Tumwe smiled and shrugged. Made no difference to them. They had beaten Chandra once and were sure they could do so again.

"Tie her up, Alyssa," Tumwe said quietly. His words barely reached Chandra's ears. "I'll keep the Seeker busy."

White light emanated from Alyssa's fingertips and her eyes glowed a haunting shade of yellow. The katarl wasted no time. Energy fueled into the rope at her side caused the tool to spring to life. It whipped through the air like an eel chasing its quarry through a reef. The length of rope bent and snapped as it wriggled toward Chandra.

Another wave of familiarity smashed into Chandra. Though this was her first time seeing it, Chandra recognized the trick that had bound her in the alleys of Eaststead. Familiarity that did not accompany an answer. The manarail spike in Chandra's hand formed an edge in time to slash at the rope as the hempen snake sprang upon her. No good. Lively coils twisted around the keen edge of Chandra's dagger and latched onto her arm. Chandra shook her arm as if to swat away a deadly wasp, but her efforts only seemed to further entangle her in the rope. When she reached over with her left hand, the rope jumped upon the new target and bound Chandra's arms together.

Chandra took a pair of panicked steps back. She waved her cinched arms about in the air, desperate to free herself from the clutches of Alyssa's spell. A glance up from her arms revealed that Alyssa stalked toward her. This further fanned the flames of panic as Chandra's mind reeled for a solution. The binding of her arms was so thorough that she could not twist her dagger to slash at the winding rope.

A dagger sliced through the air, just ahead of Chandra's hands. It was not Alyssa's weapon. The hand that bore the dagger belonged to Owen. He managed to nick the evasive rope with the fine point of his weapon. Not enough to cut through the rope by any means. All the same, Chandra felt the rope around her arms go slack. The trail that led back to Alyssa plummeted from the air to land on the ground with a lifeless thud. Alyssa's spell was shattered. A look of disgust warped her confident features into an ugly display of failure. She began to charge, her knife raised.

The charge was short-lived. Owen leveled his caster pistol at Alyssa's legs and released the spell chambered within. A jet of water flew from the weapon and collided with Alyssa's ankle. She barely seemed to notice until the water froze to her fur. The remaining water changed course and lashed out at her other leg, freezing against the other ankle. Both frozen ankles were yanked together and joined in a dense hunk of ice.

The whole event unfolded before Chandra could blink. Forward momentum carried Alyssa to the ground. Her knife flew from her hand and skittered across the cobblestones.

Chandra looked over to Owen, intending to thank him, just in time to see Tumwe strike the Seeker in the side of the head. The blow was just foul of the jaw. Still, there was enough force to send Owen stumbling backward. His defense of Chandra had left the Seeker open to a powerful blow. Tumwe launched after Owen to press the advantage.

A noise pulled Chandra's attention away from Owen. It sounded like a loaded sled dragged across a frozen lake, and it came from Alyssa. The woman had recovered from her fall. Claws extended, she pulled herself toward her dagger. A perfect tool to chip away at the uneven lump of ice that bound her ankles.

Chandra bounded toward the katarl with powerful strides. With a brutal grunt, she smashed her foot into Alyssa's face as if kicking a ball. The top of her foot collided with the tip of Alyssa's snout to produce a loud crunch.

Consciousness fled Alyssa faster than an out-of-control manarail engine, and with just as much force. Chandra was free to unbind herself. It took a moment of awkward struggle, but Chandra was able to wriggle from the ropes.

As the rope fell from her arms, Chandra turned in time to see Owen stop a sweeping punch from Tumwe. Only the strike did not stop. Owen had raised his dagger to catch the arm, but the arm slid right through the blade. Knuckle-dusters continued forward and smashed into Owen's face a second time. Tumwe's arm seemed to turn to vapor where the blade passed through. Owen fired his caster pistol as he stumbled back, but the jet of water passed through Tumwe's leg to create a sheet of ice on the stone. The same vapor-like defense. Tumwe's leg had turned to mist where Owen's spell would have struck.

How do you beat that? Chandra asked herself.

There was no time to ponder a solution. Their opponent wound up to strike another unopposed blow. Chandra could not imagine that Owen would last long if she did not do something. Anything was better than nothing.

Trying her best to advance in silence, Chandra slunk forward. Her gaze was locked on the back of Tumwe's left leg.

Maybe if he doesn't know I'm coming, Chandra reasoned. *Maybe I can get him if he doesn't know I'm here.*

Tumwe seemed intent on bashing Owen to a pulp. Another strike passed through Owen's defenses and caught him square in the face. Crimson sputtered out from his broken nose as Owen continued to backpedal.

As Tumwe closed in for another blow, Chandra drove the point of her dagger into the back of Tumwe's leg.

A new stream of crimson began to pour. This one from Tumwe. The blow from behind connected while Tumwe was distracted. His step faltered, and his next swing went wide. Owen was spared another vicious blow to his unprotected face. A blessing that allowed the Spellseeker to regain some of his balance.

The next strike was at Chandra. Tumwe swiveled and turned his hips as he drove his reinforced fist into Chandra's face. A wide right hook smashed into her ill-prepared jaw. Brute strength carried Chandra to the ground. She hit the road hard, her head bouncing on the raw stone. The world spun as bright stars flashed all around. Purple spots plagued her vision as Chandra blinked at the pain.

Something felt loose in her mouth. On her tongue. Chandra rolled over to her side and coughed. A tooth, covered in her blood, shot out with the force of the cough. Reflex placed a hand on the cheek that had been punched. Regret ripped the hand away as Chandra became fully aware of the pain in her face.

Metal sheared against metal. A piercing sound that cut through Chandra's daze. When she turned her head to look, Chandra felt the familiar sensation of booted toes smashing into her ribs. Another cough. More blood from the gap in her teeth splattered onto the street. There was just enough time for Chandra to roll over and see Tumwe rear back for another kick.

"Second time you stabbed me," Tumwe spat as he unleashed another kick into Chandra's ribs. "Won't be a third."

"Hey!"

The cry stopped Tumwe before he delivered the next kick. Chandra allowed her bleary gaze to lull toward the exclamation. Owen had re-covered and was pointing his caster pistol at Tumwe. Blood covered Owen's lips. Dripped from his chin. He did not seem to be in a much better state than Chandra, apart from the fact that was able to stand. Visible pain did not deter him. Owen held his weapon pointed steadily at Tumwe.

"Go ahead," Tumwe chuckled. He stepped away from Chandra and toward Owen. Fear and caution were absent from Tumwe's stride. He practically sauntered over to Owen. "See if it works better this time."

Owen snapped his aim from Tumwe's chest down to a leg in response. A misty circle that had occupied the center of Tumwe's chest followed Owen's aim along the body and down to the leg. The man was prepared for another spell to be launched his way.

Undeterred, Owen launched the spell at his target. There was no water this time. No chance for ice to form around the approaching attacker. An altogether different spell erupted from the caster pistol. Wind leaped from the weapon at gale force and collided with the band of vapor that circled Tumwe's leg. The Flow-infused molecules were battered by the wind and forced to disperse behind Tumwe.

Severed meat crashed to the stone road with a juicy thump. Tumwe, expecting for his weight to be caught on the leg, soon after. Arms whipped up to brace the fall. More an instinct than in response to what had happened. It was not until Tumwe tried to stand that he realized his leg was no longer connected to his body. He smashed back into the ground from the effort. There was no pain in his eyes when he looked down at the bleeding stump. Shock stepped in to dull any sensation the man might have experienced, but that did not stop him from screaming in terror. The world around him vanished. Tumwe no longer had a mind for Chandra or Owen. His lost limb occupied all rational thought until the man grew pale and crumpled to the ground unconscious.

A dirty sleeve wiped blood from Owen's nose and chin as he unceremoniously stepped over Tumwe. Deliberate strides carried him to Chandra, who still lay on the street with a hand to her side. She took Owen's hand when it was offered and allowed herself to be hauled onto her feet. It was an endeavor that neither party enjoyed. Both winced and sucked air through their teeth as they steadied themselves.

"You all right?" Owen groaned.

"I'll manage," Chandra replied before spitting out a gob of filmy blood. Her tongue prodded the gap where a tooth once rested. Too late she realized her mistake as a jolt of pain shot through her jaw. She spat another gob of blood. No matter how much she spat, Chandra could not get the metallic taste out of her mouth.

"Thanks for stepping in," Owen went on. "Gave me time to change caster charges. He would have beaten me to death if you hadn't helped."

"We helped each other," Chandra replied with her best attempt at a smile. She could scarcely imagine the grisly sight that was her teeth covered in blood while she grinned. The back of her left hand became smeared with crimson as Chandra attempted to clean her face. "So, what happens now?"

"Have to stop the bleeding."

"Are you cut somewhere?" Chandra inquired, looking Owen over for injuries. Alyssa never had the chance to get to him, but Tumwe had landed a handful of powerful blows. Most of the strikes showed as lumps of red that promised to form horrific welts or bruises. One spot had broken skin, but the injury looked far from life-threatening.

"Not for me," Owen huffed while he fought to catch his breath. He pointed a finger at Tumwe. "For him."

Owen set his weapons down and went about coiling the rope that had bound Chandra. Not another word escaped the Spellseeker. The silence gave Chandra a moment to process the mental gymnastics of what her companion had just said.

"Wait, you're going to help these people?" Chandra asked in disbelief. "They just tried to kill you!"

"Doesn't mean I want to see them dead," Owen grunted.

Owen knelt next to the unconscious Tumwe and wrapped some rope around the man's stump of a leg. Blood oozed from the hole at an alarming rate. The steady flow would surely kill Tumwe without intervention if shock did not claim him first. An improvised tourniquet of rope seemed to be what Owen had in mind. Coils were cinched tighter and tighter until the flow of blood had dwindled to trickle. Satisfied, Owen sat back on his heels and looked at his blood-covered hands.

"Just a stopgap," Owen muttered. "He might make it, but they need to get him out of here fast."

Stunned silence held Chandra's tongue while she had watched Owen work. She was still processing the thought of Owen bandaging a man that had just tried to crack open his skull. Astonishment did not begin to describe the notion. Chandra understood not wanting to be responsible for a person's death, but this was self-defense. The conflict that wracked her brain was an uncomfortable one. It was not the type of moral dilemma to be explored while under the threat of death.

"What now?" Chandra asked. The queasy argument that raged in Chandra's mind had left her numb. She did not know what to think and decided to shelf the conflict for another time.

"Well, that was quick," came a response from the dark, as if on cue. Chandra snapped her head to the edge of the light as a pair of boots strode into view. The frame of Olivia followed soon after. In her hands were the axes that had hung from her hips. She did not raise them into a guard position but rather tapped them against her legs as she walked closer and closer. That same mask of confidence took a sinister new meaning as the woman approached with weapons in hand. Olivia smirked as she said, "I guess that's what I get for sending juniors to do the chief's job, huh? Hey, Harish, cover me!"

There was no sign of the archer. Chandra could only guess where the katarl stood out in the dark. The notion of an arrow flying from any direction was not a comforting one. She gripped the rough handle of her dagger and raised the weapon. If she could help it, Chandra promised herself she would not be a liability this time.

Owen took a different approach. Quiet steps carried him from Tumwe back to his weapons. Blood-covered hands scooped up dagger and pistol without a word. Rather than reply to Olivia in some official capacity, or tell her to drop her weapons, he leveled his caster pistol at her chest and released the wind spell once more. A terrible gale ripped through the air with enough force to pull Olivia off her feet.

Except that is not what happened. Olivia did not allow herself to be struck. She raised her left hand in response to the spell. Violet light flared from a ring Olivia wore. Ruby eyes flickered to piercing sapphire for the brief moment that Olivia channeled the Flow. When the powerful gust reached Olivia, it flowed around her like a river against a time-ravaged boulder. There was no strain on Olivia's face or in her movements. Her stride slowed a touch but resumed its inevitable pace soon after Owen's spell dissipated.

"Come on," Olivia cooed, "where's the fun in that?"

Metal slid against leather. The sounds of Owen holstering his pistol and sheathing his dagger. Next to cut through the air was a sword drawn from its sheath. Purple light radiated from Owen's direction. He must have reignited the shield he bore against the ashling. Not that Chandra saw any of this transpire. She was too frightened to take her eyes off Olivia as the woman stood just outside of striking distance.

"Much better," Olivia snarled in response to Owen's change of weapon. She looked from Owen over to Chandra. Complete dispassion in Olivia's voice gave Chandra chills when she next spoke. "Last chance, amateur. Mercy falls on deaf ears after we start."

Seething pain was not a sharp enough deterrent to keep Chandra from clenching her jaw. The cold, unfeeling words of Olivia brought just as much terror as the unreal howl of the ashling. Perhaps even more. She was lean and armored. Armed to the teeth. More like a proper soldier than Alyssa or Tumwe. An unyielding force, tensed and ready to unleash itself on any who were unfortunate enough to stand in her way.

The dagger felt insubstantial in Chandra's hand. Like she brandished a butterknife in the face of a grizzly bear. Unnerved, Chandra could not stop herself from taking a step back. Precaution against the wicked violence she knew would come her way. She would not allow herself to stand down. As terrified as she was, Chandra refused to let history to repeat itself before her very eyes. She would not let Owen be crushed under the ungrateful bootheel of Arnstead.

"Take a deep breath," Owen urged. The familiar voice brought a sliver of calm to Chandra. Enough to help her focus on the task at hand. "Same as the ashling. We get on either side of her, and—"

Directions were cut short by a grunt. An uncomfortable pause snapped another handful of Chandra's nerves. She could not bring herself to cast a glance sideways but yearned to know why Owen had stopped midsentence. Fear overruled her curiosity. Chandra could not bring herself to let Olivia out of sight. Not even for the briefest of moments.

A look of confusion tugged at the wild excitement that dominated Olivia's features. She cocked her head to the side, then cast a disappointed glance back over her shoulder. Axes rose out to either side of Olivia in a show of exasperation.

"I said cover me, Harish," Olivia belted, "not shoot him."

"Wasn't me!" Harish replied from somewhere in the darkness.

This exchange was enough to break Chandra's focus. She had to know. The answer to her confusion slapped her in the face when she turned to look at Owen.

Contagious confusion had spread to Owen. His gaze was locked on his left side, the space between his breast and shoulder. An arrow shaft protruded from just below his collar bone. Grimy, black fletching twitched and rustled in response to subtle movement. Surprise continued to plague his face as his left hand worked its way up to touch the shaft. Pain shattered his confusion before he managed to touch the missile.

A skittering sound popped up between Chandra and Olivia. The sound of a second arrow with the same black fletching. Its tip was crude with a pair of vicious barbs. Chandra looked from the arrow on the ground over to Owen, imagining those same barbs ripping into his flesh. Scraping against bone. It was not the sort of arrow a person could just rip out. Reckless removal would do Owen more harm than good. Chandra watched those same thoughts go through Owen's mind as he looked from the arrow on the ground to his shoulder.

When the third and fourth arrows struck nearby buildings, Owen snapped from his pained expression.

"Cover!" was all Owen said.

"On me!" Olivia commanded at the same time. "We're under attack!"

20

Tooth and Claw

Arrows whistled through the air. What started as a sparse volley became a shower of metal-tipped death. Arrowheads click-clacked against stone streets and walls. Brittle shafts snapped into plumes of splinters. The missiles seemed to come from every direction all at once. All from on high, with archers lining the rooftops of the ancient buildings. Safe from immediate retaliation. Free to fire again and again without reproach.

The only luck to be had was that the archers attempted to replace quality with quantity. Arrows often landed feet away from any of the vulnerable targets below. Owen had suffered a rash of bad luck when he was struck by the first arrow. That same level of accuracy was not replicated as all present bolted for cover.

For Chandra, that meant a mad dash into the home where Ryleah scurried before the fight.

Primal confusion had dominated Chandra at first. She looked this way and that for the source of danger. Whatever was firing at her was concealed by darkness above the reach of her light. It was not until Owen wrapped an arm around Chandra's back that she started to move, goaded forward into cover. Barbed missiles continued to land at her feet and whip past her head all the while.

Light filled the crevices of the ancient home. Molded chairs lay on their sides. Sticks and stray rags filled a whole corner of the house. Some kind of nest. Chandra did not spare any time to think about what she saw. She crossed the room with long strides and flung her arms around Ryleah, who had tucked herself into the nest-like corner.

"What's going on?" Ryleah spluttered. "I heard shouting. Are you okay?"

"We're fine. We're fine." Chandra placed a comforting hand on the back of Ryleah's head.

"Varmints," Owen muttered.

"What? How?" Chandra asked. She craned her head back to peer at Owen. "You saw those streets. The ashling got to them."

"Well, not all of them, apparently," Owen grunted. He set his sword on the ground to free both hands. With his right hand, he steadied the arrow lodged in his shoulder. His left hand snapped the brittle arrow shaft with a violent twist. The action was illuminated by the purple shield over his forearm and elicited a grunt of pain. Chandra could not help but wince at the display. "I've seen these arrows before. Definitely varmints."

Owen looked the arrow shaft over in the light as if to be doubly sure. He pitched the splintered arrow to the ground when satisfied and picked up his sword. The shield flickered a little over his arm. Owen seemed to struggle to maintain concentration on his protective focus. Small droplets of blood began to pool on his knuckles and drip to the floor.

Chaos blared outside. Arrows continued to click and clack wherever they fell. A rush of feet smashing against stone. The occasional cry of pain when an arrow found a fleshy home. Metal and leather dropped onto the hard ground and the scrape of retrieval. All sounds of the Baylocke Battalion. Olivia had summoned them when the avalanche of arrows had begun. How many of them made it to her was unclear. It sounded like a handful, at least, had managed to get into the building across the street.

Muffled cries erupted from the opposing building. Chandra could not make out all she heard but did catch two names. Alyssa and Tumwe. Realization caught Chandra like a branch on horseback. Those two had been left out in the middle of the street. They were unconscious and unable to fend for themselves, abandoned to a rain of arrows.

The pair of them might still be alive. However slight the chance, it was true that the varmints struggled to hit their marks. Some slim possibility held that Alyssa and Tumwe might survive the volley. That they were still and prone lent more credence to the thought. They had not even presented themselves as targets to the archers. Despite how they treated Chandra, Alyssa and Tumwe were still people. Chandra didn't want to be like them. The sort of person that abandons injured strangers to the will of the world.

Dagger in hand, Chandra crept her way over to the open doorway of the house. The density of arrows had subsided. Clicks and clacks of arrowheads on stone grew less frequent. Chandra could see, as well as hear, as she willed her light spell out into the street. Over to where she estimated the fallen members of the Baylocke Battalion to be.

There you are, Chandra noted.

It took just a few moments to locate the motionless bodies of Alyssa and Tumwe. By some miracle, Tumwe had been spared the assault of varmint arrows. Alyssa was less fortunate. Two arrows were burrowed into her exposed flesh. One was lodged into her right thigh, while the other had struck a shoulder blade. Neither were fatal. All Chandra had to do was wait for the arrows to stop.

"Chandra?" Owen called out from the back of the house. "What are you—"

Now!

Arrows had slowed to a trickle. Chandra could sense that Owen was about to stop her. It had to be now. If Chandra was going to move, she had to do it *now.*

Chandra blasted out from the house. Her head was lowered, with one arm raised in protection. The target was Alyssa. She was closest to the house, and, from the look of her, Chandra guessed Alyssa to be the lighter of the two battalion members. An arrow whistled overhead. Another clicked by Chandra's ankle. She ignored the danger and pressed forward.

Adrenaline shortened the gap to the blink of an eye. Chandra chomped down on her dagger to free her hands as she slid to a stop. Alyssa remained motionless. There was no time to rouse her. Chandra knelt and hooked her hands under Alyssa's armpits. With a mighty heave, Chandra started to drag the unconscious katarl back to the house. The hope was that the motion might wake the injured woman. A hope that was not realized as Chandra continued to lug Alyssa's limp weight.

Fire roared through Chandra's back. The effort to drag Alyssa called on every muscle in her body, and not all muscles were keen to listen. Alyssa slipped out from Chandra's hand. Once, then twice. A troublesome pattern that her raw hand could not help but perpetuate. The only thing going Chandra's way was that it had grown quiet. Arrows no longer snapped against stone or bit into flesh.

"Chandra!"

Warning struck Chandra's ears the same moment something else struck her back. A living weight that latched onto her frame. Momentum from the surprise forced Chandra to the ground. Alyssa was ripped from her hands. Sharp pain sliced into one of Chandra's cheeks. The dagger had been knocked from between her teeth and clattered onto the street.

Whatever struck and clung to Chandra did not let go. She felt it squirm. A pair of arms slid around her torso as she attempted to roll over onto her back. Chandra only made it halfway. On her side, she felt something blunt dig into her arm. There was enough force clamped down to break the skin. Chandra gasped in pain as she turned her head to see a creature with matted fur and large, buck teeth gnash into her arm. Small jaws open wide to gather more of Chandra's arm for a second bite. Beady, black eyes looked everywhere and nowhere all at once.

The varmint atop Chandra wailed before it could take another bite. A steel blade doused with crimson blood erupted from the creature's side. Limp arms released Chandra as the varmint became little more than a lifeless doll. The blade wrenched the varmint from atop Chandra and slid out from whence it had come.

Owen did not offer a calm hand to pick Chandra up to her feet. Both were occupied. He brandished his sword and flickering shield against the encroaching dark and howled.

"On your feet, soldier!"

There was blood in his voice. Even as he spoke, Chandra could see another varmint leap out from the darkness and into the light of her spell. It came from above and attempted to latch onto Owen. The attempt was thwarted with a mighty cleave. Keen steel tore through the varmint's neck as Owen sidestepped the assault. Bloody gurgles trickled from the monster until its spasms gave way to stillness.

Another varmint jumped into the light. A second followed on its grimy heels. The scrape of claws and the gnashing of teeth permeated the air. Whistling arrows were traded for ravenous assault. A third and fourth varmint appeared as Chandra slid across the street to snag her dagger.

Two of the creatures had been cast aside. Dead. Owen's strikes were quick and efficient. Absolutely lethal. Still, he was only one man. The varmints appeared faster than he could deal with them. One of the creatures climbed his back as two of its kind fell screaming to the ground. Owen reached up to stab the creature as it clawed at his neck. The fourth varmint dove for Owen's legs while he was distracted.

Chandra dove as well.

The varmint after Owen's legs was caught by surprise. Chandra tackled it to the ground before it had a chance to bite. Though she had the creature pinned with her knees, the varmint still whipped its head and snapped its jaws. Teeth came alarmingly close to Chandra's thighs. A bite she was not keen to experience a second time. She drove the tip of her dagger down into the chest of the writhing mass of fur. The varmint bucked and whipped, but Chandra held it down with all her weight. She twisted and wrenched the blade until the varmint ceased to move.

Another varmint was upon Chandra before she had a moment to think. Grubby little arms wrapped around her neck. Dull front teeth dug into her shoulder. Chandra flung her left hand up to the thrash at the beast. Anything to get it to stop the attack on her shoulder. She could feel her bones creak under the stress of the bite.

Viscera trailed behind her dagger as Chandra ripped it from the varmint beneath her. She pulled her arm back to prepare a vicious strike into her attacker's skull. When Chandra went to unleash the coiled power, she found that her arm would not move. Furry limbs wrapped around her wrist. There was not enough power to rip her arm from this second assailant. The varmint had Chandra's arm fully extended and pulled behind her back. Her arm was under complete control.

More arms wrapped around Chandra's waist as she moved to stand. The combined weight of another two or three varmints added to the pile kept Chandra on her knees. She lost track of how many monsters assaulted her. Teeth dug into her right arm, her left shoulder, and near her ribs. The bites on her already abused ribs hurt the most, but there was nothing Chandra could do to dissuade the varmints that beset her.

Chandra released the varmint on her shoulder to get a better grip. A desperate attempt to make some kind of retaliation. Something before the creatures could rip her apart. When she blindly groped at the varmint on her shoulder, Chandra felt something squishy. A part of the varmint with some give.

An eye! Chandra realized.

The varmint cried out in frenzied pain as Chandra dug her thumb into the creature's eye. Teeth released her shoulder and gave a much-needed moment to move. At least, that was what Chandra had expected. She tried to pull her left arm forward and found that it could not move. Much like the varmint on her right, one of the oversized rodents had gotten a hold on her left wrist. Her struggle to break free was brought short by another bite. This time, the varmint on her left locked its teeth onto her hand. Her little and ring finger.

Chandra felt the snap of her bones. Heard the crunch of her fingers run up her arm and into her ear. With wild eyes, she looked from her left over to Owen. She screamed his name in desperation. Words that fell on deaf ears. Not only did Owen have a pair of the mousier varmints crawling all over his back and legs, but he attempted to square against a larger varmint at the same time. It stood at eye level with the Seeker, a notched blade in the varmint's hand poised to strike while Owen was occupied.

There was no help to be had from Owen. Not while he was under coordinated assault. While Chandra looked on, she felt the skin on her ribs break. Felt warm streams of blood trickle down her torso to well on her hips. The bones on her left little and ring fingers had been crushed. Teeth tore through the skin.

Chandra's left hand was free again. She drove her sad fist into the varmint on her right. Her second strike was caught and bound before she could swing. All her struggles were in vain. Piece by piece, the ravenous varmints were ripping Chandra apart.

A weight lifted from Chandra's back. Her right arm returned to her control. Without thinking, Chandra whipped her dagger over to stab the varmint that held her left arm. A solid blow knocked the creature from her side. Both arms were free and ready to strike the next varmint she laid eyes on.

By the time Chandra swiveled to attack the varmints on her back, they were gone. Over Chandra stood Olivia. Wild-eyed and with great force, the Deepkin ripped her hand axes from a pair of varmints that lay behind Chandra. The weapons were dislodged in time to strike down a new assailant, one of the taller varmints, as it charged into Olivia with a pair of cruel knives. Power and grace buried an axe head into the creature's neck. It crumpled to the ground, pliant flesh releasing Olivia's weapon as it fell. The woman readied herself for any other varmint that might throw itself her way. Seeing none, she snapped her gaze down to Chandra.

"Inside!" was the single word Olivia roared. Her commanding presence left no room for questions or doubt. New direction flooded

Chandra's burning muscles. She pushed herself up and stumbled toward the house where Ryleah hid. White knuckles remained wrapped around the handle of her dagger. The last piece of personal defense she wielded against the flow of enemies.

Olivia had not come alone. Almost a dozen others moved in and out of Chandra's light, goggles fastened to their eyes to ward off the dark. Some fought against the endless tide of varmints. A pair of others took hold of Tumwe and Alyssa and dragged them into the house where Chandra was headed.

Chandra ducked around powerful blows. She sidestepped a varmint that leaped down from on high just in time to see Owen run the creature through with his sword. His violet shield dissipated, Owen grabbed Chandra by the arm and sped her along into the house.

Strength left Chandra halfway into the house. Outside of immediate danger, her body refused to carry her any further. Both legs crumbled and carried Chandra to the floor. Owen attempted to keep her on her feet, but the sudden nature of the fall proved too much. The pair of them both tumbled into a heap of limbs. Chandra's dagger bounced over to a wall. Owen's sword flipped and flourished after it bounced, then settled next to the Seeker with a persistent wobble.

The world raced around Chandra. Sounds of violence pervaded the streets. Steel and flesh and stone all blended into a single cacophonous mass. Death rattles gurgled amid the clamor. Sounds that pierced Chandra to her core. She felt cold. Shivers wracked her entire body. Walls encroached on her mind. The house seemed to shrink and collapse around her.

"Chandra," Owen panted, "are you okay? Chandra?"

Owen had been shaking Chandra to get her attention. It sounded like he had been asking that same question for quite some time as well. Chandra was so absorbed in herself that she had not noticed.

"Fine?" Chandra asked Owen.

Fine?

Chandra asked herself the same question. Fine? How could anyone be fine after enduring such a reckless onslaught? Savage creatures bit and tore and slashed with whatever they had. All an effort to tear life away from Chandra. She was the opposite of fine. Everything was wrong. The venture was not supposed to end like this. Varmints were meant to have been dead or fled. An ashling had been vanquished. This was a plan that should have ended with wealth beyond imagination. Instead, the effort left Chandra with terror in her heart, pains that ached all over her body, and bites that delivered gods knew what sort of diseases into her system.

A halfhearted attempt to rise to her knees awakened a whole new pain. Something that Chandra's body had tried desperately to shut out. Searing agony radiated from her left hand. It was a pain too intense for Chandra to ignore. Her eyes, unfocused and wandering, peered down.

In the back of her mind, Chandra knew what had happened to her. She had not yet taken the time to look at her injury, but that snap of bone and rip of flesh still echoed like a haunting chime in her ears. Her body had convinced her to forget while Chandra remained in mortal peril. Now that combat was traded for the relative safety of the house? There was nothing to distract her from the fact that she was missing her left little and ring finger.

Tears welled in Chandra's eyes as blood spurted from her hand. The source of her shivers became apparent. Lifeblood dripping out of her body brought on a feverish chill. Sounds of battle dulled. Words spoken next to her ear had no meaning. Chandra could feel her pulse pound in her ears. She cradled her trembling left arm even as a white bandage began to wrap around her hand.

Chandra screamed.

The scream was inaudible to her. A blank cry into an uncaring void. Chandra *felt* the scream. Felt her lungs shudder as the last of her air was expelled. Felt her face swell with blood and anguish. Hot tears rolled down her cheeks. Her left hand pounded. Pounded. Pounded. Chandra could feel each pulse of blood that leaked from her hand. The bandage Owen applied was soaked through with each new wrap. It felt like a river crushing a dam made of paper.

It was too much to look at. The absence of her fingers. Crimson blood pooled at her knees, staining the once pure bandage. Chandra had to find something else to look at. She swiveled her head around the room in desperation.

Ryleah was tucked into the nest-like corner of the house. Arms pulling knees to her chest, it seemed like the acolyte had not moved from that spot since Chandra fled the battle. Chandra wondered why Ryleah did not approach. Her fevered mind imagined the acolyte crawling over to seal the wounds on her hand. Maybe restore the fingers taken by a ruthless varmint. Hopefully just taken. Chandra could not bear the thought that a part of her had been eaten.

Wonder at Ryleah's idleness vanished when Chandra realized her light spell had ceased. She was not sure at what point the white light vanished to be replaced by the pulsing red of lit flares. It seemed odd that the Baylocke people bothered to light the room, what with their goggles. That was too great a puzzle for Chandra's shattered mind. She was coherent enough, though, to realize that Ryleah must be sitting in the dark. All alone, with no way to know what happened outside the house.

The uncomfortable thought melted away as Chandra's head lulled toward the front of the house. There was nobody in the street anymore. Just the varmints, clawing and gnashing outside the open door. Olivia, haloed in red light, made some sort of sweeping gesture. One of the other people, an unfamiliar face, glowed with emerald light. They made a series of quick gestures in the direction of the door and windows. The stone portals shrank and shrank until they were sealed. A spell to keep the varmints out. To bar all points of entry.

True quiet fell over the room. All the Baylocke Battalion were still, taking advantage of the moment to catch their breath. The walls were too thick for the sounds of the varmint mob to penetrate. Chandra's head lulled back. Her misty gaze scanned the empty ceiling of the house. The last thing she remembered as darkness overtook her was the pounding of blood in her ears.

* * *

Pound.

Pound.

An ever-present thump in Chandra's hand. Sensation she could not escape. No distraction was strong enough to pull her attention away from the awful thrum. It came in waves. Sometimes so intense that it made Chandra feel like she was going to vomit. Inevitably, the pain subsided into something duller. Constant droning that refused to quiet.

The most intense pain came whenever Chandra attempted to close her left hand into a fist. Physically, it did not generate any additional pain. It was mental anguish. Her mind tried to move fingers that were no longer there. No matter how hard Chandra tried, she could not convince her brain that there were only three fingers on her left hand.

Red light from the Baylocke Battalion flares died before Chandra awoke. Concentration on a light spell helped to pull away some of Chandra's mental faculties. A little piece of her that did not focus on her mutilated hand or the fact that she was trapped inside a stone cage. Trapped with a pack of wolves who had so recently sentenced Owen and herself to death.

Across the room from the nest-like corner where Chandra and her companions rested, the Baylocke Battalion was in constant motion. They occupied half of the house near the sealed entrance. Chandra counted fourteen of them in the warm glow of her spell. Some were in better states than others. A few nursed arrow wounds that could not be treated. Others had bites and scratches they wrapped in bandages after a thorough wash. The most energetic among them prepared some foodstuffs that did not require a fire.

Blankets were draped over three bodies. Two of the battalion had not survived the battle with the varmints. The third was Tumwe, who had succumbed to the wound inflicted by Owen. That was Chandra's assumption. She had not approached the group to ask questions. There was little enough strength in her body without having to argue with lunatics. Rest was the first order of business.

Chandra felt her head bobble up and down. Arhythmic movement in response to Ryleah. Chandra's head rested on the acolyte's shoulder. At the same time, Ryleah was hunting through the pouches on her belt for anything that might be useful.

"Outright healing is not likely," Ryleah had said when Chandra first woke. "I only had the one mouse with me. Without a life to offer in return, I would have to rely on luck to get Manus to hear my prayer. Could try that, but I think I'd better focus on what I can do right now instead of what I hope to do later. Right now, I can get your smaller wounds washed and bound."

Fear had not abandoned the acolyte. A light tremor ran through Ryleah's hands as she went about her work. Near-white skin somehow seemed more pale than usual. That fear did not stop Ryleah, though. Once she had performed the necessities for Chandra and Owen, she was already digging around for more options.

What Ryleah produced, in the end, was a small handful of jagged, blue-green leaves that looked an awful lot like velvet. Sage's mint. Ryleah popped the leaves into her mouth and began to chew. Busy hands continued to rifle through her pouches all the while.

"Awright," Ryleah slurred, pulling Chandra from her almost trance-like state, "time to shainsh da bandashes on yoh hand."

"Are you okay?" Chandra asked, peering over at her friend.

"Fine," Ryleah replied. "Ish the leavsh. Numbs yoh tongue."

The thought was far from enticing: changing bandages. Chandra was not keen to see the mangled stumps that used to be her fingers. Despite her concerns, she did not fight Ryleah. Blood had soaked through the bandages that were in place. They no longer performed their intended function and needed to be replaced for Chandra to have any hope of recovery. She had already lost enough blood to feel quite lightheaded. The flow needed to stop, and a clean bandage was the best way to help without a miracle.

Chandra closed her eyes. Just because it had to be done didn't mean she had to watch. Ryleah gave Chandra a gentle squeeze on the shoulder before the endeavor began.

Wet cotton sloshed as Ryleah peeled away the first layer of the bandage. It sounded like taking off a shirt soaked with sweat after a day in the orchards. The innocent comparison did not calm Chandra, knowing that it was her blood that caused the sound and not her sweat. Each layer made that same sickening noise as it was peeled away until open air rushed over Chandra's hand.

"Braysh yohself," Ryleah muttered.

The time between warning and application was criminal. Some kind of powder was applied directly to Chandra's open wounds. It had the consistency of sawdust and burned like hot embers. Chandra clenched her teeth and sucked down a sharp breath. The urge to rip her arm away from Ryleah was unbearable.

"Thash to help clod yoh blood," Ryleah slurred. "Thish ish foh the pain."

Another substance was applied to the open wounds. This one had more the consistency of a paste. The moment it touched Chandra's flesh she felt a refreshing chill run from her injury up to her shoulder. She was able to relax her arm for the first time since the initial bite. It was like the pain had been carried away on a cool mountain stream. A sigh of relief fell from Chandra's lips and plopped onto her heaving chest.

"Mush bedder," Ryleah attempted to coo.

"Oh gods, yes," Chandra gasped. "That feels so much better."

"Good. Now, shtay shtill."

Ryleah proceeded to wrap a fresh bandage around Chandra's hand. Chandra barely felt a thing. What should have been a sharp pain felt like someone patting her hand through a thick, woolen glove. The rest of Chandra's body relaxed. Without her brain sounding alarm bells, muscles were able to release their tension. Knots in her stomach slipped undone. Toes uncurled. Teeth unclenched.

"Thank you," Chandra whispered. "So much."

A gentle kiss on the top of Chandra's head replaced a verbal reply from Ryleah. The acolyte ran her soft fingers through Chandra's hair a few times before she nudged Chandra away. When Chandra picked her head up, Ryleah stood and patted herself down. An attempt to do away with the bits of fiber that accumulated on her clothes from the nest.

"I'm gonna go shee if they need help," Ryleah said. She spoke while gazing at the huddled mass that was the Baylocke Battalion.

Concern tempered the fresh waves of relief. Chandra narrowed her eyes at her friend, then peered over at Olivia and her people. It felt like it was too soon to approach. To walk over and chat with the people would be to court danger, and there was nowhere to run in the small house. The Baylocke Battalion controlled the only entrance and exit through the Flow.

"I don't think that's a good idea, Ryleah," Chandra whispered. She felt compelled to voice her concerns.

"People are hurdt," Ryleah replied. Her gaze remained locked on the brooding encampment across the house. "I have da shee if I can help."

"Then I'm coming with you. You're not going to deal with those maniacs alone."

"No, pleash—"

Chandra stood before Ryleah could venture further protest. At least, she attempted to stand. Dizziness that lay thin overhead while Chandra sat increased tenfold when she tried to rise. She was forced to steady herself with her right hand or fall over. Sight left her for a brief window, but she was able to blink away the darkness. Chandra shook her head to push the feeling further aside.

When Chandra attempted to stand a second time, Ryleah crouched and put a hand on Chandra's shoulder. There was no force in the gesture. It was not a command. This was a request from a friend. Stay and rest, Ryleah seemed to say with softened features.

Fine.

An aura of confidence radiated from Ryleah as she stood. Not a display of menace like Olivia. A gentle cloak of purpose that was felt but not seen. Chandra did not have the heart to stop Ryleah. Healing was what the acolyte knew best, and she made it clear that she would not be deterred.

Chandra slumped back against the wall when Ryleah turned and left. If she was going to stay put, Chandra figured she might as well make herself comfortable. The nesting provided a suitable seat. With a shimmy and a small slide, Chandra was able to find a nice, cool spot on the wall. She let her hair down and ruffled the grungy, black mess. It was not until she had let her hair fall about her shoulders that she realized getting it back in place might be a struggle. Chandra refused to look at her left hand and legitimize the thought.

Rather than dwell on her hand, she lulled her head to the right. Owen rested against the wall on the opposite side of the corner. Far enough to away to have his own space. Close enough that Chandra could reach out with her foot to give his boot a gentle nudge. Chandra could not resist, even though the man's eyes were closed.

"Hey," Chandra murmured, "you awake over there?"

Owen did not speak, nor did he crack an eyelid. He took in a great sniff of air. A pronounced noise that signaled an exaggerated effort. Both eyebrows reached up for the ceiling. His cheeks pulled backward until his lips formed a thin horizontal line. Owen was awake, but he did not seem particularly pleased about the fact.

"You doing okay?" Chandra asked. She prodded his boot a second time, then a third in quick succession. Attempts to get Owen to engage. To distract her from the load of trouble they had landed themselves in.

"I've felt better," Owen grumbled after a few more taps on his boot. "Feeling muscles I forgot I had. Shoulder is awful sore."

A lazy gesture from Owen's right hand pointed up to his left shoulder. Bandages were visible through his shredded shirt. Imbedded in his shoulder was a small hunk of an arrow shaft. Ryleah had attended to Owen while Chandra slept, but the removal of the cruelly designed arrowhead was beyond either of them. It had to remain in place. Wrapped and bandaged so that it might remain as still as possible.

There was only so much a couple of bandages could do. Even the small movement of his right arm made Owen wince. An accidental transfer of energy from his right side to his left. Smaller patches of cloth were tied in place elsewhere. Bites, both from tooth and blade, dotted his arms and torso. Handkerchiefs were used where possible in place of regular bandages. Chandra guessed that was her fault. Her hand had gone through at least one wrapping so far, and would likely require more. A notion that raised a pit of guilt in her stomach.

He shouldn't have to suffer because I got hurt, Chandra thought gloomily. *Hardly seems fair.*

"Thanks for saving me," Chandra said. At first, it was a groggy mumble, but she cleared her throat and repeated herself. "Thanks. I'd probably be even worse off if you hadn't followed my dumb self out there. Might even be dead."

"Don't be so hard on yourself," Owen replied. "You were trying to save a life. That's admirable... even if I wish you'd've just stayed inside."

"Yeah, I guess."

"That was the agreement, after all. You get us down here in one piece. I make sure nobody takes pieces away. If anyone should be apologizing, it's me."

"No," Chandra replied with a shake of her head. That Owen could not see the gesture did not matter. She felt compelled to apply as much emphasis as she could. "No, you couldn't have known this would happen."

"Should have made you stay up top once we found the ashling. Should have talked to my superior and tried to requisition a task force from the 4th Federation Army. *That* would have kept you safe. Would have been the responsible thing to do."

"Hah, you couldn't have stopped me if you wanted to. I would have tagged along anyways, whether you knew I was there or not."

"I could have just thrown you in a jail cell, you know," Owen retorted. At this point, he cracked an eye to peer at Chandra. There was no malice in his gaze. Just regret. "Novice working in the middle strata without a license. Dealing with a known black-market trader— yes, before you ask, I know about Robin and her side business. Throwing you in a cell, at least until we were done, would have been the smart thing to do."

"Like a jail cell would have stopped me."

Chandra twirled her last manarail spike in her fingers. She channeled a small amount of the Flow into the spike, forcing it to bend slowly until it formed a perfect right angle. A flash of smug pride raced across her face for an instant.

A sharp snort popped from Owen. His chest rose and fell with silent laughter as he closed his eye and rested his head back against the wall. A thin hint of a smile cracked his neutral expression.

"So," Chandra began again after the moment had passed, "why didn't you? Throw me in a cell, I mean?"

"You wouldn't have gotten your share," Owen replied matter-of-factly. "You're doing this for money, right? To help your family? You wouldn't have seen a penny if I had to get other officials involved. Didn't seem fair."

"Thanks." The word was light on Chandra's tongue. No sarcasm or glib intent. Just the purest gratitude, untainted by fancy dressings and unnecessary remarks. Grim reality followed. "I don't think it matters at this point, though. We'd need an entire army to deal with what's out there. Going to be lucky if we even manage to make it topside."

"Yeah," Owen said. He took in another breath. There was something on his tongue, but he seemed reluctant to share. Chandra gave him another gentle tap on his boot. "Who do you owe?"

"Pardon?" Chandra asked.

"All this money," Owen went on. "Trying to make some money is one thing, but going through an ashling? I figure you have to owe someone an awful lot. And, whoever it is, they must be pretty eager to get paid pack."

"Guess I haven't really talked about it much," Chandra said as much to herself as she did to Owen. "Seemed personal. Sort of thing you wouldn't want to know. I didn't think you needed to know. Well... my dad has a bad habit. Ever since Mom died, he's been trying to think up new ways to make ends meet. Problem is that his ideas usually mean buying something we can't afford from Westinghouse. Orland Bank foots the bill and we get saddled with something we didn't need to chase money we don't have. Bank owns the land we farm on, too, so the hole just keeps getting deeper and deeper. Was hoping I could strike it big down here. Get enough money to pay the bank off and finally own the land we work."

An uncomfortable silence hung in the air. Chandra felt relieved to spill her guts, but at the same time felt ashamed. Like she was trying to make her problem into Owen's problem. It never did feel right to share the whole situation. To make it sound like she was begging for scraps with a sob story. At this point, though, Chandra figured it might be the last time she told the story to anyone. Only felt right to come clean to the man she had dragged down with her. Owen deserved to know the truth.

"Jacob was right," Chandra sighed. "I should have just talked to the smiths in town. Tried to find an apprenticeship somewhere. Wouldn't have been fast money, but it might have helped keep us afloat without getting me killed. Now it's just going to be Father looking after the family. That farm isn't going to last another year."

"Orlands, huh?" The speck of mirth in Owen's voice had been shouldered out by a heap of disgust. Nostrils flared as he spoke. His body visibly tensed, an act that disturbed Owen's shoulder and caused another wince of pain. "For all the good she does, I only ever seem to hear about her ruining lives."

"Huh?" was all Chandra could think to utter. The pivot in demeanor was sharp and caught her by surprise.

"No one should have to go through this much pain just to keep their home," Owen grumbled. "If we get out of here, I'm giving her an earful."

"Um, who are we talking about?"

"Cynthia Orland." Owen sighed. "She's the woman that runs the Arnstead branch of the Orland Bank. We haven't exactly been on speaking terms lately. Mostly because I don't want to hear her voice, but my disgust isn't a good enough reason to stay quiet."

"What are you talking about?" Chandra asked in growing confusion. She leaned toward Owen to ensure she heard him correctly as he spoke. "You're not making sense. How is a Spellseeker going to talk to a banker about somebody's loans? Why would she listen to you?"

There was not an immediate response. Owen brooded in place. His head tilted back to gaze up at the plain ceiling, the featureless void of stone. Some of the disgust seemed to seep away. A calmer, more even tone accompanied his words when he spoke again.

"Don't worry about it. I've got some pull at the bank. Enough to get Cynthia's attention. If we manage to get out of here, there's going to be a long talk about the Pattal household."

That was the end of the discussion. No matter how much she poked or prodded, Chandra could not get another word out of Owen on the matter. He withdrew into himself. Silent thought and dour air dominated his countenance as he gritted his teeth. The man was clearly angry about the Orlands. Understandable in its own right, Chandra thought, but it seemed odd that Owen was so moved by Chandra's predicament that it put him into a cold rage.

If Owen did not want to speak further, Chandra decided she would not attempt to pry morsels out of him. They both needed rest. An argument was the last thing Chandra wanted. Better to just let it be and allow Owen to cool off.

21

Desperation

"If you don't take her to the surface with you, I will *haunt* you."

"Excuse me?" Olivia replied to Chandra's remark. The woman leveled a blank stare against Chandra, who was seated with her back to the wall.

"I said I'll haunt you," Chandra repeated. "Leave Ryleah behind, and I'll bind my soul to yours and make sure you never get a night of peace for the rest of your life."

Furrowed brows accompanied the blank stare. Olivia cocked her head. She shifted her weight from one leg to the other, hands on her hips, as she towered over Chandra.

Chandra felt she was clear. How could she make the threat simpler to understand? If Olivia took her life and left Ryleah to fumble around alone in the dark, Chandra was willing to sacrifice the chance of a peaceful afterlife to ensure the Deepkin suffered. Not that Chandra was certain she could do that. Still, some kind of threat was better than no threat. She was seated in the nest-like corner of the house without a weapon. Owen was out like a light. Chandra only hoped to delay the inevitable.

"That's why you're here, isn't it?" Chandra hounded. "Kick us while we're down? Kill a man in his sleep, and do me in after? Come on. Let's see what an eternity together feels like. I'm ready."

"Oh. Oh! No, no," Olivia chuckled with a dismissive wave. "No. If I was going to kill you, I wouldn't have stopped to ask. No, I just wanted to chat. With your friend looking after my people, and the law taking a nap"—Olivia lifted a finger toward Owen—"I figured it was a good time."

It was Chandra's turn to be baffled. Not more than a few hours could have passed since Olivia was ready to hack Chandra to pieces. The look in the woman's ruby eyes was impossible to forget. Pure menace. Intent to kill with ruthless efficiency. Olivia had not seemed like the sort to be reasoned with. There were no apparent injuries, to limb or head, that might suggest the woman was out of sorts either.

Chandra allowed her gaze to wander over to Owen. Of all the times to be asleep, he had to have chosen the moment when the homicidal madwoman decided to saunter across the room.

The distraction was brief. Chandra did not trust Olivia enough to let the woman out of sight for long. Despite her claims of peace, Olivia still wore axes on her hips. There was no need to bring them along if her intentions were pure.

A quick twitch of the eye allowed Chandra to see past Olivia. It gave her a chance to check on Ryleah while keeping tabs on Olivia. Ryleah had been over with the Baylocke Battalion for at least an hour. Maybe more. Chandra failed to track the time. To their credit, the battalion received Ryleah in peace. They allowed her to walk among their injured and offer whatever help that was possible. The trusting streak that Ryleah put on full display somewhat irked Chandra. It felt like Ryleah's generosity gave the Baylocke Battalion a hostage.

"Tell you what," Olivia muttered. Chandra snapped her attention back to the woman, who raised open hands in reassurance. "Let me take these off and I'll have a seat with you. I don't want it to feel like I'm talking down to you or anything."

Open hands dropped to axe heads. Chandra winced in expectation of a blow that did not come. Instead, Olivia drew her axes and tossed them to either side of Chandra. The weapons sunk into the fibrous nest without a clatter. Olivia then crossed her legs and dropped into a seated position. She maintained a respectful distance between Chandra and herself. Once seated, Olivia planted her elbows on her knees. Pearly hands propped the woman's chin.

"Let's start over, amateur. Can we do that?" Olivia placed an open hand on her chest as she spoke her name. "Olivia Baylocke. I lead the Baylocke Battalion— those hooligans across the room. You are?"

Displaced fibers forced Chandra to believe what she had imagined she saw. Chandra looked away from Olivia to the weapons deposited by her sides. Timid fingers confirmed that the axes were not a hallucination brought on by exhaustion.

"What are you playing at?" Chandra asked.

"What's your name?" Olivia replied. She did not mirror the blatant hostility with which Chandra spoke. Olivia spoke with a curious lightness. It almost felt like she had pulled Chandra away from a crowd to talk gossip. The sort of thing friends might do at a festival.

"I already told you my name. What do you want?"

"To try again, like I said," Olivia hummed with that same light touch. "I'm sorry about the whole 'blood rage' thing. I start to see red when Federation folk try to push their laws on me. Puts a bad taste in my mouth. Still, that doesn't excuse me pulling you into the mess."

"Stop talking to me like we're friends," Chandra muttered. "We're not."

"What, want me to swear at you? Call you names, Chandra?"

"What I want is for you to leave us alone. Have your stone shaper open one of the windows and let us out. We'll get out of your hair and you'll never see me again."

"Come on, Chandra," Olivia huffed as she batted the notion aside like a fly. "That's quitter talk. Stick with me. Be an extra pair of hands. We're going to send out a scouting party to see what the situation is, then plan the best way to get as much loot as possible. Neither of us needs to leave here empty-handed."

"My extra hands aren't doing so great if you hadn't noticed," Chandra grumbled. A sour smile crawled across her face as she held her left hand up to Olivia. "I think I'd rather leave than lose more fingers, thanks."

Olivia wrinkled her nose at the injury. The Deepkin's ruby gaze roved over the hand as if she had just now noticed. Chandra found that hard to believe. She was not exactly trying to keep her lack of fingers a secret. Little good it would do her.

An awkward silence drove a wedge between the pair. Olivia seemed to strain herself in thought, hunting for the right thing to say. A few words or suggestions that might win Chandra's favor. Chandra was in no hurry. She could not leave, even though she desperately wanted to. All she could do was bore an uncaring leer into Olivia's face. Maybe if she stared hard enough, Chandra might get her message through the woman's dense skull.

"Chandra," Olivia finally began. She looked down at the floor, raising her gaze to meet Chandra as she spoke. The lightness was gone. "We're all in a bad way. Together. Last thing we want to do is fight each other. You and the acolyte stick with me, we might manage to get out of this cursed city. Make enough money to never have another care in the world. I need all hands on deck to pull this off."

"And what about him?" Chandra asked, tilting her head toward Owen. "Conveniently left him out of your plan, huh? What happened to all hands on deck?"

"Yeah, about him," Olivia muttered. The woman curled her lower lip and bit down. Indecision racked her features. "He got hit by an arrow, same as some of mine. Poison is going to make it hard enough to get *my* people out. We don't have spare hands for someone who's just going to throw us in a cell when we get topside."

"Wait, poison? What do you mean, poison?"

"Oh, you didn't notice?" Olivia asked. She titled her head up, then allowed her gaze to fall directly on Owen. "We stabilized my folks that got hit. Stopped the bleeding, secured the arrowheads, but they're burning up. Won't talk. Can't move on their own. One of them chucked his guts up. Takes more than a couple hours for a normal arrow wound to get infected, so… yeah. Our guess is poison."

Chandra shifted her weight. A queasy sensation gripped at her guts, something she could not readily describe. Like she felt more alone now.

It did seem odd that Owen had so recklessly passed out. Was not like Owen. At least, not what Chandra knew of him. He did not come across like the type to let his guard down when a threat stood out in the open, clear to see. This would explain how he managed to sleep through the conversation that unfolded at his feet.

Chandra stole a glance over to Owen.

Olivia noted.

"Go ahead," Olivia said. She tossed her fingers limply in Owen's direction. "Check him. Put your hand up to his head. Give him a good shake. See if I'm lying to you."

There was no doubt that something was out of place. Against her better judgment, Chandra turned away from Olivia. A feat that required all that remained of her meager willpower. Chandra could feel Olivia's piercing gaze like needles scraping her rib cage. Might have just been internal bruises pitching a fit when Chandra started to crawl across the nest. The sensation felt real enough.

Probing fingers jabbed Owen in the shoulder. First two fingers, then three. Soon Chandra had her whole palm on Owen's shoulder as she tried to rouse him. Uttering his name brought no reaction, neither when whispered nor when shouted. Chandra might have smacked Owen if her whole body was not a giant ache. Water was too precious to splash against Owen's face. Just thinking the idea felt cartoonish as Chandra peered at her unconscious partner.

Maybe Ryleah has some kind of smelling salts, I wonder, Chandra mused. *That might crack him out of whatever is going on.*

Chandra refused to believe there was poison at work. Enough had gone wrong. She did not have room in her heart for another setback. Still, she pressed the back of her hand against Owen's forehead.

"Oh gods," Chandra muttered, "it's like fire."

Beads of sweat pooled on the top of Chandra's hand. She pulled away and checked with her other hand. Same result. It felt like she had touched a stovetop that had not quite cooled. There were sweat stains beneath Owen's arms. Chandra had not thought to look until she felt the sweat on her hand. Peering closely at his face, Chandra also swore that he had grown somewhat pale.

Concern dominated Chandra. The man that had helped to keep her alive was broken. Still breaking. Cracks widened to let Owen's soul slip gently from his body. There was nothing Chandra could do for him. She could not fool herself into thinking there was some sort of help she might be able to offer. No, the only person that might be able to bring Owen out of his stupor was across the room.

Chandra rose with care. Blood loss still battered her sense of balance. Though the flow might have stopped, the fact that the blood was gone remained. She rose slowly, one leg at a time, and crossed the room with halting steps.

Confidence came with practice. Some of the trouble was in her mind. The more she moved, the easier it became to maintain a steady stride. It was like Chandra found her strength as she walked.

"Come on, almost there," Olivia murmured.

Chandra deflated faster than a skewered waterskin. Olivia walked next to her, and the woman had a hand under Chandra's left arm. The ease of movement came from Olivia. Unnoticed support. Chandra ripped herself away from Olivia's grasp, stumbling a bit as she did so.

"I'll manage," Chandra grumbled in reply.

Her steps were a little more unsure, but Chandra did manage. She wobbled and weaved her way through the Baylocke Battalion until she reached Ryleah. The girl was hunched over Alyssa, who was in a similar state to Owen. The katarl did not respond to pokes or prods. Small puddles of sweat had formed around her hands and bare feet. If not for the subtle rise and fall of Alyssa's chest, Chandra might have assumed that the woman had succumbed to her wounds.

Ryleah performed her examination by hand. Still unused to the sudden gift of sight, it was the method she knew best for assessing injury and ailment. Fingers roved over pressure points and probed the inside of Alyssa's mouth. The acolyte seemed to pay particular attention to the tongue and gums.

"Is it true," Chandra asked of her friend. "Are they… is he…?"

"Poisoned?" Ryleah remarked. She looked back at Chandra in time to see a feeble nod. "I think so, but I'm not familiar with the symptoms. Well, that's not true… more like I'm too familiar. There's too much overlap for me to know what's in their system."

"What do you mean?"

"It could be all sorts of things," Ryleah explained. "Fever and enervation are pretty common. The excessive sweating might be from the fever, or something unrelated. Gums are swollen, the tongue is filmy. Not responding to sound. I'm not even sure if they've fallen asleep or if it's more severe than that. Could be something going on in their ears. Awful close to the brain, at that point."

"Ryleah," Chandra interrupted. Each new symptom placed greater weight on Chandra's chest. She feared she might not be able to breathe if Ryleah went on. "There's something you can do, right? Something in your pouch? A miracle! I'm sure the gods could help with this if you asked."

"I could ask, true, but that might do more harm than good." Ryleah's voice soured as she went on. "Problem is that I don't know what's in their system. It's not sealing up a cut or mending a bone. If I just ask for the symptoms to go away, whatever is causing them will still be there. Symptoms will just come back. It's up to *me* to know what the gods need to remove. If I ask for something to go that isn't there, they might take something that needs to stay. The gods are powerful, but they're not infallible."

"Well, how do we—"

"What if we got you an arrow?" Olivia cut in. Chandra whirled around to see that Olivia craned over the conversation. "One that hasn't gotten stuck in somebody yet. Think you could figure out what's on them?"

"Maybe," Ryleah said without hesitation. Her hands continued to rove over the injured katarl as she knit her brows in thought. Silent lips mouthed words that remained in her head. White, braided hair swung back and forth as Ryleah tilted her head from side to side. "No, not maybe. Definitely. If you can get me a sample of the poison, I'm sure I can figure something out."

"Perfect," Olivia replied with a clap. "Millicent, open up the wall. Jeff, Samira, you're on the hunt. Find us an arrowhead that's coated in… something. Harish, provide cover when they duck out. Give the furry little monsters something to be afraid of."

Orders were followed without delay or question.

Four people shuffled, some rising from the ground and others leaning off walls, and grabbed whatever gear belonged to them. Chandra recognized Harish. The furtive katarl that spied on her while she and Owen had battled the ashling. Other names met faces for the first time. Millicent grabbed the least gear of the three. Made sense, as it sounded like she would not be leaving the house. Emerald light formed a misty haze around the Nirdac human's muscled arms. Preparation to perform her function.

The other three strapped goggles to their heads, ready to drop the focuses over their eyes the moment they left the light Chandra maintained. Harish secured a quiver of arrows to his waist and gripped a recurve bow in his left hand. Samira, a Bangeli human with a slender frame who moved like a shadow, fixed knives to various parts of her body. Inobtrusive weapons that would always be within reach. Jeff, the only other person beside Alyssa and Tumwe who did not wear a black gambeson, bounced on the balls of his large harn feet. He seemed eager to venture out into the abyss, where the other two maintained quiet composure.

Millicent stepped toward the smooth stone wall of the house after she received nods of readiness from Harish, Jeff, and Samira. The light around her intensified. A fierce aura flowed from Millicent into the wall. Solid stone liquified into a more malleable form. Walls parted as Millicent moved her hands in opposite directions. Almost like the woman was throwing open a set of curtains.

The circular opening that appeared was small at first. Just the right height for Harish to approach the wall, goggles fixed in place, and peer out into the city street. There was a pause while the katarl scanned the darkness. He stepped back from the wall and patted Millicent on the shoulder. She nodded and ripped the wall open with a jerk of her arms. Harish, Jeff, and Samira all poured out into the city. Behind them, the opening shrank back to the size of a large peephole. Olivia stepped forward to watch the progress of her people.

Sounds of hurried movement seeped through the ceiling above. Claws that scraped against stone. Chatter in a harsh language that Chandra could not understand. Varmints must have been on the roof of the house the whole time, and now they reacted to the incursion into the street.

"This was a terrible idea," Chandra muttered as she neared the front wall. She drew close enough to hear whatever Olivia might mutter in response, but well outside of arm's reach.

"Nah, they're all cowards," Olivia half whispered. "They only attacked us because we were distracted with each other. Won't attack again, not after a failed ambush."

"You sure?" Chandra asked, tilting her head upward to look at the ceiling. She imagined rows of furry little monsters lining up along the roof to fire a hail of arrows.

"Besides, Harish is going to give them something to think about."

As if the man had heard his boss speak, there came a high-pitched whine followed by a bright light that pierced the peephole. Olivia was forced to look away. Violent tremors shook the house a moment later. Bits of stone tumbled down as small fissures formed in the ceiling. There was a powerful roar and sudden rush of air, followed by terrified screams from the creatures above.

"What was that?" Chandra stammered. Hands flew above her head to intercept specks of debris that tumble down.

"A message," Olivia replied with a wicked grin.

Whatever Harish had done, it certainly left an impression on the varmints. Scrapes and gurgles trickled down through the newly formed cracks in the ceiling. Somber silence that followed suggested that none of the creatures on the roof survived.

The rest of the Baylocke Battalion that could stand on their own formed a semicircle around Millicent. Some pressed ears to the wall. A handful of pennies were pooled between the members. Some kind of bet, though Chandra could not make out the whispered stipulations. She was more focused on the people that crowded her space. None seemed to pay Chandra any mind. Neither for good nor ill did they look Chandra's way. Still, she did not care to be surrounded by the dubious squad. A couple of steps back pulled her away from the crowd and offered some room to breathe.

"All right, clear out," Olivia said with a wave of her hand. The crowd of people pulled back to make space around Millicent, but not disperse. Eager attention was paid to the portal fashioned by the stone shaper.

That was fast, Chandra mused. *Figured it would take a while to search through the mess.*

Chandra assumed there was a mess. How could there not have been? Dozens and dozens of arrows. Whatever weapons the varmints might have carried. Bodies of the varmints that had been slain, and possibly those of battalion members as well. It could not be a pleasant picture beyond the wall.

Emerald light flashed. The stone wall liquified and was ripped apart once more. Samira slid through first. Jeff bounded in after, an action that resulted in some grunts and the passing of coins. Harish followed. He backed through the hole without taking his eyes off the street. Olivia gave him a tap on the shoulder as he passed into the house.

"One more, for good measure."

Harish nodded in response to Olivia's command. He drew his bow, an arrow already knocked and resting on the weapon. Scarlet light emanated from his left forefinger. When he touched his fingertip to the arrowhead, the light slid out to coat the missile with a brilliant red sheen. Twang went the bowstring. The arrow pierced the darkness like a bloody spear. It traveled for a moment before erupting into a concussive shower of fire and smoke. The explosion illuminated the house across the street long enough to see varmints thrown from the roof. Bits of fire lingered after the explosion ceased, moving around the top of the house. Varmints that had caught fire but not been lucky enough to die. Their screams pushed across the street, quieted only by Millicent binding stone back into a solid wall.

Both Jeff and Samira presented a handful of arrows to Olivia. Five or six between them, it was hard to count through the crowd. The face Olivia made was not a promising one. A sort of disappointed grimace. She looked the arrows over and handed them back.

"I said to bring arrows that had something on them." Olivia sighed. "These ones are bone dry."

"Look again, boss," Samira replied with confidence. "These have got *something* on them. There's a line on the arrowheads, and the color changes a bit. Whatever they coated the tips with must have dried out."

"And they weren't all like that, neither," Jeff added. "Most of the arrowheads were one color through and through. These were the closest to special we could find."

"Fine," Olivia grumbled without bothering to examine the arrows a second time. "Let's see what our friend has to say."

Olivia was already walking over to Ryleah as she spoke. Her pace was almost hesitant, like she was not expecting good news. Chandra rounded her away around the crowd to get next to Ryleah. If Olivia was going to flip her lid at bad news, Chandra wanted to make sure she was close to Ryleah. Images of the madwoman's wrath were far too recent to be forgotten.

Arrows passed from Olivia to Ryleah without a word. A hand was extended to receive the arrows before Olivia had closed the gap. As before, Ryleah only gave the object of her attention a quick look. Detail was derived from senses other than sight. Curious fingers probed the barbed arrowheads. Felt the difference between the coated and uncoated surfaces. Fingernails chipped small flakes of coating. Ryleah held the substance up to her tongue. Just the tip of her tongue touched the mysterious substance, and Ryleah spat the stuff out with haste. Her lips closed and her cheeks bulged, first one and then the other. She must have been rolling the taste around her mouth, Chandra guessed.

The process was repeated for all the arrows. Ryleah even raised a couple of them to her nose, taking in a huge whiff before she shook her head.

There was quiet once all the arrows had been examined. Ryleah placed them on the ground and allowed herself to sink back against the wall. Mumbled gibberish trickled from the acolyte. Even standing right next to the girl, Chandra could not decipher what was uttered. Unblinking eyes peered at the ceiling. Ryleah tapped the back of her head against the wall with a consistent rhythm. Pensive taps to jog her memory. To shake loose some long-forgotten scrap of detail.

Restlessness wormed its way through the battalion. It started as little fidgets. A tap of the foot, or drumming fingers on a hip or pommel. Subtle mutterings came next. People passed discouraged glances. Part of the battalion even separated from the group, tired of fruitless observation. They left with a dismissive wave or kicking a bit of dislodged rock across the room.

Darkness seeped into Chandra's mind. She cast a forlorn look across the room at Owen. He was no longer upright, but had tipped over and rested on his side. Chandra had failed to notice amid all the excitement. The man looked like a pathetic tangle of limbs. A discarded doll, outgrown by its owner and forgotten by time.

"I've got it!" Ryleah blurted out of nowhere. The excitement in her voice tempered as she continued. "Well... maybe I've got it. I think it's one of two things. Either a purple witherroot extract or ground-up spotted cavecap mushrooms turned to a paste. Problem is, I'm not sure which."

"It's got to be the cave mushrooms, right?" asked one of the battalion members.

"I thought so, too, but purple witherroot grows around the memory-glass quarry. No reason to think the varmints couldn't dig some up at night. They wouldn't have to go far from the caves. I need to bring these arrows to my master at the House. Rajani will know for sure. She's taught me most of what I know."

"Can you do anything in the meantime?" Olivia added. "Something to keep our folks alive until we get back topside?"

"Yes," Ryleah replied, hands already rifling through her pouches and bags. "I should be able to tone the symptoms down a peg. Maybe get them back on their feet... but no promises there."

"Good. That's what I want to hear. All right, folks," Olivia said with a grunt as she forced herself up from a squat. "Listen up. Four hours. Eat, sleep, get some water, stretch. Whatever you need to do to be ready."

"Ready for what?" Chandra asked though she was certain she knew the answer.

"You didn't think we'd be leaving here empty-handed, did you?"

The wicked grin returned to Olivia with a vengeance.

* * *

Sleep was a battle. Not an effort to find rest, but the continued attempt to remain awake. Chandra was beaten. Battered. Slashed and bitten. Exhaustion grasped at her eyelids like rime on a windowsill. They wanted to shut out the light and drift off into well-deserved slumber. Chandra did not have the will to resist for long. The trials of the day were too great to withstand.

When Chandra woke, it was with a start. Gravity pulled her stomach up to her throat as she teetered and fell to one side. A falling dream made manifest. Arms flailed in surprise. The fibrous nest caught her wriggling frame in a gentle caress.

Panic struck. Chandra whipped her head around to take in the house. Ryleah lay close by on the nest, still burrowed in comfort. Light snores rattled out of her throat with each inhale. Owen had been set on his side with his back resting against the wall. A small pool of vomit soaked into the fibers in front of his face. Bits of the mess were stuck to his lips. Not a pretty sight, but his breathing was calm and consistent.

Color had returned to his cheeks. Ryleah's stopgap measures went a long way.

Inquiry turned from the nest to the other side of the house. The injured among the Baylocke Battalion remained asleep, but those who were well were up and about. Checking weapons, rifling through packs for snacks, a trio was playing some kind of card game. From a glance, Chandra would not have guessed they were about to venture back to the cache.

What mattered most was that they had not encroached on the nest. Chandra counted her blessings that her lapse in consciousness only cost her time. It would not have surprised Chandra if she had never woke at all.

Chandra dug through her battered pack, never allowing her gaze to leave the Baylocke folks for too long. Not all of the pain that coursed through Chandra was from the previous day's exertions. A rumble gnawed at her empty stomach. She could not remember the last time she had eaten. Well before the battle with the ashling. Sometime during the trek to the city, but the specifics evaded her. All Chandra knew was that she was hungry. She pulled a small brick of pemmican out of its cloth wrapper and took a savage bite.

Water was next on the list. The dry nature of the pemmican did not help the barren desert that was her mouth. Greedy hands pawed around until they felt a canteen. Chandra pulled it from the bag and shook it next to her ear.

Not much left, Chandra noticed.

That was true for all her supplies. Just the one manarail spike was left. There was a handful of pemmican, enough not to be worried. Water would be a problem if they remained below for much longer. As much water had gone to washing wounds as had been consumed. The clock forced upon Chandra by the lack of water was only outmatched by the poison that still coursed through Owen's veins. Symptoms would speed dehydration, which would increase water consumption. It was more than Chandra felt ready to contend with.

Chandra did not afford herself a mouthful of water. Instead, she drank just enough to help wash the food down. She felt the cold water pump through her body. A meager sense of refreshment that left Chandra wanting for more. That battle raged in her mind until a call to arms filled the ancient house.

"All right, folks, time to move," Olivia bellowed. It felt odd that she spoke so loud to a group in her immediate area. Then the woman threw a sharp glance over to Chandra and beckoned her to join. "I want everybody ready in ten minutes. If you can't walk on your own, borrow a shoulder."

A great commotion rose from the other side of the room as the Baylocke Battalion rose. The fittest threw on their gear before turning to the injured to assist. Minor cuts and bites did not prevent preparation. Even those who had been poisoned struggled to get themselves ready before they were offered assistance. Time was a precious resource that the battalion did not waste.

While her people busied themselves with preparations, Olivia walked across the house to Chandra. The woman needed no preparation. Her gear remained on her person even as she slept. Ready to move on a moment's notice.

"What do you want, Baylocke?" Chandra growled as the woman approached.

"Peace," Olivia begged. She crouched before Chandra to speak eye to eye. "Gearing up to move out, and we're not closing the wall behind us. It's not going to be safe here. Varmints won't attack a large group, but a haggard band of… let's say two and a half? Odds aren't great."

"So, you're abandoning us," Chandra sneered. "Fine. Expected as much. Too much of a coward to just kill us yourself, so you're hoping the varmints will do the job for you."

"Peace," Olivia said again, raising her hands to show her lack of aggression. "You don't trust me. I get it. At least let me apologize. Come with us and fill your bag, as much loot as you can carry."

"Uh-huh. What's the catch?"

"No catch." Olivia smiled. "I just want you to see what the rewards look like when you stick with me. Who knows? Maybe you come around after we get topside and come knocking on my door. I'd like that."

"And what about Owen?"

"Oh, the Spellseeker?"

Both Chandra and Olivia turned to gaze at Owen. Enough commotion rocked the house to cause him to stir. Bleary eyes, tired and confused, blinked at the warm light that filled the house. He smacked his lips and grimaced at what must have been the taste of dried vomit. With the back of his hand, he wiped the crusted remnants from his lips. The process of waking up did not seem to treat the man well.

"He's coming around, see?" Olivia crowed in feigned relief. "You don't need to worry about him anymore. He got himself down here, he can get himself out. Spellseekers are the resourceful type. You just worry about yourself and the House girl. Tag along and we'll get you out of here in one piece."

Olivia leaned in and offered an open hand. An unwritten contract for safe passage and potential employment. Promises of wealth and a bright future at the cost of a small evil. Chandra would have been lying if she had said she was not tempted. For all her espousing of loyalty, she could not deny the powerful desire to secure her family's livelihood.

It would be easy. All she had to do was take Olivia's hand. For all the evasive speech, she did appear genuinely interested in Chandra. Enough to offer her a cut of hard-earned spoils. Olivia could have just killed her and Owen while they slept. What would be the point in bringing Chandra along just to kill her on the way up topside? Chandra could not think of a reason. Why Owen remained alive was likely that Olivia did not want to anger Chandra further. If Olivia won Chandra over then they could just leave Owen to his fate. Why kill a Spellseeker when the World Below would do the job for free?

Cursed thoughts. The kind of temptation that would lead to a life of regret. Chandra would never forgive herself if she abandoned Owen, especially when he was in such a sorry state. It would make her no better than those who claimed the life of her mother. That thought alone smothered all temptation that had burned in her chest.

"I'm not like you," Chandra said. Her tone was frigid. Her tongue sharp. "I won't leave him here to die alone in the dark. He's making it topside, whether you want to help or not."

"Hmm." Cracks formed in Olivia's easy smile. She pulled her hand back slowly as if her arm was weighted with indecision. Strong legs pushed the woman up from a crouch to her full height. A ruby red leer fell upon Chandra from on high. "I hope you don't regret this. I really do."

Another pound of regret heaped itself onto Olivia's shoulders. The confidence she brought with her across the room deflated. There was still a clear display of pride, but the interaction had not gone as planned. She struggled to pull her gaze away from Chandra. Her head remained locked in place as Olivia turned, watching over her shoulder until it was impossible to do so. Hesitant steps carried Olivia back to her people.

The Baylocke Battalion was ready when their leader returned. Gear had been donned. Bedrolls and cookware were stashed. Blankets remained draped over the fallen. It was clear that Olivia and her people did not intend to return to the house once they left.

Emerald light mingled with the warmth of Chandra's spell. Millicent ripped open a door in the stone wall that led to the street. It was wide enough for the company to leave two by two. An effort to allow those that needed assistance to pass without further trouble. The last to leave was Olivia, who cast a final glance back at Chandra.

"Look me up if you make topside, amateur," she called across the room. "I'd like to see you again."

Silence was Chandra's reply. An intense stare that shouted her decision to remain and help her companions. She rose to her feet in defiance and refused to break eye contact. The message was clear. Olivia lingered for a few moments but eventually dipped through the door with a shrug and a chuckle. The Baylocke Battalion had vanished into the darkness of the ancient city.

"What was all that about?" Owen grumbled. He forced himself into a seated position with considerable effort. The fact that he spoke at all was a good sign. "Did I miss something?"

"No," Chandra muttered with a smile. "Nothing important, at least."

"Good," Owen sighed. "How long was I asleep?"

"Don't worry about it. You needed your rest. Still do, really, but it's gonna have to wait. Right now, we need to get ourselves outta the city. We can take our time once we're free from varmint territory."

"Yeah, that makes sense. When are leaving?"

"Now, if you can manage it."

"Oh, yeah, I'll be fine." Owen grunted as he attempted to stand. Weak knees knocked a few times, and legs like wet noodles refused to hold his weight. Chandra stepped in to catch Owen before he tumbled back down into the nest. "Okay, maybe with a little help."

"You don't say." Chandra chuckled. "Sit here and pack what you can. I'll wake Ryleah up and get us ready to go."

"Sounds good, boss."

A satisfied expression plastered over Owen's face as he plopped back against the wall. He seemed quite pleased that he was able to sit up on his own. To be fair, Chandra was a bit impressed herself.

The commotion had not raised the same alarm bells for Ryleah as it had for Owen. She remained curled in a loose ball on the nest. Gentle vibrations echoed from her throat with each quiet breath. Peace incarnate. It almost upset Chandra that she had to wake her friend, but she feared wasting more time in idle slumber. There was one truth she believed Olivia spoke. What varmints remained might be keener to strike a small group. Especially one so battered and bruised as Chandra, Owen, and Ryleah.

Chandra crawled over to Ryleah and gave her a few light shakes. Enough to wake the girl, but not enough to cause a fright. The action did not wake Ryleah. Instead, it forced her slack jaw to drop open. Quiet snores now made their best impression of a sawmill. Chandra put a little more effort into rousing her friend. The snores stopped and started without rhythm as Ryleah was pulled back into the waking world. She did not seem too pleased.

"What's wrong?" Ryleah grumbled. Propped up on one elbow, her free hand wandered up to her mouth to stifle a yawn. She blinked at the light a handful of times. Sight adjustment was still an unaccustomed struggle. "Was having a nice dream, you know. Sharing some lemon cake with father."

"Sounds delightful," Chandra snorted. "No more time for dreaming, though. The Baylocke folks have gone, and they left the front door open. We need to make ourselves scarce."

"Oh," Ryleah grumbled. The gravity of the thought struck a few moments later. Ryleah's eyes widened. She shot up straight and peered around the emptied house. "Oh. Oh, no."

"We'll be fine," Chandra said. She placed a hand on Ryleah's shoulder for reassurance. "Just need to get our stuff together and get moving. The sooner, the better. Can you carry the other pack?"

"Yeah, I'm sure—"

"I'll carry my own pack, thank you!" Owen hollered in protest.

"You will not," Chandra reprimanded. "Now hush. The rest of us have work to do while you keep yourself awake."

"Yes, ma'am," Owen mumbled in reply. Both Chandra and Ryleah got a hollow giggle out of the display. There might have been mirth, but present circumstance kept its bootheel atop any hope for joy. Fun had to wait.

There was not much to gather. Between the fight with Olivia's people and the surprise attack from the varmints, much of what Chandra and Owen had carried was spilled onto the street. Full canteens. Scraps of medical supplies. A forlorn sock tucked somewhere beneath a fallen varmint. There had not been an opportunity to stash their things away before the battles began. Nor was there time to scrounge for their belongings once the fighting had concluded. Chandra and her group were forced to make do with what was left.

The hardest part was getting Owen to remain compliant. He was still feverish, and a promise made would not necessarily translate to a promise kept. Twice he tried to secure his baggage from Ryleah. Insistence did not get the man his confused way. Chandra stepped in each time to regain a new promise that would be attacked minutes later.

One article eluded Chandra. She had hoped to find the light focus that Owen used when Chandra's spell was not enough. The little cylinder of metal was hidden well. No matter how thoroughly she dug through the pockets of Owen's backpack, Chandra was unable to locate the tool. Owen proved less than helpful. Vague shrugs were his answer when asked where the focus was sequestered. Chandra feared it might have been lost to the street like so many other bits of their supplies. When Chandra finally gave in and searched Owen's pockets, she was met with a mischievous grin.

It's like dealing with a toddler, Chandra groaned internally. The focus had been in his right front pocket the entire time.

"You just… just put your thumb on the gem. On the memory glass," Owen said, having decided to be helpful for a moment. "Flow goes in, light comes out. Easy peasy."

"Thanks," Chandra mumbled as she rolled her eyes.

With the focus in hand, Chandra was ready to move. Her bag was packed and she had a plan. All that remained was to get Owen on his feet and begin the troublesome walk to the edge of the city. A task that Chandra tried her best to minimize the danger of in her mind. She needed to be calm and steady. If she allowed her head to tumble this way and that, none of them would see the sun again.

Ryleah gave a confident nod when Chandra looked her way. The acolyte strapped Owen's pack to her back and stood tall. No rousing speech was required. Ryleah was just as ready to move as Chandra, if not more so. A welcome sight in a veritable sea of pain and disaster.

The girls both heaved a preparatory sigh as they stepped to either side of Owen. Though he was not without some control of his faculties, it still felt to Chandra like she was hoisting a bag of sentient bricks. A bag that giggled and chuckled as the girls struggled to keep it on its own two feet. This was going to be a long walk, Chandra thought in glum realization. Maybe Owen will regain some of his strength as the walk goes on? Hopeful thoughts felt miles better than the sour alternative that begged contemplation.

Coordinated steps carried Owen to the front of the house. Chandra and Ryleah verbalized their efforts to remain synchronized. By the time they reached the street, the need to speak their steps aloud had subsided. The pair settled into a steady rhythm that pulled Owen forward at a painfully slow pace. An emptied jar of molasses might have beaten them to the edge of the city without any outside provocation. Another thought that Chandra tried her best to quell. She focused instead on her steps and the light spell that bobbed an arm's length ahead.

Violence outside the house had not been so intense that it made walking difficult. The smattering of varmint corpses paled in comparison to what lay further down the road. Chandra and Ryleah were able to pick their way through the remnants of battle with relative ease. More than anything, the site of battle served as a reminder of what lay in the shadows. The creatures must have watched every step Chandra and Ryleah took toward their goal of escape.

It was not long before the grim reminders grew a voice. Collections of muffled chitters and chirps. The scrape of claws on ancient stone. Sounds poured out from darkened alleyways and rained down from sheltered rooftops. None yet dared to venture into the light of Chandra's spell, but the desire was palpable. Chandra could feel beady varmint eyes leering at her unarmored flesh. Disease-infested tongues smacked lips that drooled in ravenous anticipation. To say Chandra felt uncomfortable would have been to call the Kastkill Mountains a collection of molehills.

Light did not reach far enough for comfort. Chandra funneled more energy into her spell. She toed the line between comfort and friction burns. It was enough to capture the entire street in the warm glow of her light. Alleyways became a little less dark. Chandra was able to discern the tips of clawed fingers that gripped the edges of rooftops. The first visual confirmation that her path was watched.

Signs of pursuers did not escape Ryleah. Chandra felt a nervous hand grip her arm behind Owen's back. The acolyte's fingers trembled in anticipation. Whether or not Ryleah could see the hints of varmints was unclear, but Chandra knew the chitters and scrapes reached her.

"Chandra, they're close," Ryleah muttered to hammer the point home.

"I know," Chandra replied. She twisted her mangled left hand to touch Ryleah's arm. "I know. We're okay right now. They're keeping out of the light."

"For how long?"

"I… don't know." Chandra sighed. She could not bring herself to lie to Ryleah. If this was to be Chandra's last day in the world, she wanted to go with as few regrets as possible. The meager gains from a lie were outweighed by the desire to be honest in the end.

Screams cut through the air. From far behind, the sounds of a battle soared through the still air. Carried by the ill will of the city in place of a swift breeze. Metal clashed. Fierce explosions rocked the ground beneath Chandra's feet. There was no question in her mind as to what had happened. The varmints proved to be braver than Olivia had given them credit. Another ambush must have been launched while the Baylocke Battalion was busy sifting through the cache.

Chandra shuddered to think what might have happened had she accepted the invitation from Olivia. No amount of money was worth another roll of the dice with those vicious creatures. All Chandra could do now was hope that the battle behind would draw away some of the varmints who watched from on high.

A vain hope.

If any varmints had fled to assist in the battle with the Baylocke Battalion, Chandra could not tell. The opposite effect came to play. Rather than flee, the nearby varmints grew bolder at the sound of their brethren locked in combat. Chandra caught glimpses of full limbs creeping out from windows and around alley corners. Leering heads poked through doorways and hung down from rooftops. The warm glow of Chandra's spell began to lose its luster in the eyes of the varmints. They were no longer dissuaded by the brilliant glow.

"Ryleah, the light's going to go out in a second," Chandra whispered. She did not know if varmints could understand Federal common, but she did not want to risk the chance. "Should make these guys scatter. For a little while, at least. Just keep walking forward. I'll use Owen's light to steer us."

Reply was not immediate. Chandra felt Ryleah's grip on her arm tighten. Ryleah was not pleased by the thought of pushing through the unfamiliar territory without the blessing of sight. Chandra could not blame her. Still, it had to be done. The spell needed to flare before the varmints got enough courage to reach out and strike. Chandra would do her best to channel the Flow and build a replacement spell, but she was already close to self-harm.

"Okay," came the eventual reply from Ryleah. Her voice trembled as much as her hand. Though Ryleah did not voice her concerns, Chandra could feel them dig into her forearm. "I trust you."

"How are we doing, girls?" Owen piped in out of nowhere. Slurred words dribbled out of his mouth like spittle from an infant. "We making good time? Going to make it back in time for dinner?"

"Shut up, Owen," Chandra grunted.

"I think chicken. Do you like chicken? Of course, you like chicken."

"Owen!"

"Everybody likes chicken."

"Knock it off!" Chandra snapped. She let go of Ryleah with her left hand to clip Owen in the back of the head. A handful of expletives peppered the ground at Owen's feet, but he did not resist. Chandra's next comment was directed to Ryleah. "What did you give him? It's like he's drunk or something."

"Nothing weird," Ryleah grunted. "Might be an allergic reaction. He wasn't really in a state to be asked, you know."

As Chandra bickered with her companions, the varmints continued to encroach. The arguments made them bolder. Chandra cast a concerned glance over her shoulder to see that half a dozen varmints trailed behind. Warm light glistened in their little black eyes. Fear left the varmints. Openly they stalked their prey. Left unchecked, the monsters would soon nip at Chandra's heels.

Patience ran its course. Chandra refused to let the varmints draw closer. With a sudden surge of energy, the small orb of light ahead of Chandra swelled to three times its normal size. The warm glow vanished to be replaced by a searing glare. Light grew to a feverish intensity before there was a loud pop.

Darkness followed. The sort that left purple and yellow spots in Chandra's eyes when she blinked against the gloom. Though the flare had burned its memory into Chandra's brain, the effort was worth it. Claws scratched and skittered in all directions. Up and away. No varmint dared to creep forward through the dazzling display of light. Whether it was fear of the spell or a distaste of the light was not important. All Chandra cared about was the time that she had bought.

Chandra let go of Owen's arm and allowed it to dangle around her shoulder. With her right hand, she fished the light focus from her pocket and began to channel the Flow. The energy required was minimal. A few moments of focus drew out a piercing beam of light. Chandra flicked the device to check for assailants. As far as she could determine with the limited light source, the varmints had indeed retreated for now.

"Are we okay?" Ryleah grunted.

"Yeah," Chandra replied as she focused the light on the path ahead, "we're fine. Just keep walking. If I tug, you follow."

"Okay."

"Sounds good, boss," Owen added.

"Hush!" Chandra growled.

Without an expansive shower of light, it would be difficult to determine if the varmints returned. Chandra needed to hear each tooth that chattered and claw that scraped. The light from the focus was enough to guide their way, but it was by no means enough to keep Chandra and her companions safe.

Wasted thoughts equaled wasted time. Chandra forced herself not to dwell on how little time her stunt likely bought. Instead, she focused on channeling energy. A slow and measured effort to gather enough of the Flow to reignite her light. It had to be done without injury. Ryleah's resources were spent. Any friction burns that Chandra suffered would stay with her until she reached the House of Many. Navigation of the tunnels in the World Below with a burned hand was not a prospect Chandra wanted to consider.

As the group trudged forward through the dark, Chandra felt her senses come under assault. A gradual attack of sound and smell. Unmistakable skitters in the dark recesses of the ancient city drew near once more. The varmints had not retreated for good. They were merely frightened. A fright the creatures overcame much sooner than Chandra had hoped.

On top of the slinking sounds of clawed hands and feet was the smell of death. Slight at first, the odor of decomposing flesh grew in strength. An all too familiar smell by this point. It meant they had made it to the field of corpses where the ashling lay slain. A mile marker that helped Chandra gather her bearings of the area. They were making good time despite the stumbling drunk that weighed Chandra and Ryleah down. As awful as the smell was, Chandra was a touch relieved.

Relief that evaporated as Chandra realized the difficulty ahead. Not the varmints that hunted or the intolerable stench of decay. What lay ahead was a stretch of road choked with obstacles to navigate around or, as was more likely, trip and fall over. The fallen varmints were about to serve as a natural roadblock. Service in death to their kind that circled like vultures in the inky black darkness. Bodies here and there would not have posed a challenge and could have easily been circumvented. Streets filled to the brim? There was no way Chandra could guide Ryleah through without light, and Chandra refused to duck into an unexplored side street.

A new light spell was demanded. Demanded, but still unfulfilled. The effort to keep the light focus on was an unwelcome distraction. Owen weighed on her shoulders like a rock that threatened to pull her down to some untold, watery depths. To top it all, Chandra was tired. Not the kind of tired she felt after a day in the orchards. Not the kind of tired she felt after an all-nighter in the World Below. It felt like new muscles formed in her body just to cry out in pain. There was nowhere that did not hurt. Through it all, Chandra had to force the Flow into her ragged left hand to craft a light spell that *might* deter impending death. Maybe.

Screw it.

Scratches and scrapes were too close at hand. Chandra's comfort was not worth the lives that clung to her shoulders. Floodgates lifted. The Flow roared into Chandra. It felt like her blood came to a boil. Like needles dragged through her veins to pierce her left hand. She could hear the flesh on her hand sizzle as an orb of light burst into existence just above. Warm radiance spilled over the streets that were clogged with death. Varmints brave enough to have drawn close scurried back into the secure veil of darkness.

"Not a moment too soon." Chandra winced in appreciation.

"What did you do?" Ryleah asked as she blinked at the sudden resurgence of her sight. "Why does it smell like burning?"

"Don't worry about it," Chandra gasped. "Just keep walking."

Just keep walking, Chandra repeated to herself. *What's one more injury? It's just pain. You'll laugh about it later. Just keep walking. Keep walking. Walk.*

The new light spell was enough to carry Chandra and Ryleah through the stretch of varmint corpses. Their pace was slowed, but they did not stop. One false step might throw the group to the ground. Chandra could not imagine a more opportune moment for the varmints that yet lived. A swift strike that would end Chandra's journey in blood and death.

Signs of pursuers lessened as the group passed through the corpses. At first, Chandra thought it might have been solemn respect for the dead. That the varmints might steer clear of the area to leave their fallen brethren in peace. The notion stuck for as long as it took to come upon the hulking corpse of the ashling. There was no doubt in Chandra's mind that the ashling, dead as it was, was the true reason that the varmints steered clear. Even in death, the ashling was a horrific sight to behold. Scythe-like fingers glistened in the warm light of Chandra's spell. Blank eyes hung open and stared in all directions. Tricks of the light made the arms appear to move.

As awful as it was to see the vile creature again, Chandra was thankful for the minor respite. The slowed pace allowed her to catch a bit of her breath and adjust the weight on her shoulders. Shuffled steps supported Chandra as she drew closer to Owen for a better grip.

The readjustment could not have come at a better time. Halfway through the stretch of corpses, Owen's feeble steps lost much of their strength. Chandra felt the extra weight push down on her legs. She would have demanded more from Owen if the man had not started to wretch. He heaved and shuddered as his body attempted to purge a meal that had already been lost. It must be the smell, Chandra thought. She hoped it was the smell. There was no room for some new, hidden symptom of the poison to make itself known.

Occasional heaves continued as the group left the varmint corpses behind. Loud enough to draw attention, but not so loud that it stifled the resurgence of varmint stalkers. The creatures had not waited long to make their presence known once more. They had little to fear now that the ashling was out of sight. Bravery manifested in the form of creeping bodies that slipped in and out of Chandra's light.

Aches rolled over Chandra's thighs. Weakness had not dissipated along with the stench of decaying flesh. Owen still struggled to put one foot before the other. Heaves came in shorter intervals and increased in severity. Coughing fits followed the heaves. Violent as they were, the deep inhale before each cough seemed to be all the air Owen could manage to cram into his lungs.

"I don't know if he's going to make it the edge of the city," Chandra gasped between steps. "Not like this."

"I can't... can't do anything unless we stop," Ryleah coughed in reply.

"Guess we just have to deal with it, then, because we're not stopping."

The words tumbled out of Chandra as haltingly as Owen's steps. Words did not help. Talking just made Chandra feel that much more exhausted. It had been a mistake to ask Ryleah for aid. Chandra knew nothing would come of the request, but her lungs were desperate. Her legs needed rest.

Atop the anguished cries of Chandra's legs and the scurry of varmints in the shadows came a new sensation. This one was born of the desperation that plagued both Chandra and Ryleah. In her distracted state, had Chandra missed the chalk-marked turn that would direct her to safety? She had not paid much attention to the street as she walked. Owen's rapid deterioration offered no favors. Paranoia crawled over Chandra's sweat-soaked skin. An army of spiders that caused the hairs on her skin to prickle.

Contemplation of such horrors had to wait. The scrape of claws rose sharply behind Chandra and demanded attention. A varmint dashed into the light. With dull teeth bared, the creature barreled straight for Chandra's leg.

"No, you don't!" Chandra snapped.

Chandra unleashed her right leg like a mule. The heel of her boot dug deep in the gnashing muzzle of the varmint. A solid connection that Chandra felt up to her hip. Both of the varmint's legs buckled from the force of the kick. The creature crumpled to the ground and did not stir.

Necessity had called for the kick, but gravity was near at hand to punish. The force of the kick pushed Chandra forward. Owen's weight pulled her down. With only one leg to support her, Chandra buckled and joined the varmint on the ground. The whole group tumbled down after her. Owen slapped onto the street like a dead fish before a set of coughs wracked his broken frame. Ryleah made a valiant effort to remain on her feet. Brought down onto one knee, she managed to keep Owen's arm around her neck.

More claws scraped nearby. Opportunity presented itself. Chandra saw a pair of varmints dash toward her through the light. She thought she heard more behind her. The mistake that had carried her to the ground would now cost her the light spell. There was no greater defense available. Chandra channeled the Flow through the orb of light until it popped in another radiant shower of light and sparks.

No bites came. Claws scratched and stumbled away. Chandra hoped she had blinded the ones closest at hand. The creatures had already vanished by the time she retrieved the light focus. A welcome sight emerged amid the frantic search for assailants.

The chalk mark was visible!

"We're getting close," Chandra panted. "We turn here. Let's get him up and get moving."

"Yeah, okay," Ryleah stammered. Chandra could not begin to imagine the terror that must have swallowed Ryleah. To see a pair of ravenous varmints charge at her just for the world to plunge into darkness. That fear clung to her voice. There was no brave face left to give. "I'm ready."

"Okay. Three, two, one… up!"

Both girls dug deep as they pushed their way back to full height. Chandra grunted and clenched her jaw under the weight. Ryleah howled against the strain. A false start sent them back to their knees, forced them to double their efforts. Chandra joined Ryleah in her bitter howl. It felt like the muscles in her neck were going to snap.

"Steady," Chandra said through gritted teeth. "Now turn!"

The first steps were the hardest. Getting back in sync while Ryleah was blind took a minute. The girls pulled Owen this way and that as they struggled to find a rhythm. Once they found their stride, the pace was painfully slow. It did not help that Owen dragged his toes. All fight had left the man. He hung limp on Chandra and Ryleah's arms, stirred only by the occasional cough.

"Come on," Chandra gasped. "Come on, Owen. We need some help here. Give us something!"

Chandra had expected the words to fall on ears plugged by poison. Instead, she felt a bit of weight lift from her shoulders. She snapped the light focus down to Owen's feet to see that his toes no longer dragged. The man tried, however feebly, to step in time with Chandra and Ryleah. It was enough to bring their collective pace up just beyond a crawl.

Claws tempered elation. Varmints resumed their prowl faster than the last time. Even Chandra's exhausted mind could guess that the light spell was losing its power over the creatures. Twice now an orb of light had exploded. Both times the result was a harmless flash. What was there to be afraid of beyond a few moments of bleared sight?

Nothing, Chandra told herself.

That did not change the fact that Chandra had no other options. The light had maintained some level of hesitancy during the hellish march. Chandra could only hope that it would continue to do so.

Personal well-being was no longer a consideration. That luxury had been left behind. Chandra dug deep into the Flow and ripped forth the energy she needed with alarming speed. She felt her blood boil again. Burned skin sizzled for a second time. Chandra could not help but cry out in pain as she raised a new light spell into the air. She had to fight the urge to examine her arm. Knowing how badly she had burned herself would provide no benefit. All that remained was forward.

Walls of buildings slipped away into darkness. It required too much energy to maintain a wide radius for the light spell. Energy that could be put into each fought-for step. The light around her dwindled as Chandra continued to press on. Little by little, the light spell became little more than a halo to outline the group. Something for Ryleah to see her next step by and nothing more.

The varmints remained patient. Their claws raked and their growls rumbled, but they did not attack. Sounds of the swarm drew closer as the light spell diminished. Chandra assumed that the varmints were waiting for the spell to fail. When the light died, they could charge the battered group and tear Chandra, Ryleah, and Owen to pieces. It made sense in her head. Why charge into another flare when the varmints could just wait for their prey to collapse? They could saunter up to Chandra in grim satisfaction. Take their time. Nobody was coming to stop them.

"Whoa, stop," Chandra shouted. "Stop, stop, stop!"

Through her focus on step after step, Chandra had not noticed the cobblestones give way to something rougher. There was not enough light to see that the houses and stores had been replaced by sheer walls of stone. More importantly, there was just enough light to see that Chandra and Ryleah were about to step over a ledge. The very ledge they had climbed to enter the city.

Chandra fought against her momentum and pulled backward on Owen's relenting body. She felt Ryleah do the same, and so the trio tumbled backward onto the stone floor.

All Chandra wanted to do was lie in place and let the cool rock absorb the heat that radiated from her spent body. A desire she pushed aside. Claws still raked. Tails whipped through the air. Snarls rose from places too close for comfort. Chandra rolled over and brought herself to her knees, staring back toward the city. Energy freed by dropping Owen funneled back into the pathetic spell. Weak light clawed its way through the darkness like a castaway clambering up a beach.

A single varmint stood firm. Other varmints backed away from the encroaching light, but this one creature allowed himself to become enveloped in the warm glow. He was one of the tall ones. Maybe as tall as Owen. Definitely taller than Chandra. Under the filthy rags that adorned the varmint were lean muscles. One of his two front teeth was chipped on a corner. In his hand was a spiked cudgel that he tapped against the ground. It made a sickening echo that barely fought through the commotion from the other varmints.

Chandra had reached the end. At the edge of the city, she should have been free. Some part of her had hoped that her pursuers would have broken off to join in the battle with the Baylocke Battalion. She was not so lucky. Instead, a pack of varmints backed an absolute brute of a rat.

Panic and anger swelled all at once. If this was going to be the end, then she would not die on her knees. Chandra grabbed her last manarail spike and forced an edge upon it. Friction seared the flesh on her right arm. It wouldn't matter if she was dead, Chandra told herself, but she could not help but wince at the pain. She placed her left hand onto her knee and attempted to push herself up. A whole new pain rushed through her body. Chandra looked at her left arm and finally saw the blisters that her light spells spawned. The arm was little more than a shield.

Chandra attempted to stand without assistance from her damaged arms. An effort that proved futile. Her legs refused to cooperate. They had undergone too much stress to listen to any of Chandra's demands. A furious growl rumbled in Chandra's throat. Rage that pointed inward as much as out. She took in a deep breath and roared as she brandished her newly formed dagger.

"Leave us alone!"

What sounded like a few chuckles morphed into unified cackles. She could not see them, but Chandra could feel the ridicule emanate from the varmints. They made a mockery of her desperate last stand.

Laughter died in throats when the tall varmint raised a closed fist. An eerie calm settled over the swarm, punctuated by an occasional scrape or titter. The great varmint glowered down at Chandra amid the taut silence. Weighted steps carried him forward. Its presence alone was enough to make Chandra recoil. The air around the creature swelled with the promise of death.

The varmint stopped just outside the reach of Chandra's blade. Chandra made sure to check the distance with a few warning swipes. There was no desire to strike the varmint. This was a fight Chandra knew she did not have the strength to win.

"Stay back!" Chandra howled in desperation. She slid on her knees until she was directly between the varmint and a cowering Ryleah. The dagger shook in Chandra's trembling hand as she flicked the tip toward the varmint. "I'm warning you!"

The tall varmint knelt and locked eyes with Chandra.

"Don't. Come. Back."

"What?" Chandra asked in reflex.

A verbal warning was the last thing Chandra expected to receive from the imposing varmint. Raspy words that the varmint strained to produce. Like each word required a full breath to utter. It took a while to process that the varmint had spoken. Enough time for the creature to stand, turn around, and walk back into the darkness from which it came. Claws raked over stone for the final time before Chandra was left in a deafening silence.

Numb fingers let the dagger fall from Chandra's hand. The clatter of metal on stone was loud and stringent. Chandra felt the noise with her whole body. A noise so sharp that it sliced the tension in her muscles. Finally able to stop, Chandra crumpled to the cool ground. Pressed her cheek against the welcoming stone.

The sobs were gentle at first. Physical relief of the pain that welled up both inside and out. Pain that Chandra had been forced to suppress with all her might. Now she felt the full force of her body's wrath. A single cry of agony echoed through the spacious tunnel. It did not make Chandra feel any better, but it was what her body demanded. There was room for such an indulgence. The rest of the World Below be damned. Chandra had made it out of the city of Those Who Came Before.

Gentle, trembling fingers pawed at Chandra's arm. Ryleah crawled over Owen with tears in her eyes. Chandra and Ryleah embraced on the cold, cold ground as they let their agony and fear fill the caves with bitter cries of relief.

22

The Way Forward

All was quiet in the Pattal household when Chandra awoke. The first light of day crept through her bedroom window. There was no warmth in the light, just a chill signal that morning had come. Under the sheets, it was quite warm. Thanks in part to Omala, whose body was half splayed over Chandra. Temptation to remain comfortable in place was strong. Drool soaked into her sleeve was a minor price to pay to avoid the cold floor. Chandra wanted to settle back into position and allow sleep to reclaim her before the whole house was awake.

Not today, Chandra told herself.

With the practiced care of an older sister, Chandra lifted Omala's arm and slid out from under the girl. A seeking hand drowsily accepted the pillow that Chandra offered in her stead. Quiet grumbles filled the room for a moment as Omala adjusted. Peace overtook the young girl not long after.

Chandra swung her feet off the bed to find the floor was just as cold as she had feared. She struggled to suppress a gasp in response to the sudden change. Warm mornings had been replaced by chill dawns. Autumn was closer to winter now than it was to summer, and the weather promised to grow colder still. Not a notion over which Chandra was particularly fond. Months of green and bloom were always sorely missed when the sun brought no warmth to the farm and the days were short.

Furtive haste carried Chandra across the room to her small wardrobe. She slipped from her nightclothes into more travel-appropriate attire. Woolen socks were the first thing to go on. They allowed her to slide into solid black trousers without a fixation on the frigid floor. Black suspender straps hung down by her legs, dangling in place until they were strapped atop a dark blue shirt. The sleeves were rolled up past her elbows as a matter of course. Chandra hardly noticed herself doing it. A pair of leather boots completed the change.

After strapping a few manarail spikes to her waist, Chandra felt ready to face the world. She dusted a few scraps of lint from her pants and crept toward the bedroom door. Careful hands pried the door open without so much as a squeak. Chandra displayed just as much care in closing the door once she had passed. Omala deserved another hour of sleep. Maybe even two, if she was lucky.

"Early riser today, huh? Not even your turn for breakfast."

Hushed words gave Chandra a start. Another gasp died in her throat. Amid her efforts to make a quiet escape from the bedroom, she failed to notice her father standing by the kitchen counter. Chandra placed a hand over her rampantly beating heart to stifle its pace. The cheeky grin on Nitesh's face suggested he was quite pleased with himself over the scare.

Chandra placed a finger over her lips to hush her father, walking over to the counter on the balls of her feet. A stack of flatbread was out. Nitesh, satisfied with his effect on Chandra, turned back to the counter. He worked steadily on a bowl of ginger mint sauce. Something to help the family wake up and prepare for the day. Another reddish sauce Chandra did not recognize was off to the side.

"Eating with us today, my dear?" Nitesh asked while he worked.

"Not today, sorry," Chandra replied as she grabbed a handful of bread. "Today's the big day. Want to show up as early as I can. Make a good impression, you know?"

"That day already, huh? You ready to go back into the big city? I wouldn't say anything if you decided to wait another week, or a month... or a year, or—"

"I get it." Chandra chuckled. She gave her father an affectionate nudge before clamping down on some bread with watering jaws. Muffled words struggled to escape the chunk of bread as Chandra continued. "The bills won't pay themselves, though. Have to do what I can, especially since the last job was a bust."

Bitterness clung to those last few words. Chandra raised her left hand and waggled her remaining fingers to emphasize the point. The gesture was enough to pull Nitesh from his work. Setting down his pestle, he wiped dirty hands on his trousers and wrapped Chandra in his arms. An unexpected gesture, but not an unwelcome one.

"Just make sure you come back in one piece this time, okay? There's no amount of money in the world that's worth your life."

"I know," Chandra whispered as she returned her father's embrace. "Learned that lesson the hard way. You don't have to worry about me anymore."

Nitesh raised a hand to stroke his daughter's hair. After a kiss on the top of her head, he released Chandra and returned to his breakfast preparations. The loving smile he bore was infectious. Chandra could not help but adorn a similar smile as she turned and walked toward the front door.

"Oh, speaking of lessons," Chandra said in a glib tone, "don't buy anything while I'm gone."

"Yes, yes, yes," Nitesh sighed from across the room. He did not bother to look up from his culinary work. "Go on, get out of here already. I'm sure Alabaster is dying to get back into Arnstead. Goodness knows he seems to love that place as much as you."

This was the most Chandra and her father had spoken of the incident. When Chandra initially returned home, battered and broken of body and spirit, Nitesh had not asked questions. There was a look on his face that Chandra had not seen since the days when her mother returned home in slings and bandages. It lacked any form of judgment.

An understanding look that said more than the man could ever hope to verbalize. Acceptance of the world's cruelties without spite against transgressions.

Chandra wondered why her father kept so quiet about the matter. Surely, he had all manner of questions that he wanted to sling Chandra's way. What had kept her away for so long? Why had she returned in such a sorry state? How could she have sacrificed so much of herself and yet have nothing to show for it? That last question was one that Chandra continually asked herself, so she imagined it must be on her father's mind as well.

It took Chandra a few weeks to understand her father's disposition. That his silence was less a sign of scorn and more a show of respect. Nitesh was willing to wait for his daughter to talk, if she ever wanted to talk at all. Chandra was unsure if she would ever recall the whole story for him. There was too much to say. More pain than she wanted to remember. Horrors that still caused her to shoot up in the middle of the night drenched with sweat. Half-heard scrapes of claws on the floorboards. She might share the broad strokes when she returned from her trip to town, but Chandra decided that some details were best kept in silence. Nitesh was already sporting some gray hairs. He did not need Chandra's help to sprout more.

The doorhandle was cold to the touch. Chandra recoiled in surprise before taking a firm hold of the metal ring. She wanted to be gone before the moment of understanding and kindness devolved into something awkward. When she pulled back on the door and moved to step outside, Chandra was met with another surprise.

On the doorstep, wrapped in a scarlet scarf, was Victoria Chandler. One mittened hand was poised to knock on the door that just swung away. The other was tucked behind a clipboard that she held under her armpit. She shivered like it was the dead of winter rather than a chilly autumn morning.

"A bit early for the winter wear, don't you think, Vic?" Chandra mumbled. She was not particularly pleased to see her neighbor. "Here for collections, I take it?"

"If I can see my breath, then the snow clothes are coming out," Victoria replied. Agitated eyes roved over the clipboard, which she slid out just far enough to read. The clipboard, and the hand that held it, jumped back to the warmth of her torso once she was satisfied. "And yes, I'm here for collections. If I'd come asking for sugar, I would have waited for the sun to come up. Now, let's get this squared away. You're the first on a long list."

"Right, well, we can't pay," Chandra said through an aggressive sigh. "The new rate is too much to handle. We'll give you what we have, and I'll talk to your boss in town today."

Victoria raised a hand to stop Chandra, then curled the hand into a fist. She brought the fist to her lips and revitalized her covered fingers with a puff of hot breath.

"Rate changed again," Victoria said with a thin, green-lipped grin.

"Wait, what? What do you mean it's changed again?" Chandra stepped off the threshold, casting a disparaging look over her shoulder as she closed the front door behind herself. "What did he buy and when did he buy it? I need to know before I kill him."

"If he bought something, the loan didn't go through us," Victoria replied. She spoke with a fuller voice now that the door was closed. A show of respect for those who might have still been asleep. "No, this is a change in your favor. Your rate was dropped to five dollars."

"Wha— five? *Five* dollars?"

"That's what the paperwork says. Not sure what you said to who, but it looks like somebody at the branch listened."

"But I… I didn't talk to anyone at the bank."

Victoria shrugged. Innocent eyes scanned her clipboard a second time as her grin widened into a proper smile.

"Well, whatever happened, I wouldn't ask too many questions, yeah? If the bank makes an error in your favor, don't go bothering any- one to know more. Anyway, have you got the five dollars, or do I need to talk to Nitesh?"

Overwhelmed with questions, Chandra was unsure what reply to give. The answer to the immediate question was no. Chandra did not have any significant sum of money on her person. Rather than try to grapple with the situation in front of Victoria, Chandra cracked the front door and called for her father. She excused herself and headed toward the barn once Nitesh had struck up a conversation.

Five dollars.

Five.

Less than half of the rate Chandra had been quoted when the cider machine was delivered. Closer to a quarter of the amount. Unless Nitesh had stumbled upon some buried treasure while expanding the herb garden, Chandra could not imagine how he handed over enough money to drop their rate by such a staggering amount. Had he visited the Orland Bank branch while Chandra was stuck in the World Below? No, that couldn't have been it. The last time Chandra had checked, her father was still banned from the premises.

Confusion hung about her like a storm cloud as she walked to the barn. It was not until she had readied Alabaster for travel and hit the road that Chandra fully processed the advice from Victoria. The rate had changed. Whether it was an error on the Orland's end or the Pattal family had a mysterious benefactor was not important. What mattered was that five dollars was an almost manageable amount. If her business in town went well, the Pattal family might be able to put some money away for the first time since Chandra's mother had passed.

Thoughts shifted away from concern as Chandra continued to ponder the news. Possible explanations flooded her mind like a newly struck well.

"I wonder who it was," Chandra muttered. The farmhouse was gone from sight. Her words were directed to one of her oldest friends. "Who do you think it was, Alabaster? Couldn't have been anyone around the homestead. They've all known for ages and never said a word. *Definitely* wasn't Victoria. I'm amazed the woman didn't burst into flames when she had to share the good news. Maybe Robin? She's a respected businessperson. Not sure why she would bother the Orlands for me, though. Who else have I even talked money with?"

Alabaster whinnied, almost as if in response. The timely noise got a chuckle out of Chandra. She leaned forward and gave Alabaster a few pats on his neck.

"You don't think it was... no. No, it couldn't have been... Owen?"

Forgotten words scratched the surface of Chandra's memory. Owen had mentioned something while they lay broken in the varmint house, waiting for fate to claim them. The man said something about talking to the Orlands.

"Couldn't have been Owen," Chandra said with a laugh. "I mean, seriously, a Spellseeker? The bank's not going to listen to what he has to say, no matter how good his intentions are. Maybe I should go see him while I'm in town? Ask him face to face?"

The last time Chandra saw Owen was at the Arnstead House of Many. Workers from the memory-glass quarry had carried them out of the upper stratus of the World Below. They helped transport Chandra and Owen, though Ryleah had enough strength to make it to the House on her own two legs. It was a frenzied journey. Chandra could only remember bits and pieces. When she had reached the safety and support of the quarry workers, her body failed. Weststead passed her by in a flash. A few landmarks from Oldstead stood out, but Chandra was in the House before she had realized it.

Expert hands brought Chandra back from the brink. Ryleah worked with her mentor, Rajani, and a handful of others from the clergy. Minor miracles formed part of the treatment. They peeled away burned flesh and sealed the open wounds on her left hand. Exhaustion and blood loss, however, had to recover through more conventional means. Chandra's stay was short. Just shy of two days. Best of all, thanks to Ryleah's tale of the slain ashling, the treatment was performed free of charge.

Owen was still in the care of the House when Chandra was cleared to leave. Practical surgery was required to remove the arrowhead in his shoulder. Attention from a local apothecary was called for. A miracle closed the wound, but Rajani was not able to determine the nature of the poison that had coated the arrowhead. The information Ryleah provided proved to be too insubstantial to act on. Nevertheless, Chandra was assured that Owen would be all right given time to rest. The clergy promised to assist Owen until the poison had passed naturally under medical supervision.

It had pained Chandra to leave without saying goodbye. Her absence could not be avoided, as Rajani estimated it could take anywhere from a few days to a full week for Owen to recover. Chandra's desire to greet the Spellseeker when he woke was contested by the desire to see her family again. To let her father and siblings know that she was alive and, more or less, well. Who was Chandra to doubt the medical prowess of the House, after all? There was little doubt in her mind that Owen would answer the door if she visited his home.

"I'm sure enough time has passed," Chandra muttered. "A visit sounds like a good idea, once I get everything figured out."

A chill autumn breeze and the steadfast Alabaster were Chandra's only company until she reached the main road to Arnstead. She expected to make the ride into town alone. In the back of her mind, though, she knew there would be someone waiting for her at the crossroads.

There was no cart to speak of this time. Just a boy on a horse, gazing attentively in the direction of the Pattal homestead. Early rays of the dawning sun lit his blond hair like fire on the horizon. He flung a hand up in fervent greeting as Chandra rode his way. A confident glimmer in his eyes crowned a wide and welcoming smile. His excitement bled into his horse, who tramped and stamped in response to the sudden movement. Some of the light left the boy's eyes as he struggled with the reins to control his mount.

"Your father must have hired some extra hands, Jacob, if you can afford to be out here," Chandra called out as she approached.

"Oh, you know," Jacob grunted in reply as he regained control of his horse. "It's not too hard to think of an excuse to visit town. I learned from the best, you know."

"Okay." Chandra chuckled in response to the implication.

The pair exchanged smiles. Before long, they convinced their horses to match pace on the road to Arnstead. Silence was the first order. A tenuous ordeal punctuated by the occasional snicker as one caught the tail end of a glance from the other. Stupid looks went back and forth until Chandra and Jacob could not help but indulge in quiet laughter.

"So," Jacob asked as the laughter subsided, "how's the arm? Doing any better?"

Chandra held up her left arm and surveyed the scarred landscape that was her skin. For all the help the House was able to provide, pink scar tissue still dominated most of her forearm. A brutal reminder of how dangerous even a simple spell can be when a person is past their limits. It was like looking at a web of flesh.

"Still can't feel a whole lot with my left hand," Chandra said. Her speech was airy as if she were lost in thought. "Everything moves fine, though. The skin is stretching better too. Doesn't hurt as much when I move. Starting to get some of my natural tone back, but the folks at the House said that might take a while. It'll probably never be smooth again, though."

"Well, better is better, right?"

"Right." Chandra smiled. In the face of unwavering optimism, she had learned the only option was acceptance. "You didn't *have* to come, you know? I could have managed fine on my own."

"I'm sure you could," Jacob replied with a polite nod, "but this is the big day, right? You're finally gonna go talk to her! After weeks of ifs and maybes. Had to be there to see it."

"Yeah, yeah," Chandra muttered through a deep inhale of cold air. "Whatever you say."

"Nervous?" Jacob asked after a short pause.

"Who, me?" Chandra tilted her head toward Jacob and lifted an eyebrow. Her smile withered a bit when she returned her gaze to the road ahead. "Maybe a little bit. In a bit of a sorry state these days, after all."

"You've got the talent," Jacob offered in tender assurance. "She might have an attitude, but I doubt she'll look you over just because you're on the mend. Come on. Confidence!"

"Hah!"

Chandra slapped a hand over her mouth to stifle both her laughter and embarrassment.

* * *

"What's a Baylocke?" Jacob asked. Chandra had brought Alabaster to a stop, and Jacob pulled on his horse's reins to match. "And why do they need a battalion of them?"

"What now?" Chandra replied.

Chandra only half turned toward Jacob. Her eyes remained locked on the black shield that dangled over the doorway of a small building in Eaststead. A silvery sword served as a vertical divider between two *B*s that glittered like gold. Not a sight she expected to find. Chandra knew that the group would have been based somewhere in Arnstead, but she preferred to imagine the building had gone up in flames. At the very least she was hoping it was boarded up when nobody returned to occupy the building.

"That building," Jacob pressured. "You came to a dead stop and stared at the sign. Mouth was hanging open and everything."

"Really? I didn't even notice."

"Uh-huh. Well, you don't have to tell me if you don't want to, but we're not far from Nia's now. Let's get a move on."

"You remember I told you I got mugged in Eaststead?" Chandra looked over to Jacob in time to see him halt his arms. He had been about to snap his reins but stopped short at the subject. Full, undivided attention rested on Chandra. "These were the guys. A couple of them, anyway. Same folks I got stuck with down below."

"All the more reason to get moving," Jacob replied. The late autumn chill infected the boy's words. Spite was not something Chandra was accustomed to hearing from Jacob's mouth.

"Yeah," Chandra sighed with a nod. "Yeah, you're right. Let's get mo—"

"Finally taking me up on my offer?"

The hauntingly familiar voice came from behind Chandra and caused her to jump in her saddle. She let out an excited screech. Sudden sound and motion combined to stir Alabaster. Chandra worked in haste to settle both her rampaging heart and disturbed horse.

"Hyperios help me," Chandra called out to the sky once she had gotten her situation settled. When she looked over her shoulder at the source of the voice, Chandra was somehow more disgusted than she had expected. "How are you still alive?"

"Was thinking about asking you the same thing."

Though there was part of a black-and-gold parasol that obscured the speaker's face, there was no way Chandra could have forgotten Olivia Baylocke's voice. The woman tilted her parasol to make eye contact. A superior tone stood in stark contrast to the newly developed pair of scars that raked across her face. An eyepatch covered her left eye. The other ruby-red eye glimmered intently upon Chandra.

"I'm not here for you," Chandra sneered. "And I never will be."

"I know," Olivia sighed. Despite her words, some of the light drained from her gaze. She cast a look over her shoulder to the pair that stood behind her. "Harish, Genevieve, go on in. I'll be in once we're done here."

The familiar pair of Shikaree skirted past Olivia, both giving Chandra a nod as they passed. Neither said a word. Not to their boss or Chandra. Somber steps carried them over the threshold of the Baylocke Battalion establishment. Chandra only saw them move in her periphery. She was not comfortable looking away from Olivia just yet.

"Everything okay, Chandra?" Jacob asked. He sounded closer than he had a moment ago. Concern joined the chill that coated his words. Chandra imagined the look on his face. It was not pretty.

"I'm fine, Jacob," Chandra said. She straightened her back and raised her shoulders as she glowered down at Olivia. "She's not dumb enough to try and hurt me here."

"I wish you'd get that idea out of your head," Olivia begged. Little tassels flew through the air as the woman twirled the parasol over her shoulder. "I don't mean you any harm. I really don't."

"And I wish you hadn't tried to kill my friend," Chandra snapped, "but here we are. How many of you people are left, anyway?"

"A touch of concern? That's sweet of you."

"Fine, don't answer. I'll just leave."

Chandra did not turn to go. Not yet. Instead, she kept her gaze locked on Olivia. Something about looking down on the woman brought Chandra a modicum of satisfaction. She felt a bit dirty about it at the same time, but that did not stop her. The satisfaction increased when Olivia's smile melted into a fragile frown. When Olivia began to squirm, Chandra knew she had the upper hand.

"You saw the whole team," Olivia muttered. The thin veneer of confidence that hung about the woman dissolved, eaten away by the cruelty of the world. She broke eye contact with Chandra as she continued to speak. "Just the three of us now. Lost a lot of people down there in that city. We lived down there in the demon cities for a while you know. The Deepkin. After we got pushed out of the Kastkills. I was too young to see any of it, but the elders say it was even worse. Things were fine when it was just the varmints. When the Federation moved west and came from above? Well, that was just too much. I guess it kind of felt like I was taking back our home. Got caught up in a fantasy and my people died for it."

It felt like Olivia was moments away from tears. The shift was so sudden that Chandra felt a sort of whiplash. She wanted to ask where all of this was coming from, but that felt insensitive. That confused Chandra even more. Why was she feeling sorry for this woman at all? It should not matter what kind of story Olivia wove, true or false. What she had tried to do was heinous and should not be forgiven.

Still...

"Well," Chandra muttered with a softened tone, "we all lost something down there. Everyone paid a price."

"Yeah," Olivia replied through a hollow chuckle. She tossed Chandra a sorry look, pointed to her face, and said, "We almost match, don't we?"

"We've both got our scars."

"Chandra," Jacob interjected. "Come on. We have places to be, and they're not here."

"We really could use your help, Chandra," Olivia said before Chandra could respond to Jacob. "We're hurting pretty bad right now. What do you say? Sign on with us. We can split everything four ways. Even."

"No, I don't think so," Chandra sniffed. The decision came in an instant. Though the delivery was less aggressive than she had initially intended, her answer remained unchanged. "I've given the World Below a pound of flesh. Not gonna give it anything else."

Olivia did not sigh. She did not protest or beg. All she did was cast her gaze to the ground for a moment before looking back up at Chandra. A thin, wily smile had replaced her honest frown.

"I figured not," Olivia said. "You're too smart for all this. Well, whatever you're here for, I hope it treats you well."

"Thanks," Chandra replied with a fair share of hesitance. "Before I go... what's with the parasol? Can I ask that?"

Disbelief wiped away the smirk that had cracked Olivia's features. After a quiet moment to process the question, the woman found a genuine smile. Laughter followed. A deep bout of laughter that came from the woman's stomach. It was enough for Olivia to double over and clutch at her stomach. Just as Chandra was about to inquire, the woman raised a hand.

"Of all... all the things you could ask. That's what you want to know?" Olivia stood up straight as she sucked down a massive breath. Tear streaks glistened on her cheek, which she pawed at with the back of a hand. "It's the sun. Disagrees with my skin. Hurts my eyes. You don't see many Deepkin walking around in broad daylight, do you?"

"No, I guess not," Chandra muttered, still stunned by the reaction to her question.

"Well, whatever you're doing, good luck. See you around, amateur."

With a feeble wave, Olivia sulked inside the Baylocke Battalion establishment. Muffled words from inside were silenced when the thick wooden door creaked to a close. The street became quiet save for the shuffle of a few passersby. Strangers that paid no mind to the conversations in their midst.

Disquiet settled over Chandra. She was less sure how she felt about Olivia and her brood than she had been the day before. Deep-seated distrust still colored her perception, but a few traces of wonder slipped in through imperceptible cracks. Chandra continued to stare at the closed door to the Baylocke establishment. The noise of her surroundings faded and dropped below her attention. She wanted to believe that Olivia offered genuine kindness. It was more palatable than carrying around such ugly hate in her heart. White-hot disgust that threatened to boil Chandra's blood, to cause venom to spew from her mouth. Still, though, the image of eyes like rubies soaked in blood would not relent.

Not my problem anymore, Chandra tried to convince herself. *Leave it be and move on. I've got my own future to worry about.*

The small cluster of traffic parted around Chandra and Jacob once they started to move again. An overlooked benefit of riding a horse down a small street. Nobody got in their way, and, if they did, nobody stayed for long. A boon that made passage through the winding streets of Eaststead an almost pleasant affair.

Jacob did not resume his light-hearted speech. The boy seemed bothered by the confrontation with Olivia almost as much as Chandra. If only he knew, Chandra thought to herself. What she had relayed of her journey to the boy was largely sanitized. Half-truths extracted from the harrowing ordeal. The Baylocke Battalion were changed from murderous thugs to a pack of bullies. Presence of an ashling was omitted in full. As for her missing fingers? The result of a climbing accident, and what ultimately forced the group to return home.

The closest thing Chandra gave to a straight answer was regarding the burns. Sharing that she over channeled the Flow and suffered a severe friction burn served as the grain of truth that gave her lie roots. Jacob's reaction to the injury had been visceral enough without telling him the fingers stewed in the gut of a varmint. Chandra saw no need to make the boy more concerned than he already was.

Lack of conversation allowed Chandra to lose herself in the sensations of Arnstead. It had been almost a month since her last visit. The farm was so quiet in comparison. Here, in Arnstead, Chandra could hear deals being brokered over shipments of lumber and spices. Bickering soldiers from the 4th Federation Army popped up where disturbances evolved between merchants. Oxcarts creaked. Urchins scampered. Hosts and hostesses tried their hardest to pull people into their restaurants or taverns. A vibrant collision of the highs and lows that life had to offer, all coalesced into a single town.

"I missed this," Chandra whispered to herself.

Soft at first, but rising in intensity as Chandra and Jacob drew near, was the sound of metal pounded against metal. It cut through the dusty air like a hawk's cry. Shrill, yet powerful. The sort of rhythmic sound that shook Chandra's bones. That she could feel in her soul.

"And we're here!" Jacob proclaimed. He slid gracelessly off his horse and offered a hand for Chandra in assistance.

"Oh, put that away." Chandra chuckled. Her dismount was fluid, and she met the ground with a light footfall. Jacob shrugged in response and beckoned Chandra toward an open door. Toward the source of the metallic cry.

Heat emanated from the open doorway. A warm welcome on a chilly day. Above the door hung a wooden sign in the shape of an anvil. Golden tongs and a steel-gray hammer crossed above flat red letters that simply spelled *Nia's*. No services were listed on the doorway or the soot-stained windows. As far as Chandra could tell, there was an equal chance that the owner could specialize in armor smithing or wagon fittings.

A step inside saw a dramatic rise in temperature. Chandra followed Jacob, who had slipped through the doorway like he owned the place. The building was long and narrow. All manner of tools lined one of the firelit walls. From hammers and calipers to bellows of all sizes, the wall was packed with useful devices. Their well-worn nature was clear from the threshold.

On the opposite long wall were hung an assortment of weapons. Polished swords that glinted like silver in the light of the forge. Axes of various sizes and shapes. Finely crafted maces that looked like they could decommission a manarail engine. The weapons stood in stark contrast to the beaten and battered smithing tools.

Past the anvils and grinding wheel that filled the center of the elongated room was the forge. Even from the front of the building, the heat was unbearable. How anyone could stand to work so near a furious pit of flame was beyond Chandra. That did not stop the Zumbatran katarl near the forge from plunging a length of iron into the infernal housing. They removed another length of metal and brought it to a nearby anvil. Rhythmic pounding echoed through the whole building as the smith struck hot metal with powerful hammer blows.

"Nia!" Jacob called out. His voice was no match for the roar of flames mixed with the savage blows of a hammer. The boy tried to call again but found no better luck. His words did not reach the smith at the back of the room. Jacob clicked his tongue against his teeth and strode deeper into the smithy, beckoning for Chandra to follow.

Heat rose to an unbearable level as Chandra approached. Sweat beaded on her brow and dotted her back. It was like stepping headlong into a giant oven. An unfeeling cage that threatened to roast her alive. The constant pound of the hammer made the walk no more pleasant. Each step closer enhanced the noise until it felt to Chandra like someone was jabbing a needle into her ear. Over and over with each stroke of the tool. Occasional showers of sparks gave the impression of shrill fireworks whining through a night sky.

The approach of Chandra and Jacob did not stop the wielder of the hammer. No matter how loud Jacob called, the hammer always seemed to be louder. That the smith's back was turned to the pair did not help the matter. It was not until Jacob stepped past the smith and waved in front of her that the supreme focus of the artisan was shattered. She rose from a hunched position over the anvil to her full height. The smith lifted a pair of black goggles from her eyes to reveal an unimpressed amber gaze.

"I sharpened the Equalizer a month ago, Hartsfield," the woman barked with impatience. "The hells has your father done that it needs sharpening again? I thought he was a farmer these days."

"Oh, no. The sword's fine, Nia," Jacob stuttered. The woman, Nia, had put Jacob on edge with her unfiltered ire. She made it clear that she did not wish to be disturbed. If the disturbance was necessary, she preferred it to be handled as fast as possible. Jacob flashed a precarious smile and gestured toward Chandra with both hands. "This is Chandra. She's the girl I told you about. The one that's good with metal."

Nia directed her powerful gaze over to Chandra. It felt like the woman's attention carried the weight of the entire world. Powerful presence and curt speech combined to form an aura of intimidation.

"And?" was the sole word of reply from Nia. She shifted her gaze back to Jacob, clearly expecting a better explanation for the interruption.

"Well," Jacob began again, gathering courage as he continued to speak, "you always mention you're behind schedule when I bring in dad's sword. Stuff about not enough hours in the day and not having enough hands—"

"You're wasting some of that precious time, boy," Nia snarled.

"Right! Right. Well, I thought, maybe, you might need an apprentice? Someone to help you out around the forge? Chandra's got an extra pair of hands. Hard worker too. Used to do Shikaree work and help around her family's farm at the same time."

Chandra raised both hands with a courteous smile as if to say, "See? Two hands?" It felt odd letting Jacob drive the conversation when the topic was Chandra's potential employment, but Jacob had advised her to talk as little as possible unless directly addressed. Chandra understood the warning in full now that she stood in Nia's presence. She was more than happy to let Jacob navigate the treacherous conversation with this stranger.

The gesture of raising her hands invited a level of scrutiny that Chandra had not expected. Nia set her hammer down and stepped over to Chandra. Soot-crusted hands took hold of Chandra's own hands and turned them over. Roving eyes examined all there was to see. Thumbs probed muscles and tendons. Nia raised Chandra's arms out to either side. Taking a few steps back, Nia looked Chandra over from the top of her head to the tips of her boots.

"I don't pay for damaged goods," Nia said flatly. "Skinny little thing, to boot. Not gonna be responsible for breaking someone's daughter in half."

Goggles slid back down over prying eyes. Nia turned from Chandra, picked up the hammer, and began to pound on the cooling metal. The woman managed a few strikes before driving the metal back into the forge. Pulling another length of metal out from the forge, Nia resumed work as if she had never had guests.

Damaged goods?

Chandra looked at her left hand. An acute pain ran through her arm like the injuries were fresh and opened anew. Such harsh judgment was unexpected. The fierce woman had not asked a single question. For all Nia knew, Chandra could have been an expert with hammer and anvil. That did not sit well with Chandra.

Not at all.

"Hey!" Chandra barked through the piercing wail of hammer against metal. She positioned herself in Nia's line of sight as best as she could. With her left hand, her damaged goods, Chandra plucked a manarail spike from her hip. Jacob placed a hand on Chandra's shoulder in caution, but she shrugged the warning away. "Hey! Nia! I'm talking to you!"

An inaudible sigh expanded the smith's frame. Nia raised a single lens of her goggles to expose half of a severely agitated glare. Her hammer hung high in the air, poised to strike another blow once the present nonsense was concluded.

Though angry at being so easily cast aside, Chandra was well rested and prepared to channel. Precise thoughts delved into the Flow to retrieve the energy required to shape the iron in her hand. An ancient roar flooded her mind. The crackle of the Flow in Chandra's ears beat back the roar of the forge. Primal force, the lifeblood of the world, would not be silenced by a manufactured flame. That power combined with Chandra's will to bend the spike in her hand.

The long manarail spike softened. It condensed itself into a lumpy sphere in Chandra's palm. Soft and pliable as a fish egg, the ball rolled around her open hand. Another surge of energy shifted the ball into a flat, paper-thin disc. Simple manipulations that required little concentration. Their forms were plain, without detail to complicate the spell. Chandra finished her display with greater prowess. The thin disc of metal folded over itself again and again until it had been fashioned into a rod, which then flattened again. Contours formed to produce a pommel, grip, hilt, and blade. Though it did not glimmer in the firelight like the weapons on the wall, Chandra still held a sharp, fully formed dagger in her hand.

Chandra had not felt so proud of one of her crude daggers since she first mastered the spell. She twirled the dagger, albeit clumsily, with her three fingers before taking hold of the blade by her fingertips. A confident grin emerged as Chandra held the handle out to Nia for inspection.

"Go ahead," Chandra offered. "It's not a trick either. Won't snap back into a manarail spike in a day or if I get too far away. When I cast a spell, the metal *stays* changed."

Nia pulled her goggles down around her neck and took the dagger with a gloved hand. Once she set her hammer down on the anvil, Nia turned the weapon over to peer at all its pieces. No angle was overlooked. The smith even held the blade closer to the forge for better light. It was not until Nia attempted to bend the dagger that her stoic expression reformed in a disappointed sneer.

Chandra took the reaction as a win. The blade had not bent under the smith's assault. Even when she pressed the blade against the anvil and applied the weight of her body, Nia was unable to bend the metal.

Some sort of congratulations should be in order, Chandra thought. An apology from the smith for her brutal dismissal. Nia had the dagger onto the anvil so that it was flush with the surface. No part of the dagger hung over the anvil's edge. This would be when Chandra received rightful praise.

Instead, Nia held the dagger to the anvil by the handle and grabbed her hammer. A swift stroke carried the hammerhead down onto the dagger. The noise that followed was like a wagon axel buckling under stress. Bits of iron shot in different directions as the blade of the dagger snapped from the hilt. Fragments of the blade rattled on the anvil. Nia picked up the cracked hilt for examination, then glared at Chandra over the ruins of the weapon.

"Blade was too rigid," Nia derided. "Made the metal brittle, prone to break. I prefer repeat clients, girl, not people that die from malfunctions. Amateur's work."

"Well, what did you think was gonna happen if you smashed it with a hammer?" Chandra protested, stunned as she was.

"And what do you think happens to the person that tries to stop a mace swung by a three-hundred-pound Bangeli katarl with a sword more rigid than a gods damned mountain?" Nia asked. She jammed the broken handle back into Chandra's open hand. Condescension dripped from Nia's mouth as she answered her own question. "They *die.* Just because you can bend a rusted scrap of iron doesn't mean you can rip the impurities from the metal, or shape it into a sword that deserves a name. The best you could do is hand someone their death with a smile on your face."

A lump formed in Chandra's throat. Pride. The desire to fire back, to defend her inexperience and berate the woman that expected an unreasonable level of perfection. To defend her accomplishments as someone untrained. A self-taught spellcrafter who was never offered more than a pitchfork and a bucket for collecting apples.

Chandra forced herself to swallow that pride.

"But I can learn," Chandra retorted. "I've got talent. I just need a teacher."

"I don't teach shortcuts," Nia countered. "This smithy is a house for hammers and anvils. Fire and sweat. That sacrilegious nonsense doesn't have a place here."

"Then teach me your way," Chandra offered before Nia could continue. "Harvest is done for the year. I've got all winter."

"Hah." The single laugh contained twisted mirth. Nia almost smiled. "It'll take a lot longer than one winter to teach you everything I know."

Words were not the solution. It became obvious that Chandra was not going to win this woman's attention through argument. Something more was required. Chandra whipped her head around the smithy. A stroke of luck allowed Chandra to spot what she was looking for in the cluttered room: a stool. It was raggedy and missing its fourth leg, but Chandra could make that work.

Two manarail spikes merged into a single piece of metal in Chandra's right hand as she strode across the room. She paid no mind to the blithe comments Nia hurled at her back. When Chandra reached the stool, she jammed the newly formed metal rod where the missing leg should have been. Metal bit down on the wood and sealed itself in place. Chandra was able to shore up the length of the metal leg as she quietly walked back to the anvil. Metal screeched and wood creaked when Chandra snapped the stool down next to Nia.

Chandra seated herself with force. Momentum swung her right leg over her left. Arms crossed before her chest. Firmly rooted and unwilling to move, Chandra locked eyes with Nia and awaited a response.

The towering smith smirked.

"I'm not going to pay you until you make yourself useful," Nia said. "You get that?"

Chandra unfurled her left hand and made a permissive gesture toward the anvil. She spoke a single word.

"Teach."

"Haughty little shit," Nia replied, her smirk growing into a fiendish smile. Gloved hands pulled goggles back up to wild eyes before the woman turned to address Jacob. "Get out of here, Hartsfield. We've got work to do."

About the Author

M.J. Oelkers is nothing if not an absolute goober. He would much rather smile than frown, if only to help others do the same. When not dragging some poor soul through a fictional ringer, he is likely playing games with friends. Board games. Video Games. It makes little difference. As long as good times are had around the table, he doesn't care too much what sits in the middle. He also likes anime. Nerd.

In all seriousness, unparalleled thanks to any and everyone who managed to make it to the end. I hope you enjoyed spending time with Chandra as much as I did. Hers is the second in a series of tales about the denizens of Arnstead. If you liked this story enough to want more from this world, please rate, review, and post about Shikaree wherever you can. It's the best way to let me know you're interested. The next handful of titles are already written and ready to be polished. Your support helps them cross the finish line in style.

Goodreads: I post regularly in the blog on my author page. Follow me there if you want progress reports on my stories or feel like asking a question.

Arnsteadpress.com: My personal website. You can sign up for my newsletter to get information on upcoming releases or anything related to Arnstead.

Until next time friends.

Toodles.

396 | *About the Author*

Arnsteadpress.com: My personal website. You can sign up for my newsletter to get information on upcoming releases or anything related to Arnstead.